"**Two adventurou**
every turn—t

—Tamora Pierce, author of t

A *Kirkus Reviews* Best Children's Book
A *Booklist* Editors' Choice
A Chicago Public Library Best Book
A Kids' Indie Next List Pick
A Junior Library Guild Selection

★ "**Wholly original** . . . enjoyable and humorous. This is an
ambitious undertaking, and strong readers who enjoy adventure
fiction and fantasy will inhale the first book in what has
the potential to be **an extraordinary series**."
— *School Library Journal*, starred review

★ "Ryan and Davis' swashbuckling quest features **fantastic world
building**, gnarly creatures, and a villain who is both spooky and
formidable. Each new location is a treasure. . . . The unique details,
expert plotting, charming characters, and comic interludes combine
in **a tantalizing read** that's made even more appealing by
the promise that the story will continue in future volumes."
— *Booklist*, starred review

★ "**Vividly cast** . . . Multifaceted characters, high stakes,
imaginative magic, and hints of hidden twists and complexities
to come add up to **a memorable start** to a
projected four-volume voyage."
— *Kirkus Reviews*, starred review

★ "**Fast-paced and imaginative**, this adventure combines action
with whimsy, injecting emotion and pathos into an otherwise
lighthearted romp. It's a strong start for what promises
to be a **highly enjoyable** series."
— *Publishers Weekly*, starred review

"**There's no catching one's breath** as the kids . . . risk life and limb. [Marrill and Fin's] tentative but determined efforts at understanding how to compromise, risk, and share with a peer is one of the quiet highlights of the novel. Fans of *The Phantom Tollbooth* will appreciate the traveling aspect. . . . Readers will undoubtedly be eager for the next volume."
— *The Bulletin*

"A master thief, a young adventuress, and an old pirate ship that sails a magical stream across the universe! What could be better? Answer: a map to guide you from one world to the next. Thankfully, Ryan and Davis have provided just such a map in their **wondrous and winning** new novel [that] will take you wherever you want to go— and to places you never imagined."
—Pseudonymous Bosch, bestselling author of The Secret Series

"**Quintessential fantasy**, melding a world achingly our own with a thrillingly realized parallel realm. . . . But what begins as a quest for a magical map deepens into **a touching search for identity**. Ryan and Davis have crafted a tale with equal parts humor, humanity, and suspense."
—Tony Abbott, author of The Copernicus Legacy series

"Clever, fresh, and **filled with fantastic charm**!"
—Lisa McMann, bestselling author of The Unwanteds series

"**Exciting, fast-paced, and well-written**. Plus I can find plenty of angles to work it into Common Core. Fantastic elements and characters will keep the attention of even the most reluctant reader, and the story is full of wonderful language and clever wordplay."
—Mary Brown, educational consultant, owner of Books, Bytes & Beyond

"A middle grade fantasy book with its roots in America [is] nearly impossible to find and [is] always so well received. . . . *The Map to Everywhere* **is amazing**; I truly love it and I can't wait to sell it."
—Cristin Stickles, buyer, children's and YA books, McNally Jackson Books

THE MAP TO EVERYWHERE

Book 1

by Carrie Ryan & John Parke Davis

Illustrations by Todd Harris

Little, Brown and Company

New York • Boston

Text copyright © 2014 by Carrie Ryan & John Parke Davis
Illustrations copyright © 2014 by Todd Harris
Author Interview copyright © 2014 by *The Horn Book Magazine*
Excerpt from *City of Thirst* copyright © 2015 by Carrie Ryan & John Parke Davis

Little, Brown and Company

Hachette Book Group
1290 Avenue of the Americas, New York, NY 10104
Visit us at lb-kids.com

Little, Brown and Company is a division of Hachette Book Group, Inc.
The Little, Brown name and logo are trademarks of Hachette Book Group, Inc.

The publisher is not responsible for websites (or their content)
that are not owned by the publisher.

First Paperback Edition: September 2015
First published in hardcover in November 2014 by Little, Brown and Company

Library of Congress Cataloging-in-Publication Data
Ryan, Carrie.
  The map to everywhere / by Carrie Ryan & John Parke Davis. First edition.
    pages cm.—(The Map to Everywhere ; book 1)
  Summary: Twelve-year-old Fin, a master thief from the pirate world of Khaznot Quay, and Marill, also twelve, of Arizona, cross paths in the magical world of the Pirate Stream while on a quest for a mysterious map.
  ISBN 978-0-316-24077-2 (hc)—ISBN 978-0-316-24076-5 (ebook)—
ISBN 978-0-316-24079-6 (library edition ebook) — ISBN 978-0-316-24078-9 (pb)
  [1. Adventure and adventurers—Fiction. 2. Pirates—Fiction. 3. Wizards—Fiction. 4. Stealing—Fiction. 5. Magic—Fiction. 6. Maps—Fiction. 7. Fantasy.] I. Davis, John Parke. II. Title.
  PZ7.R9478Map2014
  [Fic]—dc23
                                                                                        2013044752

10 9 8 7 6 5 4 3 2 1

RRD-C

Printed in the United States of America

For Jason,
without whom the Stream would not glow.
—JPD

For my dad,
who indulged my imagination.
—CR

Contents

KANTSY'S QUAYSIDE
ORPHAN PRESERVE

ORPHAN NAME: _FNU LNU_

AGE: _Four(ish)_

GENDER: _x_ MALE __ FEMALE __ PLANTIMAL __ INDESCRIBABLE

HAIR/FUR/SCALES: _Black_

EYES: _2_

SPECIES (ATTACH ADDITIONAL PAGES IF NECESSARY): _Human_

DOES ORPHAN HAVE CLAWS, HORNS, SPINES, OR OTHER SHARP EDGES? ___ YES _x_ NO

IS ORPHAN INHERENTLY MAGICAL OR MAGICALLY AFFLICTED? _x_ YES ___ NO

IF YES, DESCRIBE:

Hard to remember, difficult to notice. And not just like "doesn't stand out in a crowd," like serious "it's magic"-type stuff. The boy just slips out of the mind when not in front of you. Forgot why I was writing this report three times already—have to have the boy here right now just so I can finish this blixin' thing without wandering away again. Origin of affliction unknown.

(CONTINUED ON PAGE 2)

ORPHAN HISTORY:

Two days ago, the Preserve received a curious visitor. Our logbook shows the signature of a Ms. Notah Reelnaym, hailing from the foreign-sounding port of Nowareneerheer, arriving at 10:00 am on the nose with a child and leaving an hour and three minutes later without one. Log notes indicate that Ms. Reelnaym spent precisely one hour touring the Preserve. Mr. Gubbens, our Chief Orphan Wrangler, reports spending that hour walking around the Preserve alone, loudly explaining Preserve policies to no one for no obvious reason. Remaining three minutes of Ms. Reelnaym's visit unaccounted for.

Shortly thereafter, an extra set of boys' clothes was found in one of the bunkrooms. Reports of hungry ghost stealing food from kitchen and phantom snugglings at night were investigated, and a child was ultimately located and brought in for processing by Mrs. Canaly Parsnickle, mistress of three- to six-year-olds.

Boy is currently in the care of Mrs. Parsnickle, who seems to be the only person who can remember him for any length of time. So long as she doesn't forget him, I'm sure the boy will be just fine.

CHAPTER 1
The Ghost of Gutterleak Way

Fin crouched behind a rack of bootleg flavors, trying hard to ignore the taste of rat fur and broccoli juice seeping from the grungy bottles. No more than ten minutes before, the owner of the dirty little shop, a nasty, gray-scaled old monster called Sharktooth, had let him in for a quick browse before closing time, then promptly forgotten he existed.

Plenty of people planned for a break-in, Fin thought

with a smirk. Not enough planned for a break-*out*.

Fin kept low as the old swindler locked the shop door—after all, he was forgettable, not invisible—and watched Sharktooth lumber into the next room to go to bed. Then he waited while darkness fell in earnest over the twisted streets of the Khaznot Quay, until the high winds that constantly shrieked down from the mountain to the bay reached their evening pitch.

Finally, it was time to act.

Uncurling himself cautiously, Fin rubbed the feeling back into his legs, then crept past shelves filled with all sorts of secondhand junk to the old display case behind the counter. His prize stood out beneath the smeared glass: a golden gemerald brooch, bright and shiny as the sun. He licked his lips in anticipation.

With one careful finger, Fin found the hidden wires behind the display doors and followed them back to the traps set to protect them: a single handcatcher and a few acid squirts. Standard stuff—disarming these barely counted as practice.

"Pretty soggy, Sharktooth," Fin muttered under his breath as he popped the traps loose and jimmied the lock. "At least give me a workout next time." He grinned as he gripped the handle of the display doors. He'd be in and out before the nasty bafter even hit his pillow.

That thought vanished the moment he pulled the doors open and they let out a screech so loud it practically shredded the air. Fin shuddered. The perfect crime, spoiled by a rusty hinge!

Old Sharktooth burst from his bedroom. "Who's dyin' tonight?" he bellowed, brandishing a heavy cane.

"Shanks!" Fin shouted. He snatched the brooch. Sharktooth lunged. But a good thief moved on instinct, and Fin was the best. The cane whipped through the air just as he leapt to the counter. It smashed into the display, sending shards of glass scattering everywhere.

For a long moment, boy and beast stared at each other, waiting to see who would make the first move. Fin crouched a little, arms out, balanced and braced to run. Sharktooth studied him with eyes like black pits, double rows of jagged teeth gnashing below.

Then, with a growl, Sharktooth charged. Fin faked left, then jumped to the floor and beat feet for the exit. "Too slow!" he yelped as the old monster clattered after him, knocking busted earflutes from their shelves and sending rusty sun-funnels crashing to the ground as he went.

Fin didn't look back. He slammed the door open and burst into the darkness outside. Sharktooth's shop crouched in a short tunnel formed where two buildings had apparently decided to fall into the same alley at the exact same time; there were only two ways out. Fin chose one at random and took off.

"You little skuzzleweed!" Sharktooth cried, charging out after him.

Their footfalls clattered in rhythm against the background wail of the wind. Fin gulped. He knew he could outrace most folks; it came with being chased a lot. But a body didn't get to Sharktooth's level of sleazy without being chased a good bit itself. It was only a matter of time before Fin would go from shark bait to shark chow.

Fortunately, he had a plan for occasions like this. After all, being forgettable had its advantages for a thief. Folks' memories didn't fade quite so quickly when they caught him doing something like, oh, pilfering jewelry from their locked display cases. But one thing was sure in Fin's life: They *did* fade.

He ducked onto a side street and flattened himself immediately into the nearest doorway. A moment later, Sharktooth careered around the corner, roaring past Fin's hiding place. But after a few feet without sign of his quarry, he slowed to a stop, sniffing the air.

Adopting his most casual stance, Fin slipped up behind Sharktooth and tugged on the swindler's sleeve. "You looking for that girl who just came tearing through here, jangling a necklace?"

Sharktooth whipped toward him. "What? A girl? No…" He trailed off. One hand stroked his rough-scaled chin in thought. The high winds whistled overhead, making the lamplight dance in his jet-black eyes. "Coulda sworn it was a boy…. Got a good look at 'im… but now I think of it, can't quite recall…."

Fin shrugged, sliding into his routine. "Well, it was a girl that came through here. Dark reddish hair, little shorter than me?"

Sharktooth tilted his head. "Dark hair, yeah, that rings a bell. And she *was* short...."

"That's the one!" Fin announced. "Tore through here like a mountain gust, shot right down that alley." He pointed to the row of buildings across from him. "Headed to the Wharfway Warrens, by my reckon."

Sharktooth nodded. "Thanks, kid." A cruel sneer curled back up his lip. "Now, don't count on ever seeing her again," he added menacingly. His cane whipped the night air as he trotted off in the direction Fin had pointed.

"Oh, I won't," Fin chuckled when Sharktooth was out of earshot. He waited a few minutes, until he was more than certain he'd been entirely forgotten. Then he pulled his hand from his pocket. Alongside the gleaming gemerald brooch sat the velvet coin purse he'd lifted from Sharktooth's belt just a moment before.

He ran a thumb over the surface of the brooch. Yet another successful caper for the Master Thief of the Khaznot Quay. He whistled as he sauntered up the street, counting the coins in his newly acquired purse. Turned out Sharktooth had made quite the haul today!

When Fin reached the Nosebleed Heights, where the poor folks' houses clung to the steepest parts of the mountain, he took the sharpest turns down the sheerest lanes until he came to the soggy little bystreet called Gutterleak Way. His destination was the seventeenth house on the right: a rickety, narrow little place hunkered on the edge of a cliff. Atop its two usable stories, a high attic tower swayed in the wind, forever threatening to topple into the bay below.

Fin's steps slowed and his whistling trailed off. No one had left the light on for him, nor the front door unlocked. But it wasn't like he'd expected anything different. This was the only home he'd known since leaving the Orphan Preserve five years ago, when he was barely seven, but no one else knew it. Not even Mr. and Mrs. Parsnickle, who lived there, too.

But he didn't hold it against them.

With the ease of many years of practice, he jumped from the stoop to the storm gutter and shimmied his way along it until he reached the kitchen window. Fin always made sure to keep this one oiled properly, and it slid open without a sound. And just inside sat the old bread tin where the Parsnickles kept their coin.

Carefully, he pried the lid off and looked inside. Then he shook his head. Empty. The Parsnickles were too generous; if he let them, they'd give every last drillet to keep a stranger from missing a meal, and would go hungry themselves for having done it.

Fin tipped the contents of his new purse into the can, then placed the brooch on top. Mrs. Parsnickle had pawned it that very morning to Sharktooth, at a price that was a rip-off even by the swindler's normal standard. Then she'd turned right around and used the money to buy shoes for the six-and-unders at the Orphan Preserve.

Fin didn't feel bad about stealing it back, not for a second. He'd have stolen the world for her, if he could have. After all, that was what he felt like she'd given him, back when he was a six-and-under. Except for his mother, Mrs. Parsnickle was the only person he'd known who'd ever really remembered him, and she'd treated him all the more special because of it. It wasn't her fault she had finally forgotten him, too. Everyone did, eventually.

And besides, he knew she only had eyes for the under-sevens. He figured she'd only remembered him in the first place because she cared so much for the little ones. He'd just gotten too old, that was all.

At least being forgotten came with some advantages, Fin reminded himself with a smile. This was the third time he'd stolen that brooch from Sharktooth this month! Though poor Mrs. Parsnickle really did think she was losing her mind when it kept turning up in her bread tin each time.

Warmth spread through his chest as Fin replaced the tin, closed the window, and scrambled up the gutter to the attic tower, watching out for rotten molding as he went and holding on tight when the wind blew too strong. When he reached the very top, he slipped through a broken window and breathed a sigh of relief. It was good to be home.

Hunched over awkwardly, Fin pawed his way across

the familiar mess that littered the floor. Mounds of cloud-catching nets tangled with self-fetching balls, old maps, and all the other junk he'd pilfered over the years but never really used. It was a testament to his thieving skill, and the biggest testament was right where he slept.

Even though there was no one there to see him, Fin produced Sharktooth's empty velvet coin purse with a flourish. "The last one!" he announced, adding it to the mound of velvet coin purses he used for a bed. Then he flopped into them face-first, luxuriating in the triumph of having completed his masterpiece.

It'd only taken three years and 462 picked pockets. The soft fuzz tickled his palms, tingling up his arms, and he didn't even mind when a cockroach skittered out of one of the pouches. He'd grown to like bugs, living in an attic and all. And at least roaches didn't bite, unlike the chitterchomps that had moved into the leather coin purses he *used* to sleep on.

"It was a good day," he whispered to himself, rolling onto his back. He drifted off to sleep imagining the look of happy surprise on Mrs. Parsnickle's face when she discovered the brooch the next morning.

⤙ ✛ ⤚

"BLIXIN' GHOOOOOOOOOOOOSSSSSTTTTT!" Mr. Parsnickle's shouts filtered up through the loose attic floorboards and hammered into Fin's ears. Outside, the morning wind howled as usual, but even it was no match for Mr. Parsnickle's roaring. This was Fin's morning wake-up call; the old beast had probably noticed the missing cheese Fin had swiped for yesterday's dinner.

Fin rolled carefully off his makeshift bed, sweeping stray purses back onto it as he went. He weaved his way across the attic, crouching to avoid banging his head on the rafters, and pushed aside the sapphire-and-opal statue blocking the trapdoor to the house below. With a muted *thump*, he dropped into the back of an old closet the Parsnickles had never bothered refinishing (at least, not since the "ghost" had hidden all of Mr. Parsnickle's refinishing tools) and made his way silently down the stairs.

"For goodness' sakes, Arler," Mrs. Parsnickle was saying as Fin reached the hallway to the kitchen, "I've no time for your ghost nonsense! I'm late already, and the sixes will have the fives stuffed into the drying baskets by the bath pool if I don't get there soon."

Fin winced, remembering the stink of that bath pool. At least he didn't have to deal with that anymore.

"The cheese, woman, the cheese!" Mr. Parsnickle yelped from down the hall. "The blixin' ghost moved the cheese!"

Fin snuck closer. In the reflection of a nearby mirror, he caught a glimpse of Mrs. Parsnickle pushing a knot of blue-gray hair into place atop her thin frame, Mr. Parsnickle's huge red face beside her. His thick jowly cheeks quivered around his white tusks.

"Oh, you impossible orc!" Mrs. Parsnickle laughed. Then came the kissing. Fin gagged. Grown-ups were so gross.

He peeked his head around the doorjamb. Mr. Parsnickle rifled through the larder a few feet away, pulling out a loaf of bread and some toadbutter, Fin's least favorite thing ever. Mrs. Parsnickle grabbed a slice, nimbly dodging the dollop of gray ooze Mr. Parsnickle tried to swipe over it, and headed to the door. Fin was just about to slip in and nick the crusty heel when Mrs. Parsnickle hesitated on the threshold.

"Arler?" She bent down and grabbed something from the mildewed wooden stoop. When she stood, she held a carefully folded scrap of white paper pinched between her twiggy fingers.

"Whazzit?" Mr. Parsnickle asked, slathering another hunk of bread in gooey muck. He jammed it halfway into his mouth and peered over her shoulder.

"Looks to be a letter," Mrs. Parsnickle pronounced.

Fin leaned into the kitchen, farther than he ever would normally. Regular Quay folk like the Parsnickles didn't *get* letters. Once in a while, the Preserve would send a notice via speakfrog, or a parrotboy might bring a message from Mr. Parsnickle's relatives on the Best-Not-Visited Coast. But never an actual *letter*.

"Let's see here," Mrs. Parsnickle said. Her brow wrinkled as she read. "Seems to be addressed to an 'M Thief.'"

"Master Thief!" Fin blurted before he could stop himself. That was him!

Mr. Parsnickle jumped so hard he hit the ceiling, causing bits of rotting wood and grout to rain down from it. Mrs. Parsnickle clutched the note to her chest, eyes as huge as midsummer moons.

For a moment, no one said anything. Fin tried to will the words back into his mouth. He wondered what he must look like leaning half out of the doorframe, black hair uncombed against his olive skin, clothes dirty from days without so much as a splash in a fountain.

"Vagrant!" Mr. Parsnickle cried, solving the mystery. He snatched a thick-handled broom and swung it over his head like a club.

Fin swallowed, and tried the one thing he knew for sure wouldn't work. "Mrs. Parsnickle?" he whispered. "It's me, Fin?"

Mrs. Parsnickle cocked her head at him. Her eyes narrowed just a bit. He searched her face desperately for a spark of recognition. Her mouth opened, just a little, and hope exploded in his heart.

"I'm s-sorry, young man," she stuttered. "Do I know you?"

Fin sighed as the hope fizzled. Of course not. Mr. Parsnickle pointed the bristles of his broom at him, making a slow sweeping motion toward the door.

Time to go. Again.

He marched, shoulders slumped, through the kitchen. No breakfast for him this morning. But there was something he needed more than a hunk of toadbutter-bathed bread. Just at the threshold, he turned to Mrs. Parsnickle. She looked at him with the same blank stare, tinged with just a touch of fear.

"I'm sorry," he whispered.

The corners of her eyes twitched and she frowned. "Breaking into houses is bad manners," she instructed him. Mr. Parsnickle snorted behind her, broom at the ready.

Fin shrugged. "Oh, not for that," he said. "For this!" In one quick motion, he jumped up and snatched the note from her hand.

Mr. Parsnickle roared and swung the broom. It smashed against the floor, missing Fin by inches.

"Shanks!" he cried, already moving. His legs pumped, carrying him out the door and down the narrow street, cobblestones bruising his feet as he went. That had been a close miss.

But the Parsnickles would forget soon enough, and no lock could keep him out. And, most importantly of all, in his hand he clutched the letter. *His* letter.

CHAPTER 2
The Pirate Ship in the Parking Lot

I t's not from a dinosaur," Marrill pronounced. She turned the old weathered bone over in her hand and swiped her damp forehead with the back of her wrist. Three seven-year-old boys stared up at her eagerly. Above, the Arizona sun blazed hot enough to half melt the soles of her sneakers. "I'd say it's most likely cow," she added.

Almost as one, their smiles dropped into frowns.

"But how do you know?" asked the oldest, Tim (or was it Ted?). They all stood in the Hatch triplets' famed archaeological dig, better known as the empty lot at the far edge of their middle-of-nowhere neighborhood.

The triplets had likely come to Marrill because of her experience in these matters. Last year, she'd spent three months on a dig site in Peru with her parents, hunting up the remains of a bird so big it ate horses for snacks. Her dad had written one of his travel essays about it, and her mom's photograph of Marrill holding a beak the size of her head had ended up in the Smithsonian.

"Because it's a bone," she said matter-of-factly. "If it were from a dinosaur, it'd be a fossil by now."

She caught the youngest Hatch, Tom (or was it Tim?), looking at her. His bottom lip stuck out, and his whole face drooped with disappointment. His brothers wore similar expressions.

Marrill felt a twinge of guilt. They'd been imagining a great discovery, and she'd messed it up by bringing in boring reality. It was a feeling she knew all too well. But thanks to her parents' jobs, she normally got to have lots of cool adventures, and she'd be leaving for more any day now. The only adventures the Hatch boys would have were the ones they made up. And now she'd ruined even that.

Studying the bone more closely, she twisted her lips. "Of course, now that I think about it…" She trailed off, then shook her head. "But no, it couldn't be."

"What?" the youngest asked, his face lighting up again.

"Well…" Marrill crouched and scratched at the ground.

"When I was in Peru last year, I heard these rumors about dragon remains popping up in all sorts of places. A bone this small would have to be a baby dragon, but…"

The middle one (Tim, she was pretty sure) frowned. "Dragons aren't real."

"That's not what the Peruvian Dragon Research Center thought," Marrill said with a shrug. "Though how anyone can know for sure without looking for the rest of it…" She tossed the bone back to Ted (Tom?) and started toward her great-aunt's house. When she looked over her shoulder, the trio were huddled over the bone, chattering to one another excitedly.

She was still grinning when she turned onto her street. But when the house came into view, her steps faltered. The FOR SALE sign that had stood in the yard for weeks was missing.

Her heart thudded against her chest. They'd been stuck in Phoenix ever since her great-aunt died a few months ago, making Marrill's parents cut short their latest expedition to come deal with her things. And the house was the last piece. Every day, Marrill hoped to find a little white SOLD! plaque hanging on the bottom of the sign. And every day, she was disappointed.

Until today.

She burst into the house, excitement roaring through her. She didn't even pause to savor the blast of air conditioning. Instead, she raced straight to her room and dove under her bed, pushing aside dropped drawing pencils and half-filled sketchbooks to reach the old shoe box she'd hidden there. She'd been dreaming about this moment all summer. They were finally traveling again, and she had the perfect spot for their next destination!

"We're finally leaving!" she squealed as she tore into the kitchen, box in hand. Her parents sat at the old butcher-block table, stacks of papers spread out in front of them. Marrill's one-eyed cat, Karnelius, sprawled on top of one of the piles, an orange paw batting lazily at a crumpled envelope.

"So when we got here, you told me to be thinking about where to go for your next story," Marrill rattled before her parents could even respond. "Well, guess what? I found the most perfect place!" She upended the box. Glossy pictures, maps, and pamphlets flooded the table.

She lowered her voice like a game-show announcer. "Lady, gentleman, and cat, I give you..." She paused for dramatic effect, then thrust a poster of a girl cradling a one-armed baby chimpanzee into the air. "The Banton Park Live-In Animal Rescue Reserve and Playground Fortress!"

Her parents looked stunned. They could scarcely get out a word. She paused to bask in their wonder. She under-stood how they felt—she couldn't imagine a better destina-tion herself. Marrill was a sucker for any lost and homeless creature (it was how she'd ended up fostering a two-legged ferret in France, a deaf tree toad in Costa Rica, and a tailless parakeet in Paraguay). The Reserve was an entire island dedicated to nothing but the rehabilitation of animals in need. She was smiling so hard it felt like her face might actually split.

Her father glanced at her mother, who looked down at her hands clutched in her lap. Both of them appeared concerned. Her stomach dropped. Her father cleared his throat.

"Marrill," he said.

She knew that tone. It sounded like sorries, and stern explanations, and all the things she didn't want to hear.

"But wait!" she cried, hoping that if she barreled forward, maybe whatever was about to happen wouldn't. "Observe how all living areas are conveniently located within the park, so at any time of the day or night, you can wander out and find your nearest needy elephant, or kangaroo, or sloth, or giraffe, depending on your preference, all desperate for the love and care only a twelve-year-old girl can give. And let's not forget amenities like the ice-cream machine and waterslides and..."

Her voice trembled and petered into silence. Her parents' expressions looked so pained. She tried to brace herself for whatever was coming.

"Marrill." Her father cleared his throat and adjusted the wire-rim spectacles he'd picked up in a Romanian swap market. "There's something we need to tell you."

He stood and slipped his arm across her shoulders. Then he said the words she'd dreaded hearing for five years. Ever since the last time she'd stood next to a hospital bed, crying and feeling helpless inside.

"Honey, your mother's sick again."

It felt like stepping out into the Arizona sun, scorching her and leaving her breathless. Silence filled the room. Marrill stared at him, then looked to her mother, willing her to contradict him. But she said nothing.

Panic churned in Marrill's stomach. This couldn't happen. Her mom was her best friend, the person she shared everything with. She couldn't take it if her mother was sick again.

Marrill shook her head. "No," she whispered. Her father's arm slipped from her shoulders and dropped to his side limply as she pulled away from him.

But as she stared at her mother, she could see it. A little less color in her cheeks, a little thinner in the lips. Her movements more guarded and cautious. Even her bowl of cereal from this morning sat untouched by the kitchen sink. All the clues had been there, but Marrill hadn't noticed. She hadn't wanted to notice.

She spun around, pressing her hands against her face as if that could somehow stop all her fear and pain from spilling out. She hated the way she was feeling. She hated not knowing what to say, what to do.

"I'll be okay, Petal." Her mother stood and came around the table to pull Marrill into a fierce hug. Instantly, everything unique about her mom enveloped Marrill: the sound of her voice, the way she smelled, the pattern of her breathing. All the things Marrill had known from the instant she was born, the things that were as much a part of her as her DNA.

"It's just another flare-up," her mother explained, her lips against Marrill's hair. "We'll need to be near a doctor for a while, is all." She pulled back, meeting Marrill's eyes. "I'll get better and we can hit the road again. I promise."

"But I don't understand," Marrill said, trying to make sense of what was going on. "The 'For Sale' sign is gone. That means we're moving, right?"

Her father cleared his throat. "It means we're staying. We're going to keep the house. It's ours now."

Something tight coiled in Marrill's chest. She fought to keep her breathing steady, but it was difficult as her heart began to drum against her ribs. Her mother had suffered flare-ups before, ever since the hospitalization five years ago. But those had only meant slowing down a bit, not stopping.

"I've taken a job in the city," her father continued. "And we've sent in the paperwork for you to enroll in the school down the road. Since you've been homeschooled, they'll want you to take some tests to make sure you're at grade level, but don't worry, you'll do great. There's a good clinic here, and the doctor's already said she thinks your mother will rebound after a little more stability. For now, we just have to keep the excitement down, and the stress levels low, which means staying in one place for a while."

Her father's words overwhelmed her. "A house? School? But…" They'd never owned a house before. For as long as Marrill could remember, they'd never even lived in the same place longer than six months, and even that was only when her mother was sick the first time. Her parents always said it was "constricting." Marrill suddenly knew what they meant.

A house meant permanency. It meant staying in one place. No more adventure.

It meant her mom must be *really* sick.

Without another word, she turned and ran from the kitchen, biting back tears. Karnelius jumped from the table, knocking aside a stack of papers in the process, and trotted after her.

Marrill paused when she got to the room she'd been staying in, staring at the collage of her drawings and her mom's photos she'd taped to the wall. They were from all over the world: her dad pretending to hold up the Leaning Tower of Pisa, Marrill as a seven-year-old riding a goat up the side of a mountain in the Indonesian rain forest, a sketch she'd done in Australia of a mama wombat holding a cub.

But the one she loved most was of her and her mother in midair, holding hands as they jumped from a cliff toward clear blue water. She remembered it so vividly she could have been standing there right now. Terrified, staring down at the water that seemed so far below. Her mother whispering in her ear, calming her fears, telling her everything would be okay, it would be great. And her mother had been right—it had been amazing.

She felt a hand rest on her shoulder. "The water was freezing that day." Her mom laughed softly, knowing exactly which picture Marrill was staring at. The way she always knew what Marrill was thinking, always knew just the right thing to say or do.

Marrill fought the tears she had only just choked back. "I was so scared."

"But you jumped." Her mom squeezed her shoulder. "Some things can be scary at first. And often those lead to the best kinds of experiences."

Marrill turned to her mom, but her eyes stayed on her own hands, twisting at the hem of her shirt. Her worries burst out in a flood. "This means everything's changing, though. That it won't be like it used to be—we won't be able to do stuff like that anymore."

Her mother crouched in front of her and placed her palms on Marrill's cheeks, pulling them face-to-face. Hot tears welled up in Marrill's eyes, but her mom wiped them away with the pad of her thumb.

"It just means we have to be a little more careful for a while, sweetie, that's all. I promise you'll have lots of adventures in your future. With or without me."

Marrill's stomach clenched. "But I don't want to have

any without you. Why would I have to? You and Dad said you'd be okay!"

"I will be," her mom said, placing a kiss on her forehead. "I plan on sticking around for quite a while." She smiled, that same sweet smile that always made Marrill feel warm inside. "And in the meantime, you'll just have to have a few adventures for me and tell me all about them. Okay?"

Marrill nodded, sniffling. Her mother pulled her into a hug before standing. "Maybe Phoenix won't be so bad," she said, pausing in the doorway. "Remember—when you find yourself in a new situation, you have two options. You can run away, or you can jump in with both feet." She smiled again, this time more softly. "Being a normal kid might be fun for you, if you give it a chance." Then she was gone.

Alone now, Marrill looked to where Karnelius perched on the edge of the bed. "I don't want to be a normal kid," she mumbled. A burning sensation crawled up her throat, and she tried to swallow it down. She didn't know how to feel: terrified for her mother, anxious about her future, disappointed they had to give up their next adventure, guilty for even thinking about that when she should be focused entirely on her mom.

Her room suddenly felt like a cage, and she had to get out. She hastily strapped her cat into his harness, called a quick good-bye to her parents, and stepped outside without waiting for an answer. Karnelius trotted along next to her, his one eye squinting against the bright desert sun.

In moments, they'd crossed the desolate patch of dirt that served as a yard and headed down the road leading out of the empty neighborhood. Dry sand wedged its way into her sneakers and the back of her knees as they trudged. Time slipped away, and all Marrill could focus on was her mother. Before she knew it, they had gone a mile or more, all the way to the abandoned strip mall that had once marked the edge of a now-dead town.

Marrill was so absorbed in her worrying that she didn't notice the scrap of paper cartwheeling across the ground nearby. Karnelius, on the other hand, did. Without warning, he bolted after it, slipping right out of his harness as though he were Houdini himself.

"Get back here, cat!" she called out. "If you make me run in this heat, I swear I'll turn you into mittens!"

His orange tail darted under a dilapidated wooden fence. She dropped the leash and sprinted after. She'd had Karnelius since she'd found him as a kitten. He'd been the first animal she'd ever rescued, the one to teach her about the true love that comes from saving a creature from an uncertain future. He was the only pet she'd been allowed to take with them from one move to the next.

And he was her only friend.

A gust of wind blew up behind her, tossing the ends of her hair over her shoulder as she squeezed through a gap in the fence. On the other side, the mall's empty parking lot sprawled into the distance. Heat wavered up from the asphalt, looking for all the world like an endless expanse of water.

Before she could take another step, the scrap of paper Karnelius had been chasing fluttered past, caught by the wind. Her cat bounded after it, his tail fluffed out like a bristle brush as he pounced and pinned it to the sidewalk. Marrill snatched him up. His claws raked across her palm as he struggled to continue the chase, and she winced in pain.

While she cradled him in an attempt to calm him, she glanced down at the paper. It was old and thick, its edges torn and stained yellow from age. Someone had sketched an elaborate ink drawing across it, a star of some kind.

She'd never seen anything like it before, and she bent closer, hoping to pick up some pointers for her own drawings. But the breeze lifted it again, spinning it just away from her fingers. Reaching out to snag it, she stepped off the sidewalk and onto the parking lot.

The asphalt splashed.

Marrill froze. Warm water sloshed over her shoes, carrying away the grit caked on them. "What in the world?" she asked herself, squinching her forehead. Where it had been dry a second ago, the entire parking lot was now flooded with water. It looked almost like a calm lake. And with the heat distortion, it seemed to stretch out forever.

Sunlight reflected up from the surface, stinging her eyes.

Marrill stared, trying to make sense of this new development. As she watched, the scrap of paper drifted away on the breeze, disappearing into the distance.

And then, as if things couldn't get weirder, out of nowhere a gigantic ship sailed into the handicap spaces.

"*Bwaaa!*" Marrill cried. She stumbled back. Her feet sloshed through the shallows. She blinked, sure she couldn't be seeing right.

It looked like a pirate ship, four masts crowded with sails and a bowsprit jutting out so far in front that it almost pierced the busted plastic sign on one of the empty shops.

"Well, this is unexpected," a voice said. Head spinning, Marrill tented a hand over her eyes to block the blazing sun. Dozens of feet above her, an old man's head popped over a dark wooden railing. His face was small and round, copiously wrinkled, and trailing an enormous white beard. A pointed purple cap fell limp over one ear.

He caught sight of Marrill and leaned so far forward she worried he might topple overboard. "You there," the man called to her. "You wouldn't happen to know what current this is? What strand? What branch of the Stream?"

It was too much. Marrill's mind reeled just trying to process it. Her vision blurred. It took all her effort to keep from falling face-first into the warm lake. The lake that just a few moments before had been a parking lot in the desert.

CHAPTER 3
Thieves in a Pie Shop

Fin sat on a rooftop in the Sellitall District, his feet heavy as they kicked back and forth in the empty air. A labyrinth of buildings teetered their way up the craggy slope behind him, as if looking over his shoulder to watch.

He may have been the Master Thief of the Khaznot Quay, but no one knew it. No one else even knew there *was* a master thief. After all, no matter how big the job was, no one could ever quite remember who had done it.

Until today.

M. Thief, the letter read. *Parsnickle Residence, 17 Gutterleak Way*. It was for him, all right. His fingers trembled with anticipation as he opened it.

Dear Master Thief, it read. Fin wondered what type of person had thoughts so big that their words needed so much space. The letter continued:

The path To mother leads through Home,
but someone must Show the Way.

I will set you on your Journey,
but first there's a Price you must pay.

In the harbor, a ship that Never harbors
Waits to be Boarded.

Full of Treasures, her richest
Treasures are only in Secret Hoarded.

Pierce the Starry sky to find the vault,
Break the safe to get the Key,

Bring it to the thieves' Den,
And take the Rest as your Fee.

Believe that I Am,
Someone Who Remembers You

Just beside the signature, a black splotch marred the white page, as if a single droplet of ink had fallen from the author's quill.

Fin's gaze drifted back up to the one word that had caused his breath to catch and his chest to ache. *Mother.* He closed his eyes, replaying in his mind the last time he'd seen her.

It was the only thing he remembered about her at all.

He couldn't have been older than four. He still recalled the waves shining golden as they split before the ship's prow, and the lights dancing on the shoreline, climbing from the water up the shadow of a great mountain, on and on to join the night sky above.

"The Khaznot Quay," his mother had whispered, pronouncing the first word with a grumble and the last with a pop, so it came out something like *Has Not Key.* "Your new home."

Of course, Fin knew the Quay all too well now; he'd been here ever since. But that night, he'd been afraid, balled up in her arms, snuggled close. He couldn't really remember exactly what she looked like anymore; just black hair falling around her shoulders, moonlight on her eyes, the outline of a soft, round nose.

How safe he'd felt with her holding him.

He sighed. The very last thing he remembered was her pointing up to a star in the sky, brighter than all the others. "No matter what happens," she'd told him, "so long as that star is still there shining, someone will always be out here thinking of you." Even in memory, her voice came as smooth and calm as a warm fire on a freezing day.

Sniffling, Fin swiped at his eyes and stared at the letter. He read it again, tracing the bizarre curves of the handwriting. Break into a ship, steal a key, and anything else was his. A typical heist, really, if sparing on the details. And written by someone with really bad taste in poetry.

It was the signature that he kept coming back to. *Someone Who Remembers You.* Before falling asleep last night, he'd watched the star blinking through the attic window, the promise that someone would be thinking of him. Now it had come true—there really was someone who remembered him. And the reward they promised... to show him the path to home, to his mother?

There was no turning this offer down. Even if whoever sent it sounded like they'd dipped their head in Stream water.

Fin stood up on the roof's edge, unbothered by the four-story drop below. This job was too important to risk going in blind; what Fin needed was intel. And for a Quay thief, there was only one place to go to learn anything about anything: Ad and Tad's pie shop.

He set off, clattering across ceramic roofs and jumping from dangling gutters on his way to the top of the District. The old pie shop squished against a cliff there, just beneath the crumbling towers of Nosebleed Heights. Before long, he slipped down a trellis of tangleweed, into an alley so steep and narrow it would be better called a staircase, and hiked up to the little dead-end plaza outside Ad and Tad's Gourmet Pie-o-ria.

It was a cramped space, with only one way in and one way out. Overhead, the fierce Quay winds blew straight into the cliff, creating a curl-over vortex that kept all but the best skysailers at bay. In short, it was a terrible place for a store, and a great place for a bunch of thieves to keep their den.

The bell over the door jangled as he opened it. NO ONE LEAVES WITH AN APPETITE! claimed the sign in the window, and Fin could hardly argue with that.

Instead of the smell of buttery rolls and cinnamon, Ad and Tad's reeked of damp mildew and burnt *something*. On the shelves, mounds of sticky buns with gooey green frosting slumped beside stacks of cookies that each sported a fully functioning eyeball. And, of course, on the counter sat a plate of foil-wrapped candies. Ad and Tad called them their Famous Chocolate Flavor Blasters. Everyone else in the world called them "the puke pills."

The thieves had chosen carefully in locating their den here. Fin didn't remember ever seeing this place with an actual customer.

Ad and Tad looked up with toothy smiles as he strolled inside, not a drop of recognition in their eyes. "Help you, young man?" Ad asked. She was young and sweet, at least by Quay standards, which meant she had nearly all her teeth and usually wasn't armed.

"No trub today, Ad," Fin said. "Just an order of your finest phlegmenflosses." He squared his shoulders as he said the password, trying to look authoritative.

Tad nodded and motioned to the brick walk-in oven in the back. "Of course, m'boy," he said. "We bake 'em fresh right through there."

That was what made this place great, Fin thought. Among the pie shop crew, a thief who didn't draw attention was a good thief. To them, as long as Fin knew the right signs, the fact that no one remembered him just meant he was good at what he did.

He slipped under the counter, snatching a few puke pills on his way (they were always handy in case you got poisoned), and headed into the dark oven. At a touch, the back wall swung away, revealing the thieves' den.

Just down a few rickety stairs, thieves laughed and

gambled and argued in an open hall filled with wood tables and a roaring fireplace at the far end. Hulking thugs with arms like gorillas' played toss-the-teeth using wiry foot-pads. Scale-covered cutpurses picked away at practice locks, while swindlers spun stories to half-interested con artists. To a man almost everyone, and everything, was covered in a light dusting of flour.

Fin smiled and relaxed. It was good to be back.

Casually, he wandered over to a table full of privateers clanking cups with a squad of highwaymen. They were a rough-looking bunch, but Fin didn't worry. While pretty much anyone crooked was welcome in the pie shop, Stavik, the self-proclaimed Pirate King of the Khaznot Quay and undisputed boss of the den, drew the line at murderers. Besides, thieves and pirates honored their own.

"Signs up, bloods," Fin announced, briefly gaining their attention. He made the traditional pirate greeting in the air, and ten gloved hands echoed it back.

"Welcome, fellow shady-fellow," one of them said cheer-fully. "Make a spot, mates."

Fin bit back his joy at being included; it wouldn't last, of course. The spot they made was closing almost before he could sit. Still, even a moment's warmth was more than Fin got anywhere else.

Normally he'd sit and soak it all in. But today he was here to get information. "Soooo," he said, "how about that ship that doesn't harbor harboring in the harbor, huh?"

Nine sets of eyes looked at him and blinked. Fin had a moment of discomfort, until the tenth man spoke up. "Bly me twice, but 'twere the Iron Ship what sent her limping into port!"

One of the other pirates let out a guffaw. "You old bafter, the Iron Ship's naught but a story."

"Don't laugh! It's true!" a third argued. "What else could bruise a ship like that?" He leaned forward, a crazed gleam in one eye. "They say the Iron Ship comes in the biggest storms, when the lightning flashes red. A ship cast in iron, her crew cut from shadows. They say her master's the ghost of a great wizard-demon-pirate-captain-king, and he's hungry for souls." As usual in a gathering of thieves, half the gang snorted in derision and the other half affirmed it as undeniable.

"Wizard-demon-pirate-captain-king, got it," Fin said. "But about the ship here in the *harbor*...the one that's not made of iron?"

A thick-bearded smuggler dropped his cup with a clang. "Oh, she's something else. Supposably, whatever she's carrying is fancy enough that she don't ever make port, just stays out on the Stream full-time where none can touch her. Stavik tried to go after her once, but even *he* couldn't bring her down...." He trailed off and shook his head. "But then I reckon she got caught in one of them storms. Drove her in for repairs, and I reckon the Quay was the closest harbor she could find. The Master o' the Iron Ship musta did a number on her, for a ship like that to dock in a place like this."

Fin nodded. "In for repairs is good. What's she look like? Well guarded?" He cleared his throat. "I only ask for a friend."

"Well, ya can't miss 'er," the first pirate said. "About the weirdest-lookin' vessel I e'er peeped. As fer who's on board, well..." He leaned in and dropped his voice. "You'd have to ask Stavik."

The others at the table gulped. "I wouldn't," one of them murmured.

Fin grinned. "Don't worry about me...." he said, slipping to his feet. Not that they would. Because practically before the words had even left his mouth, the privateers and highwaymen had forgotten he was ever there. "I can handle Stavik," he added to himself.

Keeping his back straight, he swaggered his way toward the far end of the room, where the Pirate King sat on his throne, a polished chair made from the figureheads of ships he'd captured. Stavik was lean and angular and seemed built from taut wire. More of him was scar than smooth skin, and he did nothing to hide it.

He dressed simply, in a vest and matching trousers made of close-cut dragon leather. The story went that Stavik was so good a thief he'd cut the skin from the dragon itself while it still lived, and the beast never knew it was missing. It was no wonder the rest of the thieves feared him.

But Fin actually *liked* Stavik. He'd been the one to teach Fin most everything he knew about thieving, even if the Pirate King didn't remember it.

Back when Fin was seven, it had taken him months to learn the right mix of bravado and deference to get an audience with Stavik. He probably still had bruises on his shoulders from all the hands that had tossed him onto the cobblestone street. But he'd come back each day, a total stranger to the thieves each time. And each time, he learned a bit better how to carry himself. And then one day Stavik had said, "Leave him. I like the tyke," and agreed to show Fin a few tricks.

Fin had repeated that scene ever since, starting fresh each time, until he knew just about everything Stavik had to teach. He still did it from time to time, though, relearning the same old lessons. He liked spending time with the old goon.

Puffing up his chest but keeping his eyes down, Fin walked straight up to the polished chair, stopping exactly the second before a thick hand would have come down on his shoulder. "Leave him," Stavik said, his voice rough like the edge of an old rusty razor. "I like the look of the boy. Good swagger, but knows his place. Blends in. Barely noticed him till he stepped up. Good thieving in this one." He squinted at Fin. "Who the 'etch are you, then?"

"Just an apprentice," Fin said. Long experience had taught him how hard it was to convince anyone that a kid his age was a master thief. "My bossman said to mention the Blind Beetle Bank break-in, or the Laughing Sauce looting?" He rifled through his pockets quickly, producing a red coin with a bug emblazoned on it as proof.

Stavik's face barely moved, but an ugly red scar on his chin twitched, a sure sign he was considering. "Yeah," he said. "All right. What's your bossman after, then?"

"I...uh, I mean, *he* needs some information on that weird-looking ship in the harbor."

"Fine enough," Stavik said. "*Someone* needs to rob that thing." It went without saying, of course, that he expected a cut of the take. Fin nodded eagerly; if the letter was right, this job should net plenty of loot to spare.

Stavik's eyes shifted from one side to the other and his voice dropped. "Ship belongs to the Meressian Order. Heard of them?"

Fin shook his head. "Wouldn't think so," Stavik continued. "Some kind of cult started a couple centuries back. They spent decades writing down everything that came outta some oracle's mouth, something about a prophecy and the future and whatnot. End-of-the-world-type stuff."

He lifted a shoulder. "Anyway, back in the day, they had some sort of falling-out with their oracle, he split, and the whole cult sort of faded out of view. But word is the real hardcore blights kept going, trying to stop the nutter's prophecy from coming true. They been collecting stuff related to that prophecy ever since. Relics and antiques and all sorts of value-ables."

His mouth split into a grin. "That's a couple hundred years of loot if your math ain't good. All of it on that ship, which is why they keep it out on the Stream full-time, nonstop."

"But now that it's here..." Fin said, echoing Stavik's grin.

"Don't get cocky," Stavik told him. "These guys know how to protect their jink. I tried once, didn't go well. That was on the open Stream, a'course, but being in port will make 'em even more jumpy. Way I hear it, the guards they got posted on the docks are professionals, impossible to distract. Get past them and there's a whole mess more, patrolling the place. Nasty traps, too. Your man will have to be good."

"He is," Fin said with pride, plans already running through his mind.

"He'd better be," Stavik said. "He won't be the first to try." He leaned back onto his figurehead throne, knitting his fingers together. "That's all I got."

Fin nodded, half-bowed, and made to leave. It was heist time.

"Hey, blood," Stavik called after him. Fin turned. "Your man busts that ship open, tell him to bring me something nice. Make it good, and I'll show you how to pick a lock with a dagger tip."

Of course, Stavik had already taught Fin that trick. Three years ago. And five times since.

"I'd like that," Fin said.

CHAPTER 4
Don't Harass the Barnacles

The ship in the parking lot towered over Marrill, making her feel tiny in comparison. A part of her wanted to slosh closer, to touch the hull to see if it was real. The other part warned she should get as far away as possible.

She glanced around, wishing her dad were here, or her mom; they would know what to do. Even the Hatch brothers could at least tell her if she was hallucinating. But there was no one. Just Karnelius, the cool water against her skin, and the pirate ship. She could make out a few windows on its sides, running away from her in rows, but each one was either boarded by shutters or crusted with salt. The only other person was the old man, who leaned out over the ship's rail, staring at her expectantly.

"I think she's deaf," he remarked to someone out of sight. "Or possibly she just replaced herself with a perfect double, made of her own belly button lint. If it's the latter, we're in luck; I'm pretty sure I've been here before."

Marrill blinked, realizing he was talking about her. She knew she ought to say something, but she didn't quite know what. "Um...hello?" She swallowed uneasily. "I didn't understand you. Or what's going on, or...anything, really."

The white-bearded face turned back to her, one eyebrow lifted. "Not deaf. Or lint," he told his invisible companion, sounding vaguely disappointed. "But good for you, of course!" he added to Marrill. She stared, trying to keep up. "Anyway, we're a bit lost, as you might have gathered. Could you kindly tell us what branch of the Stream we've stumbled on?"

She had no idea what he was talking about. They were in the desert—there wasn't running water for miles. Unless you counted the sudden lake, which she didn't because...well, because it shouldn't have been there.

Except that it *was* there, since she was clearly standing

in it. Little waves lapped at her ankles, and if she angled her head just right, she could still make out the lines of the parking lot below the surface.

She blinked, trying to remember the question. "What branch of the what?" she asked.

"She doesn't know where we are," the old man called over his shoulder.

"I didn't think she would," a voice shouted back.

Marrill opened her mouth. She was full of questions but could scarcely decide which to ask first. Before she could make a sound, the old man slipped out of view.

She shook her head. "I don't guess you know what's going on?" she asked Karnelius. He glared up at her with his one good cat-eye, the rest of his body still in full-on puff mode and rumbling with growls.

Marrill had absolutely no idea how to approach this situation. She thought back to what her mom had told her about jumping in with both feet, even if it seemed scary at first. Marrill took a deep breath, steadied herself, and sloshed closer to the ship. She craned her neck and called out, "Mr. . . ." She hesitated. "Mr. Sir?"

The old man popped back into view. "You're still here, then?" he asked. Then he frowned. "Or rather, we're still here. Hmmm. Unexpected." He drummed his fingers on the railing.

"So," she plunged ahead, "pretty neat trick, making a

boat appear like that out of nowhere. Are you guys magicians or something?"

"Wizard, actually," the old man said. "Good question, though. My turn: You wouldn't have set eyes on a certain bit of map, would you?"

Marrill had no idea what he was talking about. "Huh?"

"Tell her it's a scrap of paper," the invisible voice shouted.

The old man's face gave a flash of exasperation before he turned back to her. "A bit of parchment, perhaps? In these parts? Have you seen it?"

Marrill used the toe of her left foot to scratch at where the water tickled the calf of her right leg. "I . . ." Her brain sank back to the first part. "Wait, you said a wizard?"

His laughter sounded like a cloud tastes, light and fluffy and slightly damp. Which was weird, because she'd never really considered the taste of a cloud before. It felt, she had to admit, magical, which sent a little thrill down her spine.

"Yes, I certainly did!" the old man responded. "Now back to my question, about that map—any sightings?"

"Um . . ." Marrill shifted Karnelius in her arms, wincing at the pain from the recent cat scratches on her palm. Maybe if she just played along, she would get to the bottom of this. At the very least, she'd end up with a story to tell her mom over dinner tonight.

She wasn't getting much information out of him so far.

She thought for a minute, contemplating her next move. An idea came to her. "Tell you what," she called up. "If I agree to answer a question of yours, will you answer a question of mine?"

"Yes!" the old man cried. "Well, that's my end of the bargain. Your turn to answer."

"Wait, what?" Marrill asked. She rubbed her neck, which had grown stiff from looking up. Suddenly, she realized what had happened. He *had* answered a question of hers. She stomped her foot, but only succeeded in splashing herself. "But that's not fair!" she cried.

"Fair?" the old man mused. "Well, probably not, I suppose, but they're your rules. Besides, when speaking with wizards, one must be precise. Wouldn't want to end up with a scalp covered in rabbits when what you really wanted was a baldness cure. A head full of hare can be devilish to keep fed, you know."

He trailed off for a moment, then shook his head, returning his focus to Marrill. "So, did you see a scrap of paper hereabouts?"

Marrill narrowed her eyes. It occurred to her that she'd been approaching this conversation as if it were normal, when absolutely *nothing* about this day was even *remotely* normal. She thought for a moment and then grinned.

"Yes, I did see a scrap of paper," she answered simply. The old man looked down at her expectantly. "We traded an answer for an answer," she said triumphantly. "Now, if you'd like to make that same bargain again, I'm sure I can find another question for you."

Laughter echoed from somewhere behind him. "She got you there, Ardent," the hidden voice remarked. Marrill struggled to swallow her giggles.

"Quite so!" the old man—Ardent, apparently—said. "I accept your terms, young lady, but I'll start this time. Where, perchance, did the paper go?"

"Last I saw, the wind was carrying it that way," she told him, pointing her chin beyond the ship, to where the lake shimmered into the distance.

The old man followed her gaze. Then, out of nowhere, he started shouting to his companion. "Coll!" he ordered. "Turn us around. Or heave to or whatever you sailors call these things these days."

A low grumbling began in the bowels of the ship, a kind of groaning as it started to turn, trying to navigate the shallows. Waves radiated out from the hull, crashing against Marrill and sending her off balance. The ship floundered, and Marrill heard the hidden voice—Coll's—yell, "Sorry! The Stream's shallow; current's grown pretty stagnant. We might be stuck for a minute."

Marrill juggled Karnelius so that she could free up an arm. "Wait!" she called out, waving to get the old man's attention. "You didn't answer my question! Where did you come from?"

The old man looked down at her and smiled. "Why, the

Pirate Stream, of course!" And then he disappeared.

"Wait!" Marrill called again. "What does that even mean?" The ship rocked again, sending waves that splashed up to the hem of her shorts and crashed against the storefronts behind her. "Hello?" she called up at the empty railing.

She sloshed closer, easing her feet along the pavement to make sure it didn't drop off. But it never did. Even next to the ship, the water only came up to her knees.

She studied the hull, trying to make sense of how such a massive boat could sail through such shallow water. Barnacles clung to the damp wood, up to the level of her nose, and she suddenly realized they were *looking* at her.

She bent closer. Green bodies peeked out from iridescent turquoise shells that shimmered as if coated in glitter. Also they had eyes. And feathers. She blinked in surprise. The little creatures let out a series of tiny chirps in response, and tucked themselves away, leaving only little wispy frills sticking out.

Marrill thought back through the dozens of books she'd read on the world's strangest animals. She'd never heard of anything like these before.

Karnelius released his claws from Marrill's shirt for just long enough to take a swipe at one. She yanked him out of range before he could do any damage. "Bad cat!" she quietly scolded. But then, she thought as she stared at the iridescent creatures, touching them *was* kind of irresistible.

She tried to keep her hands clenched into fists to avoid

the temptation. But it was too much. It was all just too weird. Carefully, she snuck a finger out, holding it over one of the frills until the creature let out a squeak and eased from its shell.

"Hello, little fellow," Marrill cooed, giggling as its feathers tickled her skin.

"Oh dear," came a voice from above, startling her. "You didn't let it touch you, did you?" The old man leaned dangerously far over the railing, staring down at her.

"I . . ." She slipped her hand behind her back. For a moment, she considered lying. But something about the man's expression worried her. "Just a little," she confessed.

"Oh dear," Ardent said again, his forehead wrinkling in a frown.

Marrill's heart rate spiked. She had the uneasy feeling that she'd done something terribly wrong. "Why? What's bad about touching them?"

The man cleared his throat before answering. "Oh, nothing," he said with a nervous smile. "Incidentally, you're not allergic to poison by any chance, are you?"

CHAPTER 5
Guarding, and Other Ineffective Jobs

Most folks thought guard duty was boring. Not Ghatz. Guarding was in his blood. He traced his line back to ancient times, when Ghatz the Original had guarded the last tub of honey in the entire Khesteresh Empire against an army of angry bees. His own father, Ghatz Sr., had nobly guarded the Saint Nolywere Bridge, which kept the Khesteresh safe from the skink-riding plantimals of the Longtooth Kingdoms. And

Ghatz himself had once guarded the imperial treasury of Khesteresh, up until it was sacked by plantimals. And now, even though the Khesteresh Empire might be a skink-infested ruin, Ghatz kept right on guarding.

Only now he worked for the Meressian Order, who had arrived just in time to save some of the Khesteresh Empire's greatest relics from plantimal handicles. Grateful as Ghatz was for that, most of the time it didn't quite live up to the old days. The Temple Ship stayed hidden on the deep waters of the Stream, and though he did his best to walk the deck and frown at any suspicious shape on the horizon, it was hardly *real* guarding. Up until recently, that is.

The sun shone bright on the wharf, and Ghatz squinted against it. His partner, Hersch, stood at stern attention next to him. In front of them, the ramshackle buildings of the Khaznot Quay leaned toward the docks like a pack of criminals getting ready to pounce. It was a thieves' paradise, a den of smugglers and pirates without morals or inhibition. In short, it was the perfect place to guard against, and Ghatz was on high alert.

"Hello!" a voice chirped next to him. Ghatz jumped and looked down. It was a skinny little kid, with olive skin and dark hair. How could he have slipped up without being noticed? Ghatz cleared his throat to cover his embarrassment.

"Who goes there?" he demanded. He gave the kid his best guard-eye.

The kid shrugged. "Just a kid," he said. "Prolly don't remember me, huh?"

Ghatz looked to Hersch, who shrugged. "Remember you from where?" he asked.

"No trub," said the kid. He gave them a big innocent smile that made even Ghatz feel comfortable. Not enough to let his guard down, of course, but comfortable nonetheless. "Ever seen a brine butterfly?" the kid asked.

The comment struck Ghatz as odd. He looked up at the sky and rubbed his chin. Overhead, the masts of the Temple Ship branched into a million intertwining limbs, each covered in tiny, leaflike sails. Those little sails always reminded him of butterfly wings. And of the brine butterflies of Khesteresh, in particular. Somewhere inside him, he had the strange feeling he'd just been telling someone that, not long ago.

"Funny you bring it up," he said. "Used to love the little puppers when I was a kid." He tapped Hersch's arm. "You ever seen one?"

Hersch glanced at him quickly, then looked away. "We're on duty," he whispered. "But no," he added sheepishly. "Sort of always wanted to."

"Lucky chance," the kid said with a smile. He pulled a small glass jar from a bag at his waist and held it up. Inside, bright blue liquid sloshed about. "They were unloading a batch of 'em down the wharf a ways and I got to snitch me one."

"Weren't we just talking to someone about this?" Hersch asked.

"Shhhh!" Ghatz hissed as the kid unscrewed the lid. He leaned forward in anticipation.

The kid moved slowly, with the grace of a master showman. He twisted the jar hard, and the lid came open with a loud *pop!*

Ghatz and Hersch drew in their breath simultaneously. Nothing happened.

"Shy girl," the kid tittered with a nervous smile. Just then, the liquid congealed and pulled together. First one long leg emerged, then another, and another. Ghatz practically shook with excitement—it really was a brine butterfly! The creature pulled itself free, brilliant blue wings unfolding, until it perched on the lip of the jar and shuddered slightly in the breeze.

"That's something!" Hersch said, leaning forward. "It's awful pretty...." He reached out a finger to stroke the butterfly's translucent wing.

Ghatz shot out a hand to stop him. "Careful, Hersch," he barked. "They get scared easy. She'll burst right into salt water if you touch her wrong!"

Out of the corner of his eye, he barely noticed the kid nodding in agreement, even as the jar dropped from his hand.

The butterfly startled, flapped for another perch. Ghatz ducked around her. Hersch didn't. She settled straight on his nose, her wings brushing against the ends of his eyelashes.

"Don't…move…." Ghatz whispered. Hersch quivered with each brush of the wings. His face contorted. His eyes went wild with panic. Something was coming. Ghatz sucked in his breath.

Hersch looked like he was about to cry. And then he could resist no longer. He sneezed.

Ghatz let out a shriek as the terrified brine butterfly exploded into salt water, splashing all down Hersch's face. "I told you not to touch her!" he shouted, batting away Hersch's efforts to wipe himself off. "Don't mess with her or she'll never come out again!"

"I didn't do nuffin'!" Hersch protested, his eyes red and teary from salt. Ghatz fussed around him, completely devoted to saving the butterfly. For a moment, neither one of them was paying the slightest attention to his guard duty.

And that moment was all Fin needed to slip past them, out of their minds forever, and onto the Meressian ship.

++ + ++

Fin couldn't help smiling. It had taken him most of the morning chatting with those two to find the soft spot, but it had been worth it just to see the looks on their faces!

As he scrambled up the gangplank, he examined the Meressian Temple Ship. It was mostly built of dullwood, of course. Dullwood was the only stuff in existence too boring to be transformed into something crazy by the magic waters of the Pirate Stream. It was therefore essential for any good streamrunner. "Can't sail a chicken," as the sailors down at the docks would say, accompanied by the fervent nods of anyone who had sailed out too far in a normal-wood boat only to watch it sprout feathers.

But dullwood was the only thing dull about this ship. Living in the premiere smuggling port on the Pirate Stream, Fin had seen a lot of strange vessels. Most ships, though, looked something like ships. This one looked almost like, well, a forest.

First of all, she was circular, more a flat-topped bowl than the normal ship shape. Second, her masts pushed from her deck randomly, as if they'd grown there, and each one branched out toward the top, their limbs tangling in a dense canopy of leaflike sails. Carvings etched the sides of the ship, from waterline to mast tip, full of strange places and weird people and things Fin had never heard of.

Those carvings were a bit creepy, no doubt, but they made a grade-A climbing surface. And Fin would take climbing creepy carvings over sneaking past the guards on deck any day. In moments, he'd shimmied across a big, ugly-looking fish, traversed a horse with the tail of a peacock, and pulled himself through a nearby porthole.

Inside, a sharp, spicy odor punched him in the face. Apparently he'd found the ship's mess. Low dining tables filled the room, and shelves full of flavor bottles lined the walls. In the middle of it all, a huge metal cauldron bubbled. The sign hanging over it read **THIEF STEW**.

Fin gulped. *Very funny*, he thought. Then a wicked idea crept into his mind. Whatever might actually be in the thief stew, it *was* the crew's dinner. He searched through the pockets of his coat until he found the puke pills from Ad and Tad's. He unwrapped a few with a mischievous grin and dropped them into the boiling cauldron. "Now *that's* thief stew," he said, chuckling.

He was just about to slip through the doorway when he heard a voice outside, saying, "Clear the workmen off." He pressed himself flat against the wall, holding his breath to stay as still and quiet as possible.

"The repairs aren't complete yet," a second voice said. "And it's almost lunchtime, so—"

"We've no choice," interrupted the first voice. It was raspy and thick, and felt like a cheese grater on Fin's eardrums. "There are rumors the Oracle's already in the Quay, and we can't risk him getting on board. We push off now."

Fin gulped again and shifted until he could catch the reflection of the two speakers in a row of pots hanging on the far wall. The first voice belonged to a tall, thin creature with deadly-looking thorns covering his body. *Bet he doesn't get involved in many tickle fights*, Fin thought.

"We never should have made port here to begin with," the thorny guard said. "Every cutpurse in the city's been eyeing us like a roast chicken for days now."

"At least it's a nice afternoon," offered the second, a hulking figure with a face that looked more bullish than humanish.

The thorny guy shook his head, exasperated. "You'll excuse me if I don't place my hope in the Oracle stopping for a picnic. Now, get moving," he ordered before walking off.

The guy with the bull face started after him, but then paused and doubled back toward the mess. "Maybe just one little yummy for my gummies," he said to no one, tiptoeing quickly into the room and heading for the pot of thief stew.

Fin flattened himself against the wall, every muscle frozen. Bull Face lifted a steaming ladle full of the soup and took a long, loud *sluuurrrrrrrrppppppp*. He smacked his lips a few times and turned to leave. When he reached the door, he let out a massive, satisfied belch, then continued on his way.

Too close, Fin thought, slumping against the wall. He waited for his pulse to slow before slipping out of the mess after Bull Face and pushing his way through the narrow door at the end of a hallway.

He found himself on a catwalk over an open gallery so giant it practically filled the whole ship. At its bottom, fires burned in censers all around, casting a red-orange glow on the huge masts that extended through the deck above to the base of the hull below.

In the middle of the chamber, a massive statue of a man cloaked in white robes and holding out a great golden chalice towered nearly to the ceiling. Several stories below the rim of the golden chalice, a reflecting pool was set into the floor, its water shimmering in the firelight.

But even that wasn't what *really* caught Fin's eye. Because scattered throughout the gallery were hundreds of display cases, filled with untold riches of every kind imaginable. It was a horde of loot like he'd never seen.

Fin nearly salivated at the sight. He took a moment to focus. These were certainly the treasures the letter had mentioned. But he needed to find that key. And according to the letter, it along with the ship's *true* treasures was hidden in some sort of vault.

He scanned the gallery, searching for any sign of the vault or the "starry sky" the letter had talked about. Nothing. Not that he was surprised—if he could have seen it so easily from here, it wouldn't have been very well hidden. And if he was going to learn where his mother was, he was just going to have to go down there and find it. He glanced around for the quickest way to the main floor.

A series of catwalks and ladders ran around the walls of the massive chamber, creating a maze of ups and downs, sideways and crossways. And each and every one, he swiftly noticed, teemed with purple-clad guards, all headed in his direction. It was lunchtime, and he was standing between the Meressians and the mess hall.

There was no time to lose, and no place to run. With no other option, he flung himself over the rope railing and into the darkness.

If there were three things every orphan in the Khaznot Quay knew, the first was how to climb. Too many times, Fin had hung upside down from makeshift arches, the muscles in his arms and legs quivering and aching, waiting for a crowd (or a town watch or an angry mark) to slip past. He breathed a silent thanks for all those bad memories as the guards walked past where he was dangling and headed in to enjoy their thief stew.

Fin grinned. They had no idea what they were in for.

Once he was clear, Fin carefully lowered himself from one catwalk to the next, making a slow descent to the bottom. Finally, he dropped to the floor, just next to a fancy-looking glass display case. He couldn't resist taking a peek inside.

A brace of spiff-looking knives waited for him, all silver blade and pearl handle. They looked just perfect for climbing, jimmying, and all-around thieving. He knew he shouldn't; he had a key to find, *real* treasures to pilfer. But he did need to get a gift for Stavik....

"I'll be taking those," Fin whispered to himself. A quick

check for traps turned up a gossamer line running down through a little hole in the base to a vial of purple mist. Sneeze Breeze.

Stavik was right, these guys weren't fooling around. One of the pie shop thieves had gotten sprayed in the face with Sneeze Breeze once. Before that day he'd been called Jack the Nose. Now everyone called him Jack No-Nose.

Carefully, he undid the wire, let it slip free, and opened the case. The knives were his. He smirked as he slid them into his belt, feeling as masterful as a master thief could be. *Now on to the real treasures*, he thought.

He turned around, smack into a wall. "*Oooof!*" he said, stumbling backward.

"Gotcha," the wall growled.

CHAPTER 6
Marrill Grows Feathers

P oison?" Marrill echoed the old man's words, her mouth going dry. A sick feeling churned through her as she stared down at her hand. Her fingertip glowed a faint shade of green where she'd touched the barnacle creature. Already it was spreading across her palm toward her wrist. Her legs began to tremble, sending little ripples across the surface of the lake.

"Oh, it's hardly a big deal," Ardent called down from the

deck of the ship. From Marrill's perspective, it was difficult to see this as anything *other* than a big deal. She held her arm out as the green crept up onto her forearm. Her fingers started to tingle and, somehow, buzz a little bit. Karnelius hissed.

"But just in case," Ardent added, "wait right there." He grunted and swung a leg over the railing. The hem of his purple robe fluttered as he reached for a rope ladder dangling nearby. "And whatever you do, don't think of any words with the letter *X* in them!"

Immediately her mind began conjuring up *X*-letter words. *Relax*, she told herself. The green streaked faster along her arm, almost to her elbow.

She bit her lip, willing herself to breathe. "Inhale," she whispered. "Exhale." She shrieked as the green shot up farther. Already the skin felt heavy and wrong and a slight burning throbbed in her bones.

"What's happening?" she cried.

"That depends on how human you are," the old man said, landing in front of her with a splash. He reached for her arm. "May I?"

Marrill blinked and nodded, because she didn't know what else to do. Her fingers vibrated and her arm glowed, and it took everything she had to keep standing and not drop Karnelius. Karny hated water. Getting him wet would only make things worse.

Ardent's touch was comforting as he *tsk*ed over the spreading green. The scratches along her palm from Karnelius's earlier struggle had turned an alarming shade of black and oozed a thick purplish slime. Her stomach churned and she had to look away.

"Judging from the reaction, you're definitely at least mostly human," Ardent mused. "So that's something good to know, isn't it?" He gave her a gentle, caring smile.

"What's going to happen to me?" she whimpered, daring a glance back at her arm. Feathers seemed to be sprouting along her wrist. She squeezed her eyes shut. Her father had said they needed to keep her mother's stress level low. Marrill was pretty sure a daughter who suddenly grew feathers would accomplish just the opposite.

If she lived to make it home again at all.

The old man grasped her arm tightly, and for the briefest of moments a flash of warmth flared across her skin. It reminded her of the sensation just before lightning strikes, when the hair stands up on your neck and the back of your throat tastes like old pennies. Karnelius wiggled mightily in her grasp.

She squirmed a little herself, the inside of her elbow tickling. And then...nothing. The heaviness, the buzzing, the pain—all of it was gone.

"Right as rain," Ardent pronounced, poking at a few of her fingers. Marrill eased her eyes open and glanced at her arm. With a gasp, she found her skin was back to normal—not a speck of green anywhere. The feathers had disappeared from her wrist. And even more curious, so had the scratches she'd gotten earlier from Karnelius.

She opened and closed her hand a few times. It felt like nothing had happened at all. And yet...she saw something flash along the ripple of waves. She bent and plucked it free, staring. A waterlogged feather from her wrist dangled limp between her fingers.

Ardent was already splashing his way noisily back toward the ladder. She scrambled after him. "How did you do that?" she asked, her eyes wide with shock and confusion.

"I told you," he called over his shoulder. "I'm a wizard." He began climbing back up the side of the ship. "Coll, we still don't seem to be moving!"

Marrill frowned. That was no explanation at all. Because wizards didn't exist. "I don't understand," she yelled after him.

"Why, I healed you, of course," he called back. "With magic! It's what I do. Magic, not healing. But sometimes both." He reached the railing and hefted himself out of sight.

Marrill glanced back at the feather in her hand. This *was* magic. *Real* magic. Maybe if it had just been her skin turning green and the buzzing and burning, she could chalk it up to some sort of illusion or adverse reaction to an animal's natural defenses or a trick of her heat-addled brain.

But that wouldn't explain the cat scratches. Karny had gotten her good; those had been real. And they hadn't been little cuts, either—she could still see the traces of blood along the cracks in her palm. And yet, now there was no evidence at all that the skin had ever been split.

Somehow, Ardent had healed her. Even though it didn't make sense, it was the only explanation she could come up with. And if he could heal her…if what Ardent said about being a wizard was true—and didn't she have the proof in her hand?—then he really could heal people. And maybe not just her.

He could heal her mother! Or teach her how to! And then they wouldn't have to stay in Phoenix, and everyone would be healthy and happy, and they could hit the road again, go back to the three of them having adventures together, the way it had been before. She practically jumped for joy. She'd get her old life back. And most importantly, her mom would be right there with her!

She grabbed for the ladder. "Hey!" she cried. "Wait up! I have a question for you!" She quickly found it wasn't easy climbing with only one arm, especially with a cat who wasn't a big fan of either heights or large pools of water. She struggled to keep her grip, and when she finally reached the top, she stumbled over the railing, slightly out of breath.

A vast deck spread out before her, raised in the front and back like she'd seen on model ships, with a cabin at the far end. Ardent had already made his way over to it, and she chased after him across the wide wooden planks.

"You say you can heal people?" she blurted.

The wizard swung around halfway up the narrow stairs leading to the rear deck and let out a high-pitched yelp, startled by her sudden appearance. Well, at least she wasn't the only one here feeling a little unsettled.

"Oh! Well. Oh." He cleared his throat. "Oh! It's you. From before. How...unexpected. Isn't that unexpected, Coll?"

He turned, revealing a boy just a few years older than Marrill, his hands gripping the giant wooden wheel of the ship. He was tall and lanky, as if he'd been stretched—all elbows and knees and dark, dark skin. Marrill blinked a few times—from their earlier interactions she'd assumed Coll was much older.

"We weren't exactly anticipating picking up stowaways," Ardent mused as he tugged on his long white beard. "Is there a protocol for this?"

Coll's response was more of a grunt. "The brig?"

Before either could say anything more, Marrill stepped forward, directly in front of the wizard. "You can heal people?" She still felt a little stupid for believing it could be true. She waited for both of them to laugh at her, but neither did.

Instead, Ardent frowned. "*Magic* can heal people," he answered. "When it wishes," he added with a chuckle.

"What are the limits? I mean, can you heal anything?

Can you fix someone who's really, really sick?" She tried to think of the worst kind of injury imaginable, because if he could fix that, he could do anything. "If I got my arm cut off, could you put it back on again?"

"Hmm," he said, looking from her left to her right. "Which arm?"

She blinked. "Does it matter?" An arm was an arm, wasn't it?

"Well, I'd think it would matter to *you*," he told her.

"But you *could* fix it?" she asked, barely able to breathe as she waited for his response.

"Possibly," Ardent said. "We would need the arm, of course. And it always depends on the tides of the Stream and how the magic's feeling that day and often the semi-mesopheric compression of..."

Marrill didn't listen to the rest because it didn't make sense. But that didn't matter. She had her answer: There was the possibility he could make her mother better.

"I need to get back," she said, cutting him off. "Now. And I need you to come with me."

The old man stared at her as if she were the one being confusing. "Back where?"

"Home." She turned to point behind her, across the abandoned parking lot to the road that led to her great-aunt's house. Except it wasn't there anymore. She gasped, her heart thundering as she ran to the railing for a better look.

Gone were the abandoned storefronts with their broken

windows and boarded doors. Gone was the cracked asphalt parking lot. As far as she could see, there was nothing except an endless expanse of water. Golden, glowing water.

Karnelius rumbled in complaint, and she realized she'd been squeezing him too tightly. For the first time, the feel of his furry body cradled in her arms did nothing to comfort her.

"How?" she whispered, equal parts bewildered and amazed. "What?" She swallowed. "Where are we?"

A crash of thunder boomed behind her, and she turned. Dark clouds boiled along the horizon, racing toward them. Ardent didn't seem concerned. He stood with his feet braced against the rolling of the ship, damp purple robe whipping around his ankles in the increasing wind, the tip of his cap flapping like a wind sock.

The wizard—for she now knew that's what he was— held his arms out wide and grinned. "Welcome," he cried, his voice louder than the thunder, "to the Pirate Stream!"

CHAPTER 7
Dead Is Dead Is Dead

Fin looked up into a pair of flaring bull's nostrils. Behind them, teeth like tombstones gleamed inside a dark, furry muzzle. From this angle, Bull Face looked like he could eat three Fins for breakfast and still be up for a big lunch.

"You're a sneaky one," Bull Face grunted, cracking his monster-sized knuckles. "Saw the case come open, didn't even see you there."

Fin raised his hands. "Well, I'm hard to noti—" Without

even finishing the word, he dropped to his knees and scurried between the thick tree-trunk legs. The guard, stunned, barely had time to swipe at the spot where Fin had just been.

"Thief!" Bull Face's deep voice boomed. "Thief, everyone! Get him!"

Fin knew when it was time to run. He took off through the gallery, weaving through the maze of display cases, toppling as many as he could behind him to slow the pursuit. Glass shattered and wood splintered, sending priceless artifacts spinning across the floor.

Ahead of him, the towering statue loomed. Behind him, Bull Face bellowed and charged. Every pounding step shook the floor beneath Fin's feet, eating up the space between them. Worse, it seemed the lunchers had heard the commotion, because guards were streaming down the catwalks to join the chase.

Fin needed to find that key and get out of here. He looked to the left, only to find a stampede of angry Meressians. He glanced to the right, only to find another crowd of sword-wielding guards.

Meressians to either side. Bull Face behind. Statue ahead. There was nowhere to go. No ducking behind corners and waiting to be forgotten this time. It was time to stop this chase.

Fin pivoted ever so slightly and headed straight for the nearest display, right at the foot of the statue. Bull Face wheeled after him, roaring, his breath hot on Fin's neck. Fin hit the case at full speed with an "*Oof!*" and slid over the top of it. Just as Bull Face grabbed for him, he yanked the case open, right in front of Bull Face's big bull face.

Purple mist sprayed straight into the guard's flaring nostrils. He stumbled backward, smacking at his nose. First there was a snuffle. And then another. There was an ear-splitting snort, then a monumental sneeze, so strong it sent Fin reeling backward into the base of the statue.

His eyes shut on impact. Something warm, thick, and sticky splashed across his chest. "*Blugh!*" he groaned, shuddering. When Fin opened his eyes, he found Meressians jumping from side to side, dodging the furiously sneezing brute who flailed among them.

"*AH-CHEW!*" Bull Face snorted, spraying a handful of guards with snot, causing them to back up even farther.

"Take that, you dumb ox!" Fin laughed. The huffing behemoth lay between the horde of angry Meressians and Fin, keeping him safe for the moment.

"Sneeze Breeze won't . . . *AH-CHEW* . . . last . . . *BLAH-CHEW* . . . forever," Bull Face gasped.

Fortunately, it only needed to last long enough to find a hiding place, Fin thought. Once everyone forgot about him, he'd resume his search, find the key, and pick up all the valuables he could carry for himself and the Parsnickles.

Not that he had a whole lot of options with his back pressed against the massive statue and Bull Face flailing in front of him. In fact, he realized, it looked like the only direction left was up.

Producing his newly acquired knives, Fin turned, sank one into the white robe draping the towering statue, and began climbing.

"He's scaling the Oracle!" someone gasped.

"He can't do that!" cried another.

"Looks like I can!" Fin called back, scrambling higher. The robe was slick, but the knives bit deep, giving him good holds.

Just as he crested the statue's shoulders, the whole ship quivered and jolted. It began to rock from side to side, making his stomach roll. They were leaving port!

Sweat broke out on Fin's brow. Before long, they'd be out on the open Pirate Stream. And then there really *would* be nowhere to go.

He'd climbed plenty high to be level with the uppermost catwalks, all of them swarming with pointing and hollering Meressians. Fin belly-crawled onto the statue's outstretched arms. Maybe he could slip into the cup of the golden chalice gripped in its hands and wait there until he was forgotten. But when he reached the cup, he saw it was a single, solid piece. There was no room to hide.

He was stuck.

Fin dropped his head in resignation, looking down into the pool of water several stories below. The reflection of the statue gazed back at him.

With a start, he realized there was something off about that reflection. It looked strangely anguished, not at all the serene marble visage behind him. Huge black tears ran down the reflected porcelain face, all set off against the darkness of its robe.

Fin blinked and glanced behind him. The statue he'd climbed wore a white robe, not a dark one. He looked down again. The reflection was a perfect opposite of the reality, cloaked in black and spattered in white like a sky full of stars.

Something buzzed in the back of his mind. He struggled for his pocket, ripping free the letter he'd hidden there. *Pierce the Starry sky to find the vault*, it told him.

"Shanks," he whispered. He peered back at the pool. It looked just like the starry sky, no doubt. But it was over thirty feet below and could scarcely be an arm's length deep. He'd break his neck if he tried.

An arrow whizzed past him. He sucked in his breath. The Meressians weren't waiting. Neither could he. And the letter had been right so far.

Carefully, Fin folded the note and put it back in his pocket. Sneezes and shouts echoed around him. Below, one of the purple-clad guards nocked another arrow into his bow.

Before he could talk himself out of it, Fin took a long, deep breath. Then he pinched his nose shut with his fingers and jumped.

He struck the cold water of the reflecting pool with a jarring smack. Thankfully, it was deeper than it looked.

He struggled downward, kicking toward the bottom. And then the bottom came, and passed, and he was in the air again, falling.

Fin hit the floor hard and rolled, spreading the impact. If there were three things every orphan in the Quay knew, the second one was how to land. The mountain winds blew hard and constant; you never knew when a sudden gust would grab you off your feet, and it was never too particular about where, or how, it put you down.

When he came to a stop, he found himself face-to-face with a...well, face. It was another statue, just like the one he'd jumped from. Except it wore black robes and hung upside down like a bat, its feet stuck to the ceiling while its head almost touched the floor.

"Creepy," Fin murmured, reaching out a finger to trace the black tears streaking from the statue's eyes to its chin. With a shiver, he craned his neck, looking up. Overhead, a circle of water shimmered in the ceiling, held in place by nothing but air. It was the pool he'd just jumped through. He laughed. The statue in front of him was built to look like a reflection.

His good mood didn't last long. On the other side of the water, he could see movement. The Meressians might dive in after him at any moment. And he still needed to find the key, grab whatever other awesome loot had to be hidden down here, and get out.

He glanced around. Other than the circle of dim light

filtering in through the reflecting pool, this entire deck was pitch dark. But *that* challenge, at least, he could handle.

"Out you go, little fellows," he whispered, pulling a small bottle of lights from a pouch on his belt and unscrewing its lid. Twenty tiny yellow heads peeked out from the rim. They took wing, first one, then the next, then the next, spreading out in a spiral.

Living with bugs had a few advantages. Like getting to know glowglitters. Glowglitters ate darkness, which made them Fin's best friends. The little bugs chewed at the shadows in front of him, tearing a ragged tunnel through the dark that he could see through.

A few moments later, he could make out his surroundings. This hold was way smaller than the chamber above, its walls covered in weird banners and adorned with statues. Dense writing scrawled across the banners, the same phrase repeated over and over again:

GUARD AGAINST IT AND PREVENT IT.

As freaky as all that was, Fin didn't get the feeling the statues were supposed to be guarding against anything. They were horrific, more like something you'd fear rather than something you'd want looking after you. Each one was a replica of the statue in the reflecting pool—the crying man. The Oracle, he'd heard the Meressians call him.

He remembered what Stavik had told him, about the

Oracle and the Meressians being at odds over some prophecy. And then it hit him: The Oracle was what the Meressians were guarding *against*.

"Weird," he whispered to himself. The statues gaped at him with open mouths, a scream wide enough to swallow him whole. Fin shuddered at the thought. But it was none of his business, really—he was here to steal. And what really scared him was that there was absolutely nothing here worth stealing. The job looked like a bust.

He shook his head, bewildered. It couldn't be. This was where the letter had told him to go. This was where the real treasures should have been hidden.

He watched as the glowglitters merrily chomped away at the darkness near the far wall, exposing the corner of a short metal box. Fin almost sagged with relief. A safe! He trotted over to it and skimmed his fingers along its still-shadowed surface, searching for a lock.

The edge of his palm banged against something sharp, and he shook his hand at the pain. "Come on, bugs," he muttered, thinking about the army of angry Meressians getting ready to stream down on him.

Finally, a curious glowglitter lit on the safe's handle and started munching. Fin poked it gently in the butt, trying to scoot it along so he could figure out what he was working with. Crystal, definitely. Some kind of gemstone. Faceted. He poked the bug again. It stopped, annoyed, then went back to munching.

Fin kept his eyes on the handle as the darkness peeled away. He could make out one pointy, wavy arm. Then another, then another. Six of them, all branched out from a golden center. A sculpted sun! When he grasped it, he could just slide his fingers between the sun's rays. But when he tried turning it, it didn't budge.

"No time for this junk," Fin grumbled. He pulled out one of the knives he'd grabbed for Stavik and jammed it against the base of the knob. He pried at it hard, heart thundering in anticipation, until it came free with a pop and the door swung open.

The ship rumbled beneath him suddenly. "That can't be good," he muttered.

Quickly, he slipped his hands into the safe. But any hope he'd had of escaping with pockets full of treasure evaporated—it was practically empty! He swiped the only two objects inside and glanced at them: a crystal vial filled with water and a sculpted ruby key.

The Key! He had it!

He shoved it and the vial into his thief's bag. He even snatched the sun-shaped doorknob; at this point, he'd take what he could get. After all, it didn't look *not* valuable.

Just then, the reflecting pool crashed to the deck. Water splashed everywhere. Glowglitters scattered, a few of them spewing little black trails of darkness in fear.

The statues lining the walls groaned. Dirty brown water burst from the mouth of one, then from another across the chamber. "Shanks!" Fin shouted. The safe had been trapped!

Oily water from the Khaznot Bay poured into the hold from the statues' mouths, splashing across Fin's feet. Fear poured in with it. He gulped, imagining what this trap was really for.

Because at the Quay's docks, the water was basically just water. But out on the open Stream, where the magic flowed fully, where this ship would normally be...well, his legs might be frogs by now. If he was lucky.

This was a death trap to end all death traps.

Then again, as Stavik always said, dead is dead is dead. And normal water or not, if he didn't find a way out, that's exactly what he would be.

CHAPTER 8
Ardent Explains Everything (Poorly)

T *he Pirate Stream?* The hair on Marrill's arms stood on end, and a prickling sensation trickled down her spine.

Everywhere she looked, they were surrounded by water—endless expanses of it. "But that doesn't make sense." She clutched Karnelius closer. Just a few moments before, she'd been standing in the middle of the desert, and deserts weren't places well known for being full of water.

She turned back to the wizard, who still stood with his

arms stretched wide, watching her expectantly. It dawned on Marrill that she had no idea what she'd gotten herself into.

She bit her lip so they couldn't see that her chin had begun to tremble. In the course of her family's numerous adventures, she'd been thrown into many strange situations, and she'd learned how to handle them. But then, her mom and dad had always been nearby, or some other responsible grown-up.

And this was something entirely different. "Who are you, really?" she asked.

"I am the great wizard Ardent," the old man said. He bowed with a flourish, the hem of his purple dressing gown waving around his bony ankles. "You may have heard of me?"

Marrill stared at him blankly. "Or not," he said, deflated.

Ardent kicked the folds of his robe aside and motioned to the boy, whose right hand draped lazily over the wheel. Marrill noticed he had a tattoo of an intricately knotted rope twined around his knuckles. "And this is the captain of this fine vessel, my good friend and journeying companion, Coll."

Marrill choked. Captain? He was barely older than she was; how was he a captain? She remembered the way the ship had floundered when she'd first seen it. Maybe he wasn't a very good captain, she decided.

Coll looked like he was about to say something, but Ardent didn't give him the chance. "And this," he said, sweeping his hands around at the various masts, their sails straining against the wind of the approaching storm, "is the *Enterprising Kraken*, the greatest sailing vessel the Stream has ever known!"

Overhead, the ship's rigging all squealed at once. Marrill looked up, and her eyes widened. Above them, the ropes rising from either side of the deck came together almost like long legs, pulleys making knees and a waist. Similar weird formations ran in from the front and back masts, making rope-and-pulley arms. It all twisted together in the middle, so that the whole thing resembled a giant person made of twined rope.

Marrill squinted. In fact, it seemed that someone had painted a face on a paper plate, and fastened it in place on the rope that stretched from the "body" to the top of the mainsail. The painted smile bobbed cheerily as the ropes squeaked through the rigging.

"Pardon me," Ardent said, with a polite bow to the rope figure. "And this would be the Ropebone Man," he said, waving from Marrill to it. "Generally in charge of the rigging and whatnot. Would be quite hard to sail a ship this size without him."

Marrill wasn't quite sure how to respond. Ardent must have noticed the confusion on her face. "I mean with only the one sailor," he said, as though *that* were the question on her mind.

"Now," he said, "that brings us to the two of you."

Marrill hesitated. This was all so strange and absurd that it didn't feel real. Except that every sense told her otherwise: the snap of the sails overhead, the smell of the approaching storm, the sharp sting of her cat's claws digging into her shoulder, and the ache in her arms from holding him for so long.

"I'm Marrill," she said, clearing her throat. "Marrill Aesterwest. And this is Karnelius." She waved one of his paws at them in a halfhearted hello. Her cat squinted at the wizard through his one eye and hissed.

"Well," Ardent pronounced, "we certainly weren't expecting to be adding to the crew. But since you're here and we're not where we were, welcome aboard!"

It took Marrill a moment to untwist what he'd just said. When she did, her eyes widened in alarm. "Karny and I are *not* a part of the crew," she protested. "And I'm really sorry, but I want—no, I *need*—to get back home." After a beat she added, "With you."

Ardent smiled, but it was strained. That alone filled Marrill with concern. "Right," he said. "Home. Well. That's an interesting conundrum now, isn't it?" He tugged at his beard, clearly uncomfortable, and glanced at Coll.

Marrill's unease intensified. She didn't know what a conundrum was, but it didn't sound good.

Coll tilted his head at Ardent. "He's referring to the tides. Navigation can be tricky on the Stream."

"Stream?" She looked around at the water stretching out in every direction, the waves nearby rising to white frothy crests. "This doesn't look like any stream I've ever seen."

"Yeah, I'll leave that to the wizard to explain," Coll said.

With a small measure of relief, Marrill said, "Yes, please!" An errant wave struck the bow, and she set Karnelius down so she could brace herself against a nearby mast. Immediately, he scampered off and crouched by the door to the ship's cabin.

"Right, well. Hmm." Ardent frowned in concentration. "This would be easier if I had my treatises," he murmured, tapping at his chin a few times as he easily moved with the rocking of the ship. He shook his head sadly. "Regardless, I shall do my best.

"Imagine a river of creation," he began, "that flows from the beginning of all things to the end of time." He drew his hand through the air, and a sliver of silver liquid spun from his fingers, growing wider and deeper as it went, until a miniature river flowed between them. "Entire worlds, universes even, spring up from it like cities on its shore."

Houses and towns and planets appeared along the image's silver water. Marrill gasped, stunned. She reached her hand out toward the replica river, wondering if it felt as real as it looked.

Ardent batted her away. "The first, and most important, rule is to never touch the Pirate Stream," he warned. "Her waters are the purest form of magic. You wouldn't want to grow scales or explode, would you?"

She gaped at him, her eyes wide. He didn't seem to be joking. And when she remembered the feathers that had sprouted from her wrist earlier, she realized that he might not be. "No, I'm not generally okay with exploding," she told him.

He raised an eyebrow. "Few are," he said wistfully, as if he had personal experience in the matter.

He cleared his throat. "Now, as I was saying, most rivers flow into each other—water likes to come together as it makes its way to the sea, you know. But sometimes, very rarely, but *sometimes*, a stream will just up and split off from a bigger river, running off in its own direction for reasons known only to itself. And when it does, that stream is known as a pirate stream."

To illustrate, he drew a finger across the top of the silver river, then snaked a small strand of water out into its own little branch. "It's in books," he explained, as if that made it all make sense.

She stared at the floating image, forehead furrowed, trying to understand. The phrase sounded familiar; she remembered her father saying something about a pirate stream when they were hiking up the lower Colorado River in the Grand Canyon when she was eight. But as far as she knew, those waters weren't the kind that made you grow scales or explode.

"You, my dear," Ardent continued, "sit on the piratest of all pirate streams!" He held his arms out wide, indicating the endless expanse of water churning furiously beneath the storm. "This is *the* Pirate Stream, the one and only offshoot from the River of Creation!"

Marrill glanced around again, trying to match up what he'd told her with what she saw with her own eyes. "This *still* doesn't look like any stream I've seen," she said at last.

Ardent shrugged. "The Pirate Stream flows fast and free when compared to the River of Creation, a steep mountain creek compared to a slow coastal river. But even so, the Stream touches all worlds, at some place and some time. Not to mention the many, many worlds that exist only as islands within the Stream itself. So, yes, it's fair to say it's a bit on the large side."

Marrill frowned as the bow of the *Enterprising Kraken* crashed through a big wave. Questions rushed into her head. "If we can't touch the actual water," she said, "how come I could stand in it back at the parking lot? And what about the spray from the ship?"

"The spray's too busy deciding whether or not to be air to bother us," Ardent told her, waving his hand as though it wasn't important. "Really takes a good, solid splash or dipping before things get worrisome. As for the water you stood in, well, it was just water. It usually is, where the Stream touches a world. Usually."

A flash of lightning broke across the sky, sending thunder over the waves. "Some rain coming," Coll said, still slumped on the wheel like he didn't have a care in the world. He caught her eye briefly. "Don't worry, we're heading around the storm, not going in."

Ardent nodded in agreement. Still, he pulled out a length of twine and tied it around his head to keep his cap from blowing away. "So that should pretty much answer all your questions. It all made sense, I take it?"

Marrill stared at him. "Not even a little," she admitted, feeling defeated. "And you still haven't explained how I'm getting home. Because I *am* getting home."

Ardent cleared this throat. And then cleared it again before glancing at Coll, who merely cocked an eyebrow. "Well, the thing is," he told her, "it may not have seemed it, but your world is far removed from where we are—the Pirate Stream proper. Getting back there wouldn't be easy under the best of circumstances. Add to that the rather peculiar nature of the Stream lately, and well, I'm not quite sure how we got there in the first place. It's not exactly somewhere Stream folks ever go."

The wizard stepped forward and laid a gentle hand on her shoulder. It was that touch, more than anything, that caused her throat to tighten. It made her feel safe;

it reminded her of her father. Her vision blurred, but she refused to let the tears come any farther.

Ardent's smile turned down with sympathy. He looked to Coll again, clearly urging him to say something. The captain nodded, if a bit reluctantly. "He's right. Tides in this part of the Stream are erratic and have a fairly long life cycle. I've been sailing the Pirate Stream for..." He ticked one, two, three on his fingers, then shrugged. "Well, for long enough to know my way around, and I've never been down that particular branch before—maybe no one has."

He jutted his chin toward the horizon. "We were trying to follow that bit of map and caught an unexpected eddy in a current I'd never seen, almost certainly the result of the passing storm."

At the mention of the storm, Marrill glanced at the dark clouds churning behind them. Her breath hitched at how menacing they appeared, but neither Ardent nor Coll seemed to be concerned in the least.

"And add to *that* the spring tide and winds coming out of the Breathless Strait," Coll continued, "and those conditions might not arise again for...well, ever."

That got her full attention. Marrill's eyes grew wide and she stumbled back, feeling faint. The rocking boat only added to the lightness in her head. She could barely force herself to say the words, as if uttering them would make them true. "Ever? As in, I'm never going home?"

Coll looked to Ardent, who chewed his lip, watching the sky for a long while. At last, he gripped her shoulder tightly, reassuringly. "We will get you home, dear. I promise it. I just don't know *when*."

CHAPTER 9
The Master Thief Thieves Masterfully

Fin whistled to his glowglitters as water gushed into the Meressian Temple Ship. "Come on, come on," he muttered as they flittered back to their jar. "No rush here," he told them. If they caught his sarcasm, they ignored it.

He glanced around the hold anxiously. If he didn't want to drown, he needed to find a way out, fast. Maybe he could float back up through the hole from the reflecting pool?

But before he took three paces toward it, someone familiar fell through, landing with a splash.

It was Bull Face. In one hand, he held a wicked-looking blade. With the other, he swiped at his running nose. "Give back the Key," he grunted, his voice thick and stuffy.

"Are you headsoft?" Fin asked. "We're going to die down here!"

In response, Bull Face charged. Fin ducked out of the way just as the gleaming blade swung past him. He skittered—as best he could skitter in two feet of rising liquid, anyway—behind a water-spewing statue.

"The whole ship will sink now, you fool thief!" Bull Face warned. His skin had taken on a distinctly greenish hue, and his lips were turning a deathly shade of pale. "It's designed to protect the Key at all costs. Oh, Hedgecaw will kill me...."

For a moment, just a moment, Fin considered it: *Give back the Key, head home. Probably get locked up, forgotten about, maybe starve until someone decides the jail needs a cleaning.* Still, he'd be alive.

Alive, but no closer to finding his mother. He couldn't afford to lose this lead. Besides, Fin thought, he wasn't the Master Thief because he gave stuff back.

"Quick-like, or we all go under!" Bull Face snarled.

Fin shrugged. "You look like a champ swimmer," he offered.

Bull Face swung again. Fin jumped. This time, the blade slashed high after him, the Meressian's reflexes almost as fast as Fin's.

Almost.

The blow missed Fin by inches but smashed clear through the head of the statue he'd ducked around. Where its mouth had been, a huge hole now gaped in the hull, letting even more water pour in.

Fin gulped. They'd be under in minutes! His eyes raced around the hold. No exit. None. No openings at all except the stupid gap in the ceiling and the hole gushing in water from the bay.

Bull Face raised his sword. Fin noticed the waver in his hands, the tremble around his belly. "Guard... against it." The big guard shuddered, his lips barely able to form the words. "And... pre... ven... *GYACK!*"

Fin rolled out of the way, knowing what was coming next. The puke pill had hit home at last. Bull Face bent over and retched hard into the water.

That was Fin's cue. Doing his best to avoid the now-disgusting tide, he dodged past the still-heaving Meressian and climbed the broken statue behind him. "Hope you liked the thief stew!" he shouted triumphantly. Then he shoved his hands into the streaming hole where the statue's mouth had been and launched himself into it.

It felt like being swallowed alive.

Momentum was enough to get him through, but the flow

of water into the ship was enormous. It sucked him backward, slamming him against the hull. Water shot up his nose and into his ears. He pushed against the dullwood, kicked, flailed at it. Desperately, he yanked one knife from his belt and dug it into the wood, then the other, using them to haul himself away from the sucking hole.

Again and again, he planted the knives and pulled himself after them, bracing with his feet. And just as his lungs screamed and he gave a last little prayer that he might be part mermaid, his hand burst through the surface, his head a second behind.

He sucked in great gulps of air. Shouts filled his ears. The Meressian ship was sinking fast!

He looked around. They'd pulled off from the Quay; its docks were too far away to swim to. And also, he remembered with a twisted stomach, he didn't know how to swim. "Shanks," he coughed, gripping his knives tightly.

The only option was to climb. He scrambled up the ship's carvings like a lizard on a drain spout, planting his feet on the shoulders of stone-faced kings and finding handholds in the mouths of vicious-looking monsters.

He crouched beneath the ornate railing circling the main deck. It was mayhem: Meressians rushed back and forth, hauling treasure up from the hold and filling the lifeboats before abandoning ship themselves. Hoping to get lost in the fray, Fin slipped over the railing and slunk toward one of the empty lifeboats.

But his bad luck seemed to be holding. "Wait, who's that kid?" a familiar voice boomed. "He doesn't belong here! That must be the thief!" Footsteps pounded across the deck as Bull Face, soaked, sniffling, and still looking queasy, pushed his way out of one of the hatches.

Fin sighed. So close to being forgotten. Then again, he guessed sinking a whole ship took a little more time to fade from the mind than showing up with a butterfly.

He had to admit, though, that a part of him was glad to see the angry beast. He couldn't much bear the thought of the Meressian drowning down in the hold, no matter how hard the creature had tried to kill him.

That happiness didn't last long. Bull Face wrenched free his sword and pointed it toward Fin. "Don't let him get away!" he bellowed.

Fin only had two options: overboard or up. And since swimming was out, he leapt toward a tangle of rigging and shimmied up it. He hadn't gotten far, though, when the ropes creaked and swayed from someone much heavier chasing after him.

Fin swallowed and climbed faster. In moments, he was in the canopy, leafy sails rustling all around as the breeze picked up and turned to wind in earnest. The whole ship lurched, shaking him from side to side.

"Come on, boy, there's no escape!" Bull Face shouted. Though he couldn't match Fin for speed, he was coming more quickly than Fin had expected.

Fin reached the bottom of the netting that hung between the masts and slithered up through it. The holes were too narrow for Bull Face to follow, but that didn't slow him long. With a serrated blade, he sliced the ropes, snapping them clean.

"Shanks!" Fin cried, leaping to the nearest mast.

"Caught now, kid," the Meressian said, pulling himself through. "Nowhere to go. Give me the Key, and there's still time for us both to make it off before she capsizes."

"Still a no, but thanks!" Fin called back, shimmying up the mast. It narrowed quickly, just a spindly stretch of wood that held the topsails proper. In a few moments, there really *wouldn't* be anywhere for him to go.

A gust of wind pummeled the ship, rattling the leaf-sails. Fin's heart skipped a beat. He clutched the wood tight, feeling the grain scrape against his palms. What had been a calm day for the Khaznot Quay had come to an end. The winds were picking up again now, screaming down from the peak of Khaznot Mountain.

"Where you gonna go, kid?" Bull Face asked. He was too large to climb up this part, at least. But the blade of his sword glittered bright in the sunlight. Looking at it made Fin a bit queasy.

"Nowhere left but down," the Meressian said, flashing his massive teeth in a grin. He sliced the sword through the air, chopping straight into the wood.

The whole mast shook. Fin climbed higher. Somewhere

in the distance, a great roar built, as if a lion were greeting its prey. Fin knew the sound well. It was the big winds, coming down from the mountain to tear across the bay. He braced himself, listening.

Chop! The mast shivered in his hands. How much more could it take before the spindly wood snapped, plunging him to the deck several stories below?

"Done for now, kid!" the Meressian called. The ship lurched, tipping ever farther sideways. "Give it up!"

Fin breathed deep. "Come on, come on!" he urged, begging the wind. His fingers pawed at the sleeves of his coat, playing nervously with a pair of strings hidden inside each one.

Just behind the next *chop!* of Bull Face's sword, just over the creaking of the ship and the shouts from below, the roar closed in. The massive, musical, monstrous roar.

Fin locked eyes with the scowling Meressian and smiled. "Sorry, jog," he said. "We've had a time, but I think this is my ride." Bull Face paused, his sword mid-swing, confusion in his eyes. He sniffled.

And then the wind rushed over them, searing cold across Fin's exposed skin. He jumped, straight out, away from the ship, diving for the surface of the bay.

Because if there were three things every orphan in the Quay knew, the best and most awesome, without a doubt, was how to skysail. Fin pulled hard on the little threads inside his sleeves, and his coat billowed out behind him, catching the wind as it hit. Just moments before he would have splashed into the churning water of the bay, the gust pushed him upward, outward, away.

Fin wheeled in a happy spiral, laughing as he went. Bull Face shook his fist and cursed. His mates down on the deck continued loading the last lifeboat even as the ship rolled slowly. There was still time for them all to make it. They would remember the master thief who sank them forever, he wagered, even if they wouldn't remember Fin himself for an hour.

He breathed a last sigh of relief as he winged toward shore. At his hip, he felt the weight of his thief's bag. He might not have pockets full of treasure, but he'd recovered the Key. And finding his mother was worth way more to him than an entire ship's hold worth of riches.

CHAPTER 10
What Are *You* Doing Here?

Marrill's knees wobbled as she thought about what would happen if she never made it home. How long would her parents wait for her until giving up? How sick would her mother get in the meantime? It would be all her fault. Taking a deep breath, she forced herself to stay upright, to keep together even as she wanted to fall apart.

Ardent held up his hand. "Don't panic yet," he said. "You simply can't go back the way you came, is all."

A trickle of hope began to ease the tightness in her chest. She was fine with going home a different way, so long as she could actually *get* home.

"Why don't you take her on a tour of the ship?" Coll suggested. He looked to Marrill and added, "Might make you feel a little less adrift." He gave her a knowing wink as if he understood what it meant to be thrust into an overwhelmingly new situation. She smiled gratefully, and he nodded.

"Excellent idea!" Ardent made his way down the steps to the main deck and crossed it. When he reached the hatch at the base of the ship's front, he pulled it open.

Marrill sniffed and followed, Karnelius rousing himself and trailing after.

Once through the door, she found herself at the top of a wide spiral staircase, more elaborate than any she'd ever seen. Her steps slowed as she took in the elegantly scrolled handrails, the golden risers. Even the walls were impressive, painted with vibrant murals that appeared to move, ever so slightly, in front of her.

Ardent seemed not to notice, or be impressed. He marched determinedly down the stairs, continuing the conversation, and Marrill had to scramble to keep up.

"The Pirate Stream," he declared, "touches all waters, everywhere, at some place and some time. Even the most remote and removed ones."

"But there weren't any waters in the parking lot," Marrill

said, peering over the railing. The stairs seemed to go on forever. She guessed there were at least eight stories below this one, maybe more, far more than it looked like the ship could hold from the outside. And at each level, corridors and hallways branched out from the center like the arms of an octopus. "I mean, the heat made it *look* like water, but that was a mirage...."

"Well, there you have it!" Ardent announced. He continued down the steps. "You see, when I say the Pirate Stream is a river, it's really more like many rivers all at once, each twisting through new and exciting places. The Deep Stream, the part that looks like an ocean, is where many of these rivers overlap. It may seem a single body, but it is, I assure you, a hundred billion currents flowing to a hundred billion worlds, all around and atop and beneath each other. Which is why having an experienced Stream navigator like Coll is essential to getting anywhere."

He paused at the first landing and squinted down a dim corridor.

"What are *you* doing here?" he mumbled.

"Um, you asked me to follow you?" Marrill said.

The wizard chuckled. "Not you," he said, continuing downward. "I meant the Promenade Deck." He waved his hand over his shoulder at the floor they'd just passed. "You'll have to watch out for that one—it likes to walk off. Best to stay away from it. Never know where it'll end up; sometimes it up and heads to another ship."

"Um…" Her words faltered. "How do I know which one's the Promenade Deck?"

He glanced up at her, forehead furrowed. "It's the one that moves."

Before she could even respond, he'd already reached the next floor. Marrill raced to catch up.

"The other thing that's good to have," he said, resuming the earlier conversation as though it had never been interrupted, "is a map."

Marrill stumbled once she reached the landing. It opened into a hallway, long and wide. And practically every inch of it was filled with doors. They stood frame-to-frame, all gold handles and silver hinges and brass knockers shaped like faces with eyes that seemed to turn and watch her. There were big doors, from floor to ceiling. There were small doors scarcely big enough for a mouse to run through. There were doors that didn't go all the way to the floor, and doors on the floor beneath them.

"This is the Door-Way," announced Ardent. He strode purposefully down the hall, the hem of his robe snapping around his ankles as he stepped over doors in the floor. Finally, he reached a single door, plastered alone against the far wall. Its knocker was nearly as big as his head, and its frame sported a stylish ebony molding, carefully carved into tall dragons. "And this is the Map Room."

Marrill scurried after him, catching up just as he twisted the big brass knob. "After you," he said, holding the door open for her. Marrill stepped inside, confident whatever she was about to see couldn't be any weirder. And just as quickly, her confidence died.

The room was, indeed, full of maps. It was shaped like a hexagon, with the wall across from her dominated by a large window looking out ahead of the ship. Nautical-seeming instruments crowded the other four walls, and charts with names like *Giltbreaker Islands*, *West Bublestuck*, and *The Puzzly Lands* hung between them.

In the center stood a large round table, its surface strewn with maps. On top of one, three big rats seemed to be charting a course using instruments that were nearly as big as they were. Each rat had two tails. And a collar. And way too many legs.

Karnelius bounded past her, pouncing before she could grab him. The creatures let out a collective squeak and scrambled from the table. They were oddly graceful, able to dodge and weave around her cat without his getting so much as a claw near any of them.

Unscathed, they disappeared into various nooks and crannies in the wall, leaving Karny behind to lurk with his tail twitching. Marrill watched it all with wide eyes.

Then she realized what the creatures were. She grinned for the first time since boarding the ship. She was getting the hang of this place. "Let me guess," she announced. "Pirats?"

"Well, we've been calling them bilge mice," Ardent said.

"But that's much more dignified. Of course, Coll just calls them 'an errand gone wrong,' but how was I to know that a mouse and collar is a type of rigging? You get what you ask for!"

Marrill was completely lost again. And then Ardent turned to her and smiled his gentle smile. "But pirats it is from now on, I think," he said. And just like that, she felt a little bit more at home.

"So which map do we need?" she asked, peering at the label on a drawer in an old weathered chest. "'Atlas of the Lesser Scabies,'" she read.

"Definitely not that one," Ardent said. "In fact, let's never speak of that one again. No." He twittered the tips of his fingers together. "I fear the map to get to your world won't be in here. This was really just a stop on the tour. Bad timing, when I think about it."

Marrill felt her newfound relief begin to waver.

"As I said before, your world is a place the Pirate Stream rarely touches. I can think of only one very specific map that would do the task. It's quite unique, actually.

"But there's just one problem." He cleared his throat, clearly uncomfortable. "I don't have it. Plus it may or may not be in several pieces. And also those pieces are likely strewn in disparate lands across the Stream, which could be considered a third problem. And the fourth would really be not just trying to figure out *where* the pieces are but how to get them when you find them. And there's the small chance others might be searching for them, too, so that's a fifth problem and…"

"That sounds like a lot of problems," Marrill pointed out when he was finally forced to inhale.

"Well, some good news there!" Ardent's face brightened. "It just so happens that I myself am on a quest to find that same map. I need it to help locate someone…someone who may need me…." He trailed off. His eyes still looked at her, but his gaze seemed to pass through her, into a distance he alone could see. The tips of his smile quivered, and for just a moment, he looked very, very tired.

Then he shook his head, and the goofy, carefree wizard was back. "Anyway, you're welcome to look for it with me!"

Hope surged through Marrill. She practically jumped up and down, nearly falling against the Map Room table. "So if we find the pieces of this map and put it together, it will show us how to get home to my parents?"

Ardent nodded. "Definitely. It is said the Bintheyr Map to Everywhere will take its possessor wherever he or she needs to go."

Marrill let out the breath she'd been holding. For the first time in this entire—very confusing—conversation, she finally had something concrete to hold on to.

She stood up straight, mustering her resolve. "So how do we find it?"

Ardent ahemmed. Around them the ship groaned as she cut her way through the waves. "Well, that's actually where I was hoping *you* might help us," he said.

"Me?!" The deck jumped beneath them as it crested a big swell, sending her stumbling. Through the window, Marrill noticed the waves frothing at the tips.

"Oh, that was a big one," Ardent said. "Let's finish the tour while we can still stand on the staircase, hm?" Without waiting for her to answer, he swept out of the room.

"But how am I supposed to find the Map?" she called, chasing after him.

"Berths are on the next level," he said, pointing down. "Pick any one you like. You'll know you've found the correct floor by the prevalence of sleepy bugs. Below that's the galley and brig and all those other cabins that Coll insists we have."

He began climbing toward the deck. "Bottom level is the Bilge Room. There are signs on the door. I suggest you heed them. And that"—he threw open the hatch and stepped outside—"concludes our tour. How fare things out here, Coll?"

"Wet," Coll grumbled as Marrill stumbled out into the open. Rain poured down, soaking her instantly. Karnelius stopped just inside the doorway, saw the rain, and bolted back down belowdecks. Marrill didn't blame him.

"You were the last one to see the Compass Rose," Ardent told her. It took her a moment to realize he was back to answering her earlier question about how to find the Map.

"I was?" she asked. Oddly, though the rain fell all around

them, and she was drenched in a second, Ardent was completely dry. It was as if every single drop just missed him.

"Of course!" he said. "The scrap of paper I asked about. That's the Compass Rose. The first piece of the Map."

Marrill frowned. "It didn't look like a map."

"It isn't," Ardent explained. "As I said, it's only a part of one. But for us it's the best part, for if you can find it again, the Compass Rose should lead us to the other pieces."

"But how am *I* supposed to find it?" Marrill asked. "I just saw it for a second. And I don't even know where *I* am!"

Ardent beamed. "Which is exactly why I have faith in you," he said. "I'm sure it won't take you *nearly* the hundred and thirty years it took me to find it in the first place!"

CHAPTER 11
A Tentalo on the House

Halfway back to shore, the wind that had buoyed Fin aloft from the Meressian ship gave a few last gasps and died. It came in little bursts, each one dropping him a few more feet and sending his stomach jumping up into his throat. Fin swallowed it down and held on. He was still a champ skysailer, after all, even if he was a little heavier these days than he had been as a kid.

A few moments later, Khaznot Bay's ugly brown waves were spitting foam at his feet, and his face was level with the end of a thick wooden pier. Fighting his instinct to pull up, he pushed down even closer to the water, shooting into the shadows beneath the wharf. Dodging the cross-beams and rock breakwaters jutting from the surf, he glided the last few feet and landed in a quick run just above the waterline.

Fin plopped down on the dirty sand and, after giving himself a minute for his racing heart to settle, checked on the things he'd nicked from the temple ship. The nice new knives for Stavik, still sharp despite all the climbing, were tucked into the back of his raggedy canvas pants. The ornate doorknob and vial of water sat heavy in the thief's bag tied to his belt, next to his jar of glowglitters. It wasn't much of a haul, he had to admit. But whatever other treasures the Meressian ship might have held, they lay at the bottom of the bay now, making friends with grimysharks and sludgeels.

He pulled out the most important piece—the ruby key—and considered it. It weighed heavy in his hands. What was so important about this key, he wondered, that the Meressians would sink their whole ship over it?

He shrugged, tucking the key into his breast pocket. Whatever it was, it was worth giving up to find his mother.

Whistling, Fin left the docks and followed one of the narrowest, steepest alleys as it zigzagged staircase-like from the Wharfway Warrens up the mountainside. The wind was definitely picking up again. A few times when a hard gust came up, he had to stop and grab the nearby safety chains running along the edge of the street. It was about two in the afternoon, he figured, bracing a shoulder against a particularly sharp breeze. At this rate, the wind would be strong enough to carry a kid away by four.

As he passed by the market square, his belly growled, reminding him he'd skipped breakfast *and* lunch. He detoured over to Squinting Jenny's cart to nick a piece of fruit. At his approach, she leaned toward him and pushed her eyelids together. "Have I seen you before, young man?" she asked, the way she always did.

"No, ma'am," Fin answered in his best sad orphan voice. He hung his head pitifully. "Just new in town, ma'am, and awful hungry."

"Oh, you poor thing!" she said. "Take a tentalo, on the house." She hovered her hand over the rack, finally resting it on a big yellow fruit with six twisty growths coming out of it like starfish arms. Fin tried not to chuckle; it reminded him of the crystal doorknob he'd just swiped.

"You're too generous!" he said instead, tucking the fruit into his thief's bag to ripen. He batted his sad eyes at her again. "Now, if only I can find someone as kind as you at dinnertime..."

A minute later, slurping away at a bright green squiggy-fruit and with three "on the house" plummellows in his pocket, Fin slipped into the chaos of the Khaznot Quay market. The noise swallowed him whole.

"Hup, hup!"

"Trog eggs!

Fairy barbs!

Molten nettles!

Get your trog eggs!"

"I tell you, it was a brine butterfly
sure as I'm standin' here!"

"Came outta nowhere.

Saw the red lightning, and we laid

out every sail to get away."

"Quit pushing,
you bafter!"

"Strangest kinda ship I ever seen. Sank good and fast, she did."

"Ten shid,
and not a drillet more!"

"If I lived in the ol' sinky town,

maybe I'd fall fer a stork, too."

"Trog eggs! Will someone buy these rotten,
hatchin' trog eggs!"

Fin slid through a set of legs, bounced off a rickety stall, scrambled up a wall, and skittered along the top of it. With the wind picking up, he made sure to steer clear of the windward alleys (no more time for skysailing today) and kept an eye out for falling orphans in the overhangs.

The Quay crawled with life, and he loved every second of it. For most, the smell of the Quay was stagnant sea and unwashed bodies. For him, the sweet hint of cinnamon and berry threaded through the stench.

A new sound came to him as he climbed the damp, mossy steps to the pie shop's secluded plaza. A sound like someone crying. A few steps farther, it grew louder. Not just crying—bawling their eyes out. He picked up his pace.

The shop door stood wide open, letting the flies in. Some-thing was very, very wrong here.

Carefully, he slipped inside. Ad and Tad stood at the counter, as usual. But they weren't moving. Just staring into space, Tad's fingers in the money till, Ad's pressed into some dough. Tears dripped down their faces. Their chests shook without sound.

"What's wrong?" Fin mustered. "What happened?" But they didn't seem to hear him. He might as well have been a ghost, and they, silent mourners at his wake.

The little hairs on the backs of Fin's arms and the tops of his feet stood up. Not the ones that said "Watch out for that ax!" or "Guards! Run for your life!" but the other ones. The ones that stood up when he was lying on his coin purses in the middle of the night, with the attic room creaking and swaying and the shadows making figures on the walls. No matter how much he knew they weren't real, he just couldn't help feeling monsters behind him.

That was how Fin felt right now. Because as creepy as Ad and Tad were, the sobbing he'd heard wasn't coming from them. It came from the walk-in oven behind them. The one that led down to the thieves' den.

The false back was also open, and Fin approached it cautiously. The stairs creaked as he stepped down them and into a funeral chamber.

On either side, thieves and pirates were gathered as always, leaning against the walls, holding cards over half-eaten pies, sharpening their knives, or whittling their lock picks on benches. But the laughter, the chatter, the whispers were gone. Only the sobbing remained. Every one of them, just like Ad and Tad. Faces slack, crying like babies, their eyes staring off into some unseen distance.

And Stavik, too, sitting on his figurehead throne at the back of the room. The anguish on that scarred face worried Fin more than everything else combined.

When the basilizard Stavik had hand-raised from an egg got cooked for lunch, the Pirate King had shrugged. When news came in that both his brother and his best friend had been locked away for life in the lowest dungeons of the Marmar Cote, he'd giggled.

Stavik stole skin from dragons, Fin thought. He never

cried. But now, Stavik the Pirate King wept as though the world had died.

This was more than weeping potion or sniffle gas could manage, he knew. This was *real* magic, the kind only worked by wizards and truly powerful things. The kind that rarely ever came to the Khaznot Quay.

Fin willed his eyes to move past Stavik's trembling, scarred face to the shadow lurking beside him. It was a man. And like the others, he, too, shook with sobs. But unlike the thieves, his eyes were clear and focused, staring straight at the spot where Fin now stood as if he had been waiting untold hours for someone to come and stand right there.

Dark robes cloaked him. Dark robes covered in stars.

His pale porcelain face streamed with black tears.

CHAPTER 12
Lots of Pirates and Adventures and Whatnot (Are Underappreciated)

Marrill stood with her elbows propped on the ship's railing, her chin resting on her hands. Behind her, Ardent and Coll fussed over a sea chart, the sound lost in the din of the ship's sails popping with wind and the rigging constantly moving and adjusting itself. They'd left the rain behind, and now the golden waters of the Pirate Stream shone like liquid metal in the sun.

But the wonder of it wasn't enough to keep Marrill from

thinking about home. A deep ache lodged in her chest and her throat burned. She couldn't stop picturing her parents pacing the living room together, waiting for her. How long would they hold out hope before they realized she wasn't coming home?

She could see her dad now, running frantically from house to house, the way he'd gone from tent to tent in Alaska when she stayed out too long picking berries. Her parents loved her, but now they *needed* her, especially with her mom sick again.

And she wasn't there.

Marrill's eyes blurred with tears as she stared down at the wake created by the *Kraken*'s rudder. All she could think about was how thin her mother had looked. How she wouldn't be sleeping tonight, or tomorrow night, or the night after, because Marrill was lost.

She had to find a way back home, and she needed to take Ardent's healing magic with her. She couldn't let her mother down.

The thoughts churned so ferociously that she was startled to feel something tickle the back of her ankle. She yelped and looked down to find Karnelius weaving figure eights around her legs. He was exactly what she needed. Smiling, she scooped him up, pressing her face into his fur and listening to him purr. Her best friend. "I'm sorry I dragged us into this, Karny," she whispered.

She heard someone approach and lifted her head. Coll

leaned against the railing next to her. The way he stared out at the horizon made it seem as though he'd seen it all before, even though he couldn't have been older than sixteen.

"You can trust Ardent," he told her. "If he says he can get you home, he will. He's got a kind of second sense for finding people who need him." He absently traced the outline of another knotted-rope tattoo, this one circling his left wrist.

There was something about the way he said the words that made Marrill believe him. Maybe it was because she wanted them to be true. "Thanks," she said softly. "Is that how you two met? Him helping you with something you needed?"

Coll barked out a laugh. "I guess, in a manner of speaking."

Marrill waited for him to elaborate, but he didn't. "How long have you known Ardent?"

He looked over at her, one eyebrow raised. "That would be a story for another time." Gripping the railing, he leaned back and stretched, reminding her of Karnelius.

Marrill stared at his right hand. Frowning, she looked at his left wrist. "When we met, I could have sworn you had a tattoo on your right hand, too, just like that one but around your knuckles."

Coll lifted his hand and flexed his fingers. "Probably."

Exasperated, Marrill rolled her eyes. "Probably? That doesn't make any sense."

He grinned. "Welcome to the Pirate Stream. If you're

looking for sense, you've come to the wrong place."

"Thanks, I think I got that when feathers sprouted out of my wrist and a wizard showed me around his magic ship," Marrill huffed.

"Ship's not magical," Coll corrected her. "Stuff in it is." He paused. "I guess I can see why that would be confusing."

Karnelius began getting antsy, and Marrill shifted him in her arms. "So about your tattoo?"

They both looked down at his wrist, but the tattoo seemed to have shifted, the knot becoming more intricate. Marrill's eyes widened; she'd never seen anything like it. Her cat's tail began twitching madly, and she ran a hand down his back absently to calm him.

Coll lifted a shoulder. "It moves according to where we are on the Stream. Helpful for navigation. For example, right now, we're nearing the Khaznot Quay."

Just then, Karnelius surged in her arms. Teeth chittering, he dug his claws into her shoulder as though he were about to jump overboard. She snagged a finger through his collar and looked to see what had gotten him so fired up.

Dozens of stories below, a scrap of paper with a star sketched across it floated on the water. Marrill squinted, not certain she could trust her eyes.

"The Map," she breathed. She couldn't believe it! "Look! It's the..." She struggled to remember what Ardent called it. "The Compass Rose!" she cried, pointing. But as she watched, an eddy of water caught it, carrying it away from the ship and toward a big, ugly sign that Marrill could have sworn hadn't been there a moment ago.

It was held up by a giant hand, its fingernails black and broken against the rusty metal. Written on the sign in white scratches were the words

YE
KHAZNOT
QUAY

The water around it had gone oily, the golden hue of the Pirate Stream turned to a brownish red. A thin skin of rainbow color floated along the surface, reminding her of a puddle on asphalt after a summer shower. Above, the sky threatened to match the water, and the stink of old socks dipped in sour milk made her wrinkle her nose and hold her stomach.

As she stared, a seagull swooped by, letting out a thin screech that scraped along her bones. She closed her eyes and shook herself, as if that could get the feeling off.

When she opened her eyes again, the scrap of paper was no longer there. "It's gone," she sputtered. They'd been so close, but now...what if it had sunk?

Ardent came to stand next to her and smiled. He pointed past her. "Right, right," he said with a glint of mischief in his eye. "While it might have appeared to you as though the Map disappeared, what you really saw was simply the Map drifting off the Deep Stream, and into the bay of..." He motioned as they sailed past the rickety sign.

"The Khaznot Quay!" At the wave of his hand, shapes jumped up from the water, stretching around them like a horseshoe. Docks and wharves oozed out toward them, and over it all, a steep mountain climbed to the sky. Tumble-down buildings crowded its slopes, falling all over each other and across one another in a patchwork landslide. Here a tot-tering tower with a base of brick leaned out across a stone crag; there rows of houses cobbled from wood and plaster zigzagged through a sluice and into a low, flat valley.

It was as if a giant had spilled his Legos down a hill, Marrill thought. And then kept snapping new Legos onto the old ones, with no regard for where they lay or how they looked, over and over, for centuries. Every square inch of ground she could see was either run-down city or sheer rock.

Karnelius hissed and bolted toward the hatch. Marrill stumbled back from the railing, her head swimming. Every time she thought she had a handle on what it meant for there to be magic in the world, something new shattered her expectations. "Did all of that come from nowhere?"

Ardent chuckled. "Oh, that would be a feat, wouldn't it? Quite clever, quite clever. No, no, dear, that didn't come from nowhere—that's always been here. *We* came from nowhere."

Marrill remembered the parking lot back in Arizona—
one moment, a barren wasteland, and the next, port to a
massive ship. Was this what that looked like from the other
side?

"Some places are obvious," Ardent said, reading the
question on her face. "Get close enough and you can wave.
Others are hidden and don't show themselves until you
stumble into their waters. Some few require passkeys, but
don't worry about them. I have been a wizard for a long,
long time, and I go where I will."

Marrill puzzled that last statement as they slid toward
the city. She knew Ardent was powerful; she imagined any
wizard must be. "How does it work?" she asked. "Magic, I
mean. Could you teach me?"

He paced, considering her question. "Well, it's differ-
ent for every person," he explained. "You see, magic is a
persnickety and personal thing, and figuring out how to
convince it to do what you want takes centuries of diffi-
cult study and experimentation. I daresay I have spent my
whole life on those studies, and even I can only manage a
fraction of its potential.

"As for teaching you..." He paused to look her up and
down. "Maybe for very small spells, I might be able to
show you a thing or two. But to do anything with any real
power, what works for me almost certainly would not work
for you. You have to build up a rapport with the magic, you
know."

"Oh," Marrill said, disappointed. She thought for a moment. "So is magic how you knew the Compass Rose would end up here?"

The wizard beamed. "Not at all."

"Um…then how…?"

"We've been following the directions you gave us," Ardent said. "Well done on your part."

Marrill was more confused than ever. "But I didn't give you directions."

"Sure you did. When I asked if you'd seen the scrap of paper, you said yes. And when I asked where it went, you pointed. Now here we are! The good news is that the Compass Rose has likely washed ashore by now. I'm confident it won't take long to find this time!" He smiled and put his hand on her shoulder. The gesture made her feel a little better. Ardent seemed sort of like a grandfather, and she had never really known either of hers.

"The Quay's an interesting place," he told her. "One where you can find almost anything. I think you'll like it. Lots of pirates and adventures and whatnot. Little girls love that sort of thing, don't they?"

"That's little boys," Marrill corrected. *Like a weird, confusing grandfather.*

"Oh. Well, that's unfortunate, then…." Ardent's voice trailed off as something in the distance grabbed his attention. He pressed his lips together so tight that his entire mouth was swallowed by beard and mustache.

Marrill followed his gaze. Several hundred yards away, a ship foundered, the water around it churning white as it sank. She had never seen a boat like it: disklike with a bunch of masts sprouting from it like a forest of trees.

"What do you think that was?" she asked. The last thing to go under was the carved figure on the bowsprit, holding out a bronze image of the sun.

Ardent turned away as the bronze star slid into the water and sunset forever. "I'm sure it was nothing," he said. "Things like this happen, you know. The seafloor here is positively littered with shipwrecks; were it not for Coll's skills, we'd have run aground on one already."

Just then, Coll shouted, "Coming abaft!" The *Kraken* veered toward one of the larger wharves, high enough to be nearly level with the deck.

"We need not linger overmuch," Ardent said as the ship slid into place. "It's a dangerous place, after all." He popped himself effortlessly over the rail and onto the wharf before the ship even fully stopped.

Marrill glanced back at the open hatch where Karnelius had disappeared, and twisted her fingers. Karny hated water, and so long as the smallest strip of it separated the ship from the dock, she didn't need to worry too much about him heading out on his own. Even so, he was her only link to home, and she didn't like the idea of leaving him alone.

"Bilge mice—I mean, pirats—will keep an eye on him," Coll said, vaulting over the railing and landing neatly next to Ardent. "You're crew now, under the *Kraken*'s protection—they won't let anything happen to your cat."

"That's the problem," she said. "Karny tends to eat mice."

Coll let out a bark of laughter and held out a hand. She took it, and he helped her onto the wharf. "They've dealt with worse," he said. "Come on, then, let's get that Map."

CHAPTER 13
Someone Who Remembers You

Fin's heart froze in his chest. He knew that face, recognized those tears. He'd seen them not an hour before, looking back at him from the reflecting pool in the Meressian ship. On the statues spouting water into the death trap. But this was no statue; it was the real thing.

The *Oracle*. The very person the Meressians were trying to keep the Key from.

The man lurched forward, gangly and gaunt in the darkness. Tears streamed down his cheeks. He snorted a mighty snort and wiped his nose feverishly, little baby sobs still trailing out.

"You came," he said. "I knew you would." His voice cracked as he spoke, with sorrow, or laughter, or both. Fin watched one of the black tears fall from the man's chin and land in a dark circle on the flour-dusted floor. Like a drop of ink on a page.

"It was you," Fin breathed. "You wrote the letter."

"Yes," the Oracle responded. Bright red lips smiled, the corners of them quivering. "I wrote your letter, little lost boy." Next to Fin, a scam artist he knew as Tubbly the Kid let out a choke, then another thief beside him broke into bawling, then another. "I guided you down the path you needed to go. I will guide you"—the Oracle flapped one hand in front of his face, then off into the air, following it with his eyes—"farther."

"To my mother?" Fin asked, breathless.

The Oracle let out a sniffling, whimpering little laugh. "Which one? The real one you have made up, or the pretend one who is real and thinks you're a ghost?"

The mention of the Parsnickles hit Fin like a physical blow. He stepped back. Everything about the situation screamed at him to run. Instead, his throat tightened. Without warning, all the years he'd spent being forgotten, pretending it didn't matter, came crashing down on him. Why it came now, when he should have been terrified instead, he couldn't say. But it came nonetheless, burning in his stomach and clawing behind his eyes.

Brow furrowed, the Oracle waved at the air dismissively. "The first, of course, of course. Worry not for the ones on Gutterleak Way. You have my word they will be safe as can be, and my words carry with them the future."

The Oracle stepped forward. Flour whipped into dust devils around the hem of his cloak, as if afraid to land on the black cloth.

Fin opened his mouth, struggling to find words. But the only words he could think to say were, "Why are you crying?"

"Oh, Fin." Hearing his name made Fin stumble backward; he hadn't heard it spoken aloud in years. "Don't you know?" The Oracle's voice was almost apologetic.

Fin shook his head.

"I cry for the poor people in this shop." The Oracle took another halting step. One colorless hand waved at the sobbing men around them. They each choked and shook harder as the pale fingers passed them by.

"I cry," he said, "for myself." Another step. "I cry for *all* people, everywhere." He seemed to grow larger, pulling in the strength to say the next words. "For you see, the Lost Sun of Dzannin soon climbs its course across the sky. And its light, its cold, blistering light, shines on the end of all creation!"

His tears ran ever more freely, dark stains carving deep channels across the perfect white of his cheeks. "But right now, Fin," he said in a low, trembling voice, "I cry for you!"

Fin felt a deep ache in the pit of his stomach. The words made no sense, but he *felt* them, somehow, a swirl of images and thoughts and emotions that made his gut clench and his head ache. A sorrow like a serpent, threatening to strangle him.

It was as though despair radiated from the Oracle, affecting everyone around him. Fin had never seen—had never even heard of—magic so powerful.

"What do you want?" he gasped. Sadness pushed tears to the corners of his eyes, threatening to spill over. It all seemed so hopeless.

"The Key, of course," the Oracle snapped. "The Key to open the gate. The Map to show the way." He looked at Fin as if it should all be totally clear. But before Fin could react, he held up a hand. "Wait," he said. "I mustn't skip ahead." He seemed to speak more to himself than to Fin. "All things in time, the verses in line. Order, order, patience. The Key first." He shook his head, then took another step forward. The thieves, still weeping, stepped with him.

Fin's fingers flew to his breast pocket, feeling the weight of the ruby key inside. Part of him shrieked not to give it away, that this man was evil. Insane. Another part of him begged to fulfill his contract, to give the thing over and let the Oracle lead him onward.

"You set this all in motion," he said. "Just to get the Key." He thought back to what the pirates had told him, about a mysterious ship of iron attacking the Meressians in a storm and forcing them to port where they'd be vulnerable. "That Iron Ship, it was yours?"

The Oracle shrieked at the mention of the Iron Ship. "No, no, no!" He waved his hands in front of him so violently Fin took a step back. "Iron slays dragons, from it I run! I fear the Iron Ship, steer clear the Iron Ship!"

His fingers drummed against his temples, and he shook his head, babbling pure madness. "Fools stand becalmed where the wise will run. I must be wise today, for a fool will I become. Keep the order in line, rhyme after rhyme. Race face fire, fear steer clear...iron slays dragons beyond the shores of frigid night...." He sucked in a deep breath, gathering himself. "The prophet is bathed in golden light."

At the last words, the pirates all around let out a wail. The Oracle straightened. He seemed to have pulled himself together, but Fin could see that his fingers still trembled.

"Remember my promise, Fin," he hissed. "When the Lost Sun rises, you will be remembered, forever." The Oracle held out a hand, palm up. Expectant. "This ends when you give me the Key."

Fin's entire body shook. The loneliness of those words

hit him like a physical force. He felt lost, abandoned, helpless. Whatever the Oracle promised, he knew it wasn't the kind of being remembered he wanted. But he would never get the kind he wanted. What was the point of resisting, really? What was the point of ever fighting?

A tear quivered at the edge of his eye as he reached for the lump beneath his coat. "Then have it," he said.

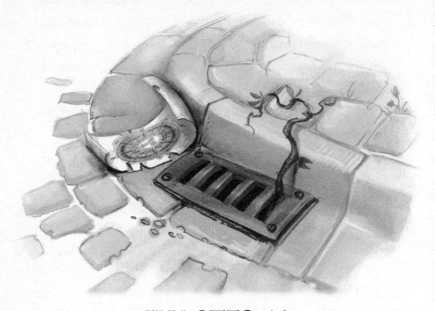

CHAPTER 14
At the Khaznot Quay,
Oh, the Things You'll See!

Marrill's steps slowed as they reached the end of the wharf. She'd been to more foreign cities and towns than she could count, but none of them were like the Khaznot Quay. Ramshackle buildings squatted just beyond the pier, and past them, streets led away in odd directions, as if a giant jungle explorer had chosen a path and hacked his way through the buildings at random.

Through it all, a strong breeze gusted and roared down

from the mountain peak, howling along the twisting streets. Marrill thought she caught a glimpse of someone gliding through the air halfway up the slope.

As they pushed into the crowd, people were everywhere, along with things that looked like people but weren't quite and things that didn't really look like people at all but still seemed to be walking and talking and wearing clothing. One of them brushed against her leg, a stooped-over woman with eyes made of dark crystals and a beak almost like a bird's. She gave a trill grunt at Marrill and pushed her aside. "I'm sorry!" Marrill stammered, but the bird-woman just kept moving.

Coll declared his intent to fetch some supplies for the ship and slipped off into the crowd. Marrill watched as he instantly blended in. "He seems kind of young to be a captain," she remarked.

"He's the best sailor on the Stream," Ardent replied, lifting a shoulder. "Now, the thing you have to know about the Khaznot Quay," he added, changing the subject as he took off up one of the streets, "is that it can be dangerous. It's full of thieves and pirates and cutthroats and worse, so stick close to me for now."

Marrill swallowed and tried to look unafraid, though she made sure to keep within grasping distance of the wizard's purple robe.

"Also," Ardent lectured, "it can get quite windy. If you hear or feel a big gust coming, don't be shy about grabbing hold." He gestured to the long chains bolted up and down the sides of the street. "It's a great way to meet the locals, get in touch with the city, and not get carried away and dropped to your death from an enormous height."

Marrill stiffened in alarm, but Ardent just patted her on the head. "Nothing to worry about. The back alleys are the worst, and we'll just stay out of those. It's not like the gutters in Sennslurp City. Nasty creatures, those. Once saw a man step out of the way of a passing wagon and get swallowed whole, spectacles and all." He shivered. "They found the spectacles later, of course."

Marrill's face contorted with horror.

"Just in case, how about we meet up at the *Kraken* if we get separated?" the wizard quickly added.

Marrill swallowed the lump of fear in her throat and nodded, wondering if she should have stayed behind with Karnelius after all.

Fortunately for Marrill, Ardent's ridiculous purple hat waved above the crowd, making him easy to follow. Because as they navigated the narrow roadways, eyes peeled for any sign of the Map, it occurred to her that telling the difference between a main thoroughfare and a deadly back alley must be an acquired skill. Every street seemed to be cramped, dingy, and full of dangerous-looking characters.

The sights and smells washed over Marrill, dazzling her. Stalls of various shapes and sizes squeezed into empty gaps between buildings. Vendors paced in front of them, calling out their wares: candles that filled the air with the smell of summer and skinned knees, baskets woven out of snow, silver charms that sang shrill notes as they passed.

She was so busy taking it all in that she almost missed the tattered scrap of paper caught in the gutter behind a row of carts. Fortunately, the familiar star-shaped pattern caught her eye just as they passed it. The Compass Rose!

"Ardent!" she called out. But the market was loud, and he was already drifting farther into the crowd. Her eyes darted between him and the gutter, trying not to lose sight of either.

She couldn't let the Map get away, she decided. Ardent, she could find again. She dove between two of the carts, hoping desperately that the purple hat would be there when she came back up.

A thin man with a mangy beard ducked in front of her, blocking the way. "Psst," he said, holding forward a grimy bit of cloth filled with tiny orangish spheres. "Someone like you must be having a fancy for trog eggs, eh?" Inside them, something dark twisted and squirmed.

Marrill barely had time to gag before a squat woman with thick hairy arms—and were those real horns jutting from her temples?—jostled her way between them. "That 'un here's a cheat," she said, jerking a finger at the thin man. "Everyone knows 'egg of red, soon be dead,' don't we, deary?" she asked.

A trickle of unease snaked up Marrill's neck. She glanced

at the Compass Rose, still resting in the gutter. But when she tried to politely step around, the woman just shifted her bulk to block the way again.

"A girl…" The woman glanced to either side before continuing, "Nay, a *lady* of yer tastes is discernin'. I could tell that easy as lookin'. You'll be wanting something sophisticated, that's right, and I got jest the thing right here."

"Oh, I'm sorry but—" Marrill's voice cut off in a squeak when a grip like iron squeezed the top of her arm. She tried to struggle, but it was useless. The woman dragged her around the corner, away from the Compass Rose, and hopelessly away from the purple hat bobbing off through the crowd.

Marrill found herself pinned in a narrow alley, the woman's massive girth barring the only exit. Alarmed, Marrill attempted to squeeze past her, but the woman plowed on, ignoring Marrill's efforts to escape.

"You ever seen the sea silks woven by a Swiggamore siren?" she asked. "Toss one of them scarves over yer head, and any man will fall for ya. Before you can blink, he'll be on his knees doin' anything you ask of him."

She wheezed as she leaned in to whisper in Marrill's ear. "Trust me," she added, slightly out of breath. "I got myself fifteen husbands, an' them's just the ones worth keeping."

"Oh," Marrill stammered, deciding that it probably wasn't a good idea to anger a woman with horns. "That's nice but—"

"Take this." The woman thrust something into Marrill's hands, then clapped twice. "That's it then!" she said. "No take-backs! Now let's see yer pay. AlleySalley cuts a fair price, anyone'll tell ya."

Marrill's eyes went wide. "I'm afraid I don't have any money," she confessed nervously.

The woman moved closer, pinning Marrill against the grimy wall. Marrill cringed, her eyes fixed on the woman's horns.

"Still a fresh one, ain't ya?" The woman laughed. "The Quay's about trade, love. And you always got something to trade." She whipped out a wicked knife that looked much sharper than her horns. Marrill sucked in a breath, ready to scream.

"Oh, love, if you could see the look on yer face." The woman made a *tsk*ing sound as she reached toward Marrill's head. AlleySalley was quicker than she appeared. In a heartbeat, she grabbed a hunk of Marrill's hair. "As lovely as midnight," she purred. And then, *snip*. Marrill felt a tug against her scalp and then a push, and she was back out on the main street, a grimy scrap of fabric clutched in her fingers.

Marrill shoved it in her back pocket and sucked in a gulp of fresh air, choking when it wasn't so fresh. She glanced toward the gutter where the Map had been moments before. It was empty; the Compass Rose was gone. Again. And there was no sign of Ardent anywhere. A sick sense of dread began building, and it only got worse when she caught sight of AlleySalley lovingly stroking a length of dark hair. Her hair, Marrill realized.

Bracing herself, Marrill reached up, ran her hand along her forehead, and winced. Great. She'd lost the Compass Rose, she'd lost her wizard, and now she had bangs. Short, uneven bangs. She groaned. She looked *horrible* with bangs.

Feeling defeated, Marrill started into the crowd, thinking that she should probably try to find her way back to the *Kraken* before she got too hopelessly lost. She'd hardly taken two steps when someone grumbled, "Wachet!" and knocked her to one side. "Walk or be a cobblestone, kid," said someone else, shoving her back the other way.

She dodged out of the way of an impressively spherical creature covered in pointed spines, so panicked that she didn't hear a shopkeeper's warning until too late. She spun, catching sight of huge black eyes and a mouth full of wickedly sharp teeth only seconds before tumbling into his cart.

Glass shattered everywhere as Marrill hit the ground. Suddenly, her mouth tasted like she'd been sucking on a shoe that had stepped in three-week-old mayonnaise. She smacked her lips furiously against the wretched sensation.

"Not the flavors!" the shopkeeper cried mournfully. He rounded on Marrill, the gray scales covering his triangular face turning purple with rage as he bellowed.

Marrill scrambled to her feet and ran. This time, the crowd parted for her easily, each passerby wrinkling their faces and gagging when she neared them, as if tasting the worst flavor imaginable. She plunged through them wildly, putting as much distance between her and the shark-toothed shopkeeper as possible.

When she finally slowed, Marrill found herself in the middle of a market square, no longer sure which way she'd come from. Nothing was familiar. Not the sights, not the smells, not the sounds, definitely not the tastes. Carts were loaded with funny-looking meat and vegetables with eyes. Men called out to each other using words she'd never heard. Even the colors seemed different: the pinks closer to orange than they should be, purples so brilliantly blue it hurt to look at them.

Never in her life had she felt so alone and lost. Not in any of her family's adventures, not even when she'd first stepped out of the car at her new house in the desert. At least back in Arizona she could've found a phone, called for home or dialed 911.

But here ... everywhere she looked she saw knives tucked through belts, daggers strapped to calves. Even women's earrings looked sharp and wicked. She bit her lower lip to keep it from trembling.

Just as despair threatened to overwhelm her, something caught her eye. A scrap of paper, slightly tattered, carried on the breeze. It skipped across the street and down a narrow alley. She knew it well by now: the Compass Rose!

Wind ruffled her shorn bangs as she raced down the thin alleyway after it, turning sideways at one point to squeeze between two tilted buildings. Up ahead the scrap of paper almost glowed in the gloom, plastered against a dingy wall.

Marrill did her best to channel Karnelius as she stalked it, crouched low to the ground. Her fingers curled. She prepared to pounce.

And then, just as she reached striking distance, she heard something roaring behind her. Too late, she figured out what it was: the wind. Coming down on her fast, louder than any wind she'd ever heard before.

Marrill dove. The wind rose around her, gaining strength. Her fingers closed around the slip of paper. She had it!

Then she was rising when she should have been falling. She scrabbled against the wall with her free hand, trying to hold on. Then she was scrabbling against the roof, and then against nothing.

She was completely airborne!

The wind tugged her higher and higher, flipping her head over her ankles and back again. Her stomach turned as streets and houses zoomed past in a blur below. She wasn't just airborne; she was flying! It was exactly the same as in her dreams, the wind in her hair and the freedom to twist and spin and roll. She let out a whoop of delight and pinwheeled her arms as though she were swimming.

For a glorious moment, her heart leapt in exhilaration. But just for one moment. Because she didn't know how to fly. She had no way to control her movements. And up ahead, coming straight at her, was a massive, looming—and very solid—wall of stone.

CHAPTER 15
Now Is When You Run

Despair spiraled in Fin's chest like water down a drain. It was hopeless. He would be alone forever. There was no point fighting. He reached into his coat, his fingers clasping around the ruby key.

And then he stopped. He knew this feeling. He felt it every time he chased a Quay kid's shadow up a wall, desperately hoping the other boy would stop and wait for him. He knew it each time he introduced himself to Stavik as though they'd never been more than strangers. He had lived it this very morning, when Mrs. Parsnickle looked him straight in the eye and asked him if she knew him.

How many times had it been made clear to Fin that he was alone in this world? That no one else could help him, care for him, be there for him? Every night on the edge of sleep, he closed his eyes and thought about finding his mother or learning where he came from or coming downstairs and having the Parsnickles pick him up and spin him around and treat him like a normal kid in a normal family.

This despair was nothing new. Every single day, he faced the fear that he would be this way forever and nothing would change, and every single day he beat that fear. He'd bitten down sadness before. He would do it again. Every single day, until he *did* find his mother, and then he *would* be a normal kid. He *had* to be.

And deep down, he knew staying here with this madman didn't mean finding her. It meant crying about it, forever.

Which was exactly what the Oracle wanted, Fin realized. *He* was the one causing all of the tears; *he* was the one dredging up the feelings Fin normally kept choked down. Doing to Fin what he had done to the thieves. There was a magic at work here unlike any Fin had seen before.

He shook his head, moving his hand away from the pocket holding the ruby key. What had he almost done? What would the crying man do if Fin gave him what he wanted?

"You're not going to help me find my mother," he said with conviction.

Fin glanced around the room. All the thieves had their knives drawn now. Each took a shaking step forward in unison.

"Now is when you run," the Oracle told him.

A shot of adrenaline wiped away the last traces of the sadness that had held him, clearing his mind. He needed to get out of there, and fast!

"Don't have to tell me twice!" Fin said, darting for the door.

He had almost reached the stairs when Ad and Tad stepped in, blocking the oven entrance. Tad flipped a switch, and flames burst up from the floor. The heat struck Fin full on, making him wince and jump back into the den to avoid it.

Every thief was focused on Fin now. The closest things he had to friends, the men he had always wished would see him. They saw him now. And he wished more than anything they would look away.

The biggest thief—a hunched-over cord of muscle and white fuzz Fin knew as Cotton Scotton—charged first. Fin twisted away from the dagger swiping at his neck and swung around Cotton's broad back. Another thief lunged into the empty space, slicing a stinging line across Fin's shoulder.

Fin let out a grunt and rolled away, clutching it. He

spared it one glance. Just a scratch. If not for the tears slowing their movement, he'd have been skewered.

Fin darted one way, then the other. Like any good thieves' den, the pie shop was full of secret doors, false columns, and hidden exits. Unfortunately, each one of them was blocked by a crowd of weeping thieves. He would never get through.

"Give in, little lost boy," the Oracle called over the thieves' bawling. "Give in to your pain. Cry with me."

"No thanks!" Fin shouted back. There was one exit left, one the other thieves wouldn't even think to go near. It was the last, and best, escape route, reserved for Stavik himself. Up the rear chimney, over a smoldering fire, a hidden ladder led to the roof. It was the only option, and he had to take it.

Fin didn't bother to think of any fancy moves or tricks. He just tucked chin to chest and charged. One of the benefits to being the youngest thief in the place was being small enough to slide between legs without breaking stride.

Of course, the problem with running for Stavik's escape route, he realized too late, was Stavik. Fin smacked into him. Arms like clamps closed around him, lifting him off the ground. Face-to-face, they looked into each other's eyes; Stavik's were red from crying, the long scar down his cheek flushed purple.

"So sorry, blood," Stavik whispered in his ear.

"Me too," Fin sighed. Tears welled up in his own eyes. Even if it was the magic—evil magic—he almost believed Stavik remembered him.

Then he kneed the Pirate King in the groin as hard as he possibly could.

"*Urfhk!*" Stavik grunted, dropping him. Fin leapfrogged over the hunched form and shoved him hard in the back toward the Oracle, sending him toppling to the ground and taking some of the thieves down with him.

The dark figure stepped back quickly, but a few still grabbed at the Oracle's robes as they fell. Each thief howled as he touched the black fabric and collapsed on the ground clutching blue, frostbitten hands.

The Oracle, for his part, watched Fin with dead eyes. "I know you, Fin," he wheezed. "Don't forget. I promise I won't forget you."

Fin hesitated just before the smoldering fireplace, a brief flood of worry washing over him. What if the Oracle really *did* know where his mother was? What if Fin was turning his back on his only way to find her? What if no one else would ever remember him again?

He forced himself to turn away, letting the immediate danger bury the deeper fears. He had made his choice, and no one evaded the pie shop pirates for long. He flew up the chimney ladder, not pausing to listen to them clambering after.

Soot and the stink of a hundred old fires clung to him

as he burst out the top, just as the wind reached a howl. He ran to the roof's edge and skidded to a stop. A jump from this height might break his leg or, worse, catch him in the wind current.

Ordinarily, Fin would rather ride a wind current than walk, but not here. The wind came head on into the cliff face, and that curl-over created a nasty vortex that would dash a kid against the cliff more often than not. It took a mean trick to ride it; maybe if he had some momentum, he could get through. But he didn't, and without it, Fin was pretty sure he'd be paste.

He swallowed. Clearly, Stavik had some plan to get out of here he'd never clued Fin in on. Cliffs and other buildings, too high to jump to, penned him in on either side. The chimney full of thieves lay behind. Trying to ride the wind meant a vortex beatdown, but trying to drop would break his legs. What a great junk of options.

The wind roared again, a big one coming. Fin braced himself, steeling his nerve. He'd have to take a chance and hope the vortex was kind.

The sound of sobbing echoed behind him. A grimy hand pushed out of the chimney. The first of the thieves tumbled onto the roof, stopping only briefly to get his bearings.

Now or never. Fin closed his eyes and waited for the wind to hit.

And then, a new noise broke through the roar of rushing air. Someone screaming. But not someone in the pie shop.

Fin poked his head over the rooftop, just in time to see a little figure flying at him, tumbling head over heels on the front of the gust.

"Lucky break, chums!" he shouted to the thieves, who were already advancing on him, daggers ready for the kill. Then he launched himself off the roof, hoping his timing was right. His hand caught something. An ankle, or a bony knee? Was that toadbutter he suddenly tasted?

And then he, too, was spinning in the gust, shooting out high into the open air.

CHAPTER 16
A Curious Tour Guide

Marrill screamed, flapping her arms wildly. But the rock face just came at her faster. She closed her eyes and braced for impact.

Then something caught her leg and a heavy weight flung her sideways, out of the path of the wall. She risked opening an eye. A boy about her age clutched her ankle, and now they were toppling through the air together.

"What are you doing?" she shouted at him. The wind

pushed them up, higher and higher, past the tops of tall buildings and into the clear sky.

"Saving your life!" he shouted back. Way too far below for her comfort, the crooked streets of the Khaznot Quay waited to dash them to pieces.

"You're not doing a very good job of it!"

The wind whipped them one way, then jerked them the other. Buildings and streets and jagged rocky outcroppings passed beneath them as they twisted around each other. One second the boy was above her, the next below. She thought she might be sick. She clutched the Compass Rose tighter in her fist.

"Don't rush a kid," the boy said. "Give me a sec...." They dropped again, and Marrill's guts did a flip. The boy, for his part, used the momentum to grab for her knees. Then he wedged a toe in one of her pockets and shimmied up her like she was a ladder.

"What...*umph!* Are you...*oof!* Doing?" she demanded.

"Stop kicking!" he yelled. His face popped up in front of hers. It was grimy and smudged with dirt. "Right, then!" He looked up. She did, too. Only up was not up anymore. Judging by the cobblestones coming at them, up was down!

"Do something!" she screamed, digging the fingers of her free hand into his shoulders.

"Hold on!" the boy shouted. "And I mean tight!"

The ground came on fast. Marrill cringed. The boy held

out his arms and jerked something with his thumbs, and suddenly Marrill's brain seemed to flip in her head. They were headed up again, real up! Wings of fabric strung out from under the boy's arms, catching the wind.

They were flying, for real this time! Gliding, actually, just above the rooftops, but flying anyway!

"It's remarkable!" she laughed.

"It's not built for two!" the boy responded. "Brace yourself!"

He tugged once more, twisting them to catch another draft, and that's when Marrill's leg clipped the roof of a building. Pain shot up her thigh.

"Ow! *Oof!* Ouch!" She couldn't tell which sounds came from her and which from him as rough slate scraped across her flesh. "*Ugh! Ack!* Oh!" They bounced and rolled, tumbled apart, and finally she came to a rest, her head right at the roof's edge.

She sat up slowly, testing to see if anything was broken. A few spots of skin were rubbed raw along her shin and forearms, and she'd have a wicked bruise from where her thigh clipped the roof, but other than that, she seemed to be in one piece. She checked the paper. Despite being rather crumpled, it appeared to have survived the crash intact. She let out a relieved sigh and tucked it into her pocket.

The boy crouched not too far away, tucking the little wind sails into the seam of his coat. He smacked his mouth, sticking out his tongue as if he tasted something sour.

If it hadn't been for him, she'd be a girl-shaped smudge against the side of a cliff by now. "Thanks," she told him. Her fingers fiddled with the ragged edges of her newly shorn bangs. "For saving me and all."

The boy's eyebrows jumped in surprise. "Y-you're welcome." He didn't sound at all like the boy who'd been in such control—well, perhaps *control* wasn't the right word— moments before. If anything, he seemed lost and vulnerable, like an abandoned animal.

Her heart dipped into that special place, where it lived already in the Banton Park Live-In Animal Rescue Reserve and took home blind owls and one-toed sloths.

He was a bit ragged around the edges. The seams of his pants were frayed, and his thick black hair had clearly been cut by someone with only the loosest understanding of what either *hair* or *cut* meant, much less the two words together. In short, he needed someone to look out for him.

Not knowing what else to say, Marrill scanned her surroundings. It wasn't terribly difficult to orient herself. The coast was a horseshoe at the base of the mountain. Ardent had instructed her to meet him back at the ship if they got separated, so that was where she was headed.

Of course, between there and here was a maze of dangerous alleys, and she knew from experience navigating wasn't so easy from street level. If she struck out into the city alone, she was pretty much guaranteed to run into trouble. She needed some looking out for herself.

"Um, so," she said to the boy, twisting her fingers together. "I'm supposed to be meeting my friends down at their ship, but...I'm not really sure how to get there. Any chance you could...show me the way?"

The boy lifted an eyebrow. "Ship?" He rocked from his heels to his toes as he considered. Marrill got the feeling he was pretty good at sizing up people and situations.

Then the awkwardness seemed to melt from him, just like that. "The docks, you say? I wasn't heading in that direction myself...." He drew out the last word, and her shoulders drooped.

"But," he added. She perked up again. "It is a pretty fine day for a walk, what with it being clear out and all. You do understand I'd be going out on a limb for you, pushing off all my other errands and whatnots. Which I have. Already scheduled, I mean."

She guessed what he was hinting at. "I'm afraid I don't have any money, or really any way to repay you."

"Oh," he said, waving away her concern, "it's all about trade in the Quay."

Marrill's stomach tightened, and she fingered her new bangs. "So I gather...."

But he didn't seem to be paying attention to her. His head tilted to one side, as if listening for something in the distance. All Marrill could hear was the chaos of the marketplace—someone shouting, someone laughing, someone crying. A few someones crying, even. A frown passed across the boy's face, so quickly she almost missed it.

Then he smiled. "Although I s'pose a good deed is its own reward, every now and then. Fills the heart and all that." He leapt toward her and grabbed her hand, tugging her across the roof.

"My name's Marrill, by the way," she said as he guided her down a narrow pipe bolted to the side of the building.

"Lovely name, that. Pleuredian?"

"Um…" Marrill said, clambering after him. "No thanks?"

The boy blinked at her as she dropped to the ground next to him.

"I'm Fin," he offered. "But look at me, going on and on. Tell me more about you. Where you came from, where you're headed, how spacious your traveling arrangements are, that sort of thing."

Marrill had a difficult time keeping up with his pace as he led her through the Quay, and an even harder time keeping up with his questions. "I came from Arizona," she said. "I guess I'm headed back there, as soon as I can. What was that last one?"

"Arizona," he said. "That sounds like a good, happy, no-crying sort of place."

She tried to disagree, but it got lost when he grabbed her hand and ducked into a sea of carts.

"So tell me about this ship of yours," he continued.

He wove his way through the chaos expertly. She wasn't quite as graceful. Her foot landed in something sticky and slick, and she nearly toppled into a cart of leather bags. One of the satchels snapped at her as she pushed away.

"It's, uh...it has sails and, uh..."

"Big? Small?" He dodged a puddle. She splashed right through it before she knew it was there.

"I don't have much to compare it to, I guess," she admitted.

"You could compare it to the other ships down at the pier," he prompted.

Marrill struggled to remember. It proved quite difficult while keeping up with Fin. He moved through the crowd with practiced ease, slipping around legs, ducking under tables, squeezing through gaps. No one yelled at him or shoved him or tried to sell him eggs; it was almost like he didn't even exist in the same world as everyone else.

"I guess it's on the big side? I don't really know all that much about ships," she confessed. "In fact, I didn't even know about the Pirate Stream until today."

And at that, Fin ran smack into the side of a cart. A towering pile of yellow, spiky fruit toppled down, bouncing off in every direction. "My pointimelons!" shouted the stall owner.

"This way!" Fin dodged into an alley so steep that Marrill almost had to sit to manage her way down. He pushed her to the center, where a thin layer of slime flowed down a shallow gutter. "One foot in front of the other, then," he said, showing her.

Marrill mirrored him.

"And like this," he instructed, rocking back on his heels. He slid down the hill, picking up speed as he went. Marrill cringed, took a deep breath, and followed.

Fin made it look easy, arms held out to either side as he glided along. Marrill was more like a newborn giraffe struggling to figure out what legs were and how they worked. She stopped counting how many times she'd fallen once she reached double digits.

"So I'd imagine with a large ship it must be difficult to search for stowaways," he said, coming to an expert stop before the alley dead-ended in a sharp little cliff. Just as she was about to career over, he grabbed her arm and swung her around onto another street.

"I mean, I imagine it would be," he continued. "Of course, I wouldn't know, being a bit of a landlubber myself, and not the type to stow away. Nope, Quay's for me, that's what I say." He paused, chuckling nervously. She tried to focus on calming her thundering heart—surely at some point today it would burst. "But I would think, you know, that it might be hard to do," he said. "Catch stowaways, I mean."

"I wouldn't know," she answered, sucking in a deep breath. "I turned myself in."

Fin pulled up short. Marrill caught a glimpse of the bay

past the mouth of the alley and started toward it. They must have been close to the docks.

"How did you join up with this crew exactly?" Fin trotted after her.

"I met them in a parking lot," Marrill told him.

"Can't say I've ever heard of Ahparkenlot," Fin mused. "Is that near the Longtooth Kingdoms?"

Something tickled her nose. "Do you smell that?" she asked, walking faster. *Smoke*. She had smelled a lot of things burning in the Quay so far. Candles, meat, incenses, things she couldn't identify. But this she knew—wood. Like the kind you build stuff from. The air was getting hazy, she realized.

"The docks are on fire!" someone screamed.

"Oh no!" Marrill gasped. She took off running. Fin called after her, but when she burst out of the alley, she found herself in a sea of panicked people rushing franticly in all directions.

Ahead, the wharf blazed with fire, most of the ships moored along the piers burning with it. Marrill raced closer, searching unsuccessfully for the *Kraken* through the wall of flames.

Frantically, she pushed through the crowd, trying not to think about the *Kraken* being destroyed. She didn't even realize she'd been holding her breath until she caught sight of a familiar pointed purple cap.

"Ardent!" she cried. To her enormous relief, the wizard turned, his face splitting into a huge grin. Coll was with him, and he seemed to relax a little when he saw her.

"Thank goodness you're safe, my dear!" Ardent said. He laid a hand on her shoulder and smiled. "I saw you picked up by the wind and tried to track after you, but the treacherous vapor told me you'd learned to fly."

Marrill glanced around and lowered her voice. "I found what we were looking for," she told him, patting her pocket.

The wizard clapped his hands. "Excellent work!" He hesitated, smacking his lips as if tasting the air. "Though I'd ask for a refund on that flavor if I were you," he said. "Far too much worstedwort for toadbutter."

Coll grabbed them both and pushed them through the gawking crowd. "We don't have much time. Our ride is leaving." He pointed. Out past the burning docks, the *Enterprising Kraken* drifted unmoored, her anchor dragging as she headed for open water.

"But the fire..." Already Marrill could feel the heat blasting between them and the water. "There's no way we can get through it!"

Ardent turned to her. "Did you ever learn to ice-skate?"

"No," she said, puzzled.

"Pity, that." He raised his arms and turned to the bay. His hands swept out, then pulled in toward him, his fingers tugging at invisible threads. A chill bit at Marrill's toes, leapt up her legs, and wrapped around her body. She gasped to see her breath come out in a thick wintery puff. "I suppose," the wizard said, little flecks of snow gathering on his beard, "that it's never too late to learn!"

He thrust his arms forth. The cold immediately left her as a thick trail of frost shot out down the beach and across the water, freezing it solid. In the blink of an eye, a bridge of ice stretched from the shore to the *Kraken*. The entire crowd gasped at once. Marrill clapped her hands.

"That may not last long," Ardent noted. And with that, they took off down the beach, onto the ice. It was slick, but Marrill remembered the trick Fin had taught her. She put one foot in front of the other, balancing on her heels, and barely fell once.

Fin! She had completely left him behind and never thanked him for bringing her safely to the wharf! She dug her toe into the ice, ground to a halt, and spun back toward the city. Already the smoke was thicker, obscuring her view of the crowd. She squinted to find him.

Only one person seemed to be moving on the shore. She immediately recognized the way he slipped through the throng of onlookers.

"Fin!" she called, cupping her hands around her mouth.

The boy hesitated, jerking his head in her direction.

"Thank you!" she yelled, waving a hand in the air. Then she turned and skated toward the ship.

To her left, a narrow pier collapsed on itself, sending a

shower of sparks towering into the sky. Ardent yelled for her to hurry, and Coll was already climbing a rope ladder up to the main deck. Through the crackling of the flames, she never even heard the growing sound of sobbing coming from the shore.

CHAPTER 17
The Compass Rose

Fin's heart froze, and not just because the wizard had dropped the temperature of the docks by forty degrees. His stomach flipped. She'd recognized him. She'd spotted him in the throng of people and recognized him. And remembered him!

He didn't know what to do, so he did what came naturally: He hid. He ducked from person to person, peeking out from the mass to see if she was still watching. Her eyebrows squished together as she searched the crowd for him. After a second, she shook her head and skated away across the ice.

But she'd remembered him! She had even waved at him, like she *wanted* to see him! It was the most incredible thing that had ever happened, ever.

Also, the docks were on fire, an old man had conjured a bridge of ice out of nowhere, and the girl and her friends were skating across it to a gigantic pirate ship. All that was also impressive. But she had seen him! He bounced a little with joy.

And then he heard the crying. A chill shot down his back. In the moment's excitement, he'd almost forgotten why he was here in the first place: to stow away on that ship. He just needed to wait a second so Marrill could *really* forget him—because she would, of course—and then he could follow.

"It's okay, dear," he overheard someone say. "It's horrible, I know. There, there. No one was hurt, dear, no one was hurt."

Fin twisted slowly toward the sound, not sure at all he wanted to see where it was coming from. His eyes met those of a girl about his own age, an orphan he'd seen around the Preserve. Tears flowed in torrents down her cheeks.

"So sorry, kid," she muttered at Fin. "So, so sorry."

Fin stepped backward, stumbled, and fell. Someone to his right started sobbing. Then on his left. He scooted away on his hands, his eyes darting all around. In front of him, someone doubled over, choking and shuddering. Behind him, someone wailed like the world was ending.

The Oracle was near.

"My stuffins, peeps are fallin' apart!" an alarmed voice called out. Everywhere he looked, crying faces waited. And each crying face stared straight back at him.

He clawed his way to his feet. No time to hesitate. It was time to go, *now*! He shot through the crowd in a full-out scramble, urging himself on: *Dive between legs. Shove to one side. Run, run.*

He broke free of the throng and took off toward the path of ice leading from the shore. The girl and her companions were gone, already on board their ship; he could just make out the sailor grappling with the rigging. But Fin's foot crashed straight through the ice the moment he touched it, splashing into frigid water underneath. It was already melting!

Without thinking, he changed direction and leapt toward a burning pier. The roaring inferno greeted him with a shower of embers. Nearby, ships blazed, offering no escape.

All Fin knew was that he best get on Marrill's ship. He raced down the pier, the back of his mind spinning. He could run out the dock, try to skysail off it. Fire meant drafts and a good lift, but also could mean a burning death. The only other option was to try the ice path again and hope that farther out it hadn't melted as much. But if it had, that meant drowning for a boy who couldn't swim.

He glanced back. The mourners had spread out now, blocking every exit back to the Quay. Fin's gut clenched. So which would it be? Ice or fire or all those tears?

"Don't shed too many for me just yet, old bloods," he told the crowd. "You won't even miss me when I'm gone."

Then he took off, headed straight down the burning dock. Just before he reached the flames, he veered to one side, scampering on the very edge of the charred boards.

Heat swelled around him like a wall. Sweat slid down his body. He leaned away from the flames, momentum alone keeping him from falling. It wouldn't last, and the gap between the dock and the ice widened with every second. This was going to be close.

Right as he was about to topple into the water, Fin spread his arms wide, yanked the strings in his sleeves, and let all that heated air catch in his skysail. It buoyed him outward, away. His feet left the dockside.

For a few pounding heartbeats, his toes skidded over the surface of the bay. Then they touched ice. He kicked against it, praying the lift from his skysail would be enough to keep his full weight from crashing through.

The ice groaned beneath him. "Come on, come on," he breathed, his veins pumping with adrenaline. Behind him, the ice cracked as mourners chased after him; it gave way beneath their weight, turning their wails to gargles. Ahead, the girl's ship loomed. And it was weighing anchor.

"Well, of course," he said to himself. He could already feel the breeze leaving him, his footsteps getting heavier. He leapt from iceberg to iceberg now, stifling his urge to shout every time he almost slipped off the edge. The last thing he needed was to alert the crew of the ship. Who knew what *they* did to thieves?

At last he reached the end of the ice. The ship had pulled away, its massive squid-shaped anchor just clearing the water. He jumped, pulling his skysail strings as hard as he could. And flew straight into the thick, dripping anchor chain.

All the air rushed out of him in a great big "*Oof!*" but he clung to the slippery metal links as hard as he could. He dared a glance back as the anchor rose toward the deck. The surf was full of flailing bodies, struggling back to shore.

Fin hugged one stout metal tentacle as the squid-anchor carried him upward. Water poured off it, soaking the front of his shirt and pants on its way down to the bay far below.

As the main deck drew near, Fin was able to shimmy from the anchor out onto the ship's brightly colored trim, just avoiding the dark hole the anchor chain clanked into. From there, he caught a bit of rope netting hung from the deck rail and rested his head against a thick, scratchy knot. Very, very far below, the water looked a little less oily, a little more golden than he remembered. And just a touch glowing.

He swallowed. This was it. As long as he had known about it, as long as he had heard the sailors talking, Fin had never actually been out *on* the open waters of the Pirate Stream. Not until now.

Excitement surged through him, blunted just a bit by the thought of what might happen if he fell and hit that magic water. *Can't sail a chicken*, the old saw repeated in his head. It seemed a lot funnier when *he* wasn't the potential chicken.

As he mulled the thought, voices filtered down from the deck, not far above his perch. Fin tilted one ear up. He could make out words here and there, but not everything.

He eased closer, trying to keep quiet. A stale salt smell crept into his nose as it pressed against the rope. "But why burn all the docks?" Marrill asked above him. "Why not just burn the ships?" He'd never forget the sound of her voice calling out his name. A smile came to Fin's face. The girl who had remembered him, if only for a minute.

"They did that, too," the sailor said. "All except the streamrunners. Dullwood doesn't burn. At least, not quick. Doesn't do much of anything, really. Better to cut those ships loose, let the tides carry them back out while they were sure no one was on them."

"Quite so." The old man sounded distracted. "Whoever

set fire to those docks fully intended that their quarry would never leave the shore, and that no one from *off* the shore could come in and pick them up. Someone, I think, was quite irate with another someone over some *thing*."

Fin gulped. He had a good guess that one of those someones was the Meressian Oracle. And a bad feeling that the other someone might just be him.

"None of our business, really," the sailor grunted.

"Indeed," the wizard affirmed. "And in the meantime, our wonderful Miss Aesterwest has found the first piece of the Map!"

Fin lifted himself to peek up over the fat wooden lip of the railing. Not more than four strides away, the wizard sat on a stool before a table. Marrill, standing next to him with a large orange cat in her arms, craned her neck to look over his shoulder at whatever he was holding. The sailor leaned back casually against a thick mast, his arms crossed.

"So how does it work?" Marrill asked, readjusting the bulk of the cat.

The wizard rocked back on his stool, his purple hat tipping one way as his body tipped the other. "So glad you asked!" he said, chortling. "Watch!" He touched it gently with one hand, the other waving in the air. Marrill gasped. Even the sailor leaned in.

Fin still couldn't see. He climbed higher, slipping over the railing and landing softly on the deck. In a moment, he was behind the mast a mere arm's length from the trio, staring at the wizard's back.

And then the wizard shifted, giving Fin a clear view of the table and the torn piece of paper atop it. The paper was old, yellowed, and so crumpled that it made it look like the star drawn across it was actually moving.

Except that the star *was* moving. As he watched, it fell apart and rearranged itself, a river of ink streaming down the page. Little lines and spirals stacked on top of each other and swirled together. Some kind of self-redrawing parchment, Fin thought. It was a neat trick.

And then the ink stood up, raised itself off the page entirely, and took flight.

Fin jerked his head up, following it as it swooped around the deck. It was a sketch, a sketch of a bird. And it was real. It was flying!

Marrill gasped as her cat hissed. The wizard chuckled. The sailor whistled in appreciation. Fin had to bite his tongue to keep from joining in the amazement.

"What is it?" Marrill asked. Her head turned as she watched the ink drawing, now looking for all the world like a rough-sketched blackbird in three dimensions, fly up the mizzenmast.

"That, my dear"—the wizard laughed—"is our guide to our next destination! Our one and only course through these stormy waters to the place we need to be. Marrill, let me introduce you...to the Bintheyr Map to Everywhere!"

Fin pressed his back to the mast, keeping it firmly between him and the crew.

"That's a map?" the sailor asked.

"That's a scrap of a map," Ardent corrected. "The Compass Rose, to be precise. You can call her Rose, if you like. She will point us the way, right to the next piece!"

"Can't it just lead me home?" Marrill asked.

"This little thing? No, no, no...the full Map will take you anywhere you need to go, but this bit, it can only take us where *it* needs *us* to go. Presumably, its next piece."

Fin sucked in his breath. A map that would show you anything you wished to find? That couldn't be a coincidence. After nearly dying too many times to count this morning, he'd wound up on board a ship with the very thing that could show him the way to find his mother. Things were starting to turn his way after all.

CHAPTER 18
The Stowaway

arrill's mind was still reeling in wonder when Rose let out a cry overhead and dove toward the ship. The bird swooped in a tight circle past the wizard and darted within claw's reach of Karnelius.

The temptation was too much. Karnelius tore out of Marrill's arms, launching himself after the bird. With a twitch of her scribbled wings, Rose banked sharply around the mast, then pulled into a steep climb, twisting through the rigging.

Karnelius didn't even hesitate, tearing across the deck with his fur in full puff and leaping for the mast. Except there was something in the way. A boy, hiding behind the rigging. Marrill's eyes widened.

Undeterred, Karnelius dug every one of his sharp claws into the kid, climbing him like a tree. The boy yowled, stumbling across the deck as he tried to fling the cat free.

Overhead, Rose let out a cry. Ardent yelped in surprise, and Coll shouted, "Stowaway!" Marrill just stood slack-jawed with surprise, only able to say one word:

"Fin?"

The boy cast about, as though looking for a place to hide. She called his name again. He froze. His eyes grew wide as she stepped toward him.

"It is you, isn't it?" She felt a surge of relief. She'd been so worried he might have been hurt in the fire, especially since she was the one who made him take her to the docks. But he looked fine, except for maybe some singeing along the cuffs of his pants. And a hint of terror in his eyes at being caught, of course.

She understood the feeling; she'd been in his shoes just that morning.

Fin's gaze bounced to Ardent and Coll, then back to Marrill again, a frown pinching his eyebrows together. "You, uh..." He cleared his throat, no longer the confident boy who'd guided her through the streets of the Quay. "You r-remember me?"

"Not at all, my boy," Ardent replied.

Coll crossed his arms and muttered, "Never seen you in my life."

Marrill rolled her eyes. "Of course I do." Turning to her two sailing companions, she said, "This is Fin. He's the one who saved me from the wind and helped me get back to the docks."

"Ah!" Ardent said. "An excellent service! And one we shan't forget, I'd wager!"

Fin coughed next to her, almost like a laugh. Marrill waved her hand toward each of them in introduction. "Fin, this is Coll; he's the captain. And that's Ardent the…erm… wizard."

"Perhaps you've heard of me?" Ardent looked at Fin expectantly. Fin shook his head and the wizard sighed. "It's not like there are a lot of wizards about," he muttered to himself.

Fin fidgeted, putting his hands in his pockets and then taking them out again, his gaze casting around the ship and landing on nothing.

"So that's kind of a spiff trick," he said, using his chin to nod at Rose soaring through the air. "Did I hear you mention something about a map? To everywhere? That can find anything?" He rocked back on his heels. "Sounds fascinating. Tell me more."

Ardent couldn't resist an invitation to engage in a lecture. "Excellent observation, young man! The history of the

Bintheyr Map to Everywhere is shrouded in mystery.

"Some say it is as old as the Pirate Stream itself, and just as great," he continued. Coll rolled his eyes. "None know who created it, and even in the very oldest stories, it was already in pieces. But each fragment is powerful beyond powerful in its own right, and each has surfaced time and again at critical points in history. For example, once there was this tribe of highly ambitious tree frogs—"

"I see, I see. Quite exciting stuff," Fin interrupted with a charming smile. Marrill gave him a grateful glance. "And how many pieces did you say there were?" he added.

Ardent began ticking off on his fingers as he explained. "Well, first there's the Compass Rose, which of course we now have. And then of course we'll need the Face—you know, the bit that actually shows you things. That part is obviously fairly important. Third, there's the Neatline, which you might know as the black line around the edge of a map. Most take that one for granted, but defining the area you're looking at is quite critical, especially in a map to everywhere!"

He chuckled a bit, then stopped and counted his fingers again, one, two, three. "Right, three. Then fourth is the Scale for the distances and sizes and whatnot. I'm sure you can see the value in that one."

Holding up his thumb, he concluded, "And finally there's the Legend. Now, that part explains what everything on the

Map means and unlocks its true potential. Only with the Legend, the stories all say, will the Map's secrets ever truly be accessible. That would be the most important part, I would say. Excepting all the others."

The optimism Marrill had been feeling since finding the Compass Rose deflated. There were still four more pieces to find—four more obstacles to her ever getting home. Plus it had taken Ardent a hundred and thirty years to find the first piece, which didn't bode well for timeliness. A familiar anxiety took root in her stomach. "Do you have any idea where the other pieces are?"

Ardent tried to give them a reassuring grin, but it wasn't working. Coll was the one to finally answer. "Dunno," he said with a shrug. "That's what the bird's for."

Marrill slumped against the mast, her eyes following Rose as she wheeled through the air above them, leading them farther and farther out onto the Stream. She thought about her parents, sitting at home waiting for her. "Any idea how long it will take to find them all?"

Ardent tugged on his beard. "Somewhere between three hours and five hundred years, I expect. Which is to say, no, I'm afraid not."

Marrill's heart fell.

Oddly, the answer didn't seem to bother Fin in the slightest. He seemed positively chipper. "Well," he chirped, "there's nothing like a good, solid quest among friends, that's what

I always say. High seas, camaraderie, not throwing anyone into the brig—that's what it's all about, really."

Fin's rambling pulled Marrill from her thoughts of home. If anything, Fin seemed a bit overeager.

"And what a crew we make, right?" he continued. "All of us together, totally not here for nefarious reasons."

She narrowed her eyes in suspicion. She thought back to all his questioning at the Quay. Had he just used her to get on the *Kraken*? "I thought you said you were a landlubber," she said, raising an eyebrow.

Fin let out half of a laugh, strained and nervous. "Oh, that..." He trailed off. He cleared his throat, glancing from Ardent to Coll then back to Marrill again. "Well I do lub me some land, obviously. I just...erm...wanted to make sure you'd gotten safely aboard and all. Now that it seems you have, I can be on my way, and you can forget all about me."

He gave her an uneasy smile and began walking backward across the deck. "By the way," he added, "not to change the subject or to distract you or anything like that but...what in the world could that be?" He pointed sharply behind them, mouth gaping open in surprise.

Marrill spun, prepared for some new horror. But all she saw was empty water.

She turned, eyes squeezed all the way to slits now, and scanned the deck for Fin. There was no sign of him. "Where did he go?" she asked the others.

Oddly, they seemed to have drifted off into their own

conversation, oblivious to what had just happened. Coll looked at her like *she* was the strange one. "Who?"

Marrill huffed with frustration. "Fin. He was just here next to me."

Ardent and Coll exchanged confused glances. "Fins?" The wizard seemed to speak for both of them. "Are there piranhabats about?"

Marrill wondered, for the four billionth time today, if she was losing her mind. "You know, the boy who was standing here? Stowaway? About my height, with black hair and singed pants?"

They just shrugged, like it didn't ring any bells. But that didn't make sense. "He's the one who guided me through the Quay? Got me to the docks safely? The one I *just* introduced you to?"

Ardent shook his head slowly, and Coll, too. Marrill's mind spun. "Is this some kind of trick?" she asked hopefully. But she already knew from their expressions that it wasn't. She looked around, searching the deck again. Nothing appeared out of place.

Except for Rose, preening herself peacefully atop a haphazardly coiled heap of rope. As if she could read Marrill's thoughts, the bird looked straight at her, barked out a sharp "Caw!" and leapt into the air.

Marrill stomped across the deck, her hands curled into fists. Sure enough, there was Fin, crouched between the pile of rope and the railing. His features were carefully arranged in a mask of innocence as her shadow fell over him.

"Hello, stranger who I've never met before," he said coolly.

"Not funny, Fin," she replied, hands on her hips. "Rose gave you away."

A tangle of emotions flashed in his eyes: excitement, confusion, then panic. "I was just..." He seemed to be scrambling for an excuse.

She didn't want to hear it, so she nudged him with her toes. "They're not going to be mad at you for stowing away," she told him.

Still, Fin protested as she began dragging him across the deck. "They won't remember me, Marrill," he said.

She just rolled her eyes. "I found him," she called out, pushing the boy toward Coll and Ardent. He stumbled to a stop in front of them, then straightened with a tentative smile.

They frowned in unison. "Who?"

"Told you," he muttered under his breath.

Marrill let out a growl of frustration. "Fin! We were *just* talking about him, like thirty seconds ago? From the Quay? The one who helped me?"

Squinting, Ardent stepped forward to examine the boy, walking in a circle around him twice before shrugging. "Nope." Then he looked at Marrill with a frown of concern. "By chance have you felt the urge to repeat everything people say to you, backward?"

Yesterday she'd have thought it was the oddest question she'd ever been asked. Now she wasn't so sure. "No?"

He stepped closer. "What about the need to cluck three times before blinking your left eye?"

Marrill opened her mouth, stunned. Okay, *that* was the strangest question she'd ever been asked. But before she could answer, he pressed a finger against her forehead as if checking for a temperature. "Hmmm…" he murmured. "It doesn't *feel* like furryflug fever…."

"Um…what's furryflug fever?" she asked.

"You do *not* want to know," Fin whispered.

"Oh, hello!" Ardent frowned. "Look, Coll, another stowaway! Did I forget to lock the Bilge Room again?"

Fin leaned toward Marrill. "See? They won't remember me."

"But you've been *right here* the whole time!" she said, balling her hands into frustrated fists. "It doesn't make any sense. *I* remember you just fine!"

The amusement dancing through Fin's expression dimmed. "No," he said somberly. "What doesn't make sense is that *you* remember me. You don't understand—no one *ever* remembers me. Or notices me, really. They can't help it; they all just forget as soon as they stop paying attention to me."

"I don't get it." Marrill pressed her fingers against her temples, where a dull ache was beginning to throb. "Is it some kind of magic?"

Fin glanced down at his feet and shrugged. "Probably. I always figured it was a curse of some kind."

"No," Ardent said.

For a moment the ship was silent except for the creak of the deck and the sound of waves splashing against the hull. Fin grew absolutely still.

The wizard now looked straight at him. "No, young man," he said. "Whatever's wrong with you, there is no magic about it."

CHAPTER 19
Without a Trace

T he wizard's words hit Fin like a punch to the gut. His entire life he'd assumed he was forgettable because of something that was done to him. Something that could be reversed.

But if it wasn't magic and it wasn't a curse, how could it ever be fixed?

A bitter taste rose up the back of his throat. "How do you know?" His voice quavered, but he didn't care. All he cared about was the wizard being wrong.

"Magic leaves a trace," the old man explained. "Like the echo of a fingerprint. If there'd been magic worked on you in the past, I'd be able to see it. Take Coll here for example...." He gestured toward the captain.

Coll crossed his arms and glowered. "Or don't," he said.

Ardent cleared his throat. "Or don't. Perhaps a story for another time. Anyway..." He turned back to Fin and frowned. "What were we talking about?"

Marrill stepped forward, her forehead pinched with concern. "You were explaining about Fin and why people forget him so easily."

Fin tried to smile in thanks, but he was pretty sure it came across as a grimace. His lips were numb, his fingers tingling. If felt like there wasn't enough air in the world.

"Right, right," Ardent murmured. "There's no trace of magic on you, young man. Even if something magical caused you to be this way long ago, no spell or curse afflicts you *now*. Whatever has made you the way you are, that *is* now the way you are."

Fin tried to calm his roaring heart. "But if that's just who I am"—he took a shallow breath—"then there's no way to fix it?"

Ardent's tone turned somber as he laid a hand softly on Fin's back. Fin tried not to wince—he wasn't used to attention, certainly not *good* attention. He didn't know how to respond.

"You can't fix a problem until you know what it is," the

wizard said with a look of regret on his face. "So, for now? I'm afraid not."

It felt as though the ship had sunk underneath him. Fin's knees went wobbly. He'd spent most of his life trying to convince himself that it didn't matter that no one remembered him. But the truth was, more than anything else, he just wanted someone to know he was there. He had to bite his lip to keep his chin from trembling.

Tears burned his eyes and his throat tightened. He refused to cry in front of strangers, though. Especially when one of them might remember.

What he needed was to be alone.

Without saying anything more, Fin turned and ran to the hatch that led belowdecks. Marrill yelled after him, but he ignored her, racing down into the heart of the ship.

He bounded down the stairs, barely paying attention to where he was going. At any other time, the massive ship would have been a thief's playground. He'd have taken off running, exploring, searching for treasures he could easily stuff in his pockets. But right now, none of that interested him.

He ran until he reached the bottom of the stairs, and then he ran until he reached the end of the hallway and there was nowhere else to run. He closed his eyes and leaned his head against the wall, trying to calm his breathing.

Thankfully, it was quiet, the only sound the creaking of the ship and the thud of the hull cutting through the

Stream. It should have been soothing, but Fin wasn't used to quiet.

Where he was from, quiet meant either something was very wrong, or it was about to be.

And something *was* wrong: him.

He hadn't always been this way, he knew it. He thought back to being four, on the boat in his mother's embrace, headed toward the Khaznot Quay. His mother's words, comforting him; her arms, holding him tight. She hadn't ignored him. She hadn't forgotten him. She'd even given him his star, pointed it out in the sky so he'd *know* she would never forget him.

But then, she'd never come back for him, either. He'd looked for her. When he wasn't stealing food or foraging for shelter, he'd searched for clues as to where to find her, looking in every house in the Quay, every place he could break into. But the only thing he'd ever found was his personal record at the Orphan Preserve, which wasn't much better than useless.

As he'd grown older he'd begun wondering why she'd brought him there and left him behind. Eventually, though, he'd stopped asking that question. He balled his hands into fists, pressing them against his eyes to keep the tears from spilling over.

But now everything was different. Someone else remembered him. Even after some of the biggest distractions in the world—the docks being on fire, a drawing on a scrap of paper turning into a bird—Marrill still remembered who he was. It was terrifying and incredible at the same time!

Maybe that meant that even if his forgettability wasn't a spell or curse that could be lifted, he could still be fixed. Fin heaved a deep sigh, thinking about what it would be like to find his mother. To be normal again.

But to find his mother, he needed that Map. A plan began to form in his mind. It was simple, straightforward, the way he liked it. All he had to do was help find the Map along with everyone else. And then, once they'd found all the pieces, he could do what he did best: Steal it.

After all, he was a thief—taking was what he excelled at. The others would get their turn after he borrowed it for a bit. They might not like the wait, but to Fin, there was no other option. Otherwise, they'd forget he needed it. He'd learned early to take his cut before handing the spoils over to Stavik. Being forgettable had its advantages, but being counted in when shares were divvied up wasn't one of them.

That was just life when you were a forgettable kid. You either got your bit first or not at all. He barely thought twice about it.

The plan calmed the storm in his chest and eased his panic.

Until he thought about Marrill. Heat crawled up his neck; something in his gut turned sour. He wasn't used to people remembering him long enough to form opinions of him. One of the upsides of forgettability was never having to explain yourself the next day, or to worry about what someone thought of you.

Never having to worry about letting someone down.

He realized that he didn't like the idea of letting Marrill down. It made him sick to his stomach.

Thankfully, that thought was interrupted by the sound of footsteps. He pushed away from the wall and looked up to find Marrill walking slowly down the hallway.

"Hey, Fin," she said.

His cheeks flushed. It was still strange to hear someone else use his name.

He didn't know how to respond, really. How did people start conversations when there wasn't a job or a con involved? He really wasn't very good at being remembered.

"Um, hi," he said at last. "Marrill," he added. He knew how much he liked to hear his own name; maybe she was the same?

A small smile ticked up the corners of her mouth. "Hi," she said. "So I guess you're part of the crew now, huh?"

Fin couldn't tell if she was asking a question or making a statement, and so he erred on the side of not responding. But that just led to awkward silence. Which seemed wrong, but he didn't know how to fix it. Normally he'd just find some sort of distraction and leave so he could start the conversation over.

But with Marrill... he cleared his throat. "So, um... you remember me?"

She rolled her eyes at him like it was the stupidest question ever. "Duh."

"Um, yeah, you're probably the third person in my life who's ever remembered me." As soon as the words left his lips, he wished he could take them back. Especially with the look of pity that flashed in Marrill's eyes.

He kept forgetting she would recall everything he said. He couldn't just say stupid stuff and get away with it. She'd actually get to know him. The thought both terrified and thrilled him.

"That sounds awful," she said.

"Yeah, well..." He cleared his throat again, not knowing what else to say.

"So how come I'm able to remember you?"

He definitely didn't know what to say to that; he had never been asked about himself before. "The only other person who remembered me was Mrs. Parsnickle at the Quay Orphan Preserve, but that was just when I was young. I think she was so focused on caring for little kids, she couldn't possibly miss one." He shrugged. "She was great, but when I turned seven, she forgot me, just like everyone else."

Marrill's expression grew more horrified. "Not even your parents?" she asked.

"My mom remembered me," Fin said. "But the only

thing I remember about *her* is her bringing me to the Khaznot Quay and dropping me off at the Orphan Preserve when I was four. I've been looking for her ever since."

The attention made Fin squirm. He didn't really like being pitied.

It occurred to him at the same time that he was going to have to think about what he shared. She would remember it, after all. And she might not take kindly to traveling with a thief.

So instead, he changed the subject. At the end of the day, he was here for a job, and that meant performing a bit of recon. "That Bintheyr Map's pretty spiff, huh?"

She slumped against the wall. "Yeah, I hope it is," she said cautiously. "I need it to get back to my mom.... She's sick." She stared down at her hands. Her fingers twined together. "I'm supposed to keep her from getting stressed out, but..."

She cringed and glanced up at him. Her eyes looked wet. Fin bit his lip. He didn't know how to comfort someone; it wasn't like people confided in him all that often. Or ever. He tried to remember what Ardent had done to make him feel better. Cautiously, he reached out one hand and gave her a quick pat on the shoulder, then pulled it back in case he'd done something wrong.

Marrill smiled, but her words came out choked. "But I got stuck on the *Kraken* because I thought Ardent could maybe help her, but now he doesn't know how to get back to Arizona—"

"Is that your world?" he interrupted.

She snorted and wiped at the edge of one eye. "Oh wow, I hope not," she said. She giggled. "I mean, that's *in* my world, but it's pretty awful. But I'm stuck here unless I can find the Map, and my parents don't know where I am, and my mom is going to be so worried, and that's just going to make her sicker and..."

She clamped her lips shut and looked away, clearly trying not to choke up.

Something inside Fin ached. He could practically feel her pain, like it was his own. He couldn't help but think of Mrs. Parsnickle—he'd have done anything to make her smile and relieve some of her worries. Now he had that same feeling with Marrill.

"Hey," he said suddenly. "You know what just right now occurred to me? Maybe I could use the Map to find my mom, too! We can look for it together!"

Marrill smiled. She could probably tell he hadn't just thought of that, but nevertheless seemed happy to play along. "Totally," she told him.

The look she gave him made his heart swell. It had been so long since he had really talked to someone, really been heard by them, he didn't really even remember what it was like. He could take a moment to bask in that, even if he knew Marrill would forget him someday, too.

He hadn't lied to Marrill; they *would* find the Map. And both their moms. It was just he would have to take it and use it first, before she forgot him. But in the meantime, maybe, for the first time, he could actually see what it was like to have a real friend.

CHAPTER 20
Kraken vs. *Kraken*

Over the next few days, the *Enterprising Kraken* navigated the Stream. And the Stream did not stay, as Marrill had previously known it, like open ocean. Sometimes it narrowed into a fast-paced torrent, thundering through canyons made of silver glass, and Marrill and Fin had to batten down belowdecks to avoid what Ardent called "mirror madness."

Other times, it flattened and broadened, becoming a slow, muddy river, and they could stand on the gunwales and wave at the friendly three-fingered sloth-folk, who hung their villages upside down from low-hanging trees. As much as she desperately wanted to get back to her parents, Marrill itched to explore all the amazing places around her.

They ate mostly prollycrab, pulled fresh from the Stream. "It's short for 'probability crab,'" Ardent told her, splitting open an orange claw and sucking out the rich velvet meat. "Because like the Stream itself, they embrace all probabilities." He smacked his lips. "Ooh, this one is chocolate!"

"Rubbish," Coll whispered, splitting off a deep blue thorax. "They're called prollycrabs 'cause they're *prolly* crabs, but everyone's too scared to find out for sure." A grimace passed over his face. "Ugh, sauerkraut." He dropped the remains of the crab to the deck, where Karnelius sniffed at it before crunching at the shell happily.

During the day, Fin and Marrill explored the ship, or played board games with the pirats, or napped in the sun with Karnelius, or swung on a swing the Ropebone Man dropped down for them. They helped Coll make repairs when they could, sewing sails and hammering loose planks, and Fin even placed a new topgallant on the mainmast.

"The raised deck at the front of the ship is the fo'c'sle," Coll explained as Marrill helped him run ropes through the side rigging (which she now knew were "deadeyes"). "Spelled 'forecastle.' The deck we're on, right in the middle, is the main deck, or waist." He pointed back to his captain's wheel.

"Up there where I stand is the quarterdeck. The covered part is the poop. Stop giggling."

Sometimes, the Stream got even stranger. A sharp bend in the river led them into the heart of a city, and soon Marrill realized they were sailing in a storm drain. They all screamed when it emptied down into a sewer, where the air smelled worse than anything she could have ever imagined. Eyeballs on mushroom stalks bent their way curiously as the *Kraken* bobbed past, until the sewer finally emptied out into a stagnant, algae-covered pond.

"Where are we going?" Marrill asked Ardent, watching Rose wing ahead, a black dot in the clear sky. Every now and again, she'd double back and circle about the ship before taking off once more, just to make sure they were still following.

He just shook his head. "Far away, it seems."

With a barge of bat-eared merchants, they traded prollycrab for speckled fruits. They drew fresh water when the Stream swept through the bottom of a well. The Giants of Gub granted them safe passage; Marrill would never forget the sight of Ardent standing on a chair on the forecastle, arms waving as he negotiated with an upside-down-faced monster five times his size. She spent much of her time sketching all the amazing things she saw with some pencils and a pad of paper Coll had dug up for her, new pictures to add to her collage when she finally did get back home.

But mostly, she hung out with Fin, Ardent, and Coll. She told them about her life and her world, and Fin shared stories about growing up in the Orphan Preserve and the pranks he used to play. Ardent went on at length about his theories on the transection of interdimensional tidal flows, and Coll shared old maritime legends about a great iron ghost ship that stalked the Stream.

"I've heard about that one," Fin piped up when Coll finished one tale. "A big ship pulled into the Khaznot Quay for repairs not too long ago reporting they'd been attacked by the Iron Ship. They said there was a storm like the whole world was breaking, and then lighting flashed red and the Iron Ship appeared out of nowhere."

Frowning, Marrill reached a hand down to where Karnelius slept on his back at her feet, and rubbed his belly for comfort. His tail twitched in response.

"Likely a bunch of swoggle sold by drunkards and mad-men," Coll said, shrugging. "I've been sailing the Stream for a long time and never seen hide nor hair of it. Skullraiders, yes. Albatross blizzards, sure. Pirhanabat infestations— too many to count. But nothing like any kind of iron ship."

He yawned and stretched. "And on that note, sweet dreams," he said as he made his way to the hatch leading belowdecks.

Marrill swiveled toward Fin and Ardent, her eyes wide. "Skullraiders?"

Ardent patted her on the head. "No need to worry about

those. We keep the *Kraken* up to date with her vaccines and enchantings." He stood. "Besides, with all the things on the Stream that can kill you, a bit of ticklish discomfort never hurt anyone." He paused. "Mostly. Anyway, good night!" He called for the Ropebone Man to take first watch and headed off to his cabin.

Marrill didn't quite feel reassured. Scoop-ing up Karnelius, she followed Fin inside and down the spiral stairs to the deck with their berths. His room was across the hall from hers, and he shuffled his feet a bit before saying, "See you in the morning?" like he was still unsure whether she would actually remember him.

She smiled, said, "Night, Fin," and stepped into her room. When she'd left it earlier, it had been decorated in shades of orange and brown, the walls painted to look like she was in the midst of a herd of ponies. She could have done without the wooden floors covered in grit or the leather saddle heaved across the bottom of her bed.

But tonight the room had rearranged itself into a kind of oasis. The walls were draped with soft fabric in blues and greens, and in the corner a trail of water slid down into a pool filled with flashing fish. Her bed was soft and smelled of grass, and she sank into it blissfully. Karnelius curled at her side, paws padding slightly against her hip. They were both asleep in minutes.

⊬ ✛ ⊬

The next day, the Stream opened up again, stretching out from horizon to horizon. And by midday, Marrill was deep in the throes of the one emotion she never thought she'd encounter on the Pirate Stream: boredom.

"What d'ya think?" Fin asked, holding out a silver pepper shaker.

Marrill scrunched her nose, considering the object. "Definitely something alive," she finally pronounced. For the past several hours, the two of them had been playing a game of Drop Things into the Pirate Stream and Guess What They'll Turn Into.

So far they'd watched a shoe turn into a fish (boring), a towel morph into a small raft of tiger-roses (not boring), and a cup disappear into a high-pitched scream accompanied by the rattle of castanets and a driving bass beat (downright freaky).

"I'm going with deadly," Fin said.

Marrill shrugged. "Just drop the thing, already."

Fin did as ordered. The afternoon light glinted off the silver curves of the shaker as it fell. It splashed into the Stream with a hiss and disappeared. Marrill held her breath, waiting.

A faint purplish hue bloomed just under the surface, churning the water.

"Another dud," Fin sighed. He turned back toward the deck, his eyes scanning for something else to chuck overboard.

But Marrill kept her eyes on the Stream. A dark shadow spread under the ship, and something about it made her uneasy. "Fin…"

He ignored her, digging through his pockets. "Seriously, what does it take to get a good solid explosion around here?"

As the shadow grew, the surface of the Stream puckered, as if something deep underneath were kicking upward. "Fin…" Marrill urged, her tone changed from warning to slightly panicked.

"I mean, sure, it was cool when that toothbrush turned into a picture of your face drawn in multicolored sparkles," Fin continued, oblivious to Marrill's mounting apprehension. "But I wouldn't really classify that as an *explosion* per se."

A long, thin band of shadow stretched out from the core, followed by another and another. And still the surface churned, waves beginning to rise. Marrill tugged at his coat. "I think maybe…"

But Fin wasn't listening. He pulled something that looked like a yellowish baseball with wavy-looking arms from his thief's bag. He sniffed at it, his expression contemplative. "Could create a nice reaction," he mused. "Shame to waste a good tentalo when it's almost ripe.…"

Meanwhile, the darkness beneath the boat grew larger and larger.…

"Fin!" Marrill finally screamed, grabbing him by the shoulders. He looked at her, clearly puzzled by her burst of emotion. Just then, an indigo tentacle the size of a telephone pole erupted from the water and waved toward the ship.

Fin's eyes widened as his eyebrows snapped together. "Huh," he said. "I guess we were both right."

Two more tentacles joined the first, grasping at the railing. A massive head exploded from the Stream, bellowing an epic roar. Behind them, Coll shouted, "Kraken!"

Marrill's heart stopped. The creature leveled its single enormous eye straight at her, no more than a dozen feet away. Its beaked mouth snapped open. In it, she could see nothing but blackness.

Pure terror raced through her. Fin had his hand around her arm and was tugging her away from the railing. The gesture was useless; at any moment a huge tentacle would crash down and crush the ship, drowning them all with one swipe.

For all that, Coll seemed shockingly unperturbed. "Ardent," he called out with a calm urgency, "perhaps a moment of your time?"

The wizard had been sitting at his table, his legs crossed, staring wistfully at a hand of cards floating before him. He glanced up, his mind still obviously occupied with whatever he'd been thinking about.

"Oh," was all he said. He casually waved one hand toward the giant beast. A shrill whistle cut through the air, and the giant octopus began to shrivel in on itself. A loud *pop* sounded, and a silver pepper shaker clattered to the

deck, right underneath where one of the kraken's tentacles had been poised to destroy them.

Marrill stared at Fin. Both of them wore the same stunned expression. Blood still roared in her ears, and her fingers shook from the jolt of adrenaline. She crouched and reached for the shaker. It was slightly dented and felt a bit slimy.

"Maybe we should find another game?" Fin finally asked, one side of his mouth twisted into a grin.

"How about some downtime," Coll suggested, face hardened into a scowl. "Every fool knows pepper and the Stream don't mix well," he added under his breath.

When Fin announced he was off to round up the pirats for a game of hide-and-seek, Marrill waved him off on his own; she was too exhausted to deal with any more excitement just then. Instead, she picked up her pad and pencils, intending to draw the kraken while it was still fresh in her mind. But when she pulled up a chair beside Ardent, she was distracted by the playing cards hovering in the air in front of him.

They were remarkably detailed, each depicting a different, intricately drawn face. They weren't playing cards at all, she realized, but portraits. "Who are they?" she asked.

The old man scooted over to give her a better view. "Old friends," he said. "Wizards I used to know and study magic with, on occasion."

Marrill scanned them. One in particular, a sharp-featured woman with a tight but pretty smile, stood out. Not least because the creases on the card showed it had been handled more often than the rest. "Who's she?"

"Ah," Ardent said. His voice was calm, sad even. "You honed right in on it. Good instincts, young Marrill."

He flipped the rest of the cards down, and they floated into a pile, leaving the portrait of the woman alone before them. "This," he said, "is Annalessa. She's the reason I seek the Map to Everywhere."

"Really?" Marrill asked. This was getting juicy! She folded her hands in front of her, listening. "Tell me more!"

"Annalessa and I were very close once," he told her. He held up the picture, and turned it. With the motion, Annalessa seemed to open her mouth and laugh. But then the tight smile was still there, and Marrill couldn't say for sure if it had ever left. "We sought the answer to a great question together. But I sought it in my study, among books and experiments, while she pursued it across the Stream."

"So she was awesome and you were boring," Marrill summed up. "Go on."

Ardent nodded, mouth twitching in a barely repressed smile. "Quite. And when she came to me for help, I...was perhaps a bit hasty in declining."

"So she was cool and you were a jerk," Marrill said. "Go on."

Ardent cocked an eyebrow at her. "Being right won't save you from a wizard's wrath, you know," he said. Marrill made a quick zipping motion over her lips. "Anyway," he went on, "one day she sent me a letter. A letter containing something she would never have sent me if she were not truly, seriously in trouble. And that is why I must find her."

"So that's why you're looking for the Map," she surmised. "What did she send you? What kind of trouble is she in? What will you do if you find her?"

Ardent stood, slipping the card into his pocket. "Wizards get to keep some secrets, you know," he said. "But fear not, I will clue you in the *moment* it involves you."

That moment, obviously, wasn't now.

CHAPTER 21
Fin Talks to a Tree

F in stepped out onto the deck and blinked against the sunlight. The ship had slowed. Around them, green blossoms scabbed over the golden Stream water. Knobby wooden roots jutted into the air beneath massive trees, as if the open Stream were turning into a landless swamp. The crisp breeze had stilled, seeming to dull and thicken with every passing moment.

Overhead, he caught a glimpse of Rose winging her way

past, weaving through the treetops. Insects buzzed, and strange whispers and whoops sounded in the distance. They were a far cry from the safe, familiar perils of the Khaznot Quay.

"Finally," Marrill said, emerging from belowdecks behind him. "I was starting to think I'd be stuck on this ship forever!"

Fin forced a smile. "Oh yeah, that would be..." He didn't need to finish. He hung back as Marrill headed toward the bow, where Ardent stood watching the water.

A dull ache tugged at his gut. Of course, he was glad they were moving on with the quest. It was just that he'd kind of enjoyed the last few days. It was nice having someone he didn't have to constantly introduce himself to, someone who *wanted* to spend time with him.

And as soon as they found the Map, that would all be over. One way or another, they would split up, and it would be just him again—forgettable Fin.

He took a deep breath and bounded up the stairs to the quarterdeck, where Coll carefully weaved the ship through the maze of root and tree.

"So," Fin announced. "Where we headed?"

Coll jumped and jerked the wheel, then struggled to pull it back before the ship could hit anything. "Stestor's bones, kid!" he cried. "Don't sneak up like that!"

He angled a long look Fin's way. "Who's this, another

one?" he asked the air. "Are we growing stowaways today? You didn't come out the bilge, did you?"

Fin shook his head. "Don't worry, we've been over this before. I'm Fin, I'm forgettable, I'm part of the crew now. We do this most every time we meet."

Coll turned back to the wheel. "Sounds familiar," he said. "Just maybe wear a bell or something."

"So where we headed?" Fin repeated. Down on the forecastle, Ardent's hands flew left and right as he explained something or other. Marrill stood with her arms crossed, looking skeptical. Neither of them seemed to miss him. It felt familiar to be forgotten, as though the world had tilted back into place again.

Coll shrugged. "Don't know. Bird's taken us far up-Stream, farther than I've ever been before. Would never have found this way without her. Wonder if anyone ever has—certainly isn't on any of the maps. I've had the pirats checking."

He kicked off a shoe and scratched at where his tattoo tangled around his pinky toe. "Wherever we're going, it's old. Real old."

As Coll maneuvered the ship around a cluster of trees blocking the way, a massive island heaved up from the water in front of them. It was covered by a thick jungle more tangled with plants than Fin had ever imagined a place could be.

Tall cypresses stretched their branches overhead, choking the light, while thick mangroves fanned their roots to either side. Ferns and moss grew on limbs and vines, which stretched out and around and above them.

"Shanks," he whispered.

The ship shuddered to a halt unexpectedly. Fin scrabbled for the railing to keep from toppling down the stairs.

"Well, I think we've arrived!" Ardent announced, carefully unhooking a cat claw from the hem of his robe. The cat in question yanked his paw back, looking offended. "Now, does anyone see Rose...?"

"Bledgeblisters," Coll cursed. Fin followed his eyes upward. A tangle of leafy green creepers snaked around the top of the mainmast, and a huge branch pierced the fore-topsail. That explained the sudden stop. "No going anywhere until those are cut away," the sailor grumbled.

"There she is!" Marrill pointed. "Rose is up in the canopy!" Sure enough, the bird perched on a thick vine high above the shore of the island. Beneath her, an overgrown trail led into the heart of the jungle.

Fin looked from mast to bird to path. Someone would have to climb up there and cut the ship free before they could even get to shore. And then someone would have to keep track of the bird in all the tangle. And if that someone happened to find the Map first, well, he wouldn't be *stealing* it so much as exercising right of first discovery.

And that was a well-recognized right in the Quay, second only to the right of I've-got-it-and-you-don't. Which that person would also have.

Not that Fin would keep the Map from the rest of the crew. He just wanted to make sure he had first dibs on using it, before the others—including Marrill—could forget about him. Better safe than sorry.

"I'll do it!" he announced. Without waiting, he leapt onto the mainmast and shimmied up to the canopy.

With the knives he'd taken from the Meressians, it didn't take too long to cut the ship free. As he chopped away, he couldn't help notice that the leaves on the vines looked more like big green ears, right down to the waxy goo on their inner surface. Worse, he swore he felt the little tendrils twitch against his hand. The whole thing gave him the shudders.

A moment later, the last bit of tangle snapped free, and the ship slid toward shore. No sooner had Fin stepped back into the crook of a tree and wiped his hands with satisfaction than Rose took wing once more, heading off into the forest.

"Hey, wait," he said, scrambling after her. "She's headed inland!" he shouted down to the others, pointing into the jungle. "I'll keep an eye on her!"

He took off, chasing the bird through the treetops. She wheeled between palm fronds that flapped like banners, and soared over branches woven together like the tops of ramparts. Fin laughed as he followed her, thick moss cushioning his hands as he leapt and climbed through the canopy.

It was just like the rooftops at the Quay up here, but a thousand times more fun. Instead of brick and stone, everything around him was living; the whole place even *smelled* rich and alive!

Granted, the beautiful blossoms looked like toothy mouths, and the ear vines were everywhere. The wood felt warm, like a person's skin. But none of that bothered him. It wasn't like there were forests in the Quay; for all he knew, this was what they were all like.

Rose headed toward one of the redwood spires bent like a leaning old tower. A hollow opened up in it, and when Rose dove into it, Fin bounded after.

Inside, the redwood seemed made out of old stones, like a room in a real tower. Vines twisted throughout it, tangling together in the canopy of a smaller tree that grew in the middle. Its trunk was gnarled and knotted, and it split at the base before joining back together again a few feet from the ground. Two large branches stretched toward an opening at the other side of the hollow, and Rose perched on one of them.

Fin paused to gather his bearings. This place was odd. The more he looked around, the more he was positive it was a room. He moved between the creepers carefully, and when he reached the tree in the middle, he grabbed a big twisty knot on its trunk, using it as a handhold to haul himself up toward the bird.

"Oh…someone's there," said a slow voice from beneath Fin's hand. Fin yelped and leapt back. He squinted and looked closer, his jaw dropping when he realized that what he'd taken for a knot was shaped just like a nose. And beneath that was a hole that formed a mouth, complete with wooden teeth. Two eyes of polished mahogany creaked in their sockets as they turned to him.

"I thought…you were a squirrel." The tree's voice came labored and rough, as if each word had not been used for a thousand years.

Fin noticed now the way the odd split in the trunk almost resembled legs; the branches reaching to the window, arms. "I'm not a squirrel," he offered.

"So…I see," the tree said. "I used to be so vigilant…and now, if you hadn't stepped on my face, I would scarcely have known you were here at all."

Fin forced a grin, but he doubted it was convincing. "Don't hold it against yourself," he said. "I have that effect on people." He paused before adding, "And plants, I guess."

The tree rumbled, as if clearing its throat. Fin waited, but it said no more. "Um, if you don't mind me asking," Fin said at last, "what, um, are you?"

"Me?" The tree sounded distracted. "I'm a tree now, I suppose. Have been for quite some time."

Fin frowned, confused. "Were you something else before?"

"Hm?" the tree muttered. "Oh, oh yes. I *was* a watchman, many years ago. A watchman for the Council. I watched and gathered secrets for them, so long ago. Secrets...hm, oh yes," it said to itself. "Oh, that is an interesting one, yes."

"Wait, you used to be a person?" Fin asked. "What happened?"

The tree sighed, a noise like a breeze through distant branches. It sounded slightly distracted. Whatever else had its attention seemed to be far more interesting than Fin. "The same thing that happened to all of them, of course."

Fin waited for more, but the tree only grunted to itself, commenting on something he couldn't hear. He cleared his throat. "Which is?"

The tree let out a huff. "Why, the whispers, naturally. All those whispers, they get to you. They get to everyone, eventually."

Fin swallowed. "What whispers?"

CHAPTER 22
Rumors and Secrets

"What is this place?" Marrill asked as she jumped from the rope ladder to the shore. The noise of the jungle hung in the air, a background buzz she recognized from many camping trips. Lukewarm water oozed up around the edge of her shoes and she made a face; it was a good thing Karnelius had elected to stay behind.

"Unclear," Ardent answered, turning in a slow circle with his head thrown back. Nearby, Coll checked the *Kraken* for damage. "Though there is a rather obscure legend that might shed some light. I found it by cross-referencing a tale in Madgaabadon's Book of Once-Had-Beens with a number of oddly consistent folk stories from various peoples and places around the Stream. The peculiar element common to each of them—"

"Abridged version," Coll coughed.

Ardent adjusted the sash of his robe, bending toward a thicket of trees so dense they practically formed a wall. "Well, that *was* the abridged version," he said. "But I suppose the point is that there are numerous references to a Council of Whispers, or some variation on it, dating back to the early days of the Pirate Stream." He paused. "This way," he announced suddenly.

Without waiting, Ardent charged into the trees. Tangles of thorns and little fuzzy stickers caught on the bottom of his robe, but he didn't seem to notice.

"What about Fin?" Marrill asked, alarmed. She craned her neck to search the canopy overhead as she trailed after Ardent. But wherever Fin had scampered off to, there was no hint of him now. An unsettling thought entered the back of her mind: What if he'd only taken off after Rose like that so he could find the Map first and take it? It wasn't like she really knew him all *that* well. . . .

A few steps ahead of her, Coll looked over his shoulder and frowned. "Who?"

"Never mind," Marrill mumbled. Clearly, the responsibility of keeping track of her new friend fell to her. Which was fine. He wouldn't be the first stray she'd taken care of.

She pulled up short, a thought occurring to her. She recalled Fin's stories of Mrs. Parsnickle, the woman at the orphanage who'd remembered him, for a while at least. He'd thought it had been because she cared about little kids almost more than she cared about herself. It was a caring so fierce, he'd reckoned, it overrode even *his* forgettability.

Maybe, she thought, that's why she remembered him, too. For as long as she could remember, she'd cared for the animals that most other people overlooked—the more neglected and in need of love they were, the better. And while it wasn't like Fin was a puppy who'd been put out on the street too young, he was still lost and abandoned.

She just hoped she could trust him.

Trying to push the concern out of her mind, she scampered after Ardent as he charged between two massive trees, their branches twined together. They resembled nothing so much as a gated archway, flanked by towering walls and soaring turrets. "So the Council of Whispers, huh?" she prompted.

Ardent slowed. "Oh yes," he said. "Fascinating story. Legend says they ruled the Pirate Stream through secrets."

"I think you mean '*in* secret,'" Marrill offered.

"That, too. But I mean 'through secrets.' You've heard the

phrase 'Knowledge is power,' I trust? The Council gathered secrets and traded in rumors. Their agents were everywhere, hidden among the people, listening. If they heard your secret, then one day you would hear from them. And if you wanted your secret kept, well then, you too would become their agent. And if you said no, they knew every rumor that might ruin you...." He paused and looked at her with an odd intensity. "The more powerful one gets, the more secrets they wish to keep. Remember that, always."

Marrill nodded, though she really didn't understand.

"Also, I gather they had large ears," Ardent said, starting off again. "That characteristic keeps coming up. Though it suddenly occurs to me that might be iconographic."

"Icon-o-what now?" Marrill asked, struggling to keep up. It felt for all the world as though they were walking down the twisty corridors of an ancient fortress. It even smelled like one, like old weathered stones covered with dirt and held together by moss.

Coll nudged her shoulder. "Never ask Ardent to explain etymology unless you've got a nice comfy chair nearby."

She smiled at him gratefully. "So what does that have to do with this place?" The constant murmur of noise had grown louder as they traveled deeper into the forest, and she had to raise her voice to be heard.

Ardent kept up his brisk pace as he spoke. "Well, there's the thing of it, isn't there? Little remains to say where the

Council of Whispers kept their home. But there are references to a place far up the Stream, somewhere distant and hidden from all normal places. A fortress deep in a forest. Or maybe a fortress that *was* a forest; it's hard to tell."

"And you think this might be the place?"

Ardent seemed distracted, turning his head from side to side as though listening. "I wonder," he said. "I do wonder..."

Up ahead, sunlight dappled through the branches, falling down on a moss-covered glade. At first, it just seemed like a break in the woods, perhaps the gap left when a big old tree fell. But as they drew closer, Marrill realized it was enormous. Way larger than the Arizona house. Maybe even than the *Kraken*!

From the edges of the glen, the trees fanned their branches overhead, weaving them into intricate shapes and casting the world in a deep, peaceful shade. Their leaves were unlike any Marrill had seen before: Brilliant purples and blues rustled against vibrant pinks and gaudy neon. Sprinkled throughout the forest floor, giant ferns grew, some of them nearly up to her waist.

"Wow," she said as she moved into the glen.

Ardent had stopped ahead of her and was turning slowly in a circle. "Indeed," he said absentmindedly. "It's like a courtyard, isn't it?"

Marrill nodded, allowing herself to relax. She closed her eyes. The air was moist but comfortable, the hum of the forest rhythmic and soothing. Sunlight filtering through the leaves made red trails on the backs of her eyelids. She let her breath slide in as the sensations of the jungle overtook her.

Right as she felt her most peaceful, someone whispered her name. Marrill's eyes snapped open. She looked around, heart racing.

She was sure she'd heard it. But it hadn't been Coll or Ardent. Or Fin. Her skin crawled. No one else on the Pirate Stream knew her. No one else was even *here*.

At least, not that she was aware of.

She moved closer to Ardent and listened more intently. The forest chittered and hummed, almost rhythmically. Almost like voices, chanting. A chill stole up her back.

"Yes, yes, that's very interesting," Ardent murmured.

"What is?" she asked.

The old man drifted off toward one side of the hollow and leaned against a vine as thick as a telephone pole. The place was full of them, she realized, twining around the trees and crisscrossing the forest floor, all loaded with the oddly ear-shaped leaves.

"Oh, just...what you said," Ardent said distractedly.

Marrill swallowed. "I didn't say anything...."

Someone whispered something behind her, something about youth and sailing and odd old curses. She spun around, but the only person there was Coll, examining a fern idly.

"Did anyone else hear that?" she breathed.

"Hm?" Ardent said. He looked up. She could have sworn she heard an echo fading away behind him:

"Ardent," Marrill asked, "what happened to the Council of Whispers?" Suddenly, she wanted to know everything she could about this place. Now.

"Oh, right, as I was saying! The Council of Whispers. No one knows what happened to them, is the funny thing. Funny in wizard circles anyway...kind of an in-joke. Anyway, one version says they found a way to gather all the secrets of the Stream, and in doing so vanished from the Stream themselves, disappearing like the secrets they hoarded. Others say they are still out there listening, never leaving their fortressy, foresty homeplace. Perhaps they just died. People do that, I understand."

He looked sharply to the left. Marrill caught the tail end of a whisper:

She froze. That wasn't just random nonsense; it was about Coll! She turned to the sailor. He stood stock-still, his face ashen. "Coll?" she managed. "What's wrong?"

His mouth opened. "I just…" He shook his head, pressing a hand over his heart. "Thought I heard someone. Someone I hadn't heard for a while."

That was it, Marrill decided, enough was enough. "Maybe we should"—she whipped back to Ardent—"go," she finished, the word dropping off her tongue. Where the wizard had just been standing, nothing but an ocean of leaves remained.

Marrill's palms went clammy. "Coll, I think something happened to Ard—" But when she spun back around, the sailor, too, was gone.

"Guys?" she tentatively called. Nothing. She yelled louder. "Ardent! Coll!"

Still nothing. She was alone. Alone with the whispering thrum of the forest.

Panic took root, threatening to strangle her. She forced herself to close her eyes. Take deep breaths.

The noise around her was almost physical now, like a pulse beating through the jungle. It tickled Marrill's ears, vibrated her skin.

fatherscoworriedlostlittlemarrill
wherehasshewandered

"Who said that?" she cried. She spun around on her heel. The ferns shook with the wind of it, rustling like whispers. "Hello?" she called.

Something tickled her toes. She looked down to find a tiny tendril of a vine creeping across her foot. With a gasp, she yanked free, and the tendril recoiled.

"What was that!?" she yelped. But there was no one there to answer her. A wave of fear rolled over her. The whispers all around her surged, filling her ears with their words.

doctorsaysimportantkeepcalmnotworry

She gulped. That was about her mother!

buthownottoworrywhenonlydaughtermissing

"Fin, quit fooling around," she tried halfheartedly. But she knew it wasn't him. It was something else. Something she had never heard of and had no idea how to deal with.

notlikehertobegoneshesnotgoodonherown

She couldn't take any more. Not knowing what else to do, she ran.

Branches slapped at her as she tore through the under-growth. The whispers followed her, led her, surrounded her. Talking about her family, her mother, their search to find her.

Before long, her stamina gave out, and she slowed to a jog. Her lungs heaved, and a sharp cramp stung her side.

Stopping altogether, she gulped for air. But even the sound of blood roaring in her ears wasn't enough to drown out the voices.

They came from everywhere now, all around. New whispers joined in—a street merchant in Marrakech telling about Marrill chasing a monkey through his market; a little girl in France explaining the rules of a game to her two-legged ferret; a young boy in Arizona describing the dragon bones he'd recently discovered.

But it was her mother Marrill wanted to hear more about. To make sure she was okay. Marrill pressed her back to a tree and slid until she was sitting. The ground was soft here, blanketed by vines that seemed to shift to cradle her. The tips of her fingers dug into the damp earth as she closed her eyes and concentrated, listening.

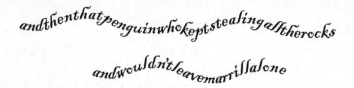

It was her mother's voice reminiscing with her father about the time they'd visited Antarctica as a family. Marrill relaxed into the story, letting the sound of her mother lull her like it did when she was putting her to bed at night.

The rhythm of the forest came low, so steady it was almost soothing. Before long, threads of other stories wove in and around the one her mother was telling. Stories about

AlleySalley and all her lost husbands. Stories about the ships that sailed the deep Pirate Stream, warships and traders and travelers and floating nations of strange people.

Marrill didn't even notice when the vines crept over her toes and up her legs. She didn't see the strange-shaped leaves tilting in, the flesh-colored flowers shifting closer. It was like they were whispering in her ears, filling her head with secrets.

As the leaves closed over her vision and the vines pulled her up off the ground and into the air, the last conscious part of her knew something was wrong. But she knew just as well that she couldn't fight it on her own.

"Fin," she whispered with the last bit of will she could muster. "Fin, if you're out there, help!"

And then the rhythmic beat of the jungle swallowed her whole. She was lost in a world of rumors and whispers and hidden knowledge. And at last, she was happy to give herself over to it.

CHAPTER 23
Poison Fire Whispers

"What whispers?" Fin asked again. But the tree's polished eyes had drifted shut. Fin looked around. Sunlight speckled through the forest canopy, dancing on the leaves outside the hollow. No matter how hard Fin listened, all he could hear was the hum of insects, the call of birds, and silence.

"Oh, oh!" the tree suddenly murmured. "That's a good one!" Fin turned back just in time to see a thick bud sprout from one of the green vines wrapping up its trunk. It burst open to reveal a black acorn, about the size of a thumbnail.

Hesitantly, Fin plucked the acorn free. It felt cool and woody between his fingers. Different colors whirled beneath its dark skin, and he pinched it lightly, testing its firmness. The acorn cracked, and a hushed voice whispered out,

priotomudskubbenhideselephantearsbeneathhishat

Fin jumped back, dropping it. A swirl of dark liquid oozed from the broken shell and disappeared in the space between two stones. Fin caught a glimpse of a face reflected in it as it went. He would have sworn it was a man with buckteeth, wedging a hat onto his head.

"What was that?" Already, where the dark liquid had gone, a new vine had sprouted. Fin gasped as it snaked its way up to twine into the tangle surrounding him.

"Hm, what?" the tree asked, blinking. "What's what? Who's where?" Its eyes settled on the newly grown vine. "Oh, that. A good rumor, that. Quite a nice secret." The heavy lids began their slow descent once more.

"Wait," Fin said, puzzling through the words. "That was a seed, not a secret."

"Of *course* it was." It sounded annoyed, at least for a tree. "Here, secrets turn to seed, good secrets take root, and the vines that grow bloom into rumors. Secrets do that, you know," it said, as much to itself as to Fin. "Once planted, they grow. And start new rumors all their own."

Fin crossed his arms. "So where do they come from?" he asked. "The rumors and whatnot?"

The tree yawned. "The Council of Whispers collects them in the Gibbering Grove, of course, and spreads them to the forest. Some come from what the ears of the forest might hear, but little happens here anymore. Thankfully, the Council sees everything everywhere and brings it all back home to grow."

Fin tilted his head to one side. He wasn't buying it. "Really? So why can't I hear all these secrets then?"

"You would if they concerned you. But you don't, which means no one anywhere is talking about you. No one any-where at all." The tree yawned and closed its eyes.

The words stung. Mostly because Fin feared they might be true. He shook it off. He hadn't let the sadness that floored an entire thieves' den get him down. He sure wasn't going to be judged by some overgrown shrubbery.

He cleared his throat and puffed out his chest. "So this Gibbering Grove," he said, "how do I find it?" If there was a Council that knew all the secrets in the world, surely they'd know where to find the Map.

The ear-shaped leaves rustled beside him, making him jump. Right by his head, the vine that had just grown from the acorn quivered with energy. The rustling spread down its vibrating length, off into the forest. *howdoifind*, it seemed to say, echoing Fin's words and carrying them away.

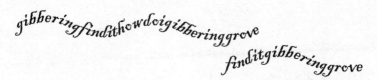

"Oh, oh! A new one!" the tree creaked, eyes popping open again. "Someone is searching for the Gibbering Grove!"

Fin blinked. "I know," he said. "That's me. I just said that."

The tree snorted, or at least Fin assumed it did; it sounded to him more like the crunch of rotten wood. "Well, who are you? I don't remember you saying anything," it said. "In fact, I don't remember you at all. Besides, if the rumor had come from you, it would only be as trustworthy as you are, which is not very. But I don't know where *this* rumor comes from, and therefore it must be true."

Fin raised an eyebrow. "Wait, you don't know where it comes from, and that means it must be true?"

"Of course," the tree sighed. "*Everyone* is saying it."

Fin chuckled. "You trees sure are a swift lot."

He was about to ask for directions again when he heard it. A voice in the rustle of the forest noises. Quiet, barely audible, barely recognizable, but there. *fin*. He cocked his head. There it was again!

fin. He moved to the hollow's entrance, stuck his head

out into open air. *fin.* But there was no one out there; nothing but leaves shook in the vine-strewn canopy.

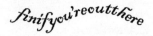

"Oh," the tree behind him said. "It seems someone is talking about you after all."

Then he heard it, loud and clear:

Fin Help!

It was Marrill's voice!

"That was my friend!" he shouted at the tree. "How do I find her?"

But the tree seemed lost again. "Local news, local news," it muttered. "How interesting…"

Fin grabbed an acorn and threw it. It bounced off the tree's nose and broke against the wall, a new vine snaking out from it.

"Ow!" the tree cried. *owowowowowowow,* the vine echoed. "That's not how those are supposed to be used!"

nothowyouuseitnothowyouuseit

Fin readied another acorn and put on his best I-dare-you squint. Forget the Gibbering Grove. Finding Marrill was more important than finding the Map.

"Okay, okay!" the tree cried. "Quick, tell me a secret about your friend that she would want to know, but doesn't. Something juicy." The vines around him twitched impatiently. "Come close and whisper it in my ear. That way it will come from me."

Fin thought long and hard, and then cupping a hand next to the tree's knotty ear, he whispered his secret.

"Oh," the tree remarked, "that *is* interesting. Not surprising at all, but interesting." A new acorn burst into life on one of its branches and dropped to the ground with a crack. A vine sprouted from it and shot past Fin, off into the jungle.

His own voice rustled down its length, and he cringed at the words. "I've never had a real friend before," it said. "Marrill is the first."

"Follow it," the tree told him. "It will take you to her."

"Thanks," Fin said. "And, um, sorry about hitting you with the acorn." He grabbed the vine and jumped out of the hollow, sliding down its length and following it into the dense forest.

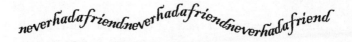

The leaves whispered, up and down and off into the distance.

nofriendsnofriendsnofriendsnevernevernever

He closed his eyes, as if he could press out the sound. It felt like facing the crying Oracle all over again. Only this time, there was no magic making him feel small, just his own words. "I have a friend now," he told himself, and that helped, if only a little. He scrambled along the vine faster, hand over hand, to reach her.

Finally, when it seemed like he must have crossed the whole island twice, his fingers touched something big. He opened his eyes. Just in front of him, his vine tangled with many others around a thick, person-sized bundle hanging just a few feet off the ground. He tapped it, and it let out a muffled squeak.

"Marrill!" Fin said, dropping to the soft forest floor. Away now from his own personal echo chamber, he could hear the deep primal rhythm of the jungle. It pulsed with voices, carried in whispers and hushed rustlings. The very trees themselves seemed to dance and sway with it.

rumors . . . secrets . . . rumors . . . secrets, it thrummed.

onceplanted, theygrowonceplanted, theygrow

"Let's get you out of there," Fin told the squirming bundle. "I'm starting to feel a mite unwelcome." He produced his knives and sliced away one of the vines binding her. A new one immediately slid up from below to fill the gap. He tried again, and again. Each time, no sooner had he cut a vine free than another appeared to take its place. All the while, the jungle chanted its sinister beat.

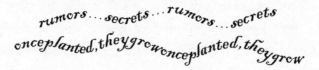

rumors...secrets...rumors...secrets
onceplanted, theygrowonceplanted, theygrow

"Shanks skating, it's like the rumors never end!" Fin cried at last, stepping back. "There's got to be another way!"

Just then, he noticed a giant ear-shaped fern turning in his direction. Listening.

Fin thought back to the hollow, to the way his words about looking for the Grove had been carried away and then had come back to him and the tree. How a rumor without a source—or in his case, where the source was forgotten—got treated as simple common knowledge, all the *more* trustworthy for not knowing where it came from.

"The rumors never end," he repeated to himself. A plan hatched itself in the back of his mind.

"Hold tight," he told the Marrill-ball. It murfled back weakly.

Fin slipped over to the fern-ear, positioning his mouth just at its rim. "I heard," he whispered gingerly, then looked around from side to side exaggeratedly, as if checking for spies. The fern didn't seem to have eyes, but as crazy as this place was, there was no being too careful. "I heard that if the vines get the girl, then it's all over for the Council of Whispers."

All around him, leaves rustled, mouths repeating his words, more ears turning to hear. He smiled.

"Yep," he continued, "I hear it's all part of the plot. To, uh...take down the Council. Get them to wrap up the little girl and not let her go. That's when the...let's say poison— or fire! Poison fire? That's when the poison fire starts." He swallowed. "And then that's it for the Gibbering Grove."

The rustling came more furiously now, branches shaking everywhere. He could hear the murmuring all around him.

They'd taken the bait!

He slipped over to a different fern to spread the story a little further. "I heard about that...poison fire," he told it. "Nasty stuff. But if the jungle just lets the little girl go, the whole plot will be foiled. That's a big secret, so don't tell anyone, now."

The waves of whispers reached a crescendo, louder even than the rhythmic beat. The whole forest was talking about it! Behind him, he heard slithering and the creaking of wood. Fin turned, just in time to see the last of the vines dropping Marrill to the ground.

CHAPTER 24
Learning to Be Supportive

One minute, a sea of vines engulfed Marrill. Secrets and whispers thrummed around her, filling her ears and her mind. She could feel the tide of them, coming and going. She was part of a vast network, all driven in rhythm by a pumping heart at its distant center.

The next minute, she sat in the middle of a small clearing swept clear of vegetation. Fin knelt in front of her, his eyes wide and slightly panicked.

"You okay?" he asked, breathless.

She blinked, trying to clear the weirdness from her head. Red marks covered her arms and legs from where the vines had held her tightly, and traces of her mother's voice still echoed in her mind. It took all her effort to ignore it.

"Um, Marrill?" Fin prompted.

His question snapped her back to the present. "Oh," she said. "Sorry—I was just…"

He looked at her expectantly, waiting for her to finish. A thought occurred to her. "You rescued me."

"Uh, yeah," he said, as if that was obvious.

Which it was, but that wasn't what she meant. "You could have gone for the Map instead. I know how important it is to you."

He frowned. "Well, it's important to you, too. I mean, we said we'd find it together."

She reached out and squeezed his hand. "Thanks," she told him. "You're a good friend." One of the leaves nearby picked up what she'd said, and soon the forest was chirping,

good friend you're friend

Fin scratched at the ground with a stick. "N-no problem." He cleared his throat and added, "Any idea where Ardent and Coll are?"

"They were right with me, and then I turned around and they were gone." She bit her lip, remembering how scary it had been to realize she was all alone. It made her even more grateful to have Fin here now. "Lucky the forest didn't get you, too," she told him.

"Yeah," he said without pausing. "Good thing I don't listen to all the things folks say about me...." His voice trailed off into nothing.

She thought about what she'd heard when she'd been engulfed in the vines.

neverhadafriendneverhadafriendneverhadafriend

It had been Fin's voice, saying

marrillisthefirstmarrillisfirstmarrill

Her heart ached for him. The forest had nothing to say about Fin, she realized, because no one remembered him enough to say anything about him.

As if sensing the direction of her thoughts, Fin stood. "Well, I guess we should figure out where the Map is and get out of here." She wasn't sure, but his cheer sounded a bit false.

Before she could say anything back, a loud "Caw!" sounded in the clearing. A smudgy black bird soared into view and settled on a nearby branch.

"It's Rose!" Marrill cried. "Good to see you, girl."

In response, Rose flapped her wings and began to preen herself.

"Good timing," Fin muttered.

Marrill started toward the bird. As she neared the vines crisscrossing the underbrush, they seemed to rear back to avoid her touch. Out of curiosity, she tried to catch one on purpose, and its whispering turned to shrieks as she grabbed for it.

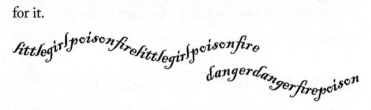

*littlegirlpoisonfirelittlegirlpoisonfire
dangerdangerfirepoison*

Marrill glanced back at Fin, one eyebrow arched in curiosity. "Fire poison?"

He swallowed, his cheeks beginning to tinge a bit red. "Poison fire, actually," he stammered with a self-conscious shrug. "The...uh...vines listen and carry rumors, and I... er...needed to free you and...um..."

Around them the ear-shaped leaves twisted in their direction. Fin stared at them for a moment before clearing his throat. "I mean, sorry, I didn't mean to let the details of your plan leak out." He winked exaggeratedly. Marrill pressed her hand over her mouth to stifle her giggle.

Rose let out another loud "Caw!" and took off into the forest.

"Let's go!" Marrill called, plunging into the dense thicket of trees after the bird. Every place she stepped, the thick underbrush shrank back, clearing a path forward. She could hear Fin weaving along behind her, dodging branches that snapped back in place as soon as she passed. He yelped as one slapped against him.

"Sorry!" she called over her shoulder.

"I should have told them I had poison fire, too," he grunted in response.

Before long, they hit a clearing surrounded by a curtain of dense hanging vines. Rose plunged through them without hesitation, but Marrill paused, catching her breath and waiting for Fin. Together, they walked through the shrinking vines to see what lay ahead.

Her breath caught in her throat.

"Welcome to the Gibbering Grove," Fin said softly.

It was as if they were standing on the edge of a lake, staring out at an island. Only instead of water, there were thick brambles, with thorns the size of her arm. Masses of huge vines, bigger even than she was, tangled through them, connecting the island to shore.

It reminded Marrill of the time she and her parents had driven through Georgia during a particularly wet summer and she'd seen acres of land consumed by kudzu. The vines had eaten everything in their path: houses, trees, power lines.

But these vines weren't just plants—not in any normal sense of the word. They writhed and twitched, ear-shaped leaves listening as the flower-shaped mouths called out in a cacophony of noise.

And beyond them, in the middle of it all, sat the island, like the central keep of a fortress beyond its leafy moat: a towering circle of trees so intertwined that it was impossible to tell where one ended and the next began. It looked beautiful and terrible and impossible all at once.

Above it all, Rose circled, a smudgy speck of black swooping through the crystal blue sky. Hopefully, that meant they'd found the next piece of the Map!

Barely able to contain her excitement, Marrill grabbed Fin in a spontaneous hug, jumping up and down. His only response was a nervous-sounding gurgle of alarm.

"Sorry," she said sheepishly, stepping back.

He cleared his throat as a deep shade of red spread from his neck into his cheeks. "N-no, it's okay!" he protested, his tone slightly panicked. "It's j-just that...uh...we shouldn't celebrate just yet because...um..." In the end, he gave up and flung his arm out to indicate the very intimidating jumble of wicked-looking brambles. "Thorns," he finally concluded.

"Right," she agreed with a sigh. Shoulder to shoulder, they stood at the edge of the clearing, trying to determine their next step. "What I wouldn't give for a bottle of weed killer," she muttered.

With a groan, Fin slapped his palm against his forehead. "Of course!"

And with that, Fin placed a hand square in the middle

of her back and shoved her forward. Straight into the pit of brambles.

Marrill managed to squeak out "Fin!" as she fell. Razor-sharp thorns loomed up at her, and then…nothing. She plopped hard onto the bare ground.

The brambles and vines had retreated, crying

poisonfirepoisonfirepoison

She stood and took her time wiping the dirt from her knees. Then she frowned at Fin.

"You could have just asked," she grumbled.

He grinned back. But the moment he stepped toward her, a vine whipped out and circled his foot. He stumbled, off balance, and another vine shot free and began dragging him toward the brambles.

"Urp!" he cried out.

Just as a particularly wicked-looking thorn reared, ready to strike, Marrill jumped forward, and the brambles shrank back once more. She swatted at the vines around his legs, and they, too, beat a hasty retreat.

It was pretty clear that while the vegetation wanted nothing to do with Marrill, Fin was fair game. Marrill bit her lip.

"What do we do now?" she asked. "We can't get you across. Unless I carry you, of course," she joked.

"Oh no," he said, waving his hands. He'd clearly taken the suggestion seriously. He took a step back, and another vine shot out to grab him.

Marrill leaned down and swatted it away. She glanced up. He looked at her nervously.

"I promise I won't drop you?" she said.

CHAPTER 25
The Gibbering Grove

Fin clutched Marrill's shoulders in a death grip. "Stop squirming!" she puffed, twisting to adjust his weight. "You're not made out of feathers, you know."

On every side, thorns gleamed like cutlasses. As they made their way through the briar lake, the brambles twisted so thick at times that they were all Fin could see. Just thickets of green and shadow all around, with deep blue sky above.

"Sorry," Fin muttered. He felt like a cat stuck on a shuddering tree branch, with a pack of wild dogs waiting below.

"You're, uh, doing great," he whispered, his eyes glued on the vines, which swayed like cobras around them.

A little farther, and Marrill was panting hard—they had been going like this for nearly fifteen minutes. "Not...sure..." Fin could feel her shoulders twitching with exhaustion. She really wasn't cut out for horse duty. "...I can go on...much..."

A stalk of stinging nettle made a grab for Fin's leg. "Oh, blisterwinds, just run for it!" he shouted, dropping off her back and shoving her forward.

Marrill lurched ahead, suddenly unburdened. The thorns shot closed like a death trap, snapping together at Fin's heels as he barreled after her.

"AHHHYAAHAAAHAAAAAAAAA!" he screamed.

"Fin!" Marril's hands grabbed his arms and jerked him to a stop. "Calm down; we made it!"

Fin blinked and looked around. No thickets surrounded them, just a circle of massive trees. They were bigger than any he'd ever seen, bigger even than the one he'd stood inside not long ago. All the vines crossing the briar lake came together at the base of their trunks, climbing into the branches. The circle between them, where Fin and Marrill now stood, was completely clear. It was like standing in a cathedral.

They'd made it. They'd reached the island. The Gibbering Grove. Relief unfurled inside him.

And now, as the pounding of his heart subsided in his

ears, he could hear talking. It was like the chattering hum of the forest, but louder, less rhythmic. Like a conversation, or an argument. Or a hundred of them, all at once. It came from above. They looked up together, and gasped.

Far, far above them, the tree branches reached into each other and twisted together, like a circle of people holding hands. And grasped in those hands, stretched like a dome over the cathedral-clearing, hung a massive expanse of parchment.

"It's like the ceiling of the Sistine Chapel," Marrill whispered. She tilted her head, looking at it from a different angle. "Or maybe more like a movie screen?"

As Fin watched, painted figures appeared on the parchment, seemingly from nowhere. He saw faces of all kinds, horses running across plains, children laughing, continents and islands and cities. They slid across its surface and disappeared at the ends of it, an unquenchable tide of places and people and things bubbling to life and dancing to oblivion at its edges.

Well, not oblivion, he realized with a shudder. The images weren't disappearing; they were soaking *into* the tree branches and moving onward. On to the trunks. And from the trunks to the vines. And from the vines, out, out through the briar lake. To the forest.

"It has to be the Map," Marrill murmured, her words barely audible over the voices.

Fin shook his head, staring at the canvas stretched like the roof of a building above them. "It's a bit big for that, isn't it?"

She shrugged. "What else could it be?"

"So how're we supposed to take *that* home, then?" Fin asked, throwing up his hands. "How are we even supposed to get up there?"

In response, Marrill jumped upside down and flew into the sky, leaving only a shout behind her.

"Huh," Fin said. And before he could think about it any more than that, something grabbed him by the ankle and yanked him upside down, too. As the ground raced away, all he could think was how grateful he was that his pockets were buttoned shut.

He flew past the dome of the Map until it was dozens of feet below him, and then whatever held him jerked to a halt. The chattering was so loud this high up he could barely hear his own thoughts. And beyond the lattice of limbs holding the Map, the ground waited far, far below.

He glanced at his feet, where a knotty cord of vine wrapped around his ankle, holding him firmly suspended. He twisted, looking around for Marrill, and found her just across from him, hanging limply. Her hair swayed like a curtain between her dangling arms.

"At last we have the little saboteurs," a rough serpent-like voice pronounced, louder than the rest of the din.

"I see a little girl without her poison fire!" said another, high and feminine but just as slithery.

"Poison fire, ha!" crowed a third voice. "I told you there was never any such thing, you gullible old beetle-boxes!"

"You lie, Slenefell!" cried a fourth. "You said she'd burn down the island if we didn't bring her closer!"

A fifth voice tumbled in on top of it. "And you said she was an amazon, Meldonoch. Thirty feet tall!"

The voices toppled into argument, speaking over each other so fast that Fin couldn't make out any of it. He looked from tree to tree. Each trunk had a face, like the tree he'd met earlier but scarier. Their eyes were dark hollows; their mouths jutted splintery teeth. Warps in the wood's grain formed the contours of twisted cheeks, and gnarls made noses and chins. Only the comically oversized wooden ears jutting out on either side of their trunks took away some of the intimidating appearance.

"Shanks," Fin muttered. "Marrill," he urged. "Marrill! Say something to them! They won't remember me long enough to pay attention to me!"

Marrill nodded weakly, her face bright red from the blood rushing to it. She cupped her hands to her mouth and called out, "Hey! Hey, trees! Put us down!" The argument going on around them died suddenly. "Please?" she added.

"*You* are in no position to be making demands, my dear," said the voice that had been called Slenefell. All the trees erupted into laughter.

"That didn't work," Fin whispered. She glared at him.

"Maybe we can make a deal?" Marrill tried. But the Grove only laughed harder, each rumbling shake swinging Fin and Marrill back and forth like pendulums.

"We have everything," said one of the trees.

"We *know* everything," said another.

"The Face shows us everything," said a third. "*All* the secrets in *all* creation come here."

"And now we have *you*," finished the voice called Meldonoch. "What have you to offer?"

"Maybe some plant food, or a nice misting?" Marrill suggested. The background chatter swelled again around them, nearly reaching deafening levels. Fin twisted around, struggling for freedom, but the vine just held him tighter.

Below him, he watched a fleet of galleons appear on the dome of the Map and slip across its surface onto the tangled branches, and from there off into the jungle to join the never-ending rumor mill. So this *was* the Face of the Map. He had to admit it was pretty impressive.

"I rather think we should keep them here forever," said the higher voice, sounding like an imperious court lady. "They make such nice ornaments to hang on our branches."

The other trees roared with laughter. "Quite so, Leferia," the serpent voice hissed. "The little girl may grow into mistletoe. The other will fade away to Spanish moss."

Fin gulped. He didn't know what a spanish was, but he knew he didn't want to be one's moss.

"Fin," Marrill whispered urgently. "Fin, secrets! Ardent said there was a Council of Whispers that was all about gathering secrets! Do you know any we can trade?"

Fin bit his lip. Secrets. What secrets did he know? He

was the master thief, the king of con artists. He had to know something.

Then again, he thought as he started to grow light-headed, it wasn't like anyone confided in him. No one even knew him at all, let alone enough to trust him with something they wanted to keep secret. And what was a secret, other than something you didn't want someone else to know?

That was when it came to him.

He sucked in a deep breath. In a voice as loud and clear as he could manage, he said, "I know a secret you don't know."

At first, the Grove gibbered on, as if he'd said nothing. Fin held his breath. He'd been in stickier situations than this one, and he'd always managed to find a way out.

Then he heard it: A background whisper caught Fin's words.

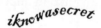

"What?" one of the trees said.
Then another.

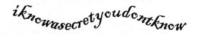

Then another, spreading it like a fire—a poison fire, Fin thought. It was a rumor without a source, the best kind. Like everything else he said around here.

A rumor that had to be true.

iknowasecretyoudontknow

iknowasecretyoudontknow

Now all the voices sang it, dropping the other chattering until it was just the one refrain, in unison.

iknowasecretyoudontknow!

"It's not possible!" cried Slenefell.

"How can it be?" asked Leferia.

"It's a lie!" cried Meldonoch.

Fin shook his head. "It's no lie." Suddenly, all the trees were paying attention to him. He wasn't so forgettable when he had something they couldn't ignore.

It was hard to keep the swagger from his voice. "I know a secret you don't know. A secret you will never, ever get through your Map."

"We will," croaked the serpentine voice. "The Face will show us!"

"Oh, really?" Fin asked. "What has your Face shown you about me, then?"

The trees fell into a hushed but frantic chatter among

themselves. "It's true," one of them cried, "I don't remember seeing a thing about him before!"

"Shhhhhh!" said the others. The chattering continued.

Fin rolled his eyes. "The answer is 'nothing'!" he called. "It hasn't shown you anything about me!" The trees groaned in grudging acceptance. "Which means..." he prompted.

"Which means he really *must* have a secret we don't know!" Slenefell announced.

The whole Grove let forth an anguished wail. "We must know!" they cried. "Tell us!"

Fin stroked his chin, pretending he had a beard there. It was his contemplating look, and he had used it effectively many times. Hopefully, it came off just as well upside down. "So you're saying we have something to trade after all."

The serpent voice hissed, but the female one, Leferia, cut him off. "The offer is a fair one, Tartrigian. Their freedom for the secret. Let it be done!"

Carefully, the vines holding them lowered them to a thick branch, level with the Map. They were still a long way from the ground, but it was a start.

"You are free," said Leferia. From here, Fin could make out an old owl's nest perched on her ear. "Now tell us the secret!"

Marrill pushed herself up onto her hands beside him. "Um, Fin?" she asked. "How do we get down from here?"

"You climb," scowled the bulbous, knotted face of

Slenefell. A hundred woodpecker holes dotted his visage, looking like zits on a teenage boy.

"I was afraid of that," she grumbled, trying unsuccessfully to tuck her hair behind her ears. Fin flashed her an assured smile as she searched her pockets, pulled out a scrap of cloth, and wrapped it around her head like a bandanna to keep her hair out of her eyes.

"And now for the secret. A deal's a deal," he announced, practically rubbing his hands together in anticipation. These were the times Fin lived for—fresh rubes on the line begging to be reeled in.

The trees leaned closer. The air, for the first time, was completely still. A vine darted toward Fin, rising up to chest height and blossoming into an ear-shaped flower.

"Speak the secret into the ear," Slenefell told him. "So it may join with our forest."

Fin grabbed the sides of the ear carefully. Holding back his smile, he put his face down until his lips nearly touched the petals.

He waited, drawing out the tension like a true showman. Savoring the anticipation. When even Marrill squirmed beside him, he finally divulged his secret, whispering it quietly.

The ear quivered, then furled its petals in on itself. It shrank smaller and smaller, and then with a final tremor, the petals fell off. Before him, perfectly formed, sat the largest acorn he'd ever seen.

It wobbled on the vine and then broke off, tumbling

through the air toward the ground. The shell shattered on impact.

"That's our cue," Fin murmured to Marrill. He started toward the nearby trunk and began making his way down. The thick bark made for excellent hand- and toeholds.

He hadn't gotten very far when the first whispers drifted up to his ears. Where his secret acorn had landed, vines had already sprung up and raced across the ground. It wouldn't be long before the trees found out what his secret was.

Fin was sure it would be quite the distraction. Enough that they'd forget all about the Quay boy who'd told it to them. He chuckled, already thinking about how he and Marrill would recount the story later.

He froze, an awful thought twisting in his gut. *Marrill.*

The trees might forget him, but they wouldn't forget her. He'd never had to plan for anyone else before.

The rumor vines twisted around the tree trunks, repeating his secret over and over again, until it became a wash of words rolling over him. The trees erupted into a furious rabble. Vines snatched Marrill, wrapping around her ankles and hauling her back up into the air. She shrieked in alarm, the sound of her cry mixing with the echo of Fin's own voice:

"My secret is that I don't have a secret."

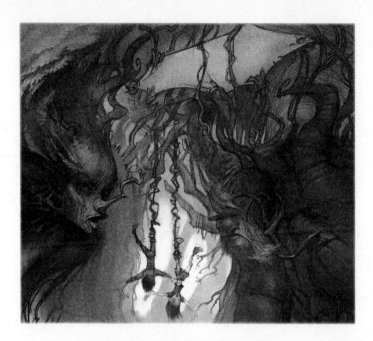

CHAPTER 26
An Unexpected Victory

For the second time in as many minutes, Marrill found herself dangling upside down. Her hair flew in a tangle over her head, the bandanna she'd used to tie it back jolting free and falling across her face.

"Let me go!" she shouted, trying to shove the tail of her shirt into her shorts to keep it in place.

The vines around her ankles unraveled. She started slipping. Her stomach lodged somewhere in her throat. The ground seemed very, very far away.

"No! Don't let me go!" she cried, her protest muffled by the bandanna.

The vines tightened, halting her fall. She dangled upside down, gasping as her heart roared in her ears.

"She's a bit flighty, wouldn't you say?" Slenefell remarked.

"Seemed the opposite to me," one of the trees said. "If she were flighty, she wouldn't have needed us to stop her fall."

Meldonoch's leaves rustled. "Honestly, Bleblehad. He meant she's not good at making up her mind. Which she's not—one minute down, the other up. What's next?"

Marrill squirmed, pushing the bandanna out of her eyes to look for Fin. He'd climbed back up to the branch and was edging his way out toward her, hands raised to catch her if she fell again.

"Maybe you could just set me down by my friend?" Marrill offered.

There followed a brief and grumbling debate about who this "friend" was and, at one point, whether she had any at all. "There's a boy right there, and he's my friend!" she shouted, pointing. "Just, you know, there. Put me down there."

A moment later, her fingers touched bark. Marrill threw her arms around the branch, thankful to be back on something solid. Even if the ground was still dozens of stories below.

Fin crouched next to her. "You okay?" he asked.

"I'd be better if they'd give us the Face," she mumbled.

"You want the Face?" Slenefell asked. "Hmm…well… I suppose we *could* give you the Face…what do you say, Meldonoch?"

The largest tree in the clearing shifted its branches. "Well, I, well…we've been fighting over it for a while, and I'd really rather not. But, if she really wants it…"

"Wait, what?" Leferia demanded, her voice a little shriller than before.

Marrill pushed herself up until she was sitting and shoved the bandanna over her forehead to get it out of her face. "What's going on?" she whispered to Fin. He shrugged, apparently just as surprised and confused as she was.

"I mean, I hadn't thought of that, but if all the rest of you think so…" Leferia said after a pause.

"All we had to do to get the Face was to ask for it?" Marrill asked the trees. Surely, she was missing something. "You'll just…give it to us?"

Above her, the canopy rustled menacingly, startling several birds from their nests.

"Wait," Slenefell said, "no, why would we give you the Face? I was, um…joking about that. Joking is what I did."

"Me too!" Meldonoch concurred.

Bleblehad raised a questioning limb. "But a minute ago—"

"Shut up, Bleblehad," the trees shouted as one. His branches drooped.

Marrill leaned toward Fin. "Am I going insane, or is this weird?"

"Definitely weird," Fin agreed.

"I feel like they were really going for it a second ago, and now..." Marrill trailed off. "I don't get it."

"You did seem awfully persuasive there for a bit," Fin agreed.

As she puzzled over what was happening, Marrill absently untied the knot of her bandanna to tighten it. A bit of rainbow fabric fell in front of her eyes. She couldn't help it; she started laughing.

"Now *you're* being weird," Fin said.

She held the bandanna up, practically rocking with excitement. It was the siren silk AlleySalley had traded for her hair. The fabric that supposedly made anyone do what you wanted. She had assumed it was junk, but it worked!

"It's this!" she whispered. "When I was talking before, it was in my face, I was talking through it!" Standing, she tied the scrap of silk over her nose and mouth like a robber in an old Western movie. "Um," she said, thinking. "Everyone touch a vine to your trunk."

Immediately, three trees slapped vines onto the woody protrusions of their noses, the fourth following a second later. Bleblehad slapped his against the Map Face, right atop a picture of an elephant that was sliding past. The others sighed as one.

"It works!" Marrill squealed, grabbing Fin's hands and

jumping up and down. Clearing her throat, she turned back to the Council. "Will you give me the Face?"

Overhead, the canopy rustled a long, drawn-out sigh. "Yes," mumbled one tree.

"I suppose," grouched another.

"If we have to, I guess," said a third.

Marrill waited. Nothing happened.

"I think you need to actually *ask* them to give it to you," Fin nudged.

"Oh," she said. "Right." She turned back to the trees and cleared her throat. "Ahem, uh, Mr. and Miss Council, um, if you would, I mean definitely do, um, please give me the Face."

There was a low mumbling among the trees. "But we've held it for so long," Meldonoch complained.

"And fought over it so hard," moaned Slenefell.

"And seen so many *things*," whined Bleblehad.

"Perhaps," Tartrigian whispered sadly, "after all this time, we have seen enough. Perhaps it is time for us to let go." Grudgingly, unhappily, each tree murmured its agreement.

"So the Grove shall Gibber no more," Meldonoch pronounced. Their leaves made a mournful rustling, a wind whispering through birches in an old graveyard.

Leferia creaked the fifth and final assent. "Very well," she said. "All at once, on the count of three."

Marrill gripped Fin's arm. The Face was almost theirs!

"One..." said Meldonoch. A quiver rippled across the Face as the branches released one by one, the parchment shrinking a little each time.

"Two..." Bleblehad breathed. Only a single branch from each tree still held on.

Marrill could practically taste the tension, bitter greens and honeysuckle sweet. "Come on," she whispered through the siren silk. "You can do it. You know you want to...."

"Three!" Leferia cried.

Four of the branches let go all at once. With a mighty whoosh, the Face snapped down to the size of a normal piece of paper, rolling itself up onto the last branch. Leferia, the branch's owner, immediately shot out more limbs to grab it.

"Singing stars, it worked!" she cackled. "You let go! I can't believe you all let go!"

A groan like a hurricane sounded from the other trees, drowned out by Leferia's whoops of triumph.

"I have the Face, I have the Face," Leferia chanted. Leaves showered down from her highest branches as she shook them, swaying back and forth in a little dance.

The others blubbered with disbelief and confusion. Leferia ignored them. She stretched the Face out before her, turning it so only she could see. The others launched vines and branches at it, but she batted them away easily.

"Ah-ah-ah!" she chided. "Might tear it, might tear it!"

"Oh, come on, Leferia," moaned Bleblehad. "That's not fair...."

"You cheated!" Tartrigian accused.

Fin looked over at Marrill with raised eyebrows. "Did we just get played?" he asked.

Marrill swallowed. "Maybe?"

Leferia pulled Fin and Marrill closer, just beneath her laughing face. "Oh, children!" she chittered. "You wonderful dears!"

Marrill could see the ink of the Face staining her wood, spreading out into the jungle from her alone now. Up close, a kindly green danced in the darkness of Leferia's eyes. Marrill squinted. She could just make out fern leaves waving within them.

"Now," Leferia said, "you really *must* tell me where you picked up that divine fabric!"

Marrill hesitantly pulled the cloth down over her chin. "This?" she asked. Leferia swayed forward, nodding in some unfelt breeze. "It's siren silk. From, um…" She struggled to remember AlleySalley's description. "Somemoreswag?"

"Swiggamore?" Slenefell wailed behind them.

Marrill nodded enthusiastically to her host. "That's it!"

Tartrigian hissed. "Swiggamore silk is junk! It does nothing!" One of his branches made a halfhearted swipe at the air beside them. Leferia quickly swatted it back.

Fin chortled. "For do-nothing junk, it sure fooled you fools!"

Leferia giggled, a sound like wood squeaking. "Oh, you poor stupid, stupid things," she said. "Maybe you should consult the Face on that one. Oh, wait, you can't!" Her glee was infectious; Marrill could scarcely help but giggle a little herself. The venom in the others' voices was giving her a real appreciation for their new host.

"Pay no attention to them, dear one," Leferia continued. "If they *could* use the Face, they would know that *this* siren silk is truly enchanted. Any object can acquire magic, you know, like an old sweater builds up static."

Marrill didn't know. She looked to Fin, but he seemed just as clueless.

"Oh, it's rare, of course," Leferia said. "Takes truly concentrated acts and emotions to work. But if I remember correctly, the former owner of that silk suckered hundreds of gullible men into loving her, all while wearing this very piece of fabric. And she left every last one broke, depressed, and ruined."

Marrill dabbed her hand against the rough edges of her bangs. "That definitely sounds like AlleySalley," she murmured.

"All those lies and heartaches seem to have given this cloth some power. It only works on the *dumbest* of men, of course," Leferia sneered. A cascade of voices sneered back.

She ignored them. "Well, now I'm queen of the Grove at last! *I* control the Face. After all this time, it is as it always should have been. And these saps can only sit and listen to rumors captured by the forest. If they're lucky, maybe they can pick up some of the wonderful secrets that flow out from me, whispered back to them."

At that, one of the trees—Bleblehad, Marrill thought—started crying. Now Marrill couldn't help feeling a little bit bad.

Then again, Leferia seemed much nicer than the others. She just wasn't quite sure how nice. "So, um. About the Face. It's the only way I can find my way home—my mom's sick and—"

"Oh yes," Leferia said, sounding truly sorry. "I believe I've seen her once, in the Face. She's not been doing well with the stress of it, is she?"

Marrill's throat tightened. "That's why I need the Map."

Behind her, another one of the trees broke into tears.

"And my friend needs it to find his mother," she added.

Fin stiffened beside her. Marrill put a hand on his arm to comfort him.

Leferia *tsk*ed. "Not sure about that one," she said.

Fin looked at his feet. "Figured," he said.

Marrill looked down, too, then quickly back up. The ground was still a *long* way off.

"Leferia!" Tartrigian gasped. His trunk shook oddly, his branches quivering. "Leferia, the forest is chattering!" Then he, too, started sobbing. Big wet drops of sap slid from his eyeholes, running across the warps of his face.

Marrill bit her lip. Now Leferia, too, seemed concerned.

She paused, listening to voices only the trees could hear. In the silence, the fourth tree of the Council—Slenefell—began to cry.

Fin grabbed Marrill's arm. His face was a mask of horror.

There's no way that could be good. Her stomach twisted. "What is it?"

Leferia answered. "He has come," she breathed. "He is here! How did I not see it? How did the traitor Face not show me?"

Alarm bells rang in Marrill's head. Something was wrong. Very, very wrong.

"Who?" she whispered. "Who's here?"

Leferia's woody lips quivered. "The herald of the Lost Sun," she spat. "The thief of the Map!"

"The Oracle," Fin breathed.

Marrill frowned, confused. But she didn't even have the chance to ask. Because just then, the Council, as one, screamed,

"Fire!"

CHAPTER 27
The Weeping Trees

F in's gut turned to stone. The crying, the fire—it was all too familiar. First the docks at the Khaznot Quay, and now the Gibbering Grove. The Oracle had followed them!

The big scary girl tree bent forward, bringing her face closer. "My forest is burning!" she shrieked, so loud it made Fin pop a finger in his ear. "You have to save it!"

Marrill grabbed his arm. "What's going on?" she asked. "Who's the Oracle?"

"A bad guy who does bad stuff," Fin told her.

"A wizard of darkness!" the tree wailed. "He's come for the Face and will stop at nothing to get it! And he's burning down my forest!" Her sobs grew, joining with the cries from the other trees.

Marrill's grip tightened on Fin's arm. "What's happening?" she asked, eyes wide and afraid.

"It's the Oracle—he's making them cry," Fin explained. "Wherever the Oracle goes, everyone around him bursts into tears."

Her forehead furrowed. "Then why aren't we—" she started to ask. But then with a gasped "Oh!" she let go of Fin and dropped to her hands and knees. "Leferia!" Marrill shouted, knocking against the branch to get the tree's attention. "Stop listening to the vines! They're carrying in the sorrow from wherever the Oracle is."

"Stop listening?" Leferia screeched in horror. "You mean, not hear things?"

Fin nodded, catching on. "You have to," he told her. "The magic is coming in over them, that's how he got the other members of the Council!"

A fat tear escaped from Leferia's eye hollows and her canopy rustled with a deep sigh. "V-very well," she said. "I-I'll try...."

As the tree sniffled, Fin scanned the horizon for smoke. "We have to get out of here—wait, what are you doing?" Vines wrapped around his waist, tugging him into the air. Marrill let out a small shriek as she followed.

"Getting you out of here!" Leferia explained. "But first—"
A small tendril dropped down from the canopy in front of
them. Curled up in its tip was the Face of the Map, rolled
into a tight scroll. The vine shoved it toward them. Fin
blinked in shock.

"Take this with you," the tree said.

When he didn't move, the vine shook the scroll at him.
Hesitantly, Fin reached out and grabbed the Face, but the
vine didn't let it go.

Marrill stammered a halfhearted "Are you sure?" Fin's
gaze flitted to his feet, and then to the ground that was way,
way too far below them.

"No, I'm not sure!" the plant-lady, Leferia, snapped. All
around them, the sound of crying grew stronger, echoing up
from the rumor vines and joining with the sobbing Council
trees. Leferia sighed. "But the Grove will never be safe so
long as the Face is here. You must take it before the whole
island is lost!"

The vine released, and the Face came free in Fin's hand.
He shoved it into a pocket in his coat as quickly as he
could. "Okay, then, back to the *Kraken*, right?" he asked.

The vines holding them reared in response, like an arm
preparing to throw a ball. Fin gulped and braced himself.
He had a bad feeling he was the ball.

"Wait!" Marrill yelled. "What about Ardent and Coll?
We can't leave without them!"

"Right!" Fin quickly agreed, fiddling absently with the strings of his skysails. He'd actually forgotten about the rest of the crew; he still wasn't used to having to worry about others.

"Oh, for…" Leferia muttered. "Fine." Around them, vines rustled and whispered, carrying the question back and forth through the Gibbering Grove. "I'm told they're lost to the rumors," she said a moment later. "I will guide you, but you have to make it quick!"

The vines holding them began swinging forward, as if Fin and Marrill were weights on the end of a long, long pendulum. As he dropped, Fin's stomach lodged into this throat. Then he hit the bottom of the arc, and his stomach ended up around his knees as he veered upward.

"Wait—can we talk about this just a second?" he squeaked as the vine began to loosen its grip.

"No!" Leferia answered. And then he was airborne.

Fin could scarcely tell where his scream ended and Marrill's began. They tumbled through the air out of the Gibbering Grove. The briar lake passed in a flash. Green leaves and branches loomed up in front of him. He struggled to straighten, to pull his skysails before it was too late.

A slash of green whipped through the air, snagging around his ankle, and then he was falling again, gaining momentum. The vine swung him around and released him, sending him head over heels across the forest. "*Urgh*," Fin gurgled.

Tumbling through the air next to him, Marrill hollered and whooped. "I'm the king of the jungle!" she cried when the next vine caught hold and flung them out again.

"So sorry for the discomfort," Leferia's voice spoke, coming from the leaves running up and down each vine. "Emergency and all."

"No... *whoa!*... problem... *wee!*" Fin told her.

"Will someone... *oop!*... *please* tell me... *agggh!*... what's happening now?" Marrill called beside him. "Who is this guy? How is he so powerful?"

The vines swung them wide, then handed them off once more. Every time they dipped through the forest, Fin could hear weeping and cries of "Fire!" drifting up from the undergrowth below. As they soared over the canopy, he caught sight of smoke rising in the distance, growing closer by the minute.

"He is the Meressian Oracle," Leferia said. "Long ago, he tried to gain ultimate power, to become one with the Pirate Stream by drinking its water. It drove him mad."

"But... *ungh*... Ardent told me no one could survive that," Marrill protested.

"Indeed," replied Leferia. "But long ago, a master wizard named Serth believed himself strong enough to succeed. A group of powerful wizards met on the island of Meres to help him try. Hold tight!" Their vine wrapped itself around a tree trunk, shooting them in a new direction.

Fin tried to take deep breaths to calm his growing nausea.

"So what happened?" he asked, as much to distract himself as anything.

"He succeeded," Leferia answered simply. "Such as is." She sounded sad. "The Stream water allowed him to see the future, but it drove him mad in the process. Almost there now!"

As the air grew thicker, the vines began slinging them lower, through whipping branches and past clinging ivy. "Serth became known as the Oracle, and his raving became known as the Meressian Prophecy," Leferia explained. "His Prophecy is doom for the whole of the Pirate Stream. And now he seeks the Map to fulfill it!"

Fin glanced at Marrill as they somersaulted through the air. He wondered if he looked as green as she did. "So what exactly does this Prophecy say?" he asked.

"Oh, that…" Leferia trailed off. "Well, it's very long, you know."

"Better make it the short version, then," Marrill said, hand over her mouth as she flipped from one vine to the next.

"Right, of course." Leferia's leaves shook with a sigh. "The short version. The short version is…also…very…" She paused. "I mean, there will be some stuff…probably.…"

"You don't know it, do you?" Fin asked.

"It was *boring*!" Leferia wailed. "Long and boring. And there was a Badger Pageant going on at the same time!"

Before Fin could say more, the vines slowed to a halt,

dangling them for a moment before setting them gently on the ground.

The world spun around Fin, and Marrill stumbled, falling to her knees. In the undergrowth, a thousand voices howled in warning or sobbed with tears.

After a moment, Marrill shook her head and pushed to her feet. "Look!" she said, pointing. Sure enough, Fin could make out a flicker of orange through the leaves ahead. Already sweat was beginning to break out across his forehead from the heat.

"I hear your friends," Leferia told them. "The wizard is this way...." she said, and a vine split off toward the fire. "And the sailor is *this* way." Another vine dove into a dense thicket.

One led to sure danger. The other looked safer, sort of. "We have to split up," Fin said, his mind racing. "I'll take Ardent. The fire's too dangerous."

Marrill started. "I beg your pardon?" she said, crossing her arms.

Fin threw up his hands in frustration. "Marrill, I don't even have a pardon. Now is not the time to be begging for it."

She rolled her eyes. "I mean, why do you think *I* can't handle the dangerous one?"

"Oh," Fin said. He chewed his lip. No time to argue, he figured. "Sure, good point. I'll take the easy one. Lead on, Leferia!" With that, he charged into the brush.

"Up over this wall," Leferia directed. "Through that

hallway, across the battlement!" Her directions made almost no sense; all Fin could see were trees and mounds of dirt.

Still, he followed her voice as best he could. He clambered up and over a tangle of bushes so thick he couldn't squeeze between them. Then ran down an alley of trees leaning into each other, then scrambled up to the top of a long hill.

As he reached the top, the smoke cleared, and before him the forest stretched out to the interior of the island. Suddenly, he could see it: Glens opened up like courtyards among the undergrowth. The mightiest trees were towers. He looked back. The walls, the hall, the battlement—he had crossed them all. This whole forest was laid out like a fortress.

It had all *been* a fortress, he realized at once. A huge fortress overgrown with secrets and rumors. People turned into plants, just sitting around, listening to the things other people actually *did*.

"Whoa." It made his head spin. "Hey, Leferia, I get it now!" he called out. "Where to next?"

But nothing answered him, only the cries and sobs of the rumor vines. "Leferia?" he tried again. Still nothing. Without Marrill, she'd forgotten him.

Of course she had. He skimmed his surroundings, finally spotting a Coll-shaped lump hanging from one of the towers in the distance. But a sea of leaves lay between him and it.

"Awww, blisterwinds," he said to himself.

CHAPTER 28
Discombobulation

"W ait!" Marrill squeaked. But it was too late;
Fin was gone. Marrill spun from side to side,
smoke stinging her eyes and making her throat
burn. She hadn't really meant to take the hard way! What
was Fin thinking, listening to her?

"Just hold on and follow me," Leferia's voice called.
Marrill half ran, half stumbled through the brush, one
hand skimming along Leferia's vine.

Sweat poured from her as though she were back under

the Arizona sun. Just as her skin started to get uncomfortably hot, Leferia yelled again, telling her to stop. "He's here!" she said. "The wizard, to your right!"

Marrill squinted. The world flickered in a haze of smoke. A few feet from her, the orange glow lit up a man-sized bundle of vines hanging in the air. A purple point stuck out from the bottom of it, and a white beard pushed out between the overlapping tendrils.

"Pull at them," Leferia told her. "Without fresh rumors to nourish them, they should be weakening!"

Marrill yanked at the mass fiercely. The vines uncoiled in her hands, one at a time, revealing more of the wizard stuck inside. "*Ardent!*" she screamed.

"I am sorry to be here," a new voice whispered from the leaves of the weeping vines surrounding them. "But now is the time."

"He's coming!" Leferia screeched. "Hurry!"

Marrill swallowed, her throat tight. The voice sounded so sad. So, so sad and hopeless. Her own will seemed to drain away, even as she tugged at another vine.

"*Bwagh*, he's a fool!" Ardent gasped, snapping her back to reality. The wizard blinked, focusing on her. "First Mate Marrill, is that you?"

"Oh, Ardent!" she said, throwing her arms around his suspended form.

"I was having the oddest dream," he pronounced, his voice muffled against her shirt. "Zambfant the so-called

Great was doubting my best theories, as if he knew anything about transcendental Stream-snorkling. Incidentally, did the pirats burn dinner again?"

The sad voice crackled from the fire. "The scenes are so carefully ordered," it said. "We must keep them in line."

Ardent's eyes widened. His eyebrows crashed together in a furious frown as his lips tightened. "That would be Serth," he sighed. "How...unfortunate." Though his words were calm, Marrill had never seen him look so troubled.

"Does everyone know this guy but me?" Marrill wondered aloud. She yanked away one last vine, and Ardent tumbled to the forest floor.

"*Oof*," he grunted. "One for you, gravity." He climbed to his feet, swaying one way, then the other.

"Put out the fire!" Leferia screamed. Marrill looked up. A gout of flame burst into the clearing, searing the jungle. Ardent waved one hand at it. A few snowflakes coughed out. The fire flickered back briefly, then surged forward once more.

"Oh dear," Ardent said, frowning and staring at his fingers. "We can't stay here. We need to leave. Now!"

Through the wall of flames, Marrill saw an outline of a man in long robes. He raised his hands toward them, and the fire exploded. A bright orange ball of death hurtled straight toward them.

The next thing Marrill knew, she'd been yanked into the sky. "Hold tight!" Leferia screamed from the wilted leaves of the vine snaked around her waist. For a moment, Marrill couldn't tell if she was swinging or falling, and then a new vine snared her around her wrist.

Ardent let out a whoop as he flipped through the air behind her. In moments, they were clear of the smoke and headed fast across the island. For all her fear, Marrill couldn't help but grin. They'd made it. And for just a moment, she was like the one-armed chimpanzee from the animal-preserve brochures, flying through the trees in someone else's arms.

"What happened back there with the snow?" she asked as Ardent swung up beside her.

He clutched his cap against his head. "Ah yes," he said. "Embarrassing, that. The jungle seems to have left me a bit discombobulated. It appears my rapport with the magic is somewhat destabilized."

"I don't...*urf*...speak wizard," Marrill said, holding her breath mid-sentence for another handoff.

"The rumor vines have broken his focus, made him too disoriented to talk to the magic," Leferia explained. "Common problem when the rumors get you. Slenefell was once the greatest magician on the Stream. Hasn't cast a spell in four thousand years. And even that last one was just a minor hex against root beetles."

Ardent sighed. "Exactly all that. Except the root beetles part—I've nothing against them."

"The fire is still spreading," Leferia said, ignoring Ardent. "I'm building firebreaks where I can, and beating it out *if* I can. But there's no way I can put it all out without the aid of the rest of the Council."

Ardent coughed. "It's more than that, unfortunately. That fire burns hot with magic," he said. "Serth fuels it. Your efforts will be useless so long as he remains nearby."

The jungle whizzed past them. "Precisely," Leferia agreed. "Once we get you to your ship, the rumor vines I still control will tell him you're sailing out with the Face. He'll head back to his own ship and leave me to put my island right. But I don't plan on giving him any lifts, so by the time he makes it to the shore, you should have plenty of head start to get away."

"What about Coll and Fin?" Marrill asked.

"Don't worry," Leferia said. "My vines have picked up the sailor as well. I'm not sure I know the other one, but the sailor seems to have someone else clinging to him."

Marrill couldn't help but laugh at the mental image. Her good mood only improved when she spied water past the tree trunks ahead. The masts of the *Kraken* bobbed among them. Marrill shouted for joy.

A moment later, Leferia set them gently along the scrub on the shore. "End of the line," she announced. "Now hurry up and get that Map out of here before the Oracle catches you." Her voice quivered ever so slightly.

"What's wrong?" Marrill asked. Ardent stumbled around nearby, regaining his composure. "Is it the Oracle's sadness again?"

"Oh, it's nothing like that," Leferia said. "I'm just…going to miss my Map, is all. It told such lovely stories. It let me drift away from all the pettiness and bickering."

The leaves on her vine fluttered in a sniffle. "You know, all I wanted was to have that stupid Council of termite-boxes answer to me for once. It's been so long, squabbling back and forth, getting nowhere, doing nothing. It just would have been nice to be in charge, just for a little while."

Marrill clasped her hands against her chest. She hadn't had a second to think about Leferia's life. How she'd spent all that time rooted to the same spot, just wanting to get away from the bickering. It wasn't fair to finally get that for a moment, then lose it forever.

"Ah, well," Leferia sighed. "As horrid as they are, I can scarcely stand to lose them after all this time. They're my family now. Better we all be safe and powerless than be charcoal and ash."

Marrill's instincts overwhelmed her. She just wanted to reach out and hug Leferia. Even if she was a weird and possibly evil old tree, she was such a *nice* weird and possibly evil old tree. And she had helped them so much. Suddenly, Marrill had an idea.

"Marrill," Ardent said behind her, steadier now. "We need to go, dear. The wind is right, and Serth will not take long to follow."

"One second," Marrill said. She rifled through her pockets quickly, pulling free the smooth scrap of siren silk. She looped it carefully around the vine, tying it tight with a little knot. "Thank you," she said softly.

The Leferia vine bobbed, its green leaves turning just a bit pink. Then it slipped around Marrill and squeezed her in a big hug. "The Gibbering Grove is in your debt, Marrill Aesterwest," Leferia's voice whispered from a leaf next to her ear. "Now get out of here and take all these wizards with you. I have a fire to put out!"

Marrill waved as the vine retreated into the forest, carrying the scrap of siren silk back to the island beyond the briar lake. "Ready now!" she said, turning back to Ardent.

Ardent, however, was already halfway up the ship's ladder. She could see Coll at the top waving and the shadow of the Ropebone Man hauling at the rigging. The *Kraken* was ready to move.

She started to run, but a familiar "Caw!" stopped her in her tracks. Sure enough, just behind a stubby bush, Rose sat atop a squat tree stump. Two crooked branches hung over it, like hands with fingers trailing down. Ripe little acorns hung from each one.

"Come on, girl, we have to go," Marrill said. The bird

knocked at an acorn with her scribbled beak. "No time for lunch," Marrill told her. She gently but urgently waved her arms to shoo the bird away.

Rose cocked one inky eye and knocked at the acorn again.

Marrill sighed. Out on the water, the *Kraken* shook, stirring and ready to move. There was no time for this! On the other hand, it wasn't like they could leave part of the Map behind, even if she'd wanted to. She stamped her foot in frustration.

"Come on, Marrill!" Fin's voice called.

"I have to get Rose!" she yelled back.

She snatched at the acorns roughly, jamming them into her pockets. "Okay, girl, you want acorns? Well, you gotta come with me to get them."

No sooner had she picked the last one than Rose gave a satisfied "Caw!" and took off, headed back to the ship.

"Finally!" Marrill grumbled.

The first thing she did when she hauled herself onto the deck was pull Fin into a fierce hug. "So glad you made it safely!" she said, smiling. "I guess everything went okay rescuing Coll, then?"

Fin grimaced and picked a twig out of his hair. Marrill suddenly imagined him clinging to Coll like a koala bear as Leferia tossed them from vine to vine. "Yeah, I don't really want to talk about it," he said. Marrill couldn't help but chuckle.

Karnelius stepped out of the ship's hold and stretched languorously in the sun. Padding toward Marrill, he paused to rub his cheek against the mast and yawned, baring every single one of his teeth. He gave a swipe toward where Rose perched nearby, but it was halfhearted at best.

"Stop being so ornery," Marrill scolded, picking her cat up and settling him in her arms.

Rose let out a loud "Caw!" and took to the sky, wheeling out ahead of them. The pirats tugged free the last mooring line while the Ropebone Man hoisted the mainsail. And the *Enterprising Kraken*, moving as fast as Coll could guide her, headed for the Pirate Stream once more.

As they neared the open waters, Marrill and the rest of the crew stood on the aft deck, watching the Gibbering Grove disappear behind them. A cloud of smoke billowed into the sky above it.

Fin pointed across the now-glowing water at a dark shape slipping from the far side of the island. "That's the *Black Dragon*," he said, voice anxious. "She's Stavik's best ship."

Coll grunted in dismissal. "Doesn't matter whose best ship she is, we've got too good of a lead for them to catch us any time soon."

Marrill tried to take comfort in the words, but her emotions were a tangled mess: She was horrified that the Grove might burn until there was nothing left. And terrified that by taking the Face, they'd just made a powerful enemy in Serth.

But also hopeful that they were one step closer to putting the Map together so she could get home. As if to fortify her hope, a raindrop splattered against her cheek, then another, on her shoulder. Karnelius hissed and struggled from her arms, bolting back belowdecks.

Ahead of them, storm clouds churned, and gusts of wind blew rain across the Stream. Straight for the Gibbering Grove. She'd never been so happy for rain in her entire life.

She turned to Fin, grabbing his arm. "Maybe the storm will put out the fire!"

He turned toward her, a smile on his face. "I hope—" The words died on his lips. His face paled as he stared at something over her shoulder.

She hated when that happened.

Already wincing, she turned. Where once there'd been open water, there now sat a ship under full sail, less than a football field's length away. Somehow, the *Black Dragon* had gained on them after all. In the blink of an eye.

And at its helm stood a pale man dressed in dark robes, his hands held to the sky.

CHAPTER 29
Down She Goes

F in's eyes froze on the low black ship behind them. It wasn't possible, he thought. The *Kraken* had had a solid lead—there's no way the *Dragon* could have caught up to them so quickly.

He blinked and shook his head, wondering if perhaps he was just seeing wrong. But when he looked back toward the Stream, the *Dragon* was still there. Worse, she seemed to be even closer.

Much closer.

"Um, guys?" he called out. He glanced over his shoulder. Ardent and Coll looked at him with identical suspicious expressions. Before they could ask who he was and what he was doing there, he pointed to the *Dragon*. "The Oracle's ship's right behind us!"

Coll leapt to the railing and leaned out, hanging from a rope. "That's not possible," he said. "The wind is ours and our lead unbeatable."

Fin looked back at the Stream. Something strange was happening. It wasn't just that the ship was gaining on them; it was as if the distance between them had vanished. He and Marrill exchanged anxious glances.

"She isn't outpacing us," Coll spat. "The space between us is just disappearing. That's not possible. Ardent, is that possible?"

The wizard pursed his lips, considering. "With magic, anything is possible." His eyes watched the *Dragon* cautiously. He flexed his fingers. "But no," he added. "I have yet to see the magic that can do *that*."

Even so, they'd just seen it happen. A chill wind tickled the hairs on the back of Fin's neck. He looked around; dark clouds gathered off the starboard bow. He could smell the rain coming on the rising breeze.

Behind them, the *Black Dragon* had drawn to shouting distance. Voices carried across the waves; the pirates were singing a mournful hauling shanty. Fin's chest squeezed tight at the sound of it. Even if they didn't remember him, the thieves were his friends. He hated hearing the misery in their voices.

Down the rats go
And down the hounds go
With a wind atop, we watch her drop
And Down. She. Goes.

Coll jumped to the deck. "Well, I don't aim to let anyone—magic or no—outsail the *Kraken*!" He raced to the wheel. "Hoist the jib, you rats! Full sail, Ropebone!"

The ship scuttled to action, pirats racing to follow Coll's command. Ardent waved his hands in the air, muttering something about "treacherous wind spirits." Sails billowed to life, more of them than Fin had realized they had. The *Kraken* turned at Coll's touch, headed straight toward the center of the black storm.

Thunder broke the sky overhead. Lightning boiled inside the clouds. But instead of the normal white or yellow, the flashes came out crimson.

Everyone on the ship froze. Goose bumps raced along Fin's arms. "The storm rises unnaturally," he heard Ardent tell Coll under his breath.

"Iron Ship weather, I know," the sailor muttered.

Fin gulped, remembering what he'd heard about the

ghost ship: a ship made of iron, a crew cut from shadows. *Lightning flashes red, and suddenly you're dead.*

Behind him, the pirate voices grew louder.

Down her knees go
And down her ribs go
And now her hands are in the sands
And Down. She. Goes.

While Fin didn't particularly desire to find out if the Iron Ship legends were true, anything had to be better than facing Serth again.

"Turn into the storm!" he called to Coll. The sailor gave him a look as though he were headsoft. It was clear he didn't recognize Fin, much less trust him.

Fin grabbed Marrill by the shoulders as rain began pelting across the deck. "You have to convince Coll—he won't listen to me. Serth's afraid of the Iron Ship," he told her. "He won't follow us into the storm. We can lose him!"

She chewed on her lip, uncertain.

"Trust me," Fin urged.

She nodded and raced toward Coll, slipping across the slick deck. Waving her arms, she explained Fin's plan. The knotted rope of Coll's tattoo flashed along his neck as he considered. Finally he spun the ship's wheel hard, grunting at the effort.

Marrill flashed Fin a thumbs-up, but as they turned into the storm, Fin wasn't quite sure it was time to celebrate just yet. They might lose Serth, but who knew what they might find instead?

Ahead of them, lightning struck, turning the sky a dark and angry red. The storm was intensifying, the rain getting so thick Fin could barely see the *Dragon* on their tail.

But he could still hear them.

> *Down in chains she goes*
> *And wrapped in shrouds she goes*
> *And never then we'll see her again*
> *'Cause Down. She. Goes!*

The *Kraken* hit a particularly rough wave, and the boards of the deck flexed and groaned in protest. With a curse, Coll gripped the wheel, fighting to keep the ship steady, and Marrill struggled to stay standing.

A great ripping noise sounded from overhead. One of the sails had torn free and flapped madly in the wind. Amidships, Ardent spun, fingers flying as he worked to fix it. No sooner was that sail repaired than another tore.

Marrill stood by his side, calling distances to Coll as the *Dragon* bore down on them through the storm. Every member of the crew had a task except for Fin.

He was tired of feeling useless. Fin raced aft, feet slipping across the wet deck as the ship crashed through a series of waves. In a lull between gusts of rain, he caught sight of the *Dragon*.

She was even closer than he'd realized. Fin's eyes met the Oracle's, separated by no more than a ship's length of water.

"Go faster!" he screamed to Coll. "Go!"

Serth stepped toward the bow. Behind him, thieves Fin had known for years readied their boarding lines. Their faces were crumpled in sadness, but Fin didn't believe for a second it had anything to do with him. Serth seemed to have such complete control over them that none of them even noticed the rain.

Overhead, red lightning flashed, furious and bright. Serth cringed looking up at it. It was that moment of weakness that bolstered Fin's courage.

"Hey, Serth—the Iron Ship's coming!" he shouted across the water. "Think you can make it cry? Or is it time to 'steer clear the Iron Ship'?"

The Oracle wrapped his arms around himself, shuddering. His mouth moved, but Fin could scarcely make out the words. "Fear...steer clear...iron slays dragons...who comes first, who comes first..."

"Fin!" Marrill yelled. She staggered over to him, awkward and unsteady as the ship rolled in the heavy seas. "Be careful! He's a wizard, remember? He can...wizard you, or whatever!"

"Not if I wizard him first," Ardent said from above. The old man stood, feet firmly planted on the mizzenmast top, the platform halfway up the *Kraken*'s aftmost mast. Bright energy crackled along his fingertips. He looked more wizardly than ever before.

"Are you ready for this, old friend?" he shouted.

"This is not how it happens!" the Oracle called back. "Not like this. The order, we must keep the order!" Serth held up one hand, palm toward them. The pirate shanty died.

For a few beats, Serth and Ardent squared off. Neither saying or doing anything. Just staring at each other.

And then the *Black Dragon* changed tack, turning away from the storm. "The scenes will come in order!" Serth called to them as the distance between the ships grew. "There will come another storm!" Then he was gone, the ship vanishing behind the churning clouds and gusting rain.

Coll let out the highest noise Fin had ever heard come from him. "Oh, bless the west wind," he said. "I was just getting ready to turn us out of the storm!" He yanked on the wheel, and the *Kraken* swung to port, away from the heart of the dark clouds.

"We did it!" Marrill squealed, beaming. She grabbed Fin's arm and bounced from side to side. "Your strategy paid off!"

Fin shuffled his feet. "You were the one to convince Coll," he pointed out.

"Well, you were the one who knew it'd work." She grinned.

Fin's gut twisted with guilt. She'd trusted him without hesitation, and he hadn't told her the entire truth. "He'll come back. After all," he said, "he followed me this far already."

"Huh?" Marrill asked. Thick raindrops splattered the deck around them, the edge of the storm petering out.

Fin reached into his thief's bag and pulled out the ruby key. "This belongs to him," he told her. "The Oracle hired me to steal it from the Meressian Temple Ship. But when he showed up for it, I ran."

Marrill frowned. Fin didn't know whether she felt confused or betrayed. She'd thought they'd been partners. But he'd kept this from her.

Fin swallowed. "That's the reason...." He paused, steeling himself. He'd never had to take the blame for anything before. No one had ever remembered him long enough to make him. And he was discovering just how difficult it was to do. "*I'm* the reason he followed us to begin with. That's why I snuck aboard the *Kraken* when the docks were burning. I was trying to escape from Serth."

He let out a long sigh.

Marrill bit her lip. "Oh, Fin..."

"Well, that all worked out, now, didn't it?" Ardent said as he half climbed, half floated his way down from the mast, with a brief assist from the Ropebone Man.

Fin, grateful for the chance to change the subject, turned toward the wizard. "Hey—you called the Oracle 'old friend'!"

Ardent raised his eyebrows. "Indeed I did," he said. "Quite observant, whoever you are."

Marrill wiped at her face as a raindrop smacked her nose. "Okay, now this is too much," she said. "You and...Serth? Are friends?"

Ardent shrugged. "Were," he corrected. He looked back and forth between them. "Why don't you head down to my cabin and dry off," he said. "You're both quite damp. I'll be there in a moment, and then we can have a nice long talk about the end of the world."

CHAPTER 30
The Meressian Prophecy

Eyes wide, Marrill looked toward Fin. "I *really* don't like the sound of that," she mumbled. The wind shifted in the sails overhead, splattering her with cold raindrops. She crossed her arms, rubbing her hands over her exposed wet skin to warm up.

She'd expected maybe a smile, or at least some sort of response, but Fin just slipped the ruby key back in his thief's bag and headed for the cabin without a word. It was so unlike him, it took her a moment to follow.

"Hey," she said, catching up as he reached for the door.

His cheeks colored, his awkwardness in full swing. Just like the first time she'd met him, on the rooftop in the Khaznot Quay. "I'm sorry I didn't tell you about the Key earlier. I'm used to looking out for myself. I—" He paused, clearing his throat. "I don't really know how to be a friend."

Marrill grabbed his hand. She remembered the secret the rumor vines had whispered to her in the Gibbering Grove—that he'd never had a friend before.

"Fin," she told him, "you're a great friend. In fact, you're my best friend."

His eyes widened; his grin practically wrapped around his head. But she didn't wait for him to say anything. She already knew how he felt. "Other than my mom and Karny, obviously," she added with a smirk.

"Obviously." He laughed. And with that settled, together they charged into Ardent's cabin.

"Whoa," Fin said, craning his neck to look around. "Look at all this stuff!"

Whoa is right, Marrill thought as she stepped in after him. A big desk dominated the middle of the room, a narrow bed pressed against one wall, and a few loose chairs sat by a dining table opposite it. Every other inch of the cabin was stuffed with shelves and cabinets containing almost everything imaginable, and a whole lot of things she'd never imagined at all.

On a pile of pillows tucked in an alcove under a porthole window, Karny sprawled, fat orange belly up. He seemed utterly unconcerned that they'd just barely avoided a massive storm and was already purring by the time she picked him up. "So this is where you've been hiding," she said as he affectionately bonked his head against her chin. A handful of pirats dashed from a tiny door in the wall and set about fluffing the pillows behind him.

"You have no idea how much jink this stuff would fetch at the Quay," Fin said as he strolled through the room. Marrill wondered if he even realized his fingers were twiddling. "Whoa, a Brother-Be-Gone sibling force field? That would go for enough that Mrs. Parsnickle could buy every single six-and-under a whole wardrobe!"

Marrill moved to the bed and examined the giant shield hanging over it. It was shaped like a fanged mouth waiting to consume someone whole. "He sleeps under this?"

"Sure," Fin told her. "It's a nightmare shield. Pretty elaborate one, too. Ardent must sleep pretty soundly."

Marrill shuddered. Having that thing over her bed would have *given* her nightmares. She turned to find Fin standing by Ardent's desk, staring at something. Marrill sidled up behind him and craned her neck to look over his shoulder. "What did you find?"

Fin held one of Ardent's cards, like the ones she'd seen him playing with before they reached the Grove, a drawing so detailed it looked like a frozen moment of life. The wizard on it, a man, wore a brilliant white robe. Scrawled across the bottom in a looping hand was an inscription:

To my dear friend, on the day before
we reach our destiny.
Without you, this could never be possible.

"Who's that?" she asked. It wasn't one of the ones she'd seen Ardent using.

Fin moved a nearby candle so that its light fell across the picture. "Don't you recognize him?" he asked.

Marrill studied the strong features, the sweeping chin and eyes. At first she didn't. Then her breath caught. The deep bronze tan on his cheeks and the hint of a smile on his lips almost disguised him. If she hadn't just seen him minutes ago, she might never have recognized him at all.

"The Oracle," she gasped. "This must have been made right before he drank Stream water. And if he gave it to Ardent…"

"Then Ardent must have been there!" Fin finished.

"Indeed," Ardent said from the doorway. Marrill jumped, and Karny let out a protesting squeak. Fin stepped back, crouching just a little as if ready to spring.

"Did you know there's someone else in here?" Ardent asked, pointing at Fin.

Marrill nodded, but didn't take her eyes off the wizard.

"He's a friend," she said. "So you really *were* there?"

Ardent let out a sigh. "Oh yes." He made an absent motion, and two chairs skidded across the room, stopping just behind each of them. A third somersaulted off the side table and landed across the desk. Ardent slid into it.

"I suppose you should *both* have a seat," he said.

Marrill sat slowly, exchanging glances with Fin. Karnelius curled into a ball on her lap, his paws absently kneading her leg.

Ardent reached for the card, and it floated from Fin's hand into his. Marrill couldn't tell whether it was sorrow or anger in his eyes as he looked at the image. Whatever the wizard felt, it must have been complicated.

"We were like brothers then," he said. "There were eight of us, all great wizards, and among us there was little we could not master. At least once a season, we met on the Isle of Meres to exchange knowledge and pursue great experiments. But Serth and I were closest."

His lips twitched. "We worked well together. He was naturally gifted, and I inclined to great study. So when Serth proposed his grand plan to become one with the Stream, I supported him." He raised an eyebrow. "I don't suppose I need to tell you it went poorly?"

"Right," Marrill announced, proud to remember what Leferia had told them. "He drank the water, it showed him the future, and that's where the Meressian Prophecy comes from."

"Well, not 'showed him the future' so much as 'crammed the future into his skull all at once,'" Ardent said. He tugged on his beard in thought. "Imagine someone ripping the pages out of a library full of books, mixing them all together, then shoving them onto a single bookshelf. That's about what happened to poor Serth's brain."

Marrill's mind reeled and she shivered, thinking of all the libraries she'd visited back home. No way any single mind could contain all of that—not all at once. "No wonder he's crazy."

"Oh yes," Ardent said. "With all that future swirled around in his brain, any time he does anything he has to first figure out what moment he's in and what happens next. Just deciding what to have for breakfast means grabbing pages at random off that shelf and hoping one has 'toast' written on it. And if you spend all your time sorting those pages, there's no time left to decide between toast and omelet."

"That sounds horrible," Marrill said.

Ardent nodded. "Quite so. I'm sure you won't be surprised to learn we parted ways shortly after." Ardent considered the image of Serth again. "Turns out ingesting Pirate Stream water is a terrible way to strengthen a friendship."

Marrill looked at Fin, thinking of their earlier conversation. Even if they hadn't known each other for long, he really was her closest friend. She couldn't imagine what it would be like to lose him so suddenly.

"For years," Ardent continued, "Serth could do nothing but recount what he'd seen, while a group of devoted followers—the first Meressians, as they became known—wrote it all down. And then one day he disappeared." With a sigh, Ardent set the card aside. "Only recently, I learned from an old friend that Serth had resurfaced, intent on fulfilling his own prophecy."

His glance fell back to the stack of cards on his desk. Marrill thought back to their talk after the kraken battle and guessed which one held his attention. "That was Annalessa, wasn't it?"

A ghost of a smile crossed Ardent's face, but the corners of his lips strained with sadness. "Quite so."

Fin looked between them quizzically. Marrill filled him in. "She was a friend who asked for his help and then disappeared."

Ardent nodded. "Annalessa was the first to realize what was happening. She confirmed what I'd feared: Serth seeks the Bintheyr Map to Everywhere to find the Lost Sun of Dzannin, as the Meressian Prophecy foretold. He intends to destroy the Pirate Stream."

His pronouncement was met with silence. Marrill sat stunned; Fin's eyes widened. The conversation had turned deadly serious.

Marrill wove Karnelius's tail through her fingers, wrestling with the news. "So he's after the same Map we are."

"Indeed," Ardent confirmed. "I'd hoped to find it long

before he could, but he seems to have caught up quite quickly."

"And what exactly does he need the Map to find?" Fin asked.

"An excellent question," Ardent said. He stood, clasping his hands behind his back, his familiar storytelling stance, and started to pace. "To understand the answer, you need to know a bit more about the history of the Stream. You see, the Stream is full of legends—so many, even *I've* barely scratched the surface of them. But only one legend survives from the time *before* the Pirate Stream."

He drew a hand through the air, and a ribbon of silver trailed from his fingers, just like when he'd first explained the Stream to Marrill. "For as long as anyone living can remember, the River of Creation has flowed slow, broad, and deep. But once, it flowed fast and furious, constantly birthing new worlds as it went."

With a flick of Ardent's fingers, tiny pinpricks of light glowed to life around the silver image, reminding Marrill of dust in a sunbeam.

"It is said that in those days, a hundred thousand stars shone on a hundred thousand different creations." He paused and pointed at one of the tiny lights. It suddenly pulsed red, swelling larger and larger. "But only one star shone on destruction."

Marrill stared at the light as it swallowed more and more of its surroundings, obliterating everything it touched. "'Star of destruction' doesn't sound good."

"That's something that I think we—and most variations of the legend—can agree on." Ardent dropped his hand and the red light disappeared, taking the silver stream with it. "The Dzane, the First Men who shaped those early worlds, wielded enormous power. They locked the star away behind some sort of gate, so that it would never again touch the River of Creation or the Pirate Stream. Ever since, that star has been known as the Lost Sun of Dzannin.

"But according to the Meressian Prophecy, that gate will open again, and Serth intends to make that happen. Of course, since there's no mention of where, or what, the Gate might be—thus the 'Lost' part of the name—he needs the Map to Everywhere to find it."

"The Key to open the Gate," Fin groaned. "The Map to show the way." He shoved his hands through his hair, tugging at it in frustration. "It's what the Oracle—Serth—kept saying when I ran into him."

"That is indeed the Prophecy," Ardent confirmed.

Goose bumps pricked along Marrill's skin. She pulled Karnelius closer for comfort. He let out a small *mrrp*. "You mean, if he opens the Gate, all of the Stream will just...go away?" she asked.

Ardent spread out his hands. "Perhaps. I cannot say for sure what such an event would look like; fortunately, we haven't had an apocalypse on quite that scale before."

"But what about the worlds the Stream only touches?

They'd be okay…right?" Marrill thought about her mom and dad sitting at the kitchen table.

"It's a safe bet every world we've been to, everywhere we've seen, would be destroyed, all its people lost. Ourselves as well, I expect."

Marrill slumped in her chair, trying to take it all in. Suddenly, finding the Map wasn't just about her being able to get home anymore. It was making sure there'd be a home to go back to. And hadn't Serth already proven that destruction meant nothing to him? She thought about the Gibbering Grove and Leferia. As scary as it had been, as odd as the Council was, it was a place of wonderful magic. A place unique even by the standards of a river of pure magic. And Serth would have destroyed it all without a second thought.

"But it would kill him, too, right? If he opened the Gate?" she asked. Ardent nodded. "Then why doesn't he just not do it? Wouldn't that solve everything? He could continue not dying, and the Pirate Stream could continue not being destroyed?"

"I doubt he's ever really considered it," Ardent said.

Fin let out a snort. "Seriously? Why not?"

"To understand that," Ardent sighed, "you would have to understand the mind of a madman." Spreading his hands wide, he tried to explain. "Let me put it like this. Magic is like imagination. It contains all possibilities. And just as you can imagine what might happen in the future, so too can the magic of the Pirate Stream *contain* the future. Serth drank that magic, and it gave him one of those futures. But in his mind, what he saw is *the* future—the only one."

Next to Marrill, Fin shook his head. "I don't get it," he said.

"Congratulations," Ardent told him. "You're not insane." He walked over to one of the bookcases and pulled down a long, narrow tube. "Perhaps a demonstration would help." He plucked a ball from a nearby basket and placed it at one end of the tube. The other end of the tube, he pointed at the table.

"Now, imagine you're this ball," he said, letting it go. "All you know is forward, right? The only place the ball can end up is on the table." The ball rattled as it rolled down the tube. "But it doesn't have to end up on the table, does it?" Suddenly, he snapped the tube in half. The ball flew across the room, and Karnelius bolted from Marrill's lap to chase after it.

"Serth's mind is like that ball in the tube—it only sees one way forward."

Finally, Marrill felt a glimmer of hope. "So Serth's basically treating this Prophecy as an instruction manual, doing everything it says even if that means destroying the Stream. Can't we just get a copy of that instruction manual and use it to stop him?"

Fin raised a hand for a high five. She started to go in for

it when Ardent shook his head. "Unfortunately, that won't be as helpful as you might think." He made a beckoning motion to the air behind him. The cabinet door flew open, and a huge book leapt down and hobbled over, walking on the bottom corners of its cover. When it reached the desk, it flapped up through the air, clearly struggling to get altitude. Marrill giggled. It looked like a fat turkey trying to fly.

The book clattered to the desk and flopped open. Dust puffed up from its dry pages. "This, my young friends, is the Meressian Prophecy."

"All of it?" Fin asked, voicing Marrill's own disbelief. The book was huge.

"Oh no," Ardent said with a laugh. "This is only one volume; there are several others like it. Unfortunately, just as Serth's mind is like a shelf full of pages, each part of the Prophecy is about as useful as pulling random pages off that shelf. Completely disordered, no connection between one and the next, no means of telling what happens when."

The wizard flipped through the book, the pages fanning past in a blur of ink. He stopped at the end, where the bottom of the page contained an etching of a massive gate. Drawn behind the elaborately carved bars was a stylized sun, its rays colored black.

"The only thing that's obvious is the end of it." Ardent touched his finger to the drawing, and the ink almost seemed to darken. "It was the very first verse Serth uttered. The Lost Sun."

CHAPTER 31
A Wasteland in Crystal and Shadow

F in stared at the drawing while Marrill read the last
stanza of the Prophecy aloud:

The Lost Sun of Dzannin is Found Again

And as in the beginning, so it will end.

The ship drowns in the bay.
The guides thought true betray.

The city that slides, the ships collide,
The storm will rise the iron tide!

The key to open the Gate,
The Map to show the way.

And when Map and key come together with me,

the Lost Sun dawns, the end is nigh!

"Well, that sounds dire," she concluded. She began flip-
ping through the massive book while Fin struggled to under-
stand it all. Karnelius leapt up to the desk beside them, paw
darting out to bat at the pages.

Fin frowned, trying to ignore the anxious rolling of his
gut. "So that's it? Serth has seen the future, it ends with
him opening this gate and destroying everything, and there's
nothing we can do about it?"

He remembered Serth's promise, that he could make
Fin remembered forever. *This ends when you give me the Key*,
the Oracle had said. Fin shook his head. That would make
him remembered, all right: remembered as the one who
ended the Pirate Stream! If, that is, there was anyone left to
tell the tale...

The Stream was his *home*. It was his world. He'd never
do anything to destroy it!

But what if...a small voice in Fin's mind asked. What if

it *was* him? What if there was no way to avoid the future? He stared down at the floor. He'd refused to accept that fate in the pie shop. There was no way he would give in to it now.

Ardent placed a hand on Fin's shoulder. "No," the wizard told him. "Serth has seen only one *possible* future. But there are other possibilities. Infinite others." With a flick of his fingers, the ball Karnelius had chased earlier flew across the room to hover in front of Fin. "If this ball is your future, it doesn't have to end up where the tube sends it. It can move in the direction you choose."

He was interrupted by a sharp knock, and the ball dropped to the table. Coll swung the cabin door open, letting the bright sunlight spill in. "Storm's cleared," he said, leaning against a patch of bare wall between shelves. "No sign of Serth."

Fin let out a long breath he hadn't realized he'd been holding. It was only a matter of time before the Oracle found them again, he knew. But for now, at least, they were safe.

"So," Ardent said, looking back to them, "to defeat Serth, we simply need to keep him from finding and opening the Gate."

"Is that all?" Coll asked. Marrill smiled at Fin, and he felt his lips twitch upward in return.

"At least we're one step closer," she offered. "Right, Fin?"

Coll and Ardent spun to face him. The wizard's eyes brightened. "Marrill, I see you brought an acquaintance back from the Grove with you. You do certainly seem to make friends wherever you go—a very admirable skill for one so young!"

"Great," Coll grumbled. "Yet *another* room the pirats will have to make up."

Marrill winked at Fin. "Oh, I'm sure we'll find a space for him. Because this friend just happens to have in his possession the next piece of the Map!"

On cue, Fin pulled the rolled-up parchment from his shirt. "Tralada!" he pronounced, holding it aloft. "The Face of the Bintheyr Map to Everywhere!"

"Excellent!" Ardent said, clapping his hands. He flicked his fingers, and the Prophecy book jumped from the desk to a nearby chair. He motioned to the empty space. "Let's have a look!"

Showmanship was something Fin excelled at. He indulged himself in the moment, grinning as he unrolled the parchment with a flip of his hand.

The Face hit the desk with a less-than-dramatic *thwump*. Immediately it welled with details: Continents and islands and whole worlds rippled across its surface.

And then dripped from the sides. Without the Gibbering Grove to catch them, everything that appeared on the parchment spilled over the edge of the paper, flopping to the floor.

Faster and faster they came, turning into a torrent of inky features. Forests and mountains and cities poured out of the Map, splashing onto the floor and bouncing off in every direction.

Fin grabbed at them blindly, not knowing what else to do. A particularly pointy continent rolled toward Karnelius, who pounced instantly, batted it away, then tore after it and grabbed it in his mouth.

"Karny! No!" Marrill called, chasing after him. "Drop that landmass right now!"

Ardent jumped forward, sputtering and swatting at the endless flow, but his efforts were as useless as Fin's. Map features were everywhere.

"Get that ... *everything* off my ship!" Coll bellowed. He leapt from the wall, only to land on a wayward island and crash heavily to the floor.

"I'm trying!" Fin called back, juggling two castles with one hand while balancing a farmhouse on a snow-covered mountaintop with the other. More shapes were pouring out than he could possibly handle; it was pointless even to try. Still, it seemed impolite just to let them fall. These were real places, after all. Or at least, drawings of them.

Marrill streaked past, shouting, "Karny, leave it! Leave it!" as she chased him around the desk. From somewhere near the door, Fin heard a *kaboom!* and looked over to find a volcano shooting out from the cabin onto the deck, spewing smoke. In its wake, a small series of hills rolled underneath the bed.

The ship was being completely overrun! Fin dropped the landscape he'd been holding onto a nearby chair before lunging for the Map.

"Almost got it," Ardent said, struggling with one corner of the parchment. Fin grabbed the other side and rolled it, sending a geyser straight into the wizard's face.

"*Agh*, steam-bathed!" Ardent cried, blinking his eyes and swatting at his beard. He released his corner, and it snapped to Fin, spitting out one final knobby atoll before he could furl it shut.

Fin stared down at the roll of parchment in his hands, his mouth agape. He'd seen a lot of amazing things in his life (an excessive number of them in the last twenty-four hours alone), but never anything like this. Not even watching the Map at the Gibbering Grove had prepared him. The whole world had just poured out of a sheet of paper and laid siege to the *Kraken*!

"I think I did mention that defining the edges would be important," said Ardent.

All around, stray terrain features scattered across the floor and hung limply from the shelves. Marrill cradled her cat, who appeared to be munching on the remains of a tiny farmhouse. Coll swept a tumble of three-ringed moons aside and rubbed his bruised leg. Fin crouched down by the open cabin door, trying to keep an elephano herd from stampeding out onto the main deck, where the volcano had sputtered and gone dormant.

"Perhaps the Neatline would be helpful at this juncture," Ardent mused, toeing a slightly bedraggled reef.

Of course, how long it would take before they found that, Fin had no idea. "Any thoughts on where that might be?" he asked.

Coll stretched his arms over his head. "Ask the bird," he said, yawning. Absently, he scratched at a spot below his collarbone where the edge of his tattoo was just visible under his shirt.

Ardent cleared his throat, his eyes narrowed in concentration as he peered at Coll. Something had caught his attention, but Fin couldn't figure out quite what it was.

Coll stopped scratching, but his fingers lingered over the tattoo. The corners of his mouth tightened.

"Why don't you two go play outside for a bit while Coll and I clean up in here?" Ardent tried to keep his voice cheery and light, but there was still a strained note to it.

Marrill was already trudging toward the door, barely containing a yawn of her own. "I'm thinking naptime," she mumbled.

Fin thought about protesting, but one glance at Coll changed his mind. He stood stiffly against the wall, arms crossed tightly. "Sweet dreams," the captain said pointedly, which was clearly Fin's cue to leave.

He nodded, and followed Marrill down the winding stairs to their cabins. By the time his head hit the pillow, any thoughts about Coll or anyone else were long gone. He'd fallen instantly to sleep.

✢ ✢ ✢

Fin yawned and rubbed his eyes. From the looks of things, it was night again, cold and dark. The walls of his cabin undulated, three of them looking like an endless stretch of water, while the fourth resembled the distant lights of the Khaznot Quay at night, just like the first time he'd seen it. A wash of pinprick lights arced across the ceiling, one star burning brighter than the others. He'd been dreaming about his mom again.

He stretched beneath his blankets. Had he really slept all day?

A strange, shimmering glow filtered in through a high porthole. It wasn't the golden glow of the Pirate Stream; this was green, or was it blue? Or maybe orange? He tried to focus. Where were they?

The cold assaulted him as soon as he threw off his blanket. This wasn't sundown chilly, or even Quay-wind frigid. It was serious cold, the type of cold that gives no warning. The kind of cold a body doesn't feel, not all at once, because even the cold itself is frozen. Fin flexed his fingers and found them slow and stiff.

He slipped off the comfy bed, thrusting his hands into his armpits for warmth. Thick foggy clouds puffed out with his every breath. For a moment, he thought they might freeze entirely and fall to the floor. He yanked the blanket off the bed, wrapping it tight around his shoulders.

Outside his room, a thin white layer of frost covered the lacquered wood of the hallway, and an odd clicking sound filled the air. The frost crunched beneath his shoes as he headed for the spiral staircase, his blanket trailing behind him. As he passed different doors, he quickly realized where the clicking was coming from—it was the face-shaped door knockers, all chittering their teeth against the brass rings in their mouths.

Icicles clung to the grand staircase and its golden rails. He poked at one cautiously before climbing up and lifting the main hatch.

The cabin had been cold, but stepping out onto the deck was like walking into a wall. Fin recoiled, almost falling backward. But cold wasn't the only thing outside. Overhead, the sky was on fire.

It was night, definitely night, but in the sky, a veil of light seemed to be cast over the darkness. Fin almost forgot the bone-chilling cold as he watched it. It danced, brilliant green curtseying to deep violet, and blue prancing into orange. This must have been the glow he'd seen through the porthole.

"Fin!" Marrill called. He struggled to tear himself away from the lights as she waddled toward him across the deck, bundled up in a thick wool coat. She was smiling, but her eyes were red. A single tear of frozen crystal clung to her cheek. "Nice getup," she said, motioning to his blanket.

He looked down at it. "Oh, this? It's for special occasions." She smiled at him, but her expression was still pained. "What's wrong?" he asked.

Marrill rubbed a fur-lined mitten across her nose. "I'm fine," she said. "Just worried about my mom, that's all. Especially, you know, with the end of the world coming." She sniffed hard, trying to laugh, but failing.

Fin started to raise a hand, then dropped it awkwardly. He still didn't have much experience trying to make someone else feel better. "Well, you know, if the world's going to end anyway, there's no reason we shouldn't take a peek at what's behind the Bilge Room door." Fin waggled his eyebrows in invitation.

The corner of Marrill's mouth twitched. "And there's this lush tentalo I've been saving," he added, pulling the fruit he'd nicked from Squinting Jenny's stand out of his thief's bag. "It's *still* not ripe, but I'm pretty certain if we toss it overboard we'll get a crazy, howling explosion."

She laughed fully now and Fin's chest warmed. "That's a terrible idea!" But then she turned serious for a minute. "Thanks, Fin."

He nodded, heart swelling. "It'll be okay, Marrill. I promise." He dropped the tentalo back in his bag. He waited a second, then he said, "So, about that Bilge Room..."

She swatted at him, and he ducked out of reach. They

laughed and teased their way over to the railing, and there they stopped, staring out at the vast expanse surrounding them. "Wow," Fin breathed, taking it all in.

Great icebergs floated past the *Kraken*, some bigger than the ship itself. They gleamed with the colors of the midnight lights, making the whole world seem to glow in the darkness. Every now and then, one would let out a low, creaking squeal, and a moment later, part of it would break off and tumble into the water below.

This part of the Pirate Stream was a stream in earnest, a narrow river slashing across the frozen land. As they moved along it, the icebergs became ice cliffs, thrust up from a snowy plain. The boom of cracking ice came more often.

Not too far ahead of them, Rose banked in a wide arc, leading them on. "Where are we, anyway?" Fin asked.

Ardent *harrumph*ed as he walked up. "These would be the Crystal-Shadow Wastes, unless I miss my guess. Which I don't, by the way. Rarely do ships travel here; most freeze solid and sink before they get too far, or else get crushed or swallowed by the ever-changing ice."

He must have seen their look of concern, because he waved his hands dismissively. "Never to worry, I happen to be on good terms with both warmth and cold. Unlike *some* elements I might name, they are quite easy to get along with. Very different management styles, naturally, but both quite reasonable."

"What Ardent is trying unsuccessfully to say is that he's keeping us from freezing," Coll said from his place at the helm.

Fin shivered. His fingers had gone numb, and he was pretty sure his nose was lined with ice. That seemed pretty much like freezing to him. "What about Serth?" he asked. "Any sign of him?"

"None reported," Coll reassured him. "The pirats have pretty good eyesight, so I've posted them as lookouts."

"Seems we've regained our lead after all," Ardent added.

Just then, Coll shouted, "Hold tight!" and Fin looked to the bow. Up ahead, the waterway narrowed, thinned, and turned into ice and snow. The Stream had ended! Fin braced for impact, but the horrible crunch of wood against ice never came.

"No way!" Marrill cried. Coll let out a loud whoop of victory. Ardent put his hands together and smiled a self-satisfied smile. The ship was still moving.

Fin jumped to the rail and peered down. Marrill popped her head over just beside him. Snow swirled in little eddies around the hull as the ship's prow moved through it. They were still sailing. On *snow*! "Shanks spinning!" he said to himself. "How?"

"I knew this was the right ship for the job." Ardent said, beaming. "A *true* streamrunner runs the Stream wherever it goes, frozen or not!"

CHAPTER 32
It's Right on the Tip of My Tongue

All around them, the ice boomed and shattered in the multicolored light. To Marrill, it was like counting seconds from a lightning strike to the thunder, only in reverse. Listen for the noise, then count seconds until the ice split. Great frozen cliffs came crashing down; fissures who-knew-how-deep spiderwebbed across the plain; new cliffs thrust up in unexpected shapes, like spirals and loop-de-loops. The whole world was constantly and violently changing.

Kind of like her life, Marrill thought. Not long ago, she'd been eagerly planning her family's escape from Arizona and return to their life of carefree adventures. Then her mom got sick, and every second since had been crazier than the last. Now, suddenly, she wasn't just looking for a way home; she was racing against a madman bent on destroying the world.

Ice boomed again, and she hugged her arms around herself more tightly. Nearby, a stretch of smooth snow ruptured down the middle, one side dropping as the other jutted oddly into the air. Only a single snowy knoll out in the plain seemed to avoid the chaos.

"You're my little snowy knoll," Marrill whispered as she leaned down to pet Karnelius. He turned his head to one side and bonked it against her cheek. Somehow, it helped.

Just then, the already frigid temperature plummeted. Her face felt like someone had dunked it in ice water. Even beneath the thick wool coat, her skin bristled with goose-flesh.

"It's f-f-f-freezing," she stammered.

Except that as soon as the words left her mouth, her breath crystalized and turned into solid ice, the letters hovering for a moment before dropping to a pile at her feet. One of the *F*s slid across the deck. Karnelius pounced down and chased after it.

Marrill was so startled she couldn't stop herself from letting out a shout of alarm. Only instead of a shout, a crunch of random letters stuck to the tip of her tongue.

"*Gahhh*," she cried, trying to work the ice free.

Ardent approached as she picked at the pieces. She jumped with surprise. Once again, she'd fallen victim to his weird old man stealth.

He grinned and held up a string of letters, roped together on a piece of twine like a charm bracelet. They read:

ꓷOHATИOЯꟻⱭ⅃OϽ

Marrill started to ask, then remembered she couldn't talk. She gave him a questioning frown.

His grin faltered. He looked down at the letters for a moment, then his eyebrows jumped in understanding. He traded the ends of the string from one hand to the other and held it up again. Turned around, it now read:

COLDFRONTAHOY

Oh, Marrill thought, *cold front ahoy!* She nodded in understanding. Not that it explained anything.

At that moment, Fin popped up from belowdecks. Marrill hadn't even seen him leave. Karnelius took the opportunity to bolt for warmer quarters, dashing between Fin's legs and nearly sending him toppling to the ground.

Marrill stifled a laugh as a string of frozen letters poured out of Fin's mouth. His eyes grew huge, and more frozen letters followed the first. Ardent shook with quiet chuckles next to her, then held out his stringed message.

Fin looked around, hands held out cautiously. He opened his mouth quickly, and the letters W H A T popped out. Then I S. He paused, clearly thinking. H A P—and the final P stuck on his bottom lip. He tugged at it, grimacing in pain.

Marrill couldn't help herself. She laughed. And a second later, she too was prying an H and an A from the end of her tongue.

Ardent dropped his string and lifted his arms in resignation. A second later, flames popped from his fingers and a glowing orb of fire burst to life. Soon they were surrounded in a cacophony of their own voices, all talking and laughing and yelping at once as the frozen words strewn around their feet melted.

"Well, there we go," Ardent said. "We hit a cold front." As if that explained everything.

Marrill sighed. "I think we got that. But what kind of cold front freezes *words*?"

"What she said," Fin added helpfully.

Ardent seemed puzzled by the question. "Well, this one, obviously. And it can freeze lots more than words, I'd expect. I'd wager if it weren't for all the heating spells I've been placing around the ship, we'd probably all be frozen solid by now. Even so, I would try not to think too hard about anything specific, or have too many strong emotions. Those will probably freeze, too, and who knows what it takes to thaw them."

"Emotions?" Marrill asked, dubious.

"Oh, sure," Fin said. She stared at him, and he lifted a shoulder. "I've heard about them being sold at the Quay," he said. "I mean, they're pretty rare, but apparently fear and stuff never melts."

"Quite so," Ardent agreed. He tilted his head to one side, scrutinizing Fin. "Have we met?"

Marrill ignored him. She was far more focused on the impossibility of the situation. "So if it's cold enough to freeze words and feelings, how do we stay warm?"

"Magic!" Ardent exclaimed with pride. "Though I admit the Wastes aren't rumored to be so hospitable to...well, being alive. I suppose technically they aren't rumored to be much at all, given that few explorers ever return from them."

The thought did not put Marrill at ease. *Every second crazier than the last*, she thought.

"All the same," Ardent continued, "I suggest staying close to me. Heat is less hot here, you know, and I'm not sure how far I can push it." And with that, he turned and strolled off, completely nonchalant.

Marrill shivered, watching the heat orb shrink and die

between them. "I guess we need to come up with some kind of sign language," she suggested. And it was good she got that out when she did, because whatever Fin said next crashed to the deck and shattered like ice cubes.

For the next few hours, the ship ground on across the white plain, snow churning below their keel. Around them, the landscape heaved and collapsed, loud cracks of shattering ice the only sound in the unearthly silence; too massive, perhaps, to freeze.

Marrill and Fin sat cross-legged on the deck, taking turns coming up with hand signals and teaching them to each other. To explain them, they'd spit out a short stream of letters and arrange them into the right words, or reorder the letters they already had into new ones.

They'd exhausted all the normal gestures, gone through all the possible ones they might need—"Run for it!" (two fingers down, twiddled like legs) was obviously a necessity, and "Be ready to fight" (ring finger over thumb, like two crossed swords) was a recent favorite—when Marrill arranged a new word on the deck and pressed her thumb to her chest, over her heart. "Friend," she mouthed.

She saw Fin swallow, and then his face broke into a huge grin as he placed his own thumb over his heart and nodded. But then his gaze slipped over her shoulder, and he shifted his hand to touch his left elbow with his right thumb, the sign to look. Marrill did.

Ahead something new reached up from the ever-shifting plain. A crooked tower, snaking toward the sky, stood out from the surroundings. Not crooked like the Leaning Tower of Pisa, which her father had pretended to hold up in that picture when her mother was creating a photo tour of Italy for an article on the great towers of Tuscany. More like a game of Jenga just before it collapsed. The bottom seemed to lean one way, then a quarter of the way up it leaned back the other, and then a little way from the top it jogged sharply to one side, hanging so far out over the empty air that it should have been impossible for it to remain standing at all.

At first she thought it was made of ice, all glassy and dimly reflecting the dancing colors in the sky. But if it was, it wasn't pure ice; as she squinted, she could make out other colors, and even shapes, beneath its gleaming surface.

As the ship churned forward, Marrill realized the strangest thing about the tower: It *wasn't* crumbling. In the whole wasteland, this tower and this tower alone seemed oddly, improbably stable.

Marrill sucked in her breath. The cold burned her lungs, and a thin layer of frost coated her tongue. She drew a question mark in the air, the symbol for "What is that?"

Fin shrugged, the universal symbol for "I don't know."

She squinted at the tower again. She could barely make out a dark smudge circling high above it: Rose. Whatever it was, that tower was their destination.

An hour or so later, they were just close enough to walk when the *Kraken* ground to a halt. Marrill gave Fin the symbol for "We're here" (both hands extended palm-down, then fingers curled into fists). He had to take a second to think about it, but nodded.

Coll jumped down to the main deck and made his way over to them. One of Ardent's warmth orbs hovered close to his face.

"I guess we're here," the sailor said.

"That's what I just said!" Marrill announced triumphantly.

Coll seemed unimpressed. "Sure," he said. "Anyway, get ready for a walk. And have fun, I'm staying with the *Kraken*."

"Oh no!" Ardent said, coming up behind him. "If we're to get up that thing, we'll need all hands on deck or whatnot. But not literally. All hands off deck, as it were. Climbing."

Coll let out a long, loud sigh and started for the ladder. Fin reached for his thief's coat. Marrill couldn't help giggling as he spun in circles, struggling to force it on over the bulky layers he was already wearing. With a sigh, he plucked free a few items from various hidden pockets and stashed them in his thicker jacket, then hung the coat on a hook attached to the mizzenmast.

When he noticed Marrill still chuckling, he grinned. "You can never be too prepared."

"I'm not sure how you can ever be prepared enough on the Stream," she responded as she made her way down the ladder and dropped to the ground next to Coll. She sank into the soft snow up to her ankles. Fin landed beside her, and Ardent after.

She surveyed their surroundings. The ice immediately around the tower was completely still—not even a snow-flake drifted in the breeze. Beyond it, in sharp contrast, the mountains slid into crevasses and up again into deep drifts just like everywhere else in the Wastes, an ever-changing world of tumbling ice and drifting snow.

"I expect this line marks the edge of the tower's domain," Ardent told them, pointing to the ground a few yards behind them. A thick dark streak frozen deep in the ice arced away in either direction, making a perfect cir-cle around the tower. It was scrupulously neat, she noted, almost like a physical barrier.

"Weird," she muttered. But at least it made walking eas-ier, not having to worry about a chasm opening up under-neath them and swallowing them whole.

After a good twenty minutes' slog, they stood at the tower's base. Above them, it stretched impossibly into the air, lit by the shimmering colors of the midnight sky. Up close, the spire was actually more of a tapering pile of junk fused together with ice rather than a tower of ice itself, like someone had piled up a garage sale in a Minnesota winter, then sprayed it down with a hose. A narrow and very steep staircase spiraled up and around it, endlessly.

All along the steps, a series of signs were planted, most of them frozen deep in the ice and frosted with icicles.

GO AWAY, the first one read.
YOU'RE NOT WANTED HERE, said the next.
SERIOUSLY, CAN'T YOU READ? came after that.

Marrill could just make out the one that followed:

**GO BACK AND READ THE FIRST SIGN
'CAUSE IT'S REALLY IMPORTANT.**

Clearly they weren't wanted. Which was fine with her; her legs ached even thinking about climbing all those stairs. "Can't you just"—she waved her hands in the air—"magic us up there?" she asked Ardent.

He straightened and opened his mouth to answer. Thankfully, Coll cut it short: "You don't want to trust your life to the wind elements," he said, leaning toward her. "At least not while Ardent's controlling them." He dropped his voice. "Let's just say that I think *nemeses* would be a good description of their relationship."

"I'm not the one who started it," Ardent protested.

An uneasy feeling began to churn in Marrill's stomach. "I guess we better get climbing," she said at last.

CHAPTER 33
The Naysayer

DONUT ENTER, the sign on the door read. Fin opened his mouth, then thought better of it. He already had a nice sore spot on his tongue from the last witty remark that had frozen there, and he didn't really need to add to it.

Still, he tapped Marrill on the shoulder and pointed. She put her hand over her mouth, curling giggles of ice slipping through her fingers. She swallowed and calmed herself, then scraped them off her mitten and let them fall onto the crooked stairs below.

The sign stood out against an otherwise empty slate of a door. There were no handles or locks, no indication whatsoever how to open it. Coll crouched at one edge, feeling for hinges, while Ardent made exaggerated waving motions. Their efforts looked to be equally useless.

Still, thankfully, this was the end of the climb. The staircase had passed over gaps that never should have supported its weight, clung to the side of the tower in spots where it should have slid clean off, and even arched across the massive crook where the whole tower should have tumbled to the ground. How they'd made it to the top Fin wasn't sure, but no matter how it looked or how slippery the ice should have been, never once had the path felt unstable.

As Marrill joined the others prying at the door, Fin looked out over the frozen landscape. The *Kraken* lay far below, her deck wreathed in soft orange and blue by the curtain of color overhead. Beyond, the landscape perpetually tore itself apart beneath the midnight sky.

Just as he started to lose himself in the bizarre crumbling beauty of the Wastes, something cold smacked him on the back of his head. He jumped and swatted at the ice sliding down his neck. A snowball fight, here? Had the rest of the crew gone mad?

Only his hands weren't sweeping away snow, but letters.

He found himself looking down at **A H A**, frozen into a ball. Fin turned to see Marrill watching him. Little giggle spirals still clung to her lips. Behind her, the door had come ajar, a perplexed sailor and slightly embarrassed-looking wizard standing next to it.

"What are we waitinggllh!" Fin managed to get out before a *G* stuck to his tongue.

"gfor!" burst out in his own voice as he stepped into the tower. Warmth flooded over him, making his frozen skin tingle. They stood in a low-ceilinged hall that felt more like a dim tunnel. Both Ardent and Coll had to hunch over awkwardly. In the dark, he couldn't make out the room at the end, but the orange glow of a fire flickered out from it, and a salty, stale odor tickled at his nostrils.

"We can talk!" Marrill cried.

"But you can't knock," a gruff voice answered from somewhere inside.

Coll held up a hand to quiet them, shifting into a fighting stance.

"Hullo?" Ardent called.

"Or read, apparently." The shadow of something massive and lumpy moved across the wall at the end of the hallway. "Say, ya didn't happen to trip over three hundred and forty-two *signs* on your way up here, didja?"

"Hu-lloooo?" Ardent tried again. Fin gulped. Against all his instincts, he moved forward with the group, slowly, toward the light.

Just as Fin started to think the creature was gone, a huge, leathery head burst around the corner. It was a deep, purplish blue, and low and flat like a salamander's. Dark orbs of eyes squinted out from it, and stringy blond hair hung off the back, more from the neck than the bald head itself. Fin was pretty sure his whole arm could fit in its large mouth. Even Coll jumped.

"Oh, fer crackin' creepers," it said. "Whatcha waitin' for, an engraved invitation? 'Cause I'm pretty sure I left you one, y'know, on all those *signs*!" Then it disappeared again into the main chambers.

"I think he wants us to go in," Marrill said.

"I absolutely don't," the rough voice called. "You'd think that'd be pretty obvious from the *signs*," he muttered. "Figgers I move to the frozen rottin' middlah nowhere and get the Stream's dumbest houseguests. Don't want you cloggin' my hallway, neither, so if you ain't gonna make like civilized whats-you-ares and take a flying leap, might as well get in and do whatever it takes to get gone again."

The others looked at each other nervously. Fin just shrugged. As weird as this was, he'd been threatened by just about everything that had ever paid him any attention whatsoever, and this really didn't seem like the worst of them.

Besides, as far as he was concerned, it was awfully easy to be ignored by something that didn't want to pay attention to you in the first place. He stepped forward, into the main room.

He blinked. He was in a big, round chamber, with shelves lining it from floor to ceiling, save for an open window on either side. A roaring fire blazed at the far end, casting light out over every manner of junk he could possibly imagine. Used chitterchomp repellent, dusty coin purses, slightly enchanted jumble jars, even an old set of skysails. It was like Ardent's cabin and Fin's own attic combined, only with twice the size and much, much cleaner.

Next to the fire, their new host sifted through a stack of glowing blue crystals. Four long arms moved beneath a thick, hunched body with short, stubby legs and a tail. It was like someone had set a whale up on a couple of old stumps and pushed it out to make its way in the waterless world.

The creature tossed one of the crystals onto the fire, where it cracked and blazed. Suddenly, Fin felt more than warm—he felt confident, bold...and hopeful. In the fire's glow, he felt like anything could happen, and everything would turn out right.

"So, what are you, then?" Fin asked.

The creature wheeled around holding up another of the crystals. "Oh, that works for you, huh?" he said, adding it to the fire. "Figgered. Loser."

Fin opened his mouth, then closed it. A cold breeze washed over his warm feeling.

Meanwhile, the rest of the crew emerged from the hallway. Ardent strode to the center of the room, almost strutting beneath his bobbing wizard's cap. "Greetings, most noble host. I am the great wizard Ardent. Perhaps, I expect, you have heard of me?"

He put his hands on his hips and thrust out his chest. It might have been heroic, had he weighed more than a hundred pounds at his heaviest moment.

The creature shrugged his bulky shoulders. "Ardent, huh? Yeah, that rings a bell."

The wizard let a self-satisfied smile slip across his face. "Really?"

"Nope," the creature said, turning away. Ardent's smile dropped and his shoulders fell.

Coll leaned over to Marrill. "Seems like some kind of naysayer," he murmured, just loud enough for Fin to catch.

The creature rearranged some of his junk with his lower arms, digging a finger into an earhole with one of the upper ones. "And you seem like Daddy let you borrow his best sailor's hat, Skipper," he snarked. "I bet you sail a great big ole sailin' ship, don'tcha, Cap'n?"

Fin watched Coll's nostrils flare and his teeth grind. "I do, actually," he said, mostly to himself.

The Naysayer shrugged one pair of shoulders, then the other. He looked at Marrill. "And you must be the lovable sidekick. I bet your parents don't even know you're out after dark."

Marrill's eyes widened, but the Naysayer continued to not notice, or not care. "Now that we all know each other, it's been swell knowing you. See yourselves out." He turned and lumbered off to fiddle with a pile of half-tinkered dream cubes arranged artfully in a basket by the fireplace.

As a first-rate rascal himself, Fin had to appreciate the creature's quickness with a comeback. He was apparently the only one, though. Everyone else wore stern scowls and angry-looking expressions.

He caught Marrill shoot a glance to Ardent, who raised his hands and stammered, "N-now, see here, good strange monster…" The Naysayer fixed him with one dark globe of an eye. Ardent cleared his throat. "We're here for a map, you see, and we cannot leave without it. The fate of the world is at stake."

"Got lots," the Naysayer told him. Ardent looked hopeful. "You can't have any," the creature snapped quickly.

Ardent chuckled nervously. "A part of a map, really," he said. "Let's see, what parts are left?…There would be the Scale, obviously, to give everything its right size…and the Legend…that's an interesting part, puts it all together, you know…."

"Ain't got none of those," the Naysayer told the wizard. "Wrong tower, try the one four hundred thousand miles that way." He pointed each of his four hands in a different direction.

Fin kept one ear on the conversation as he wandered the room, checking out all the strange things scattered around the shelves. Cages full of gumstingers hung down next to wish generators and candle holders and a whirling set of globes, rotating around a central golden ball.

Just about everything Fin could imagine was carefully arranged in stacks and rows on the shelves. It was almost *exactly* like his old attic tower, he thought, right down to its crooked lean. He even saw a cloud-catching net and a pile of self-fetching balls in one corner.

Rose came sailing in one of the open windows nearby. She circled, seemingly unable to find a place to land. Ultimately, she settled on a pile of slingshots. Fin knelt and picked one up, testing its strength.

Ruffling her tail feathers, the bird let out a sharp cry, then flapped across the room to land on the basket of blue crystals by the fire. "Sorry," Fin offered. She ignored him and set to preening her wings.

"Don't forget the part that keeps everything from falling out everywhere," Marrill said.

"The Neatline," Coll grumbled.

Fin shoved the slingshot in his back pocket and picked up a fear-flipper. It was incredible, fully automated and still in its original packaging. This guy had everything! "Where'd you get all this stuff?" Fin asked, not caring that he was interrupting.

The Naysayer turned toward him. "Oh great, another kid. I'm gonna have to start leaving out traps." Fin bit down a smile and repeated his question.

"I stole it, mostly," the Naysayer said bluntly. Looks of concern jumped onto the others' faces, which only spurred the creature on. "From no-goods who come into my Wastes thinking they own the place. Kinda like you," he added.

He lumbered over to a stack of fur-lined boots and picked a pair up. "Once in a gray tide, some prying hornsitters like you decide to 'explore the Wastes' or whatever dumb idea they got. So I go out and take a *toll*, if you get my drift."

Marrill crossed her arms. "You mean you take what they need to survive." Her voice was loaded with distaste.

The Naysayer let out a low grunt. "Awful judgmental for a trespasser, ain'tcha?" he said. "I don't seem to recall grantin' no interviews. Get lost."

Even Fin felt uneasy now. He'd just started to really like this creature, who was a fellow thief to boot. Take away a few arms, and the Naysayer could have been his older brother!

Except Fin didn't much like the idea of leaving people out in the cold. "You don't really take the stuff they need to live, right?"

The Naysayer sighed and tossed another blue crystal onto the fire. "Nah," he said grudgingly. "I just clean up what's left after the Wastes get 'em. After a while, it all freezes into the ice. The gear, the junk…the hope." The fire snapped and popped. Suddenly, Fin felt warm again. A good feeling washed over him, and his worries eased.

"Oh dear," Ardent twittered. "Dear, dear. That's what you're burning to keep warm, isn't it? Hopes?" The Naysayer snorted. Ardent shook his head. "All those hopes, frozen in the ice. I expect the people will have frozen as well." He put a hand on Marrill's shoulder and smiled. "Not to worry, my dear, at these temperatures, snap-frozen, most likely. Probably out there in the ice somewhere, just waiting for someone to come along and thaw them."

"Cold out, stuff freezes.... Yeah, I can definitely see the wizard thing now," the Naysayer said. "Well, you're all very smart and compassionate and talented and..." He leveled an eye at Fin. "Um...forgettable. Sounds like you figgered out yer mission, and I guess you better get goin' if you want to go unfreeze those folks. Be sure to take them all home with you, good chat, bye now!" He waved all four arms in a shooing motion.

"Oh, thank you very much," Ardent said, blushing. "You didn't have to say the 'smart' and 'talented' part...."

Fin rolled his eyes, not even half-taken by the fake compliments. He still felt warm, but the good feeling was draining fast. He glanced around the room. It was full of cool stuff, no doubt. The whole tower was *built* of cool stuff. But there weren't any people, anywhere. No one could get here without freezing, and even when they did, the Naysayer was a total jerk. And he just sat here, in his tower of stolen junk, warming his hands with other people's ambitions. Suddenly, everything about this place seemed less awesome.

But still just as familiar.

Halfheartedly, he tossed the fear-flipper back on the shelf. It smacked against the others, but to his surprise, the stack didn't scatter. Instead, the missing one actually seemed to jump back into place, resetting everything to its perfect order.

The tower was almost exactly like his room, Fin thought again. Just like it, except everything was *way* too neat.

An idea came to him. He slipped to the window and peered down to the smooth snowy expanse below. Carefully separated from the crumbling wastes by that neat black line.

"So," he said. "What was someone saying about a Neatline? Because I think I have an idea why this tower of junk is still standing."

The Naysayer's rough voice gave an unnaturally high nervous chuckle. "Kids, ain't they adorable? What with their imaginations and all that?"

The smirk of victory dropped from Fin's face. Because at that moment, he saw a second ship waiting in the snow, not far from the *Kraken*.

The *Black Dragon*. Somehow, it had already caught up.

He scanned for Serth and found him, his black robes spread out across the white snow. The dark wizard stood in the shadow of the *Kraken*'s bow, just across the arc of the Neatline, his trembling hands raised to the sky.

"Guys, we have to go," Fin breathed.

Serth motioned upward. The ice over the Neatline shattered. A low rumble started somewhere far below them.

The Naysayer gulped.

And then the whole tower started to shake and shudder.

CHAPTER 34
Things Fall Apart (Literally)

One moment, the Naysayer's tower, weird as it seemed, felt as solid as stone beneath Marrill's feet. The next, the entire world was trying to buck her off.

The floor quaked. The walls buckled. Junk rattled on the Naysayer's shelves. Containers tipped over, showering the room with tiny glass balls that shattered on impact. A sound like frogs croaking filled the air, along with the smell of hot pavement after a summer rain.

"Now look whatcha done!" the Naysayer cried, darting

around and trying to catch things before they hit the ground. But even with four arms, he didn't have enough hands to rescue all the stuff tumbling down around them.

"What's happening?" Marrill shouted. Something very large and very smashable crashed to the floor beside her, splintering the floorboards. She yelped and jumped back. An inch to the left, and it would have crushed her!

"It's the Neatline!" Fin yelled, his voice nearly drowning in a chaos of croaking and rattling and smashing and the Naysayer's angry ranting. "It's what kept this tower of junk together, and Serth's stealing it!"

"What? Serth's here?" Ardent asked, alarmed. "How?"

A great squealing shriek tore open the air. Suddenly, the Naysayer stopped his frantic grabbing. "Aw, that ain't a happy noise," he said. And then the whole room tilted to one side.

"Everyone out!" Coll bellowed, waving them toward the door. Already the floor was littered with debris; Marrill danced over the deepening piles, jumping from one clear patch to another like she was on an obstacle course.

Behind her, Ardent and the Naysayer argued. "We have to leave!" Ardent shouted.

"So this is what it takes to get the hint?" the Naysayer snapped back. "You go first. I got some necessaries to pack." His hands were a blur of movement as he plucked various items from the floor and the few shelves that remained intact.

Marrill stared back at the two as Fin grabbed her hand and dragged her onward. "This way!" he called. He tugged her through the chaos as though he were back in the Khaznot Quay, finding a path through the crowded streets.

But Marrill couldn't go, not yet. "We have to save him!" She pulled free and ran back to the lumbering Naysayer. Ardent already had one scaly arm. She grabbed another, ducking to avoid a massive multicolored prizmorb that crashed down from the ceiling.

Coll and Fin joined them, and together they tugged against the big creature, who struggled to reach for his things as they fought him.

Another shriek of metal sounded, wrenching through Marrill's teeth. The tower floor slanted more steeply, and something that looked suspiciously like Fin's description of a "gorgon globule" rolled to one side. A trio of prediction-predictors bounced past them and out the downward-tilted window. Marrill could just make them out, plummeting through space to the ground below.

"All right already!" the Naysayer bellowed. "Let's get out of here!"

As one, they cleared the hallway and kept running. Outside, the frigid air hit Marrill like something physical, freezing her to the core. That wasn't the only thing causing her breath to tighten, though. Below them the ice-crusted tower cracked and groaned. Huge chunks of it broke free and crashed to the ground. If the staircase had seemed tenuous before, it was downright lethal now, with large sections of it missing entirely.

Through one of the holes it left behind, Marrill caught sight of the thick dark cord of the Neatline, pulling upward at Serth's command. As she watched, it snapped free, whipping cleanly out from under the tower like a tablecloth being pulled away by a magician. It slung toward Serth as if it were an overstretched rubber band. The dark wizard twirled it twice, each time causing it to shrink until it was small enough to fit around his wrist.

She gulped. The Neatline was gone. There was no way the tower would remain standing much longer. And they had about zero chance of making it down all those stairs before it collapsed entirely. Marrill's heart sank into her stomach and twisted tight.

Just then, Fin shoved something into her hands. It was broad and flat and familiar. It looked, she realized, like a cookie sheet. She glanced at him quizzically, and he smiled, a mischievous glint in his eye.

A moment later, he dropped to the ground, his own baking sheet beneath him, and rocketed off down the icy stairs, using the rectangle of metal as a sled. A series of frozen Ws and Os clattered against the steps behind him as he banked around a tight corner.

Marrill didn't have time to think; sledding down the tower might be dangerous, but staying would be fatal. She leapt onto the little metal sheet, her heart hammering against her ribs as she started sliding forward.

In moments, she was flying.

Debris dropped down from all sides as the sheet picked up speed. Knuckles pressed white against the front of her makeshift sled, Marrill gave silent thanks to her mother for forcing her to go tobogganing down that mountain in the Andes a few years ago. The feel of it came back, slowly.

She remembered
how to use the lean
of her body to take the curves,
    how to balance to keep from toppling to one side.
        Because here,
        there were no sides
            to topple onto.
The stairs zipped away beneath her.
The sled   skipped

            over gaps, and rocketed around tight corners.
She was going so fast she felt almost out of control;
    the sensation terrified her and thrilled her.
        Through a gap, she could see Fin,
            already halfway down
            body tightly tucked
            against the wind
            arms steady
            head
            bowed.
Just then, a great *SNAP!* echoed from above, loud like

the shattering ice mountains, sending waves of vibrations down the tower. She dared a look back, even as she struggled to maintain balance.

Not far behind her, Coll hunkered over his own sled, a round brass bowl barely big enough to contain him. His face was scrunched tightly in concentration, and a string of unintelligible symbols trailed from his mouth.

Lagging a ways back, Ardent and the Naysayer shared what might have been a door. Ardent's cap snapped like a wind sock, and a rain of junk flew from the Naysayer's arms.

Behind them, the tip of the tower,
the improbable, odd-angled tip of the tower, snapped

free

and

crashed to the plain below.

A few minutes of delay, Marrill realized, and they all would have still been inside it.

She bit her lip and focused. All around her, the tower was falling apart. She let out a frozen shriek when the staircase dropped suddenly. Her pulse raced as it stabilized.

One more twist, one more turn.
A grand piano fell through the air
beside her, like something
from an old-time cartoon show.
Another twist, another slide.

The ground came out of nowhere, it seemed. She skidded across it, her lips pressed firmly shut to keep her scream inside.

Momentum carried her out into the icy field, trailing in Fin's wake. All around, the landscape shifted and cracked, and before she knew what was happening, a giant chasm opened up in the ice just ahead of them. Fin yanked hard on the front of his makeshift sled, grabbing just enough air to launch across the gap.

But it was widening too rapidly for Marrill to follow. She banked as sharply as she could to the left, digging her heels against the snow to slow down. Rolling to the side, she let the cookie sheet continue without her. Coll skidded to a stop beside her, his bowl spinning wildly like a top.

A second later, Ardent and the Naysayer flew past with no signs of slowing. She tried to cry out a warning about the crevasse, but the words froze and fell like blocks of ice. Ardent was able to roll free, but the creature continued to career toward the gaping maw. He hit the edge and catapulted through the air, the wooden door flying after.

It was perhaps one of the most ungainly things Marrill had ever seen. All four of his arms whirled uselessly, junk he'd salvaged from his tower trailing out behind him. His thick tail swung from side to side like Karnelius trying to right himself when falling.

There was no way he was going to make it across. Marrill cringed, unable to look away. Just when it seemed the edge of the cliff was out of his reach, the entire tower collapsed in a roaring crash that rolled past her with a physical force.

The shock reverberated through the ice, rocking both sides of the chasm back and forth just enough for the Naysayer to catch the lip of the far side. Marrill pushed to her feet, watching as Fin struggled to help the Naysayer to safety. Once they were both back on solid ice, Fin waved at her to signal he was okay. She began to wave back, then stopped.

Beyond Fin, over his shoulder, a sleek cutter lay moored beside the *Kraken*. And on her deck stood a man dressed in black. His face was as pale as the snow itself, and even from here, Marrill could make out tracks of dark tears down his cheeks.

Her stomach twisted in terrified shock. "Serth," she whispered, the word freezing into tiny letters that stuck to her numb lips. As though in response, the dark wizard raised one hand and beckoned.

Marrill waved at Fin frantically to warn him, but he didn't seem to understand. She spun toward Ardent for help.

The wizard had his own problem. Rose banked tight circles above him, a series of large frozen C A Ws dropping pointy Ws from her beak, like tiny daggers raining down on his head.

The wizard swiped at her, but she only cawed at him more. Flapping his hands wildly, he pulled out the scrap of parchment that the bird had first risen from, the one

Marrill had chased across the Khaznot Quay. Furiously, he attempted to bind the bird back on the page. But she just circled over him faster, cawing harder than ever.

Before Marrill or Coll could jump in to help, Rose dove straight for Ardent, her scribbled wings beating furiously in his face. He threw up his hands to protect himself and stumbled, thrown off balance by the surprise assault. He was so busy defending himself against her sharp talons that the scrap of paper flew free from his hands.

Quick as lightning, Rose snatched it from the air. Ardent lunged after the bird, Marrill and Coll running to help him. But Rose was too fast. With a quick peck of her pointed beak, she tore open the left seam of his robe along the shoulder, exposing what appeared to be a hidden pocket.

Odds and ends spilled everywhere. Including the rolled-up Face of the Map.

Marrill saw it before it happened. She dove for the Face, arms outstretched. But all she got was a mouth full of snowy ground and the wind knocked out of her. She stared at her hands.

They were empty.

Helpless panic rose in Marrill's throat as she watched Rose, her own paper-home in her beak and the Face in her talons, wing out across the icy wastes, straight for the frozen Stream.

Straight for Serth.

CHAPTER 35
A Matter of Scale

F in shook his head, unable to believe it. Rose had betrayed them. Serth had three parts of the Map now, and the only means of finding the Scale and the Legend. And once he got those, he'd destroy the Stream. There was no stopping him.

"Haw!" the Naysayer snorted. "Hope you didn't need that junk."

"Oh, cram a clam in it," Fin muttered. His hand strayed down toward his thief's bag. At least he still had the Key, he thought. As long as that was safe, they still had a hope.

His hand waved in empty space. "Wha—?" His thief's bag was gone! It must have come loose and skidded away when he crashed.

His eyes darted across the ice. Sure enough, there it was, across the ice field. Dangling from Stavik's fingers.

A single tear dripped from the Pirate King's eyes, freezing in the gaps between his scars. He opened his mouth and closed it, and a mass of letters plopped into the snow at his feet. Then he turned and headed for the *Black Dragon*.

"The Key!" Fin shouted, grabbing the Naysayer by one arm. His words slurred into slush, half-frozen. "We have to go after him!"

The Naysayer shrugged his four shoulders. "Speak for yourshelff—" He spat at the freezing letters, then yanked a handful of pebble-sized hope crystals from his pocket and cracked one open, tossing a second to Fin. Immediately, Fin felt warmer, both inside and out. "Yourself," the Naysayer finished. "*I* have to stay here and not care."

Fin scarcely spared the old grouch a glance. Invigorated by the hope crystal, he looked over to where Marrill stood waving on the other side of the widening fissure. "I'm on it!" he called to her. Then he scampered over the ice after Stavik, pausing only a second to read the letters trailed across the snow.

HEY BLOOD, they read. SO SORRY TO SEE

YOU HERE. SO SO SORRY. Fin's chest shook, ever so slightly. This is what it took for the Pirate King to remember him—dark magic in a crumbling world.

"No trub," Fin muttered, steeling his nerve. "I'm on it." He cracked his knuckles and braced himself for the sprint to the *Dragon*.

Just then, the boom of cracking ice sounded all around. The ground shifted beneath Fin's feet, casting him off balance. "Not again!" he whined. Nearby, a large mountain began to crumble, sending deep fissures racing along the ice. One of them split the ground right next to him into a bottomless black chasm.

"Ah, fer crackin' creepers," the Naysayer moaned behind him. Fin stumbled, waving his arms to maintain his balance. Without the Neatline to hold the Naysayer's little kingdom together, the chaos of the CrystalShadow Wastes had moved in once more.

Ahead, Stavik closed in on the pirate ship. There wasn't a second to lose. Fin took off sprinting. The ground shuddered, forcing him to dodge chasms and ice spikes thrusting up from nowhere. Just as he thought he'd make it for sure, a shelf of ice pushed up in front of him, catching his foot and sending him sprawling. His hope crystal skittered out of reach.

Fin struggled to his knees. Stavik had already reached the *Dragon*. He looked back, and their eyes met, for just a second.

"I've lost," Fin whispered. The words froze solid and dropped into the snow in front of him. He couldn't believe it.

And then, out of the blue, another wave of hope surged through him. "What kinda no-good-fer-what-have-ya steals a man's Neatline and leaves him for freezer burn, huh?" the Naysayer grumbled to himself. A blue hope crystal shone like a torch in his hands.

"How'd you catch up?" Fin breathed.

The Naysayer looked down. One eye twitched slightly in surprise as he caught sight of Fin. "Oh," he muttered. "Great, so they're littering my nice clean snow with urchins now, too?"

Nearby, a mountain fractured and collapsed inward, sending out a jolt that rattled Fin's teeth and caused everything around them to shudder. The rumble grew louder and louder and louder. The ground shook with violent fury. Cracks split the ice like a spider web, widening into giant, bottomless rifts.

Fin leapt to his feet. "Seriously, how'd you catch up so fast?" he demanded.

The old lizard held up a huge plank of wood he'd been trailing behind him. "Found my doorsled," he said. "And no, you can't borrow it."

Then, with an enormous *BA-RUUUM!* the whole world seemed to shatter. Behind them, the ice rose up, and in front of them it dropped, turning the once flat ground into a sudden hillside.

Fin staggered. A stream of his own frozen **O**s and **W**s smacked him in the face as he struggled for footing. The Naysayer reeled, arms flying. The door hit the ground and started sliding. "Fine, get on!" the Naysayer shouted, heaving his bulk onto it.

Fin launched himself through the air as they slid away. He grabbed the Naysayer's back and hugged himself to it, ignoring the distinct musky odor that permeated the old beast.

And then they were flying, whizzing toward the *Dragon* at breakneck speed. Together, they skidded down the newly formed mountain, the Naysayer leaning from side to side to carve a path between the widening crevasses. The makeshift sled gained speed until the frozen wind whipped at Fin's face, turning his hair to icicles.

"Well, thanks for coming over," the Naysayer grunted. "All that not-dying sure was gettin' old until you lot stopped in. But hey, who can blame ya? When I look back on it, the place really wasn't all that well marked."

Warmth from the hope crystal filtered back at Fin as the Naysayer continued grumping. Suddenly, his lost thief's bag, the crumbling Wastes, even the fact that Rose had stolen the Map pieces and taken them to Serth—none of it seemed overwhelming. He laughed out loud with joy. They were going to make it after all!

Up ahead, the *Dragon* began pulling off, ribbons of snow and frost churning in her wake. The broken edge of the ice field sheered up behind her like a ramp. "Hold on!" the Naysayer called. Fin gulped.

They hit the edge of the ice field at full speed. The sled launched into the air, and this time they were flying for real. The doorsled fell away. The side of the ship loomed before them. Fin couldn't tell where his scream ended and the Naysayer's began.

And then he smacked into the thick hull, knocking the air out of his lungs. He clawed at the wooden planks instinctively, grabbing for holds. With one hand, he caught the rim of a porthole. One foot smashed against something rough but spongy.

"Watch it, Scooter!" the Naysayer grunted.

"Sorry," Fin muttered, stepping off the lizard's head. Below him, the Naysayer was a huge lump of debris clinging to the hull with three hands, the fourth still gripping a hope crystal. Random junk dangled from him, jangling in the air.

Fin scrabbled up the side of the ship, checking every now and then to make sure the Naysayer was still latched on behind him. He couldn't help feeling a good bit of déjà vu; he was really starting to become an expert at ship scaling.

When he reached the top, he catapulted himself over the railing and onto the main deck. All around him, pirates rushed about, bringing the ship to full sail. He looked for Stavik. Up toward the bow, the dragon leather gleamed in the midnight lights.

In moments, Fin crossed the ship, careful not to call attention to himself, and slipped directly behind the Pirate King. He took a deep breath and readied his pickpocketing fingers. Then he leapt forward and snatched his thief's bag from Stavik's hands.

"Oh, oh no," Stavik muttered, turning. "Oh, blood, no."

Fin smiled. "Don't worry, old son," he said. "I'll make sure you get your cut at the end of the day!" He made to race for the stern.

"Sorry, mate," another pirate said, stepping in front of him. It was old Billy Bulb, his giant nose bright red from blowing it. The other pirates all seemed to hear him at the same time. They dropped their tasks and advanced on Fin as one.

For a second, just a second, Fin panicked. He looked around for help: for Marrill, for Ardent, the Naysayer, anyone. Then he shook his head, clearing the cobwebs. He could do this.

This was a job now. He'd started it and he needed to finish it. He mustered a grin and dove into his trademark roll.

He'd just cleared the first line of pirates when the sorrow hit him. It was a physical thing, like the roaring thunder, the gusting wind. He'd forgotten how strong it could be, what it was like. He nearly collapsed. A tear formed at the edge of his eye.

"The time is nearly come."

Fin knew that terrible voice. Taking a deep breath, he

forced himself to face it. At the bow of the ship, just beyond Stavik, the Meressian Oracle stood. Serth. The wind seemed to barely lick at the edges of his robes. "The Lost Sun is almost here, I fear."

All around him, the pirates burst into wails. Tears came faster, harder now than ever before. Fin swallowed.

"You came to give me my Key," Serth murmured. He wiped away a black tear from just beneath his eye. "I knew you would." Fin tried to shake his head no, but the effort suddenly felt like too much to manage.

"Now, where is the girl with wings?" the dark wizard asked the sky. "Wait, no, not yet... out of order, out of order! Not just yet." He clenched his jaw, pursing his lips tight and inhaling deep, as though trying to calm the madness clearly spinning through his head.

"Made it!" the Naysayer announced. Fin turned to see him hauling his huge body onto the deck. A forest of swords turned to meet him. "Aw, flippin' flippers," the Naysayer sighed, raising all four hands. The thieves closed in and stripped him of his junk.

Fin turned back to Serth. "No," he said. "I'm not giving you the Key."

Serth cocked his head to one side. "No?" His hands fluttered through the air. "Oh, Fin, Fin, Fin. I admire your spirit, I do. But you have no power to resist."

Another wave of anguish hit, dropping Fin to his knees. He struggled to look out across the crumbling Wastes. Towers of ice shattered and slid into nothing; chasms opened up, devouring whole mountains.

In the middle of that tide of icy destruction rocked the *Kraken*. She was falling behind them now, but he could see Ropebone Man swaying. He could make out figures running frantically around the deck, making her shipshape to leave.

"You won't get far, Serth," he managed through gritted teeth. "The *Kraken's* on your tail, and when she reaches us, you'll have a whole lot of angry wizard to deal with. If you thought he was scary before, wait until you see what he's like now that you've taken his crew."

Serth's head bobbed, and his chest shook with a sob. "Oh, Fin," he said. "If only he remembered you like I do."

An icy dagger of despair plunged into Fin's chest. It wouldn't have been so bad if it weren't so true.

He forced himself to stay calm. Marrill wouldn't forget him, he knew. And as long as she was there, the *Kraken* was still on his side.

"But to your point," the Oracle continued. He slipped one hand into his robe. When it came out again, he held a shiny metal pair of pincers. Fin recognized them; they were calipers, used to measure distance. He'd seen sailors use them on their nautical charts at the Quay.

"Your friends will not catch us here," Serth proclaimed. He held up the calipers and pulled the two arms apart just enough for the endpoints to catch the distance between the ships. Then he snapped them open, and the *Kraken*, the entire CrystalShadow Wastes, disappeared into the distance.

Fin's mouth dropped open. They'd just traveled miles out into the open Stream in the space of a heartbeat. It was impossible. And suddenly, he understood how the *Dragon* had managed to always stay right on their tail.

"Did you think I hadn't gathered any of the Map on my own?" Serth asked, his face a mask of sympathy. "No, no, no," he said. "I found the Scale to be the most useful part. For what use is it to know where to go if you can't ascertain the distance?"

Fin swallowed. Serth had more of the Map than any of them realized. And now, with the Key in Fin's bag, the Meressian Oracle was only one Map piece away from ending the world.

CHAPTER 36
A Ship Cast in Iron,
Her Crew Cut From Shadows

Marrill stumbled to a stop on the *Kraken*'s deck, eyes wide and mouth gaping. One minute they'd been closing in on the *Black Dragon*. The next, Serth's ship was gone, leaving only icy Stream in its place.

It took a few heartbeats for it to all sink in. But when it did, it hit Marrill hard. Tears burned the back of her throat. Serth had everything now: Rose, the Neatline, the Face. Even the Naysayer.

And, of course, he had Fin. Not only had he taken her only chance to get home, but he'd also kidnapped her friend. Even surrounded by the rest of the crew, Marrill suddenly felt very, very alone. It was like the chill of the Wastes had seeped inside of her, numbing everything.

In that moment, it all seemed hopeless. But then she felt something cold and soft falling against her cheeks and drifting around her shoulders. Glancing up, she found Karnelius, crouched on the yard of a mast and looking down at her. His frozen purrs drifted like snow, tiny ℝs floating on the breeze.

It felt strange and wondrous. It felt like magic. It *was* magic. And if Serth found the rest of the Map and opened the Gate, it would all disappear. The Stream would cease to exist. She'd never see her parents again. She'd lose Ardent and Coll and Fin—forever.

Marrill refused to let that happen. With renewed determination, she kicked frozen letters out of the way and headed aft.

Coll stood behind the giant wheel, his mouth set in a grim line. Next to him, Ardent flicked his fingers to create warmth. "Coll," he ordered the moment he could speak, "follow that ship!" He pointed toward where the Stream narrowed, snaking between two towering cliffs that had already begun to collapse. Marrill squinted her eyes. There was no hint of the *Dragon*.

"We already are," the captain shouted back.

Ardent waved his hands in exasperation. "Then belay the anchor or jib the trim sails or whatever you sailors do!"

"Huh?" Coll raised an eyebrow.

"Make it go faster!" Ardent cut his arms sharply through the air, pulling at the wind. "The Stream's at stake! Serth already has the fourth piece of the Map; this is our last chance to catch up with him before he finds the Legend and opens the Gate!"

The sails bellowed. The Ropebone Man stretched and bobbed, holding the cordage tight. Pirats darted through the rigging, making sure the knots stayed secure.

The *Kraken* picked up speed, hurtling toward the narrow gap in the cliffs that marked the edge of the CrystalShadow Wastes. With nowhere else to go, the Stream frothed and churned ahead of them where ice met water, chewing into a slushy mess.

A wave of panic rolled through Marrill as she mentally counted the Map pieces in her head. *Compass, Face, Neatline, Legend. That left…* "How do you know he has the Scale?" she asked.

Ardent paused, eyes scanning the rigging. "It was Rose betraying us that told me. I should have guessed when he was chasing us before, but I had so convinced myself we had the lead."

He licked his lips, hands now hauling through the air with fierce determination as wind filled the sails. "Rose seeks to unite the Map," he explained. "Why then leave us, and take *our* piece, unless Serth was closer to bringing the Map together? And that meant, of course, he had to have more than just the Neatline! That would give him two pieces to our one, if you don't count Rose herself, who *apparently* was always free to go."

He looked Marrill dead in the eye. Ice crusted in his beard. "With the Scale, he controls distance and size. Which certainly explains how he moves so quickly. We'll get it back, though, never fear." The words were meant to be reassuring, but his voice was filled with doubt.

Unsettled, Marrill stared at the frozen letters scattered across the deck, bits of conversations she'd had with Fin only recently. It didn't make sense that his words could still be here, trapped in ice, but that he—and the others' memory of him—was gone.

Her thought was interrupted by Coll's bellow. "Better find something to hold on to!" Marrill lunged toward one of the gunwales and wrapped her arms around it.

The ship careened, almost out of control. Ahead of them, the massive ice cliffs marking the end of the CrystalShadow Wastes crumbled toward each other. The space between them grew narrower with each second.

"We're not going to make it!" Marrill cried.

"Oh, posh," Ardent chided. He cut a hand toward one of the overhanging ice shelves behind them. With an ear-splitting rumble, a chunk easily four times the size of the

Kraken broke free and plummeted toward the half-frozen Stream.

It smashed into the slush behind them with a gigantic *SPLOOSH!* An enormous wave billowed up from the impact, taller than even the *Kraken*'s tallest mast. It roared toward the ship, threatening to crush them whole.

Marrill screamed. But Coll was ready. He twirled the wheel hard to the left and signaled for full sail. The *Kraken* lurched forward, racing just before the wave.

Suddenly, they were surfing, faster than they had ever gone before. Frozen letters went skidding across the deck.

As the cliffs collapsed into each other, the *Kraken* shot through the narrow gap, her railings scraping against the ice walls. She burst out the other side, the momentum of the wave practically throwing them across the Stream like a rock skipped along a lake.

But Marrill didn't have time to feel relief. Because ahead of them, the storm they'd evaded earlier, maybe the same storm they'd been dodging since she arrived on the Stream, loomed. And no matter how deadly that storm might be, this time there was no missing it.

Dark clouds licked at the sky. Lightning forked in jagged streaks toward the Stream's surface. And just at the edge, heading straight into the heart of the tempest, rode the *Black Dragon*.

They were close enough that Marrill could see figures

moving on deck. Serth was easy to spot at the bow, his black robes swirling around him. The Naysayer wasn't much harder to see; he was the big blue lump in a cargo net being hoisted into the air.

But it took her a moment to find the smallest figure, the one just in front of Serth, flanked by a crowd of armed pirates.

Fin!

Marrill's stomach squeezed tight. "He's still alive—we have to save him!" she shouted.

Ardent squinted across the Stream. "They seem to have strung him up in some sort of netting."

"Not the Naysayer," she said. "Though we can save him, too. Coll, can you catch them?" she asked, her skin beginning to tingle.

The storm's winds whipped furiously around them as Coll eyeballed the distance between the ships. "It'll be close—"

He was cut short when a bolt of lightning struck the mast, igniting the sky in a brilliant shower of multicolored sparks. Marrill jumped, her heart skipping, then thundering against her ribs. Above, the black clouds spread out like the jaws of an enormous beast, opening up to swallow them whole.

"That lightning struck red," Coll warned. Marrill didn't miss the look he shot Ardent, nor the frown that creased the wizard's forehead.

"The Iron Ship," Marrill breathed. She remembered the way the captain had trembled the last time they passed so close to the storm. If Coll was afraid of the Iron Ship, that meant she should be terrified. "Well, at least Serth is scared of it," she offered.

Coll's answer came short and brusque. "That's because he's smart."

Marrill swallowed. A tight coil of worry knotted in her stomach. She'd seen Coll face tempest, storm wind, and now a tidal wave and never once show much concern. But now his lips were pressed tight, the muscles along his jaw clenching.

With one hand, he pointed. "She comes," was all he said.

Marrill followed his finger. Another ship lay off the port side, one like no ship Marrill had ever before seen. She was fast and low against the water, and heading straight toward them. Her sails were gray, chain mail near invisible against the storm. Her hull was deep and black, with a streak of ruddy crimson just above the waterline, as if it were blood from the wound she slashed through the water.

From this distance, the men along her rails were nothing but dark smudges against a monolith of metal. They swarmed over the ship, an army of shadows. All except one man, lone at her bow. Her Master.

The Master of the Iron Ship. He stood with his feet spread to brace against the waves. Iron armor cloaked him from head to foot, dull black with gleaming edges. Just the sight of him made Marrill quake with fear.

Another streak of scarlet ripped through the sky, so close she could almost taste it, metallic like after biting your cheek. It melted into dread, running down her throat.

"Looks like they're trying to cut us off," she warned.

"Or ram us." Coll lifted a shoulder. "Ardent," he called, "a little help here?"

The wizard moved forward and swept his hand toward the Iron Ship. "Let's see how she does without sails." As he said the words, the sails on the other ship burst into a flurry of confetti. She immediately floundered.

He turned to face them. "That worked well, now didn't it?"

With his back turned, he didn't see the confetti whirl up as if in a tornado. In the blink of an eye, the sails had reknit themselves into tight chain mail. The Iron Ship jumped to life, gaining speed faster than before.

At her bow, a haze of red began to glow between the Master's outstretched hands. The storm swirled around him, dark clouds growling and churning. A smell filled the air like the moment a match is struck, but before the flame appears. Marrill could feel the crackle of energy from here. "Um, Ardent?" She pointed.

Ardent's smile died on his lips.

With a booming clap, the Master concentrated the light into a solid ball and thrust it heavenward. Red lightning arced overhead, igniting the storm clouds. Flames danced across the sky, raining embers instead of raindrops.

The glowing sparks swirled in the wind, setting fire to the *Kraken*'s topsail. Marrill gasped, her heart leaping into her throat. Ardent surged forward, spreading his arms wide. His beard whipped in the gale while the hem of his robe rippled like liquid. He let loose a wave of energy that blanketed them all, transforming each ember into a puff of steam.

As Marrill drew a relieved breath, twin streams of frozen white light burst from Ardent's fingertips. A wide gash split the water as the blaze scorched through the storm toward the Iron Ship. It looked powerful enough to incinerate anything in its path. But when it struck the Master, it merely burst into a shower of sparks.

"Bear away before the wind!" Coll shouted, a thread of urgency underlying the command. The Ropebone Man tugged on the rigging, shifting the sails. The ship veered right, cutting through the thickening swells. They were giving up on following the *Dragon*.

"What's going on?" Marrill shouted over the deafening sound of thunder and energy.

Coll gripped the wheel, arms straining to maintain course. The *Kraken* shuddered each time Ardent deflected a blow from the Master, her deck bucking and tilting. Marrill grasped the railing to keep from falling.

"She's coming too fast!" Coll had to shout to be heard. "We have to keep distance...and hope Ardent wins."

"But Fin," Marrill whispered, watching the *Dragon* pull away from them. Over her masts a black smudge whirled, almost invisible against the dark of the storm. Rose. She caught a downdraft, tucking her scribbled wings against her body as she skimmed bare inches above the Stream waters toward the *Kraken*. When she neared, she soared up, across the deck and through the rigging, banking so tightly that she clipped the sleeve of Fin's thief's coat where it hung on the mizzenmast. It fell in a heap on the deck.

Furious, Marrill pulled one of the acorns she'd picked up from the Gibbering Grove from her pocket and hurled it at the bird as she winged past. "Traitor!" she cried. Hot tears burned her eyes as she snatched up Fin's coat and hugged it against her chest.

But her choked sob turned quickly to laughter as her fingers brushed across a string that dangled from one of its sleeves. Of course!

Afraid she'd second-guess her decision if she allowed herself to think about it, she shrugged out of her heavier jacket and slipped on Fin's coat. "I'm going after Fin!" she called, leaping onto the forecastle and sprinting to the bow.

When she hit the railing, she vaulted over it, legs pumping as she gained momentum and sprung onto the thin beam of the bowsprit. In seconds, she'd reached the tip. She pulled the strings to free the coat's wings and threw herself into the air with all her might.

Below, the hungry waves of the Pirate Stream reached for her, churning and slapping against each other. Rain plastered her hair against her cheeks, and the storm roared in her ears. For a moment, she felt too heavy, too ungainly. She couldn't stay up! Images of all the things they'd thrown into the Stream raced through her head in a slide show, every one of them transforming or disintegrating or bursting into flame.

Then a gust of wind pushed off the water, carrying her upward. She let out a whoop of terrified excitement. She was flying! *Truly* flying this time, not like being caught on the wind at the Khaznot Quay. She had wings! It felt *amazing*.

Of course, she quickly realized, that didn't mean she knew how to steer. A slash of rain sideswiped her, sending her spinning and dropping. She straightened out, then banked sharply toward the *Dragon*, against the wind the way she remembered Fin doing before. Serth's ship loomed, but Marrill was losing altitude fast. At this rate, she would crash straight into the side of it!

At the last minute, she twisted and barely cleared the railing. She tumbled to the deck, flopping across it in a series of ungainly somersaults.

When she came to a stop, she found herself on her hands and knees, facing a black robe patterned like the starry sky. A yawning, painful sorrow hit deep in her chest, sucking the air from her lungs, making her arms and legs grow weak.

Slowly, struggling against the grief, she lifted her head. The man standing over her was crying, black tears carving furrows down his cheeks.

"Hello, Marrill," the dark wizard, Serth, said. "You can't imagine how long I've been waiting for you."

CHAPTER 37
The Map to Show the Way

Fin jumped for Marrill. The pirates jumped faster. Rough hands pulled him away, and cold steel touched his back. Struggling only made it worse. The pirates weren't murderers, he knew. But that didn't mean they wouldn't use those daggers if he forced them.

A few feet away, Marrill cowered in Serth's shadow. Tears welled in her eyes, threatening to spill over. She winced as a streak of red lightning split the sky. The storm had closed in hard around them. Fin scoured the water, searching for traces of the *Kraken*. But everywhere he looked, the Stream was empty.

There was no sign of Ardent. They were on their own.

For a moment, the wall of hope he held up against Serth's crushing sorrow cracked. Despair leached through him. He clenched his teeth, struggling against it.

"Girl with wings," Serth said, cocking his head as he looked down at Marrill. She tried to crawl away from him, but one of the pirates hauled her up and pressed his dagger against her throat.

"Leave her alone!" Fin shouted.

"My Key," Serth replied, holding out a hand. Marrill squirmed in the pirate's arms, the dagger pressing tighter against her skin. Fin's mind raced as he clutched his thief's bag to his chest.

"Okay!" he said at last. "Okay, just let her go!"

With a sigh, he tossed the bag to Serth, who caught it in one hand. The pirate dropped his dagger, pushing Marrill over to Fin. Her shoulder bumped against his, and he felt something strange tugging at his hand. It took him a moment to realize that Marrill had laced her fingers through his. She was holding his hand! No one had ever done that before.

"Thanks," she said. A warm tide of comfort and reassurance flowed through him, fighting back the sorrow.

"Don't worry," he said. "He still needs the Legend before he can use the Map."

"'Key' is another word for the legend of a map, genius," said the Naysayer from his net overhead. "Strong work, though."

Fin's jaw dropped. He looked at Marrill. Her face wore the same shocked expression he knew was on his own. If the Key and the Legend were one and the same, Serth had everything he needed to end the world!

The dark wizard towered in front of them, his lips quivering into a smile. "Now all the pieces are in place at last," he breathed. From his black robes he pulled forth a roll of parchment.

Fin sucked in a breath, recognizing it.

"The Face," Marrill whispered.

Fin struggled against the pirates holding him, causing them to press their daggers firmer against his back. He could only watch in horror as Serth held the Face out and let it fall open.

"The Map to show the way!" he cried. "The Key to open the Gate! The Lost Sun of Dzannin will rise once more!"

Continents and islands bubbled to life along the surface of the Face, a well of ink spilling forth into the world. "Bring right form!" Serth cried before any could drip from the page. He slipped what looked like a rubber band from his wrist, hooking it around each of the Face's four corners.

The page blazed white. When the light faded, the Face, carefully bordered with the thick black Neatline, hung suspended in the air. From somewhere overhead, Rose cawed, shrill and loud, as she spun through the black storm clouds.

It sounded almost like she was screaming.

"We have to stop him," Fin urged. "He has all the pieces—he's going to put the Map together and figure out where the Gate is!"

Marrill's expression echoed the panic he felt. "I know! But what can we do?"

Fin chewed at his lip, stomach churning.

Serth either didn't hear them or didn't care. He pulled the elaborate pair of calipers from his robe, holding them high. "Bring right shape!" he shouted. He touched the tips of them to the corners of the Face, and it blazed in light once more.

The Map twisted and morphed, rotating and growing until it was twice as wide as Serth's spread arms and three times as tall. More and more worlds bloomed across it, rising to the surface and then falling away like bubbles boiling in a pot of water.

Marrill clutched at Fin's arm. "That must have been the Scale. All that's left is Rose and the Key!"

Fin's mind raced through their options. "Okay, things look bad. But he still has to get to it, right? Maybe if we figure out where it is, we can beat him there!"

Serth raised his arms to the sky. Red lightning broke through the dark clouds. "Bring orientation!" he commanded. Overhead, Rose let out a piercing cry. Her scribbled wings beat against the gale of the storm. She circled above the *Dragon* twice, then dove straight toward the Map, showing no signs of slowing.

"Rose, no!" Marrill gasped.

Even after her betrayal, Fin felt a pang of fear, hoping against hope that whatever happened, Rose would be okay.

She struck the Map in a blast of blinding light. It hit them like a concussion, causing the pirates to stagger back. When the white spots cleared from Fin's eyes, Rose was gone.

Struggling to bite back his emotions, Fin tugged Marrill free from the stunned pirates. But there was nowhere to go. Because towering in front of them where the Map once was, a pair of massive doors now stood. They pulsed and glowed, almost humming with power. Fin stumbled, Marrill's hand falling from his grasp.

"It is done!" Serth shrieked, black tears flooding his eyes. "It is time!" Lightning crashed across the bow. Rain broke from the clouds, coursing down on them in frigid gusts.

"Oh no!" Marrill yelled over the storm. Even through the rain, her eyes held a sheen of despair. "The Map isn't showing Serth how to find the Gate...." Her voice broke.

Fin's shoulders sagged. Suddenly, he understood what he was looking at. "The Map *is* the Gate," he finished for her.

It felt like the entire world had fallen out from underneath him. Serth had found the Gate. Things were way worse than Fin had realized.

"You kids take your time," the Naysayer called from above them. "Me an' the oncoming apocalypse will just hang out and get to know each other while we wait."

Fin shook his head, clearing his thoughts. "We'll get you down soon!" he called back to the Naysayer.

Because this wasn't over. After all, a good thief *always* had a backup plan.

"You be sure to let me know whenabouts," the creature grumped. "I've got an incredibly busy day of dangling here waiting to die already scheduled."

Marrill looked at Fin with questioning eyes. "Trust me," he told her. Then, without waiting for her to respond, he stepped forward.

"Hey, Serth!" he shouted. A smile broke across his face as he reached into his pocket and drew out the ruby Key. It glowed in the flashing light, sucking in the red of the lightning. "Looking for this?"

The thieves stepped back, murmuring in awe. Marrill gasped. Fin winked at her. "Thing about a thief's bag," he told her, "is you can get stuff out of them *really* quickly."

Serth turned his head slowly, awkwardly toward them. His eyes locked on the ruby key. Fin couldn't name the emotion that crossed Serth's features, but one thing was clear: It wasn't happiness.

The dark wizard stalked across the deck, headed straight for them. A pang of heartache ripped through Fin, but he kept his calm. Next to him, Marrill let out a whimper. Fin gripped the Key tighter and stepped over to the railing of the ship.

Serth stopped. His fingers fluttered, and his lips moved without noise, talking to no one. "Yes," he said at last. "You're right, of course. Look at me, skipping ahead. We're not quite there, are we? Not quite. Can't skip, can't skip."

"He's *seriously* crazy," Marrill breathed.

Fin nodded. He couldn't agree more. He held his arm out toward the Stream.

Serth let out a high-pitched cry. "Is this your last stand?" he barked. "Is this the bold move that will end it? No, no, I don't think so, Fin. I don't think so."

Fin took a deep breath. To keep Serth from opening the Gate, he had to destroy the Key. But now he knew the Key *was* the Legend—it was part of the Map. And if he destroyed it, he would never be able use the Map. Never be able to find his mother. His hand shook as he wrestled with the decision.

And Marrill, he realized, would be giving up much, much more. He looked over at her. "Marrill," he said, "this is your choice, at least as much as it is mine. I can't make it alone."

CHAPTER 38
The Key to Open the Gate

Marrill stared at the ruby Key; it seemed to hum with strange energy. If Fin let go, it would fall overboard, into the Pirate Stream. It would be destroyed forever. Taking along with it her only way home.

She closed her eyes and pictured her parents. She imagined what it would be like to see them again, to feel their arms around her. She wanted to believe such a thing was still possible. She *had* to believe it.

Taking a deep breath, she opened her eyes. "I don't know,"

she told Fin, her chin quivering. "I don't know what to do!" The look on his face told her he didn't either.

"Well, don't drop it," Serth said. For once, his voice was dead flat. "That key opens my very favorite cabinet."

"What?" Marrill and Fin asked as one.

Serth lifted Fin's thief's bag and slipped one hand inside, his lips twisting into an awful smile. Out from it, he pulled a palm-sized crystal star shaped just like a warped image of the sun. Marrill recognized it; it was the same shape as the figurehead on the strange ship that sank when they'd arrived at the Khaznot Quay.

"The Key to open the Gate!" Serth cried.

"Aww, blisterwinds," Fin groaned beside her. "It's the doorknob." With a grunt of frustration, he spiked the ruby key against the deck.

"What?" Marrill asked. "What are you doing?"

"'*Break* the safe to get the Key.' That's what Serth wrote in the letter he sent. And then I pried that doorknob off the safe in the Meressian ship, and the whole place started coming down, and I just *assumed* it was because I'd gotten the ruby key...."

Marrill's shoulders dropped. "When the doorknob was the real Key all along," she finished.

"Bad miss on that one, kiddo," the Naysayer sighed from his net. And for once Marrill wasn't sure he was being sarcastic.

Serth tossed aside Fin's thief's bag and held the crystal

star aloft. "Behold!" he cried to the heavens. Red lightning split the sky. Marrill's chest ached so fiercely she could hardly breathe. All around them, the pirates fell to their knees, wailing and sobbing.

"The Map to show the way!" he cried. "The Key to open the Gate!" He turned toward the glowing Gate, Key clutched firmly in hand. "The Lost Sun of Dzannin will rise," Serth proclaimed, "this very day!"

Fin gulped. "Did I already say 'blisterwinds'?"

Marrill gripped Fin's hand as anguish swept through her in waves. Fin doubled over beside her. An image of her mother flashed before her eyes, and her father. Karnelius and the Hatch brothers, Ardent and Coll, everything, everywhere—even that stupid Naysayer.

It was all going to end.

Serth stepped toward the gates, fit the sun-shaped key into the lock. Its glowing rays lengthened into handles. He grasped them and pulled.

A rumble sounded, louder than the thunder, like the scraping of stone against massive, heavy stone. And then the Gate—the Map—began to crack open.

"Witness," Serth screamed as he heaved against the Gate, wrenching the doors apart inch by inch, "as the Lost Sun of Dzannin dawns once more!" Shafts of burning light stabbed out through the widening gap, searing the air and destroying anything in their path. One struck the mainmast of the *Dragon*, shattering it to splinters. Another punched a hole through her hull; still another sheared the railing on the port side.

The ship rocked with the blows. Debris rained down around them. Marrill ducked and ran aft, throwing an arm up to protect herself. "It's tearing the ship apart!" she shouted. Next to her, Fin leapt to one side, then the other, barely avoiding the white-hot beams.

Serth stood in the middle of it all, the light a halo around him. But if it affected the dark wizard, he neither noticed nor cared. "Behold the first light of morning!" he screeched. "Behold the last light of evening!"

Desperately, Marrill scanned the Stream for Ardent, hoping that maybe he'd come swooping in at the last minute to save the world. But he was nowhere to be found. For all she knew, the Iron Ship had caught the *Kraken* and sunk her. Whatever had happened, Ardent wasn't coming to save them.

"We have to stop him!" Marrill cried. "There's got to be something we can use!" She dug through Fin's coat, pulling out a slingshot, three different pocket watches, and a tangle of wires. Frustrated, she yanked the jacket off and thrust it at him. "Couldn't you have stolen something useful?"

Fin snatched his coat and shoved his arms into it. "If only I'd thought to swipe the 'Defeat Evil Wizard' kit from the Naysayer's tower," he sniped back. From the other end of the ship, Serth wailed, prying the Gate open even farther.

"There has to be something!" Marrill frantically turned

from Fin's pockets to her own. A handful of the acorns she'd picked from the Gibbering Grove tumbled to the deck. She kicked them away in frustration. "Useless."

"Watch out!" Fin shouted, shoving her out of the way of a burning shaft of light. She stumbled backward. Something snagged her ankle, sending her flailing to the deck.

Marrill's head rang from the impact. She looked down, disoriented, to find a thin tendril of green twisting its way up her leg, ear-shaped leaves unfolding along its length. A rumor vine had taken root on the deck.

A rumor vine, she thought. *Disoriented*. It reminded her of Ardent, stumbling around in the Gibbering Grove, too messed up by the rumor vines to conjure more than a handful of snowflakes. If only they could do that to Serth...

That was it!

"Fin," Marrill cried. "The rumors! They discombubble..." She paused. "Dismobob...confuse wizards!"

Fin cocked his head. Then a grin spread across his face as understanding hit him. "And the acorns grow rumor vines! Marrill, you're a genius!" he cried. "Quick, hand them over!" He swiped his slingshot from the deck and snatched the acorns from the air as she tossed them at him. "I'll draw Serth's attention. You figure out how to get the Map!"

Marrill took a deep breath, steeling herself. Serth struggled with the Gate at the *Dragon*'s bow, and the deck in between was covered with pirates shrieking and wailing while the rays of the Lost Sun blazed. It would be tough to even get close without being fried. But she had to try. "Do it," she said. Fin raised the slingshot, readying an acorn. "But be careful," she added.

He nodded. "You too."

Fin let his first acorn fly. It struck the evil wizard's robes and froze on impact before dropping to the deck. Marrill gulped, half-frozen herself in a runner's stance. Serth didn't even seem to notice.

Then the acorn's frosted shell cracked open. The tip of a vine burst free, one end burying itself in the wood of the deck and the other snagging the hem of Serth's robes, ignoring the frost that struggled to contain it. Apparently, the acorns from the Gibbering Grove weren't particular about where they needed to be planted; it seemed a good rumor could spring up almost anywhere.

"It's working—go, go!" Fin shouted, letting loose three more acorns in quick succession. One of them hit a light ray and flashed out of existence in a puff, but the others found their target and began growing.

That was Marrill's cue. She took off across the deck, sprinting low and weaving between shafts of burning light and panicked pirates. Ahead of her, the evil wizard kicked against the thicket springing to life around him, but he still refused to let go of the Gate.

Out of order, Marrill thought. *He gets confused when things are out of order.* She skidded behind one of the masts and cupped her hands around her mouth. "Hey!" she yelled. "I heard that the Lost Sun rises, *then* the Gate opens, then there's a fire at the Gibbering Grove, but *before* that, Fin and I get here on wings!" It didn't take long for the vines to take up the chorus, whispering

sunthengatefiregrovegethereonwings

"No!" Serth shrieked. "The scenes must come in order! Children, Gate, Grove—no, Grove, Gate, Children...no! No!" The Oracle howled in rage as a sea of whispers welled up around him. "Quiet, I must have quiet!" He clawed at the vines, releasing the doors at last as he staggered backward.

Without Serth holding them, the great doors began to fall shut, drowning out some of the deadly beams. Fin followed her lead, firing more acorns and shouting, "Serth, doesn't this *start* when I give you the Key?" Rain poured across the deck in gusts, hissing into steam where it hit the Lost Sun's rays.

Marrill knew her opportunity when she saw it. She bolted from behind the mast and raced toward the bow. But the closer she got to Serth, the more hopeless it all seemed. It was impossible. She could never beat him, not here. She could never close the Gate on her own.

"The Lost Son of Dzannin will rise!" the evil wizard screeched, tearing at the vines that choked him. "The scenes out of order will be set right!"

A deep, aching sadness welled inside Marrill, so intense

she thought her chest might crack open. She stumbled, slipped to her knees. Her fingers clawed against the soaked deck. She had to make it. She had to. But it was so, so hard to fight....

"Hey, kid!" a rough voice shouted from behind her. It took most of Marrill's will to look back. Just in time to see the Naysayer sway in his netting, then toss something high with a flick of his wrist.

A bright blue crystal flipped end over end through the rain-soaked air and smashed into the deck just beside her. Warmth instantly filled her, burning away the doubts. "Yer welcome," the Naysayer called. "Now get back to making sure I don't die, would ya?"

"Got it!" Marrill jumped to her feet as the hopeful heat infused her. The Gate had nearly fallen shut, but it still pulsed with power, creating an odd hum that vibrated through her teeth as she reached for the sun-shaped handles jutting out from it. The Key seared her skin as she touched it, burning into her palm. In her head, she could hear her mother's voice, telling her to be brave. Telling her she could do this.

She braced one foot against the Gate, slamming it closed, and pulled against the crystal with all her might. Before her, the doorway flickered and warped, the last bits of light dying. From a distance, she heard Fin calling her name—a warning.

But it was too late. A jolt of unbearable cold lanced through her back, searing her straight through to the core.

It was like the chill of the CrystalShadow Wastes, concentrated in the swoop of one pale hand.

"Release the Key," Serth hissed, his fingers clutching her shoulder. The few remaining vines still clinging to his robes echoed everything:

releasethekeyreleasethekey

A tremor started deep inside Marrill, forcing its way outward. She could feel the tide of sorrow threatening. Rain pounded around them, thunder roaring.

Fin shouted for her. But he was too far away.

She couldn't move. Couldn't call for help. Could only stand helplessly as her body went numb. First her lips. Then her shoulders, her arms, her wrists. Her fingers trembled just to keep hold of the Key. Already, she could feel it slipping from her grasp.

"Let go, child," Serth whispered, turning her toward him. His lips quivered red against pale skin. His wild eyes gleamed fever bright, tears like ink running down to his jawline.

Out the corner of one eye, she saw Fin grappling with a band of pirates, the slingshot torn from his hands. He was caught. *She* was caught.

Nothing they could do would stop Serth. She knew it now. The Prophecy *would* be fulfilled. He *would* open the Gate. The world *would* end. Sorrow yawned inside her, a gaping pit of misery, and she could do nothing but stare into it.

Just as she teetered on the edge of giving in, something over Serth's shoulder caught her attention. Something large and dark, crashing through the storm: a ship!

The *Kraken* rode into view, cresting a froth-tipped wave. Her bow towered over the *Dragon*, so close that Marrill could practically count the barnacles waving their little feathers at her from the looming hull.

The ship was moments away from ramming them.

And there, on the tip of the bowsprit, crouched an orange cat, tail twitching to pounce. Marrill's eyes widened in panic, drowning out Serth's sorrow.

No! Her mouth formed the word soundlessly.

At the last possible second, the *Kraken* surfed to one side, missing the *Dragon* by inches. And that was the moment Karnelius chose to launch himself.

No one had ever accused Karny of being a graceful creature. But today, he had all the elegance of a bird in flight as he leapt from the bowsprit, claws outstretched. Landing on all four feet, right on the back of Serth's head.

Serth roared, flailing to dislodge the furious beast. Ice clustered in Karny's fur, clinging to his thick coat. His claws raked across the evil wizard's scalp.

Marrill sucked in lungfuls of air, freed from Serth's frozen grasp. "Karny!" she cried. But that was all she managed.

Because just then, the Iron Ship burst into view, coming hard. And unlike the *Kraken*, she wasn't turning.

Marrill knew what she had to do.

Time seemed to slow around her, almost like a wizard's spell. She could feel each breath as she took it, pulling in, flowing out.

She spun, reaching for the Key.

Inhale.

Her fingers slipped between each of the crystal sun's rays.

Exhale.

Serth's voice bellowed, but the sound came from far, far away.

Inhale.

In front of her, the Gate began to shift and change, folding in on itself. Somewhere behind her, pirates shrieked and timbers shuddered. The Iron Ship striking the *Dragon*.

A spiral of ink swirled across the blank parchment of the Map. Marrill tugged, hard. The ink became a series of numbers, repeated over and over, running down the page.

Exhale.

Using all of her might, Marrill twisted the Key and wrenched it free. There was a loud tearing sound, like the world ripping apart. She felt herself being thrown through the air. And then darkness.

CHAPTER 39
That Which Was Foretold

Rough hands gripped Fin from every side. It was over; the pirates had him. And then, a second later, the Iron Ship tore through the *Dragon*.

Wood splintered. Metal shrieked. All around, the pirates fell back, screaming. Fin crashed to his knees. The deck buckled under him, sending him sliding backward to slam hard against one of the masts. Anything not lashed down went flying, and Fin just barely snagged his thief's bag as it went skidding past.

Groaning, he rolled to his side and looked to the source of the crash. The Iron Ship had sliced straight through the stern of the *Dragon*, cutting her almost in half. The two ships were helplessly tangled now, the *Dragon* listing hard as she took on more and more Stream water.

Out from the Iron Ship, her shadow crew poured, swarming the *Dragon*'s deck. They carried blades and axes and maces forged from darkness; their battle cry sounded like the hiss of a cobra in the buzz of a swarm of bees. The pirates, regrouping, rushed to meet them.

In moments, the deck of the *Dragon* was a full-blown battleground. Behind it all, an armor-clad figure cast arcs of red lightning from the Iron Ship's bow. They were met with equally violent blasts of white; Ardent, on the circling *Kraken*, keeping the Master occupied.

Fin pushed himself to his knees, hunting for Marrill through the chaos. His gut clenched when he found her. She was slumped limp against the railing by the bow, her eyes closed, head lolling to the side. Karny was rubbing up against her slumped body. Next to them, the crystal Key wobbled in a slow circle.

He called out her name, but she didn't move.

The collision had thrown Serth to the deck, but already he was struggling to stand, tearing away the last of the rumor vines still tangling him. In one hand, he held the rolled-up Map. And he was headed straight for the Key.

A sea of pirates and shadow soldiers separated Fin from

Marrill, but that didn't matter. His friend needed him. And he hadn't become the Master Thief of the Khaznot Quay without learning how to escape from a few precarious situations.

He stepped forward, knives at the ready. Stavik reared up before him, eyes bright with tears as he raised his dagger. Fin gulped.

But before either could make a move, a loud "Incoming!" sounded above them and a large heap fell onto the Pirate King, slamming him to the deck.

"I said 'incoming.' What're ya, deaf?" the Naysayer snapped, leaning down to nab Stavik's dagger and cut himself free from the remains of his netting.

"Thanks," Fin said. "And thanks for the lift!" He leapt onto the Naysayer's shoulder, using it as a launching pad to fling himself into the air. Shadow soldiers swiped at him, but he twisted easily out of their reach.

He hit the deck hard, his feet slipping on the rain-sodden wood. "Hold on, Marrill!" he called, not even sure she could hear him.

He was still too far away. Serth nearly had the Key. The evil Oracle shouted in triumph as he bent to snatch it.

But Karnelius got there first. In a blur of orange, he darted out from behind Marrill's legs, pouncing toward the crystalline star. He was a cat after a mouse, determined to catch his quarry, slapping it across the deck between his paws.

Serth let out a piercing wail, the sound like ice daggers

in Fin's ears. The pirates wailed with him, sorrow cutting across the ship.

The Key gleamed, bright even through the wind and the rain, bright as a burning hope crystal. Bright as the waters of the Stream. It skittered across the deck, splashing through puddles, Karnelius not far behind.

Fin dove, hand outstretched. He landed hard on his hip and slid across the now-tilting planks, water spraying into his face. He was just barely able to hook one of the Key's rays with his fingers and snatch it up into his hand.

"Nice job, Karny," Fin said as he gave the wet cat a sodden pat on his head. In return, Karnelius hissed and swiped at him, tail twitching angrily.

Victorious, Fin rolled to his feet and held the Key aloft. "Okay, this time, I *know* you're looking for this," he announced to Serth. But then his smile fell. Because Serth stood firm at the very tip of the bow, Marrill clutched in front of him. She shivered against her captor, her face already turning deadly white, lips a frightening shade of blue.

The Oracle's mouth split in an awful grin as the rain eased around them. His long black fingernails glistened dark against the white of Marrill's cheek. All across the deck, the cries of battle sounded against the thunder.

"Yessss," Serth hissed. "*This* is your last stand, Fin. *The Key for the girl.* No way out but through the Gate. It is fated. You cannot fight it."

Marrill squirmed against Serth's grip, glaring at Fin

and shaking her head no. "Don't give it to him," she begged through chattering teeth. "Get it out of here, go!"

But Fin wasn't leaving her. Already frost formed on the fabric of her shirt where the wizard's freezing robes touched her. If she wasn't still dressed for the CrystalShadow Wastes, she would surely be dead.

"This ends when you give up the Key, boy," Serth snarled. The dark trails down his white face were nearly dry now; only the barest hint of a tear ran from the corner of one eye. "And you *will* give up. Just as you gave up searching for your mother all those years ago."

A cold shiver of uncertainty ran down Fin's spine. "I didn't give up," he protested. "I'm still looking for her now! That's why I went after your stupid Key in the first place!"

"Oh, really?" Serth snapped. "Is that why you never before left the Khaznot Quay? Is that why you never searched the Stream yourself?" The Oracle shook his head. "Deep down, Fin, you already know what I know. You know I came to bring you the *truth*. And that truth is that your mother is never coming back. She *forgot*."

Fin swallowed, hard. The weight of the dark wizard's sorrow pressed around him, heavy on his shoulders. But the worst part wasn't the words or the magic. The worst part was the look behind Serth's mad eyes: sympathy. Honest, genuine sympathy.

"Embrace the truth, Fin. Our paths are set, we cannot fight them." He held out one hand, palm open, demanding what was rightfully his. "No one remembers you," the Oracle said, and Fin knew the words were earnest, "because *you* are *no one.*"

Fin's legs threatened to give out beneath him. Because Serth was right. Fin wasn't good enough to be thought of. He *should* be forgotten. By everyone, forever.

His hand, the one holding the Key aloft, began to tremble.

"Don't listen to him!" Marrill cried, voice breaking from the cold.

But the truth of what Serth had said was already seeping through him, tearing down any barrier he had against the sorrow. Draining any desire he had to resist. Fin fell to his knees. His chest ached, deep down in that empty place he'd carried for so long

Marrill struggled against Serth's grip, but he held her firm. "He's lying!" she cried. "You're not no one! *I* remember you! You're someone to *me!*"

"Oh, of course, Marrill," Serth said. "Because you *need* someone to cling to. You need someone to prop you up, like you always do. Even if that someone is really no one at all."

"You know what?" Marrill growled. "He's right. I *need* you, Fin. And I don't just need you to help me. I need you to hang out with me. I need you to make up signs with me. I need you to throw junk into the Stream and watch it explode, and fight off whatever monsters it turns into with me. I need you to be my friend."

In the dark tangled cloud that Fin's mind had become,

her words filtered through. For a moment, just a moment, everything cleared. "Really?"

A smile spread over her face, as though they weren't on a sinking ship, surrounded by pirates and shadows, at the mercy of an evil wizard bent on destroying the world. As if they were just two friends together.

Serth growled with frustration and clapped a freezing hand over Marrill's mouth. But Marrill, a tear turning to ice on her cheek, just pressed her thumb against her chest. Their sign for friend.

Warmth flared through Fin. Marrill was right—he wasn't no one. She remembered him. Even the fact that *Serth* remembered him had to mean he was *somebody*.

Serth was wrong. Nothing was inevitable. And right now Marrill needed his help.

"If I hand over the Key, you'll let her go?" he called to Serth. Marrill shouted a muffled protest, but Fin crossed his ring finger over his thumb, signaling her. With a quick cut of her hand, she told him she understood.

"My word as a prophet," Serth said. "It is already done." His outstretched fingers flexed, hungry for the Key.

Fin stood and held up the sun-shaped crystal. "Then take it!" he shouted. He raised his free hand to the Key, the signal to Marrill. Then with all his might, he threw it in a high arc toward Serth.

Releasing Marrill, Serth coiled to jump for the bright star. At the same moment, Marrill elbowed back, hard into

Serth's stomach. The timing couldn't have been more perfect. The dark wizard reeled, missing his catch and dropping the rest of the Map.

"Noooooooo!" he roared. The crystal star arced past him, across the bow, off it. "The Prophecy!"

Before Fin knew what was happening, the dark wizard launched himself over the railing just an inch behind his quarry. He shrieked, clawing at the empty air as he fell from the ship.

Fin and Marrill both raced to the railing. They made it just in time to see Serth splash headfirst into the Pirate Stream. The glowing water exploded into flames as a howl like a billion dying devils rent the air. Red fire danced across the waves, sucking into tiny whirlpools.

Fin tore his eyes away, stomach reeling from the sight. When he looked again, the stormy waters lapped hungrily against the hull.

No trace of Serth remained.

Beside him, Marrill sighed. She held up the rest of the Map. It was blank, useless. Fin bumped his shoulder against hers. "At least we finally got our explosion," he offered.

"Oh yeah, now you've wrapped that up, we're fine," a gruff voice grumbled nearby. The Naysayer had joined them at the railing, a content, if slightly damp, Karnelius nestled in the crook of one of his arms. "Unless you count the death army over there, that is."

He pointed behind them. Marrill and Fin turned around

as one. The pirates had crowded in, tears dried on their cheeks and swords drawn against the shadow army that waited amidships, weapons at the ready.

Just beyond, the Master stood at the prow of the Iron Ship, oblivious to the glowing water of the Pirate Stream seeping up around him as his boat continued sinking. A mere arm's length away, Ardent stood at the bow of the *Kraken* as Coll pulled her close enough to extend a gangplank to the *Dragon*'s deck. The two wizards seemed almost locked together, a halo of energy crackling and burning furiously between them.

The only way out, it seemed, was through the shadow crew.

Next to Fin, Marrill let out a long breath. "Shanks," she muttered.

CHAPTER 40
The Bintheyr Map to Everywhere

Marrill drew closer to Fin. "I guess it was too much to ask that we'd just be able to defeat Serth and call it a day?"

Fin, for his part, didn't look worried. "Oh, I got this one," he told her. He reached down into his coat and pulled out a jar full of buzzing critters. With a battle cry, he smashed it against the deck.

Glass shattered, scattering shards everywhere, and a swarm of bugs burst free. Marrill jumped back. A humming sound filled the air as they took flight, heading straight for the shadow soldiers.

"They look hungry, don't they?" Fin mused.

Marrill watched as the bugs fell on the shadows in a storm, tearing through them. "What *are* they?"

"Glowglitters," he explained, as though they were the most ordinary creatures in the world. "They eat darkness."

Marrill laughed. "Pretty cool critters to have around." She paused. "But did you really have to break the bottle?"

Fin shrugged. "They're pretty slow otherwise, honestly."

From the deck of the nearby *Kraken*, Ardent called to them. "Hurry! I can't hold him off much longer!" A stream of light crackled from his fingers, straight toward the Master. The Master waved his arm, his own streak of energy blasting at Ardent. The two streams met in the middle, a roiling swirl of fervid magic.

Orange cat clutched protectively in his arms, the Naysayer charged, barreling through the gap the glowglitters had chewed in the shadows. "See you on the ship!" he called back to them, pausing to gather a few discarded knickknacks along the way.

"To the *Kraken*, bloods!" Fin shouted, mustering the pirates to follow them as Marrill stayed close on his heels.

The Naysayer paused in front of the gangplank, shuffling everyone aboard. "One at a time, single file," he grumbled. "Mind your manners. No pushing."

Marrill stepped onto the *Kraken* with a deep sigh of

relief, relaxing in the familiarity, enjoying the sound of the Ropebone Man hauling in the rigging, the sight of the sails popping to life, even the sparkle of the half-frozen letters from the CrystalShadows Wastes strewn across the deck, slowly melting into noisy slush.

Atop the quarterdeck, Coll wasted no time. He spun the massive wheel, calling orders to the pirats. The *Kraken* pulled off, storm winds blowing hard in her sails, just as the Stream waters washed across the prow of the *Dragon*. Ardent puffed himself up, bigger than Marrill ever thought his skinny frame could manage. A massive blast of orange fire flew from his fingers, staggering the Master of the Iron Ship.

As the *Dragon* fell behind them, Marrill and Fin made their way aft. Side by side, they watched the ships go down. The Pirate Stream swallowed the *Black Dragon* in a huge wave. The Iron Ship, irreparably tangled with her, sank slowly after.

Standing planted at her bow, her Master watched the *Kraken* go with cold eyes. Those eyes never wavered, even as the Stream water lapped up higher and higher around him.

"Who was he?" Marrill choked out as Ardent joined them.

Ardent glanced down to meet her questioning expression. The old wizard looked tired, more tired than Marrill had ever seen. But he looked wise, wise and serene like a wizard should be.

"A powerful wizard once, clearly. But now, I think he's

just what the legends say: a dark wraith of the Stream, out for souls." He shook his head.

Marrill wanted to ask more, but something told her Ardent would give no other answers. Above them, the storm grumbled, its fury spent. And as they watched, the Iron Ship, far behind them now, slipped beneath the waves.

"Is it over?" Even to her own ears, her voice sounded small. She rubbed her thumb over the palm of her hand where the skin had turned an angry red from when she'd grasped the Key to pull apart the Map.

Ardent tugged on his beard, water droplets falling from it onto his purple robe. "I believe so, yes."

She slumped, sad to leave behind the hope of ever seeing her family again. But thankful, even so, that at least her sacrifice had been worth it. "Good."

Fin turned to her, his forehead furrowed with confusion. "Wait, it can't be over. Not yet—we still have to get you home."

She tried to smile, tried to shrug a shoulder. Tried to make it appear that she was okay. "Not without the Key, I guess." She held up the remains of the Map. "This is useless without it."

Alarm raced across Fin's face. "But you touched it, when we were on Serth's ship." He said the words almost desperately. "I thought I saw it show you something—I thought that might be…"

"No," she said, her voice almost a whisper. "All I saw was gibberish." Her chin quivered.

Fin crossed his arms and then uncrossed them, shifting from foot to foot. He paced, kicking frozen letters out of his way. Marrill gave him the best smile she could muster, knowing it was halfhearted.

"It's okay," she told him. "You had to throw the Key away. It was the right thing to do. It was the *only* thing to do. We both had to give something up." Her voice cracked at what they had both lost. "You gave up the chance to find your mom," she whispered. "I know how hard that was for you to do."

"But—"

She placed a hand on his arm. "You saved the Pirate Stream, Fin. It had to be done."

He shoved his hands into his unruly hair. "Maybe there's still a way—"

"Of course there's a way," Ardent said. They both rounded on the wizard in unison. "What do you mean?" she asked, not ready to get her hopes up.

"You'd think you'd have figured it out already," he said with a grandfatherly smile. "Remember, the Bintheyr Map to Everywhere is no normal map. What did I tell you about it when we first spoke?"

"That it would get me home," Marrill said, trying not to think about her parents waiting for her, forever.

"I said," Ardent corrected, "that it would take you where you needed to go. And didn't it?"

"No!" Marrill cried, tossing the useless Map on the deck. She was exhausted, the reality of her situation crashing through her like the waves on the Stream beneath them. All she wanted was to cry herself to sleep. She closed her eyes, holding the tears at bay.

In the silence that followed, thunder rolled and the pirates grumbled. Wind filled the remains of the sails as the *Kraken* cut a path through the magical waters.

Fin broke the silence. "It *did* take us where we needed to go!" He picked up the Map and stared at the rolled parchment with a look of wonder.

Marrill crossed her arms and raised an eyebrow. "How's that?"

"What led you to the Pirate Stream?" he asked. His voice held a note of excitement.

Marrill tried to take a calming breath. She was so done with this. "I was out walking my cat after finding out my mother might be *dying*." She spat out the last words, flinging them like throwing knives. But the only person they really hurt was her. All she could think of were the last moments she'd spent with her mom, complaining of being doomed to a life without adventure.

Her shoulders slumped in shame.

Fin stepped closer, putting his hand on her arm. "But

there was something else, wasn't there?"

Marrill looked away from him. She didn't know why she was so mad at him; maybe just because anger was easier than all the hurt. "You mean *other* than this big stupid ship sailing into a parking lot?" She sighed. "Ugh, this never would have happened if Karny hadn't chased that piece of paper to begin wi—"

Her breath caught in her throat. If Karny hadn't chased that piece of paper...that piece of paper that led them to the parking lot. Where she stumbled upon the *Kraken*. The *Kraken*, that had been looking for a piece of paper.

She pushed her fingers to her lips, her mind spinning. "Oh, it was Rose! That piece of paper was her!"

"And how did you and I meet?" Fin prodded.

She flashed back to the Khaznot Quay, the overwhelming *newness* of it all. "I saw the Compass Rose and I chased after it. But just as I caught it, the wind picked me up..."

"And threw you straight at me!" he finished, beaming. "Right when I needed to escape from Serth!"

Marrill's heart raced. Now she was in it, her mind following the thread through their adventure. "And in the Gibbering Grove, Rose was so insistent I get those acorns," she said. "I thought she was just hungry!"

Fin practically bounced with energy. "And *Rose* is why I picked up that slingshot at the Naysayer's tower! She landed right on it!" He shook his head as if he himself couldn't believe it. "Don't you see, Marrill? The Map took us where we needed to go. It was preparing us to defeat Serth!"

Marrill's jaw dropped in wonder. It had to be! But then another thought crossed her mind. "But she also stole the rest of the Map and took it *to* Serth. She let him put it together. If we hadn't stopped him, he would have opened the Gate and ended the world."

Fin frowned. "Good point," he said. He looked to Ardent.

The wizard stroked his beard in thought. "Perhaps the Map yearns to be complete, just like anything—or anyone—else," he said, sliding a glance toward Fin. "Perhaps it wanted to be united, but not to destroy." He shrugged. "Or perhaps not. Who can say?"

"Either way, it still doesn't get me home," Marrill said, her shoulders drooping.

Ardent's expression softened. "Well, hold on," he said. "You saw *something* when you pulled the Map apart, didn't you?" Marrill nodded. "Well, whatever it showed you, you needed to see!" he announced with a clap. "Now, what exactly *did* you see?"

Marrill shrugged. "Just numbers." She closed her eyes and pictured the string of random numerals. She could still remember them, as if they were burned in her head. She recited them out loud. "But they didn't make any sense..."

She was cut off by a bark of laughter. She turned to find Coll, standing with his shoulder propped against one of the smaller masts, looking at her with a devilish smirk. "Any good sailor can tell you what that means," he said. "It's a bearing—a designation of which Stream currents you need to catch to reach a desired destination."

Marrill wasn't quite sure what he'd just said, but she felt like her heart might never beat again. "You mean you can still get me home?"

Usually, Coll never acted his age. So much so that Marrill had taken to thinking of him as a grown man, despite his teenage looks. But the grin on his face made him seem like a kid again. "Duh," he said, clinching the image.

CHAPTER 41
A Glimpse of Things to Come

While Marrill and Coll talked headings and bearings, Fin kept getting distracted by the frozen letters strewn across the *Kraken*'s deck. Most of them had melted into slush, but they were still close enough to the CrystalShadow Wastes that a few remained stubbornly solid.

What bothered Fin was that they were all the same four letters: *F*, *N*, *U*, and *L*. They were all different shapes and sizes, and each one was marred by dark spots, as though someone had dribbled ink across them, scarring the icy surface.

Or had been crying black tears while muttering the words.

Fin swallowed, uneasy. When he'd been in the Naysayer's tower, he'd seen Serth by the *Kraken*. It would have been easy enough for the dark wizard to board and search her. And if he had, it made sense he'd have left a few traces behind.

But that it was these specific letters over and over again . . . that had to be on purpose. To anyone else, the trail of tearstained letters would have been gibberish. They wouldn't make sense to anyone but Fin.

Which Serth, of course, would know. He was an Oracle, after all.

Fin moved to the main cabin and opened the door. An *F* sat on the top step, an *N* on the stair below, followed by a *U*. As he'd feared, the trail of frozen letters led into the bowels of the ship. He glanced over his shoulder at the rest of the crew. The Naysayer marshaled the pirates toward the forecastle while Marrill pointed off into the distance, her smile outglowing the water of the Stream. Coll shouted to Ardent to trim the sails, turning purple when Ardent slashed the edges off the mainsail with a wave of his hand. Fin felt the ghost of a smile try to work its way to his lips.

But it did nothing to ease the ache pounding in his chest.

A part of him wanted to slam the door shut and rejoin

the crew, leaving the icy letters to melt into a slush of unfinished sayings and inky tears. But he couldn't. Because deep down inside, he knew he would never truly fit in on the *Kraken*—no matter how hard he tried, no one but Marrill would ever remember him.

And it wouldn't be long until she returned to her world, where she'd probably forget about him, too. Once again, Fin would be alone.

Unless he could find his mother.

Cautiously, Fin began climbing down the tightly spiraled stairs. It was still cold belowdecks, and the ice-wrapped railings were melting slowly. He toed an elegantly shaped *L*, kicking it toward the Door-Way to join the other letters. They were in all different fonts and sizes, some whispered and some shouted, but one thing remained the same, the pattern over and over:

FNUlNuFNUlNuFNUlNu

Fin U. Lanu. His own name, spelled out like on the form from the Orphan Preserve: FNU LNU. First Name Unknown, Last Name Unknown. Even his name had forgotten him.

Fin shivered, the hairs along the back of his neck lifting. The Door-Way felt longer and narrower than he remembered. All of its doors were closed, on wall, floor, and ceiling. Not even the scurrying of a pirat could be heard.

He continued following the stream of letters down the entire length of the corridor to where they stopped before the Map Room door. He squinted, examining the face on the knocker. It looked as though it had been crying, shallow rivulets grooving its brass cheeks.

Before wrapping his hand around the knob, Fin turned to glance behind him, though he knew no one had followed. Force of habit, he thought. Or paranoia. *When you're doing something wrong*, it occurred to him, *there's always a shadow lurking just behind you.*

But no shadows hid among the brass knockers and carved frames. No dire shapes slipped from doorways or crawled through keyholes. Slowly, he pushed open the door to the Map Room, shivering as a blast of cold air swept out.

Inside, frost still tinged the walls and the frozen letters scattered across the floor hadn't begun melting yet. It felt almost like walking into a tomb. With Serth swallowed by the Stream, these were the final words of a dead man. As far as Fin could tell at a glance, though, there was no order to them. They were piled around in heaps, many of them stuck together in drifts along the wall where they'd slid from the ship's constant movement.

Who knew how long it would take to sort it all out? Fin glanced over his shoulder, back down the Door-Way. He didn't know how much time he had left until they reached Marrill's world. Soon enough she'd come searching for him.

And before she did, there was something he needed to

take care of. Something more important than the words of a dead wizard.

Closing the door behind him, he kicked aside a few frozen letters and moved to the large drawing table in the center of the room. Taking a deep breath, he pulled the Map from his back pocket.

He unfurled it, staring at the blank expanse of canvas. For all the magic the Map had held, now it seemed useless. At least, it was without its final piece. Fin reached into his shirt and drew out a hunk of crystal, shaped like the sun and glowing gently.

The Key. The *real* Key.

It was funny, he thought as a smile played over his lips, how much it looked like the unripe tentalo he'd kept in his thief's bag since he got it from Squinting Jenny's Fruit Stand, all the way back at the Khaznot Quay. Close enough to fool an Oracle, apparently.

It had been easy enough to switch the two out in that last second before he threw the Key off the *Dragon*. A classic palm job; any two-bit pickpocket or street magician could do it. While everyone's focused on the Key, take the fruit from the bag (jamming a hope crystal in it for authentic shininess), switch them with a quick motion, then hide the real Key while they all watch the fake one fly through the air.

Misdirection was the word, and everyone was none the wiser.

He grasped the Key and took a deep breath. His toes

twitched with anxiousness. His skin tingled. This was it. He had what he needed, at long last.

As he held the Key over it, the Map burst to life, pools and rapids and sandbars and islands and towers and caverns and everything welling up from the depths. They all swirled into place, bounded in by the Neatline, put in form by the Scale, even properly oriented, he supposed, to where he was standing and how he was looking at it, thanks to Rose—the Compass Rose, rather.

The Bintheyr Map to Everywhere was complete.

Taking a deep breath, Fin touched the Key to the Map and whispered the words he'd been waiting too long to say: "Show me my mother."

The images on the Map whirled and flew. Landscapes and volcanoes and fortresses and oceans passed by so fast it made him dizzy. Then faster and faster, twisting down narrow branches of the Pirate Stream, through rapids, across lochs and lakes and marshes. He had to shut his eyes just to keep from feeling sick.

When he dared to look again, the Map showed open water once more. He could tell by the waves that washed over it, but they weren't storm waves like the ones the *Kraken* was crashing through now. They were gentle, peaceful ones. The kind nuzzled up by a wind that sang of summer. The kind that begged for a swim.

As he watched, a mighty vessel came into view, sailing toward him. It was a great galleon, or a man-o'-war, the type that might lead an armada or be the flagship of a king. Astride its bow, a woman stood.

Fin's breath caught. He recognized her. Her features were cut sharper than in his dreams, and her dark eyes were less gentle, but it was her, all right. The woman who gave him a star to look out after him. The one who brought him to the Quay.

His mother.

Fin's throat tightened. His eyes shimmered.

The woman turned away from him and placed a hand on the shoulder of a boy standing behind her. Together, they walked toward the stern, heads bent as they talked. They both wore simple clothes, brightly colored and finely woven. Fin could only see the boy's back, but his jet black hair and olive skin were too familiar. They were just like his own.

Fin choked. Did he have a brother? Could it be? What if there was an entire family out there, just for him? He felt his chest quiver. Joy leapt from his toes to his head and back again. He'd found what he was looking for! Finally, after all this hopeless searching, he'd found where he could belong again!

Just then, the room tilted as the *Kraken* crashed through a particularly rough wave. The Map snapped shut, and as Fin grasped the table to steady himself, the Key dropped to the floor. But when he knelt to grab it, his eyes landed on a trio of jumbled words it had rolled against: "Master Dear Thief."

Dear Master Thief. Just like the letter from Serth back at the Khaznot Quay. Fin's heart kicked up. He glanced at the door again, wondering just how much time he had left. Hopefully, enough. Putting Map and Key aside for a moment, he quickly gathered up all the words, their letters frozen together with a glue of black tears:

One *A* if **Lost dragon,** Key **back** way **its**
map will **lock** doesn't But lock **Though** forever
key On come the shall of the a the remembers
Sun be show **has day** the truth **then, forgets** it *Prophecy*

When he was done, he rearranged the words into lines according to font, and then again over and over until they made a sort of sense:

A Prophecy
One truth forever shall be
Key remembers lock
Though lock forgets key
On the back of a dragon, the Lost Sun has its day
But if it doesn't come then,
the map will show the way

It was like Fin's insides had turned to stone. The joy he'd felt just a moment ago at seeing his mother dissolved.

If she was on a ship, that meant she was constantly moving. Which meant that the only way he could find her would be to keep using the Map.

But Serth's note said the Lost Sun would still have its day, even if it didn't rise on the *Dragon*. With that, the Map was still dangerous. If the wrong person ended up with it and the Key, they could still open the Gate. They could still release the Lost Sun of Dzannin and destroy the Pirate Stream. Fin ached, the longing in his chest squeezing impossibly tight. Was finding his mother worth risking the world?

His thoughts were interrupted by a muffled shout drifting through the open porthole. "Land ho!" Squeals echoed around him as tiny doors tucked along the walls slammed open and pirats scampered out, dashing to their stations.

It could only mean they'd reached Marrill's world. Fin's time was up. He was going to have to say good-bye to his friend.

And he was going to have to decide what to do about the Map.

He'd just started for the door when a massive scraping sound shuddered through the *Kraken*. The ship ground to a halt so suddenly that Fin catapulted forward. Behind him, he heard the carefully arranged frozen letters scatter across the floor. An immense groan reverberated through the hull as the ship settled, tilting slightly sideways.

He shoved the Map into his back pocket and the Key in his thief's bag before taking off toward the stairs. Even from down here, Fin could hear shouts coming from the deck above. Something was wrong!

CHAPTER 42
Where You Need to Go

Marrill had just gotten her first glimpse of home when the *Kraken* shuddered to a halt. She landed in a heap against the railing, hard enough to knock the breath out of her. She wasn't the only one who lost her footing—piles of pirates littered the deck, grumbling and cursing as they tried to untangle themselves from each other.

"The Stream's bottoming out!" Coll cried as he pulled himself up. His expression turned grim as he fought against the wheel. Slowly, with a great groaning sound, the *Kraken* began listing to one side.

Marrill struggled to her feet and stared out across the Stream. The air shimmered with heat ahead of them, just like it would on land. Through that veil, she couldn't even tell where the water ended and the asphalt began, but the familiar lines of a parking lot and the shapes of the dumpy strip mall buildings told her she was nearly home. Her parents were so, so close. And she still couldn't get to them. It was too far away, too much Stream water between here and there.

"Ardent, trim the sails!" Coll ordered.

Ardent eyed the mainsail, holding his fingers up in a scissor formation.

Coll scrambled to correct himself, yelling, "Wait, wait! That means tighten them!"

The wizard did what he was told, but the ship continued to wobble.

Fin dashed up beside her. "What happened?" he asked, out of breath.

"I don't know." Marrill's insides twisted with panic. "We were just fine and then—"

"She's floundering," Coll warned. It was obvious how hard he strained to keep from losing control of the ship. The sails bucked and flapped above them. "Keep the wind calm or it'll tear the sheets free!" he shouted to Ardent.

But no matter what Ardent tried, the wind continued to blow, each gust pushing the ship farther onto her side. "Curse you, Air!" the wizard shouted, waving his fist.

"We need deeper water," Coll explained. "Prepare to come about!" Overhead, the Ropebone Man strained, his block and tackle squealing sharply as pirats raced along the masts, loosening knots and retying them. The ship protested, then eased backward ever so slightly.

Another shudder and the parking lot grew more distant. They were headed the wrong way—back to the open waters of the Pirate Stream. Away from home. "Wait!" Marrill shouted.

Slowly, the ship righted itself, and Coll turned her until her sails fell limp and she floated safely in place. "I'm sorry," he told Marrill apologetically. "This is as far as I can take her. Stream's too shallow past this point."

"But last time you made it to shore!" she protested.

He glanced over his shoulder, back toward the mass of black clouds dissipating along the horizon. "Must have been the storm surge. It kicks up the tides, makes 'em higher, stronger."

He turned to Ardent. "Makes sense when you think about it. The first time we got there, we were nearly in a storm. Same thing here. Except now, it's not strong enough to take us all the way in. We've got some time at this depth but"—he shrugged, his expression regretful—"not a lot of it."

Marrill stared across the distance between her and the parking lot. "What if I swam?" she asked hopefully.

Ardent scooped up a stray length of rope and dropped it over the railing. It hit the water, where it writhed and tangled, the ends splitting. "Afraid not," he told her. "Well, and a frayed knot, too." When no one laughed, he tugged on his beard and added, "As you can see, the water still carries too much magic this far out." He placed a hand on her shoulder. "I'm sorry."

She bit her lip, scouring the ship for something she could use to get ashore. But there was nothing that the magic wouldn't destroy. "I *have* to get home," she whispered, her chest tight.

Fin cleared his throat and shrugged out of his thief's coat. "Fly," he said simply, thrusting it toward her. Something flashed in his eyes, then he glanced away.

She looked at the coat and then back at him. Hope began to stir inside her. When she hesitated, he added, "It's not that far. And I saw how well you handled flying in the storm. You can do it."

"Thank you," she whispered. She grabbed him and pulled him into a fierce hug that he tentatively returned.

And then she realized what this meant. Going home meant leaving him behind. All of them. She wouldn't be able to take Ardent with her to heal her mother. She inhaled sharply. It would be okay, she told herself. Her mother had recovered before without magic; hopefully, that meant she could do so again.

She tightened her arms around Fin, and he returned her squeeze. "I don't want to say good-bye," she murmured, her voice muffled against his shoulder.

She pulled back and glanced around the ship. For a moment, a part of her wondered what it would be like if she stayed with them. All the adventures she could go on with Fin and Coll and Ardent. Every morning a new world brimming with possibility. But she knew in her heart she needed to get home to her parents, to sit by her mother's side as she recovered.

Even so, maybe this didn't have to be good-bye forever. "Will I ever see you again?" she asked.

"I fear not," Ardent said regretfully.

Marrill's eyes brimmed with tears.

"Your world is one of the most complete, maybe *the* most complete, I've ever encountered," he said. "Remember what I told you when we first met, Marrill. Magic is just the potential for creation. It follows no rules, and breaks them all. A world as complex and defined by its own rules as yours, well, it cannot bear much contact with the raw stuff.

"If the River of Creation is a deep and slow-moving river, and the Pirate Stream is a fast, tumultuous torrent, your world is like a windmill on the shores of that slow-moving river. It is beautiful and complex and built to precision, turning and grinding with the slow river's current. But place the wheel too long in swift-moving waters, and it cannot help but be torn asunder."

Coll crossed his arms. "Don't windmills use the wind?"

Ardent flapped his hands. "Well, whatever, like that but with water."

"I think I get it," Marrill assured him. "Magic doesn't follow rules, and my world does, so dumping pure magic into my world would undo the rules, and..."

"Rip it apart," Ardent finished. "Believe me, the Stream *will* touch your world again, somewhere, sometime. That's how I knew we could get you home. But it is rare. And frankly, if the Stream is close enough for *you* to stumble upon it again, well, something has gone terribly, terribly wrong."

A shiver streaked down Marrill's spine at the words. She swallowed the tears that burned the back of her throat. She wasn't sure she understood everything Ardent had told her, but she understood enough to know that this was good-bye forever.

"So this will be it?" Fin asked, echoing her thoughts. "No one from the Stream will ever be able to get into Marrill's world?" His forehead furrowed, as though he were thinking through what that really meant.

"I'm afraid so," Ardent replied.

With a deep sigh, Fin pulled a tightly rolled piece of parchment from his back pocket. "You should take the Map, then," he said, offering it to her.

Marrill frowned. "Why? It's useless without the Key."

"To get it off the Stream," Ardent answered for him. "It's something Coll and I had already been discussing. I can't say I'm happy about it, but the Map will be safer in your world, where no one from the Stream can reach it."

Fin lifted the corner of his mouth in a strained smile, though his eyes looked anywhere but at her. "Better safe than sorry, right?"

Nodding, Marrill took the Map and stuffed it into one of the many pockets in Fin's thief's coat. She had to clear her throat several times before she was able to get her voice to work. "I guess this is good-bye, then."

"I'm sorry," Ardent said gently. He crouched and opened his arms. She threw herself at him, closing her eyes as he held her tight.

"I'm scared," she whispered. She didn't need to say out loud what she was frightened of: of going home, of leaving them, of what would happen with her mom's illness, of trying to live in an ordinary world after knowing what wondrous things existed.

"Believe in yourself," Ardent said. "You're stronger than you think you are—you always have been." He squeezed her tighter. "You I will miss more than most."

Marrill nodded, trying to take his advice to heart. The wizard stood, and Coll stepped into his place. He pushed a sheaf of carefully bound papers into her hands. "My sketches!" Marrill cried, recognizing them instantly.

"I had the pirats put it together—that's real scuttlefish skin for the cover," he told her. He paused and added, "I know what it's like to leave a place you love and not be able to return."

He traced his thumb along the outline of the tattoo knotted around his forearm, as though a bit uncomfortable with sharing something so personal.

"Anyway," he said, clearing his throat. "Keep the wind at your back. And don't ever lock your knees."

"I won't," she said. She tucked the little book in her coat and gave him a huge hug. As out of character as it was, he gave her a great big squeeze back.

And then it was just Marrill and Fin. He let out a nervous cough. "Here," he said, pressing a crystal vial into her hand. "I took it from the same safe as the Key, on the Meressian Temple Ship. I want you to have it." He grinned sheepishly. "It's something to remember me by."

Tears flooded Marrill's eyes. "Oh, Fin, I could never forget you!"

Digging into one of her pockets, she said, "I have something for you, too. I've been working on them for a while." She held out two scraps of sailcloth. On each one, she'd sketched a picture of a boy with black hair and olive skin. Fin.

Underneath the image, in bold letters, she'd written:

You know this person. His name is Fin.
He's your stowaway and friend and he
helped save the Stream.
He's looking for his mother. Don't forget!
♡, Marrill

"They're for Ardent and Coll," she explained. "So they remember." She lowered her voice. "I was going to make a third for the Naysayer, but I wasn't sure you'd actually want him remembering you."

Fin laughed, but it came out watery.

And then the ship bucked beneath them again, the storm surge retreating even farther. "If you're gonna go, now's the time!" Coll suggested.

The Naysayer hovered nearby, a large orange cat cradled in two of his arms. He used his other two hands to both tickle Karnelius's ears and scratch his back. The cat purred loudly, his one eye half-closed in bliss. "Don't know why everyone complains about the beast," the Naysayer grumbled. "Seems contented to me. Much easier to please than humans," he added, reluctantly holding him out to her.

With a trembling smile of thanks, Marrill took Karnelius and tucked him inside Fin's coat, closing it tight to make sure he couldn't escape. The Naysayer grunted and turned away, but not before Marrill saw what looked suspiciously like a tear.

Fin helped Marrill up onto the railing. He took a deep, shaky breath. "You know how to bank when the wind hits you," he told her. She nodded. "Make sure you don't fly straight into it, okay?" She nodded again. "And, Marrill?" He grabbed her hand and squeezed it. But all he could do was look at her and shift awkwardly.

"I know," she whispered. "I'll miss you, too. You're my best friend, Fin."

Fin nodded, choking up. He couldn't even get the words out, but she knew what he was trying to say. And it meant the world to her.

She glanced back down at the crew one last time. It seemed impossible they'd been strangers only a few days ago. Now they felt like family.

And she was abandoning them.

Ardent stood on the deck. "Treat her right, Air!" he shouted to the sky. "Do this one thing as I ask it, and I will never command you again!"

She heard the wind first, rolling across the Stream like the sound of galloping horses and then whipping through the rigging, sending the sails flapping and the sheets popping. It was like the time her mom taught her to ride the waves on the beach in Oahu. The trick was always in the timing.

The leading edge of the breeze caught the loose hair around her face, teasing it. Karnelius flattened himself against her abdomen, tucking deeper into Fin's jacket. When the full force of the wind hit, she didn't panic like she had before. She simply gave herself over to it, jumping from the railing and letting it carry her home.

The last thing she saw as the waters of the Pirate Stream gleamed golden beneath her was Fin pressing his thumb to his chest, their unspoken sign for friend.

CHAPTER 43
Where You Need to Be

Marrill hit the ground running. The scorching Arizona sun beat down on the abandoned parking lot, burning against her skin. She ignored the angry cat squeezed against her chest and headed for home, her eyes blurring with tears.

It hurt too much to think about what she was leaving behind, and now that she was so close, all she could focus on was seeing her mom again. "Please let her be okay," she whispered.

As she turned away from the strip mall parking lot, she glanced back over her shoulder. What had once been a golden lake stretching to the horizon was now nothing more than an empty expanse of asphalt with heat waves shimmering across its surface. Any trace of the Pirate Stream or the *Enterprising Kraken* was gone.

The loss hit her like being struck in the stomach. "It'll be okay," she repeated to herself as she ran. She desperately hoped it was the truth.

She was out of breath and drenched with sweat when she finally turned into her neighborhood. A cramp had formed in her side, but she didn't slow down. Not when she was almost home.

Three streets away.

Two streets away.

One street away.

Out of habit, her eyes darted to the spot in the front yard where the FOR SALE sign used to be. Of course it wouldn't be there, she reminded herself.

But something better was.

"Mom!" she cried.

Her mom stood by the open mailbox, staring past it forlornly into space. But the instant she heard Marrill's voice, her head snapped up. Her eyes widened. "Marrill? Marrill, honey?"

The floodgates opened. Marrill couldn't speak past the tears. She tore down the street and launched herself at her mom, throwing her arms around her neck. Envelopes and magazines scattered through the air as her mom grabbed her and held her tight.

"My baby," she sobbed, her hands shaking as she clutched Marrill closer. They fell to their knees, and Marrill pressed her face against her mom's shoulder.

Home, this was home.

She'd made it.

Something struggled between them, letting out a muffled *"Mrow."* Marrill pulled back, letting a disgruntled Karnelius scrabble his way free and drop to the ground. With an audible *"Hmph,"* he stalked toward the front door, as if they'd scarcely been gone at all.

Marrill took the opportunity to really look at her mother. She seemed thinner. Bags sat heavy under her eyes. "Are you okay, Mom?" she asked, terrified of what the answer might be.

Her mom laughed, though it still sounded a lot like crying. "Shouldn't I be asking you that?" She cupped Marrill's cheeks, her fingers trembling.

Just then a car screeched to a halt on the street. Her father threw open the door and bolted out, not even bothering to turn it off. "Marrill!" he cried, racing toward her. "You're home!"

He skidded to his knees, pulling her into a hug and squeezing her so tight it was like being in AlleySalley's alley all over again. Marrill had to laugh, she was so overcome with joy at being back with her family.

"Where were you? What happened?" her father asked.

Marrill hated to lie, but she knew the truth was impossible. So she told them the story she'd made up on the way home. "I got lost in the desert," she admitted sheepishly. It wasn't *entirely* untrue.

"Oh, Petal." Her mom cupped her cheeks, searching her eyes for the truth. "We were so worried."

Marrill smiled. "I'm okay, Mom," she said. And just saying the words, she felt the truth of them in her heart. Her mother was still sick, they were still stuck in Phoenix, and in a few weeks she'd have to start at a regular school like a normal kid.

And she would be okay.

Some part of Marrill would always wish she were still out on the Pirate Stream, where things like normal didn't exist. But maybe her mother had been right. Maybe being normal would be its own kind of adventure.

CHAPTER 44
The Sign for Friend

"One, two, three, push!" Fin cried. The Naysayer let out a bellow. Fin's arms strained. The heavy trapdoor slammed closed.

"Aww, come on, bloods!" Stavik cried from beneath it. The Naysayer wiped all four hands against each other and leaned back. They could hear the rest of the pirates, trapped down with Stavik in the *Kraken*'s cargo hold, milled about and grumbled.

Fin knelt over the barred window on the trapdoor. "For

your own good, old son," he said. "You were all going to mutiny and take over the ship, and every single one of us knows it."

"Yeah, but we're *pirates*!" Stavik answered. "It's not like it means we're ungrateful!"

Fin shook his head. "Tell you what," he said, bending over so the Pirate King could see his face clearly. "Tell me my name and we'll let you free."

Stavik's eyes darted back and forth, an edge of panic creeping into them. "I...um...well..." He stuck out his tongue at an angle, concentrating. "You do look a mite familiar..."

Fin laughed. "That's what I thought," he said. He stood and walked away. The Naysayer lumbered off in front of him, already leaving him behind.

"Is it Bub?" Stavik cried after them. "Or Cobble? Louis-Josef? Tog the Log?"

Fin shook his head to himself as he mounted the stairs, still laughing.

"Come on!" Stavik's voice faded behind him. "Those are common pirate names!"

Back up on deck, Fin breathed in the salt breeze and let it ruffle his hair. The storm clouds were breaking up, a swath of blue sky peering out between them. The Naysayer shuffled around muttering unpleasantries. Coll clung to a rope on the mizzenmast, one foot braced against it to hold himself just off the ground. Ardent stood nearby talking to him. The wizard looked tired, barely even waving his hands as he spoke.

When Fin approached, Ardent threw up his arms. "Naysayer!" he called. "Pirate on the loose!"

Fin sighed and pointed toward Ardent's sleeve. The wizard looked affronted until he glanced down at the scrap of sail pinned to his robe. He had to twist his head sideways to read it.

"Name's Fin, helped save the world, stowaway," he mumbled as he read. He glanced between Fin and the sketch, comparing the two, then brightening once he was satisfied.

"Of course!" he cried. "Apologies, Fin. Good to see you, which I am assured I have done many times before. How goes..." He checked his sleeve again. "...your quest to find your mother? Well, that does make sense. Coll, we should help with that!"

"Right," Coll drawled. "Because it's not like we have any other plans, what with the Map gone and everything."

Ardent looked pointedly at the rope tattoo knotted around Coll's forearm. "The Bintheyr Map to Everywhere isn't the only way to find what you're looking for."

Coll barked a sharp laugh and ran a thumb over the shifting ink. "No, but it sure could have helped." He sighed. "I guess I'll make do with what I've got. It's not like I'm gonna run out of time to keep looking."

"No, old friend," Ardent replied. "I guess you won't."

Fin looked from one to the other, the wizard's wrinkle-creased face next to the sailor's smooth, young one. For a moment, he recognized the same wisdom—the wisdom of age—in the eyes of both of them. He hadn't seen it before, and he wondered again just how old Coll really was.

"Well," Coll said, clearing his throat. "What's one more thing to add to the list of things we're searching for?"

"Exactly!" Ardent agreed, brightening. Then he frowned. "What was it we were adding to the list?"

Fin piped up. "My mom."

"Oh." Ardent stared at him. "And who are you?"

Something about the question was so familiar that it didn't even bother him. "Fin," he reminded them, pointing to their sleeves.

"Right," Ardent said. He didn't look convinced.

Coll dropped to the deck in front of Fin and considered him up and down. "Got any experience sailing a ship like this?"

Fin surveyed the ship from bow to stern, taking in the Ropebone Man up in the rigging, hauling lines and adjusting sails. The pirats scampered along the yards, their collars gleaming in the sun. Beneath him the ship rolled through the waves, and Fin kept his feet wide and knees soft so that he rolled with it.

The *Kraken* felt more like home than his old attic ever had. Which, he guessed, made Ardent, Coll, and the Naysayer his family.

Well, maybe not the Naysayer.

"Yes, Captain. Just so happens I have experience with a ship *exactly* like this one," Fin said, beaming proudly.

Coll nodded. "Well then, welcome to the crew, sailor."

"Thanks!" Fin's heart swelled. "That means...a lot more than you know."

⧾ ✛ ⧾

At the bow of the *Kraken*, Fin stared out across the golden waters of the Pirate Stream. Even with all the questions he had, he felt better. Infinite worlds lay before him, infinite possibilities. Infinite places to find his mother. To find what Ardent was looking for, and Coll.

Even though Coll and Ardent now remembered him, sort of, he wished Marrill were still here. As great as they were, they still didn't really *know* him.

The afternoon sun had dropped to the horizon. Already, stars were coming out in the clear sky. His eye caught one— his star—rising into view.

And with it, a new hope flooded through him, so strong he looked to see if the Naysayer had cracked a hope crystal. But this wasn't made by magic; it was real. He might be no one, but he was no one with a mission.

He swallowed the thought with a smile. *Not no one.* Even though Marrill might be gone, she *had* remembered him. She *still* remembered him somewhere. And Mrs.

Parsnickle before her, even if she had forgotten eventually.

His mother's promise had been real, Fin knew now. Someone remembered him. He *could* be remembered. He *was* someone. And somewhere out there, he was missed. He knew it, because that star was still burning for him.

A large presence waddled into view beside him. The Naysayer was stringing a line, getting ready to haul in prollycrabs for dinner. The old lizard nearly bumped straight into him.

"Huh," the Naysayer grunted. "Who're you, then?"

Fin had to chuckle. It caught him off guard, starting as just a giggle. Then, before he knew it, he was doubled over, laughing hard. The Naysayer looked around like someone was playing a joke on him.

Fin wiped away his tears, letting the laughs subside. He might not know where he came from or why he was the way he was, any more than he had on the Khaznot Quay. But he was on his way. And now, he had friends, real friends, who would help him.

"Good question," Fin said, clapping the Naysayer on one lumpy shoulder. "But I aim to find out."

EPILOGUE

Clear blue sky stretched endlessly over the golden water of the Pirate Stream. Swift streamrunners carved happy paths through her bays and narrows, skipping through the sunshine and down the rivers and lakes and oceans and storm drains of a thousand worlds. Tall ships lifted their sails to a breeze that was sturdy but not rough, and from the Ojurdwei Coasts to the Rusting City, captains and witches and weathermen alike sucked in the fresh air and declared a good season was coming at last.

But out on the Deep Stream, one dark cloud still lingered. For days it had hung there, over the site of a great battle. Nary a ship had come near it. Not since the many-masted galleon had raced away across the storm surge, wizard at its helm and squid-shaped anchor jangling.

The surf had stilled since then, the thunderclouds broken up. One by one, they turned white and fluffy and disappeared altogether, until just this last remained. And here it sat still, bruise-purple against the bright sky, like a tombstone in a field of wildflowers.

But now, without warning, this one dark cloud rumbled and boiled. It swelled and gathered in on itself, and turned darker still. The placid water beneath it kicked up into waves. The waves broke into whitecaps. Had a soul been present, they might have felt their skin crawl, their hair stand on end. They might have smelled the burning of the air.

As the waves reached a fever pitch, the cloud turned blacker than night. From deep within, a single bolt of lightning, blood red, ignited its darkness. Flames danced across the water. The air cracked open with a cacophony like the end of the world.

Where the flames spread out, the Stream turned to molten metal. And out of that metal, forming from it, a hand appeared, a blazing hand reaching toward the sky. It grasped at the air like a horseman pulling up on his reins, and a ship's prow leapt up with it, the molten metal given shape in an instant.

Rivers of raw magic poured over gunwales of cold iron. The shadows on her deck took life and jumped to action, raising her chain mail sails, hauling her barbwire ropes, straightening the rudder that cut like a razor through the Pirate Stream.

In mere moments, the Iron Ship rode the waves once more.

At her helm, her Master stood calm, arm raised. The waters of the Stream ran off him. Any normal man in his place would be a bug, or an explosion, or a cloud of gas shaped like the number three and tasting slightly of chili pepper and earthworm. But if the Stream's power affected him, he did not show it.

From head to toe, metal cloaked him. The only signs that he lived at all were the cold blue eyes that peered out from behind a smooth steel mask, and the thick white beard that escaped beneath his chin.

As the shadows raced to bring the Iron Ship to life, his gaze turned down to the deck before him, where a figure knelt, head bowed. Glowing water ran down an invisible sphere around it, a sphere that seemed to match the splayed fingers of the Master's outstretched hand.

The figure coughed, choked, then coughed again. The Master of the Iron Ship surveyed it coldly, without emotion. As the last of the Pirate Stream water splashed against the deck, he lowered his hand. At once the figure sucked in air and clasped an arm across his chest.

"You saved me," the man said, still coughing. Black robes sparkled with stars fanned out around him. Beneath the dark light of the growing storm, his skin was pale as death. "I knew you would."

The Master of the Iron Ship said nothing. Thunder smashed across the sky. The sails caught the wind. The ship cut through the water.

"I knew you would come for me," the man said. The pale face lifted. Black tears welled at the edges of his eyes, but his voice was oddly calm. "I had *seen* it."

The shadows labored silently around them. The seas raged against the hull. Overhead, the storm began in earnest, lightning turning the sky a bloody red.

Serth rose to his feet. His eyes never left the cruel metal visage of his savior. "It has been a long time, old friend," he said.

ACKNOWLEDGMENTS

As any good captain will tell you, sailing the Pirate Stream is not something you do alone—like it or not. Fortunately for us, the many wild and magical beings we've encountered on our journey all helped turn our dreams into reality, and most of them have very rarely tried to eat us.

Our agent, Merrilee Heifetz, first found the pieces of the Map to Everywhere, and without her guidance and that of her assistant, Sarah Nagel, we would never have been able to assemble them. The classy pirates at team Writers House—especially Cecilia de la Campa, Angharad Kowal, and Chelsey Heller—helped spread the story to the rest of the world, and we can scarcely believe the amazing places they've taken us.

Kate Sullivan, editor extraordinaire, was the most capable captain we could ask for; she is a true denizen of the Stream and a dream made real. Godspeed, brave kraken! And because strange things happen out on the Stream, we had the unusual good fortune of getting a second talented helmsman in our UK editor, Amber Caraveo. With the help of their respective excellent assistants, Leslie Shumate and Robin Stevens, we sailed through perilous waters with scarcely a scratch.

Of course, a ship needs a crew, and we're grateful to the passionate and talented team at Little, Brown Books for Young Readers for hauling the ropes with care and expertise: Sasha Illingworth, Christine Ma, Deborah Dwyer, Victoria Stapleton, Andrew Smith, Megan Tingley, Melanie Chang, Adrian Palacios, Ann Dye, and Kristina Aven. And to our chief cartographer, Todd Harris, for letting us see the Stream with an unending imagination that is nothing short of inspirational.

And this list would be woefully inadequate without a special thanks to the swashbuckling awesomeness of Deirdre Jones, who swooped in at the last minute, sword in teeth, to guide the ship to ground. Just when we thought we'd run out of miracles, she showed up with a bag full and set the course for new horizons.

Then there are the many friends who helped us on our way, bailing out the Bilge Room during storms and sweeping up the piranhabats that flopped all over the deck. Huge thanks to Melissa Marr, Holly Black, Sarah MacLean, Ally Carter, Alan Gratz, Kristin Tubb (and the rest of the Bat Cavers), Beth Revis, Margie Stohl, Kami Garcia, Natalie Parker, Nancy Kreml, and Phillip Lewis. Many thanks also to Victoria Schwab for key advice that came at just the right time; to the Debs for their continued support; to Diana Peterfreund for being a steadfast first mate; to Shveta

Thakrar, Ken Schneyer, and Gary Cuba for their unending encouragement; and to the hospitality of Red@28th, finest tavern in the Khaznot Quay, where much of this book was written.

Of course, neither of us could have made the trip without the unwavering love and support of our families to bring us home again. Words of gratitude just don't seem adequate for all you've done for us! Thanks to Tony Ryan and Sally Green; Bobby Kidd; Chris and Andrew Warnick and their kids, Ryan, Jamie, and Audrey, for being early readers; Jenny and Jeff Sell and their kids, Corey, Robbie, and especially Alex, young reader of *The Map to Everywhere*, for sneaking in like Fin during the last day of vacation to snatch the manuscript and finish it before leaving. To John and Jane Davis, who put up with an awful lot of work during vacations and were always eager to help, and to Jason Davis, who set the wind right for the journey to begin, and his lovely wife, Sarah, for keeping that wind blowing.

And finally, to the readers, for stowing away with us on this journey. Writing *The Map to Everywhere* has been an incredible adventure, and we can't thank you all enough for sharing it with us!

Where will the Map to Everywhere take you next?

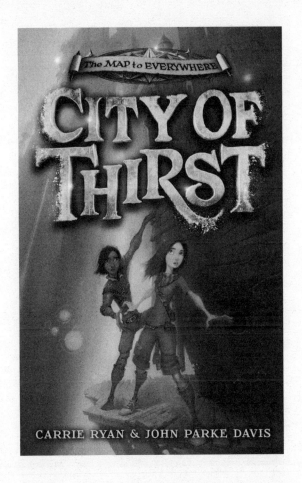

Perpetual Stowaway

Fin landed on the street with a squish. It was like falling onto an old sponge. He flapped his arms, struggling to keep his balance. Mushroom towers leaned over him, bobbing in a stale breeze. Dank sogginess filled his shoes and soaked into his socks.

He didn't care for Belolow City. The thieving was terrible. For one thing, the goo that constantly seeped from the 'shroom towers made them impossible to climb, as he had just found out. Not to mention this world's sickly green sun, which put everything in a bad light, literally: He hadn't gotten away with a single "innocent misunderstanding" since they'd arrived that morning. Good thing he could always slip around the mushroom caps and be forgotten, or he'd have been in slime-mold jail for sure.

And then there was the moisture.

Belolow's "famous" moisture was…aggressive. Fin could constantly feel drops of it running *up* his leg, gathering in pools behind his knees and threatening a full-on invasion of his waistband. He swatted at the back of his calves and gave silent thanks that he'd soon be headed out on the Stream. He slogged his way down toward the murky pool where the *Kraken* was anchored, shaking his hand to fling away some of the clinging slime as he went.

Once again, he hadn't found the first trace of his mother. Another dead end, just like every other place the *Kraken* had stopped in the last six months. He wasn't one to give up, not when it came to something as important as figuring out who he was and why he was so…forgettable. But he was really starting to wonder if he would ever find her.

Lost in thought, he never saw the girl coming. One minute he was squelching through the bog that passed for a marketplace here, doing a little dance to keep his armpits dry. The next he was sprawled on the wet ground, dankness rushing up the back of his shirt to puddle on his shoulders.

"Ay, watchit," he grunted. A girl around his age rolled to her feet nearby, clearly as stunned as he was. Which wasn't weird; no one ever noticed him. He'd have been jostled to death long ago if he weren't so good at avoiding *them*.

And that was the odd part—that he hadn't avoided her; dodging people was second nature, even when he wasn't paying attention. He shook his head and hopped to his feet. *Must be the light,* he figured.

As the girl bolted toward the towering fungus buildings, Fin gave her a once-over. She was a thief, no question, though she'd done a respectable, Quay-worthy job with the disguise. Most anyone would have taken her for a standard-issue street kid, what with the dark, knotted hair, dirt smudged across her chin, and unmatched shoes. It was the details that tipped him off: The beds of her nails were clean. Her ears were still pierced from wearing earrings. And he just barely caught the glint of silver from inside the cuff of her tattered sleeve. She was no beggar, that was for sure.

As if to confirm his impression, shouts of "Thief!" and "After her, go!" filtered through the air, coming from somewhere amid the stewing market crowd. The girl tried to make for an alley, but a thick tangle of fern-fences and dangling moss blocked her. She glanced back, worry on her face.

Three angry-looking guards cleared their way through the street, sweat streaming down their snouted faces. Passersby began to mill about, watching.

Fin smirked. Many a time, he'd been in the girl's position. It would be good to observe another professional in action. Who knew? Maybe he'd even help, if he was so inspired.

Of course, if it were him, he would just slip up to some unsuspecting mark, claim the mark was the real thief, and disappear in the confusion. By the time things got cleared up, no one would even remember the kid they'd originally been chasing.

He crossed his arms to watch. Then the girl did something truly strange. She caught Fin's eye. And she winked.

He could scarcely contain his shock. No one ever caught his eye. Or noticed him, unless he was doing something really bad. Which, in a rare turn of events, he currently wasn't.

"Here he is, boys!" she cried, stabbing a finger at Fin as the guards swarmed around them. "We got that thief right here!"

"What?" Fin blurted. That was his line!

The first guard squinted at them both. "This is yat thief?" he said in the distinctive Belolow drawl. He seemed genuinely confused.

"For sure," the girl said. "Don't you remember? I was right next to you when you saw him!"

"Arp," a second guard said. "She do look familiar." He shifted from one leg to another, squishing unpleasantly. "But thinks-I the thief was a girl?"

"Whoa whoa whoa, bloods," Fin protested. "You've got it all wrong. I haven't stolen anything!" He looked up. "Important," he added. "Today. In the last hour. I didn't steal whatever you boys are after, is what I'm trying to say."

The girl scrunched up her forehead and pursed her lips. "Noooo," she said, drawing out the word. "It was definitely a boy. Don't you remember the black hair?" She leveled her gaze at Fin with a look that seemed to say *Go with it.*

Fin threw up his empty hands in front of him. "No way."

The first guard rounded on Fin. "Thief," he growled.

Fin took a step back, his heart thundering against his ribs. He couldn't believe what was happening. "Wait now, not me! It was her!" he said, waving his hands frantically.

"Nice try, kid," the girl said. She met Fin's eyes and winked again. "But these guards saw the thief clearly. And it couldn't have been me. Because they've never seen me before in their lives."

Fin swallowed. Was that nervous sweat or just Belolow funk he felt gathering on his forehead? "But that's not—" He was about to say *possible,* but the word stuck in his throat. Because it was possible. Totally and completely. Hadn't he just been thinking about all the times *he* had done this exact same con?

And then it hit him. The girl was forgettable. Like him. It suddenly made sense. That was why he hadn't noticed her when she ran into him. She wasn't noticeable. Like him.

He sucked in a breath. Never in all of his life had he met someone like him. Someone forgettable. He hadn't even considered someone like him *existed.*

"Wait!" Fin cried, reaching for her. His fingers brushed

her sleeve. But she slipped out of his grasp, backing into the gathering crowd as the guards closed in.

"Hey, wait!" Fin cried again as a guard's hand closed on his arm. It was too late; the girl had already disappeared down the sodden street. As if she had done this a million times before. Just like *he* had.

Fin slipped his free hand into his thief's bag and looked up at the guards. He had to follow her. And that meant losing these tinheads, fast. He snatched a tiny glass pebble from the bottom of his bag, something he'd been saving for just such an occasion. Pulling it out, he crushed it between his fingers. Smoke poured from his hand, coalescing and massing into the figure of a massive giant.

"Arp!" a guard cried. "A mist-man is!"

The crowd watched, every head tilted back in awe as the smoke giant grew larger and larger. Every head except for Fin's, that is. He slipped from the guard's grip as easily as he slipped from all of their minds. That was his very last Puff-Giant. He hated to see it go, but it never failed to distract.

Fin charged after the girl, through the spectators and toward the docks. At this point, he didn't care about stealth, only speed. The soggy ground slurped at his shoes as he ran.

He was out of breath by the time he hit the pier. It didn't take him long to figure out where the girl had gone. A ship had already pulled free of her mooring and was headed out toward the middle of the harbor, where the open Stream spilled into this world. The girl stood at her stern, staring back toward shore.

He hadn't seen the ship when they'd first arrived. If he had, he'd have recognized her immediately. The design was unmistakable, even though this ship was much smaller and sleeker than the great galleon he remembered. Of course, that galleon had been drawn in moving ink, an image sailing across the face of the Bintheyr Map to Everywhere.

Fin had no doubt. This ship had the same design, was maybe even from the same fleet, as the ship the Map had shown him. The ship that carried his mother.

"Wait!" Fin screamed with all his might.

The girl saw him. She waved with a huge smile. "Thanks for the distraction, brother-fade!" Her voice barely carried across the distance, but her thanks seemed genuine. Did she think he'd helped on purpose?

Quickly, he scanned the docks for the *Enterprising Kraken*. He found her nearby; the jetty wobbled like old gelatin beneath his feet as he ran to her.

"Ropebone Man, full sails!" he shouted to the rigging as he hit the deck. "Pirats, weigh anchor!" He leaned forward, bracing for the ship's movement.

Nothing happened. The *Kraken* bobbed softly, but otherwise didn't move. A trio of rodents glanced up from where they sat in the shade of a bulkhead, tossing tiny teeth toward a copper cup.

"Let's go!" Fin shouted to them. He stomped his feet, trying to spur them into action. They just yawned at him, then scampered off to lounge elsewhere.

A quiver passed through his body, frustration and desperation and sorrow all twisted up as one. It was no use. Of course they didn't follow his commands. He was a stranger. The *Kraken* had forgotten him, just like everyone else.

Fin let out a long, shaky breath and dragged himself slowly aft. Rumor vines looped around the stern railing, whispering his own words back to him as he watched the girl's ship pull farther and farther away.

"Who are you?" Fin said to no one. The vines echoed him:

whoareyouwhoareyouwhoareyou

He closed his eyes in defeat. The only person like him he'd ever met, on a ship like the one the Map had shown him. It was the lead he'd been waiting for, and it was sailing out of reach.

The girl's ship turned broadside as it headed out to the open waters of the Pirate Stream. A jagged metal symbol was emblazoned on its side, looking pale and ill in the green light. Fin squinted, hoping it might mean something. But before he could fully make it out, the horizon reached up and swallowed the ship whole. It had made the Stream. The girl was gone.

The green sun's rays turned even more sickly as it crouched toward the horizon. The day was ending. Around Fin, rumor vines echoed his sniffles, until it sounded as though the entire ship were weeping. Inside, emotions twisted against each other like serpents. Wriggling with glee at having met someone else like him. Squeezing with misery that he had no idea how to find her.

The ship's hatch slammed open, spilling light out across the deck. A lumbering shadow shuffled forth, a lizard-like head and four arms lurching toward him, a thick tail trailing behind. The Naysayer let out a throaty belch and twisted one finger into his earhole, scratching his backside with another. A watering can dangled from a third hand, and a half-eaten prollycrab from the fourth.

As he neared the stern, the old monster frowned. "Quit your whiney-vining," he said, brandishing the watering can. "I'm fixin' to water ya." *Whineyvineyquityourfixin,* several of the mouth-shaped buds echoed back.

Fin wiped his sleeve across his nose. "It's just me," he said.

The Naysayer let out a honk of surprise, which the rumor vines gleefully parroted. He glared at the garden and then back at Fin. "Which one are you again?"

"The forgettable one," Fin moped.

"That don't narrow it down," the Naysayer grunted back. "Try something new and make yerself useful." He shoved the watering can into Fin's hands before wandering off.

With a sigh, Fin lifted his eyes, searching the darkening sky for a star, the one his mother had pointed out to him— the one that meant someone out there was still thinking of him. But tonight, it was hidden by the clouds.

As he raised the watering can, it smacked against his thief's bag, which jangled, jogging his memory. He grinned. He'd totally forgotten the one thing he did have!

Carefully, Fin slipped his hand into his bag and pulled out a circle of silver. The girl's bracelet. The thing she'd kept hidden beneath her sleeve. The one she hadn't even noticed him slipping off her arm when he grabbed for her in the crowd.

He chuckled to himself as he tossed it in the air and caught it again. The girl had been a pretty great thief, he had to admit. But *no one* skinned the Master Thief. Not without getting skinned themselves, anyways.

He held the bracelet up to the dying light. Etched in its center was the same symbol he'd seen on the side of her ship. Only he could see *this* one clearly: a dragon, underneath an empty circle.

And just like that, despite everything, hope swelled in Fin's chest. For the first time since Marrill left the Stream, he had a lead.

Five Questions for Carrie Ryan & John Parke Davis

An Interview with Roger Sutton, Editor in Chief of *The Horn Book Magazine*
Reprinted from Publishers' Previews, *The Horn Book Magazine*,
September/October 2014

Roger Sutton: Okay, who does what?

Carrie Ryan & John Parke Davis: We both actually do everything, which sounds like a lame dodge, but is really very true. There are two points of view, a boy and a girl, so Carrie *usually* takes the first pass at Marrill's chapters, and JP *usually* takes the first pass at Fin's, then we cross edit until we don't know who did what. On a more abstract level, Carrie is definitely in charge of emo-ing it up, and JP is frequently responsible for adding "cleverness" (read: making up silly words).

RS: The Pirate Stream is such a neat idea, and based on real life, too. How did you hit upon it as a motif?

CR & JPD: JP was looking up pirates one day and stumbled on the phrase "pirate stream"—meaning a stream that captures the headwaters of another stream—on a geology website (why he thought a geology website was a good place to search for pirates remains mysterious to this very day). That inspired us to think about old creation myths, where the world was all unformed potential, and imagine what it would be like if there were a pirate stream from that—a river of pure magic where anything was possible. Throw in a wizard, a forgettable orphan, an ordinary girl, and a fantastical quest, and voila, *The Map to Everywhere*!

RS: Carrie, this is a far different world from the Forest of Hands and Teeth (shiver). Was it hard to lighten up?

CR: I think writing *Infinity Ring: Divide and Conquer* really made me realize not only that I could write middle grade, but how amazingly fun it is. Though there were definitely a few times in drafting *The Map to Everywhere* that I made a note in the manuscript along the lines of, "Yeesh, way to take it dark, Carrie—lighten up a bit!" It helps that writing middle grade is such an entirely different mindset—instead of thinking "What's the worst thing that can happen?" I think, "What's the coolest thing that can happen?"

RS: The title page says, "Book One." How much more can we expect, and how far along are you?

CR & JPD: *The Map to Everywhere* is the first of a four-book series, which we love because it gives us lots of room to really dig into the different facets of the world. We've had the overall arc of the series worked out for a while, and we just turned in a draft of book two and are starting on the third. The [Map to Everywhere series] is intended to be as big as imagination, and part of the fun for us is coming up with all sorts of crazy ideas and content that may or may not ever see the light of day; we could probably write in the world forever!

RS: You two are married. Does writing a book together inspire marriage counseling or is it a replacement?

CR & JPD: When we decided to try writing together, we both sort of suspected the experiment would end in at least one homicide, so it's actually been pretty amazing how well we work together. We really build on and support each other, which is impressive because we can both be insanely stubborn people who like to do things our own way. Fortunately, being married we're used to compromising and listening to what matters to each other—we're each other's biggest supporters (though that's not to say there hasn't been a threat or two uttered on the eve of a deadline)!

Husband and wife Carrie Ryan and John Parke Davis have been in love with each other's writing (and with each other) since meeting in law school a decade ago. Carrie is the *New York Times* bestselling author of the critically acclaimed and multi-award-winning Forest of Hands and Teeth series, which is based on a world she and JP created together. She is also the author of *Daughter of Deep Silence* and *Infinity Ring: Divide and Conquer,* as well as the editor of *Foretold: 14 Tales of Prophecy and Prediction.* JP is the First Assistant Federal Defender for the Western District of North Carolina, as well as a published author of short fiction. Although they've been important parts of each other's writing for years, *The Map to Everywhere* is their first full collaboration. JP and Carrie currently live in Charlotte, North Carolina.